James Spedding

Evenings with a Reviewer

Vol. 1

James Spedding

Evenings with a Reviewer
Vol. 1

ISBN/EAN: 9783337418212

Printed in Europe, USA, Canada, Australia, Japan

Cover: Foto ©Andreas Hilbeck / pixelio.de

More available books at **www.hansebooks.com**

EVENINGS WITH A REVIEWER

OR

MACAULAY AND BACON

BY

JAMES SPEDDING

WITH A PREFATORY NOTICE BY

G. S. VENABLES

"Nam isti homines, stylo acres, judicio impares, et partis suae memores, rerum minus fideles testes sunt."—BACON

IN TWO VOLUMES

VOL. I.

LONDON

KEGAN PAUL, TRENCH & CO., 1, PATERNOSTER SQUARE

1881

PREFACE.

It has been thought desirable to publish one of the most characteristic writings of a man of letters who made no effort to acquire popular reputation. In the opinion of competent judges, Mr. Spedding was second to none of his contemporaries in power of reasoning, in critical sagacity, or in graceful purity of style; nor had he any superior in conscientious industry. No one has hitherto possessed so complete a knowledge of the subject to which his life was chiefly devoted; and it is improbable that future students should throw additional light on the career and character of Bacon. In the course of his indefatigable researches, Mr. Spedding deduced many independent and original conclusions from the profound familiarity which he had acquired with the history of the time. The relation of the "Evenings with a Reviewer" to Spedding's exhaustive "Life of Bacon" will be noticed hereafter. It may be convenient, in the first instance, to give a short account of his own quiet and laborious life.

James Spedding was born at his father's residence, Mirehouse, in Cumberland, in June, 1808.

He was educated at the Grammar School of Bury
St. Edmund's, where among his friends and contemporaries were some of the sons of Sir Samuel
Romilly, and John Kemble, afterwards eminent as
a philologist and antiquarian. In 1827 he began
residence at Trinity College, Cambridge, of which he
became a scholar, and in later life an honorary
fellow. His success both in his own college and in
the University examinations would have been more
brilliant if he had possessed the gift of rapid composition and translation. It was his nature to be
in all things deliberate ; and he was neither willing
nor able to struggle against his characteristic temperament. At a later period of his life he gave as
a reason for declining a high appointment in the
public service, that he should have found it intolerable to turn his attention to ten or twenty
unconnected matters in the course of a single day.
His power of sustained labour has rarely been sur-
passed, but in his intellect and his temperament
there was no versatility. Though he neither took
a high degree nor obtained a fellowship, Spedding
was an accomplished classical scholar. A Platonic
dialogue, in which with dramatic fitness he resolved
Falstaff's disquisition on honour into a series of
questions addressed to a puzzled interlocutor by
Socrates, resembled his model almost as faithfully in
Greek style as in thoroughly congenial reasoning.
No member of the well-known society of Cambridge
apostles was more heartily respected and beloved
by his many friends within and without that body.

The manner which faithfully represented his disposition was already formed, and it never afterwards varied. Calm and unimpassioned, he contributed his full share to conversation in a musical voice which never rose above its ordinary pitch. The ready smile with which he welcomed humorous or amusing remarks was singularly winning. His imperturbable good temper might have seemed more meritorious, if it had been possible to test his equanimity by treating him with negligence or harshness. The just impression of wisdom which was produced by his voice, his manner, and the substance of his conversation, was well described in the form of humorous exaggeration by one of the acutest and most brilliant women of his time, Harriet, the second Lady Ashburton. Lord Houghton, in his "Monographs," quotes her as saying, " I always feel a kind of average between myself• and any other person I am talking with—between us two, I mean ; so that when I am talking to Spedding I am unutterably foolish—beyond permission." While his closer intimacies were warm and lasting, his relations to those with whom he associated, in all degrees of acquaintance, were cordial and kindly. Among his contemporary friends and companions at Cambridge were Mr. Charles Tennyson, Mr. Alfred Tennyson, Lord Houghton, Archbishop Trench, Dr. Thompson (now Master of Trinity), Arthur Hallam, Dean Merivale and Dean Blakesley, Thackeray, Edmund Lushington, and Henry Lushington. In irresistible humour none of them rivalled Brookfield, of whom

Spedding said, in a graceful contribution to Lord
Lyttelton's Memoir, "In him a new and original
form of human genius was revealed to me." One
of the few survivors may be pardoned for retaining,
after fifty years, the opinion or prejudice that the
society in which Spedding and his Cambridge
friends then lived was extraordinarily interesting
and genial.

After taking his degree in 1831, Spedding resided principally at Cambridge, till in 1835 he
entered the Colonial Office on the introduction of
Sir Henry Taylor, who was to the end of Spedding's
life one of his most valued and most appreciative
friends. Sir Henry Taylor has kindly allowed me
to insert in the present account a notice, which he
had written for another purpose, of Spedding's short
official career. But for Sir Henry Taylor's unques-
tioned authority as a competent and interested
observer, I should have thought that, for the reason
expressed by himself, official life was not well suited
to Spedding's tastes and habits of thought; but
perhaps his business in the Colonial Office may not
have been as various as that of an Under Secretary
of State.

"At this time" (1835), says Sir Henry Taylor,
"I obtained another relief [in the work of the
Colonial Office], and in obtaining it obtained a
friend for life. James Spedding was the younger
son of a Cumberland squire who had been a friend
of my father's in former days, though I think they
had not met in latter. In the notes to Van Arte-

velde I had quoted a passage from an admirable speech spoken in a debating club at Cambridge when he was an undergraduate. This led to my making his acquaintance ; and when some very laborious business of detail had to be executed, I obtained authority to offer him the employment, with a remuneration of £150 a year. He was in a difficulty at that time about the choice of a profession ; and, feeling that a life without business or occupation of some kind was dangerous, was glad to accept this employment as one which might answer the purpose well enough, if he proved suited to it, and, if not, might be relinquished without difficulty and exchanged for some other. I wrote to Mr. Southey (24th January, 1836), ' Spedding has been and will be invaluable, and they owe me much for him. He is regarded on all hands, not only as a man of first-rate capacity, but as having quite a genius for business. I, for my part, have never seen anything like him for business on this side Stephen. . . . When I contemplate the long labours of Stephen and one or two others, I am disposed to think that there are giants in *these* days.' For six years Spedding worked away with universal approbation, and all this time he would have been willing to accept a post of précis-writer with £300 a year, or any other such recognized position, and to attach himself permanently to the office ; but none such was placed at his disposal. Stephen had once said to me, when advising me to depend upon the public and upon literature for advancement, and not upon the Government, 'You may write off the first joint of your fingers for them, and then you may write off the second joint, and all that they will say of you is, "What a remarkably short-fingered man."' They did not say this of Spedding, but they did nothing for him, and he took the opportunity of the Whig Government going out in 1841 to give up his employment. He then applied himself to edit the works and vindicate the fame of Lord Bacon."

Two or three years ago Spedding republished from the *Edinburgh Review* some articles in which he had defended the Jamaica policy of Lord Melbourne's Government, which was, I believe, in great measure directed by Sir Henry Taylor. It was impossible to revive, after a lapse of forty years, the interest which had been felt at the time in a controversy long since forgotten. Curious readers who remembered the contemporary discussion had no difficulty in recognizing Spedding's forensic ability as advocate of a cause which he would not have undertaken to defend, if he had not believed it to be just. No other record remains of his official career, except in Sir Henry Taylor's eloquent tribute to his merits. In 1842 Spedding accompanied the first Lord Ashburton as private secretary on his mission to America for the settlement of the dispute on the North-West Boundary. The only public employment which he afterwards undertook was that of secretary to the Civil Service Commission when it was first instituted in 1855. As soon as the office was brought into working order, he lost no time in transferring his duties to Mr. J. G. Maitland, whom he recommended as his successor. It was by his own choice that he passed his life in gratuitous literary labour. "In 1847," says Sir Henry Taylor, "on Sir James Stephen's retirement, the office of Under Secretary of State, with £2000 a year, was offered to him by Lord Grey (before it was offered to me), and he could not be induced to accept it. He could not be brought to believe, what no one else doubted, that he was equal to the duties. Be this as it may, the fact that this man, being well known and close at hand for six years, who could have been had for £300 a year in 1841, should have been let slip, though he was thought worth £2000 a year in 1847, if not a rare, is a clear example of the little heed given by the Government of this country to the choice and use of instruments. It was at my suggestion that the offer was made; but I am not sorry that it was declined. He has devoted his singular abilities and his infinite industry in research, during a long life, to a great cause, and Lord Bacon will become known to posterity, gradually perhaps, but surely, as the man that he truly was—illustrious beyond all others except Shakespeare in his intellect, and, with whatever infirmities, still not less than noble in his moral mind. . . . James Spedding was well quit of the Colonial Office. His friends, it is true, were highly dissatisfied with his decision to refuse the office of Under Secretary of State; but he maintained that he knew his own deficiencies better than they, and observed, with the

quiet humour which was characteristic of him, that
'it was fortunate *he* was by when the decision was
taken.'"

His own judgment must be accepted; but of all
others who could form an estimate of his qualifications for the office, the man best entitled to be heard
is he who was leaving it, Sir James Stephen. Owing
to the state of his health, he was absent at the time
when the questions of this or that successor were·
discussed; but Sir Henry Taylor was in correspondence with him, and on the 20th October, he
wrote: "It is a perfect cordial to me to hear of
Spedding. How could I be so stupid as to forget
him?—so gentle, so wise, so luminous, and, in his
own quiet way, so energetic is he, that I would
rather devolve my functions in his hands than to
any person I know or have known."

It would be difficult to find another instance in
which a man of great ability and of considerable
official experience has declined a high position and
a liberal income for the sake of a laborious and
unremunerative literary enterprise. The desire of
fame or of any other personal advantage had no
share in his deliberate choice of a career. His sole
object was to dispel prevalent delusions by vindicating the character of Bacon. His own estimate of
his unfitness for the office which he declined was
undoubtedly sincere. Disinclination to a rapid succession of matters to be dealt with in public business
shared with his devotion to Bacon in the determination of his course of life.

It is not known that he at any subsequent time regretted a decision which appeared to many fanciful and perverse. His life before and after his rejection of official rank was uniform and uneventful. His habits were active and manly. He was a good walker and an excellent swimmer; and till after middle life he regularly shot. Spedding for some years occupied chambers in Lincoln's Inn Fields, which were the frequent resort of many of his contemporaries, and of younger friends whose acquaintance he was always ready to cultivate. In his later years he lived with some members of his family in Westbourne Terrace. His habits continued to be sociable; and in the intervals of his literary labour he practised simple recreations for the occupation of his leisure or the benefit of his health. He became moderately proficient in archery, and he was a persevering, though scarcely a successful, student of the art of billiards. A growing deafness, which was the only infirmity caused by advancing age, tended to depress his spirits, but there was to the last little change in his habits of life.

Like many literary predecessors, Spedding had probably formed an insufficient estimate of the magnitude of his projected undertaking. His edition of Bacon, with the accompanying Life, occupied him for nearly thirty years, to the regret of some who thought that the exclusive devotion of a long life and of ability approaching to genius was a heavy price to pay for the attainment of a not inconsiderable object. On the other hand, competent judges, among whom Sir Henry Taylor is perhaps entitled to the highest rank, have thought that the task which Spedding perfectly accomplished is worth all the sacrifice which it involved. On the publication in 1861 of the first two volumes of the "Life and Letters of Lord Bacon," Sir Henry Taylor, in a letter to a friend, did justice not only to the book, but to the diligence and genius of the author : "I have been reading Spedding's 'Life of Bacon' with profound interest and admiration—admiration, not of the perfect style and penetrating judgment only, but also of the extraordinary labour bestowed upon the work by a lazy man; the labour of some twenty years, I believe, spent in rummaging among old records in all places where they were to be found, and collating different copies of manuscripts written in the handwriting of the sixteenth century, and noting the minutest variations of one from another—an inexpressibly tedious kind of drudgery, and, what was perhaps still worse, searching far and wide, waiting, watching, peering, prying, through long years for records which no industry could recover. I doubt whether there be any other example in literary history of so large an intellect as Spedding's devoting itself with so much self-sacrifice to the illustration of one which was larger still ; and doing so out of reverence, not so much for that largest intellect as for the truth concerning it." At a later period Sir Henry Taylor entered more fully into the difficulties which Spedding had to over-

come, and into the reception of the book and its
effect upon the author: "Fourteen years' more
labour were to follow [after 1861] and five more
volumes. And his heroic perseverance had to maintain itself against divers discouragements. As long
as books last, and philosophy is cared for, and there
are human beings who care to investigate human intellect and human nature in one of its most wonder-
ful manifestations, the most elaborate and authentic,
and, I will say also, most impartial ' Life of Lord
Bacon ' will be read by the studious and highly
cultivated classes in each generation. But these
are the few, and popularity is not to be expected for
biographers such as these. To the popular mind
impartiality is not interesting. A story told by a
bold and vigorous partisan, fastening upon the
features and incidents which are sure to take effect,
finding no difficulties, or, if finding them, keeping
them sedulously out of sight, rounding off everything into a factitious clearness and consistency—
such a story of a life will have a much better chance
of popular acceptation than the other. Popularity,
therefore, had never been in question; and in so far
as some of the facts he presented ran counter to
long-established misconceptions and prejudices, there
was perhaps an element of *un*popularity. But, in
some cases, not popular sympathy only, but the
sympathy of personal friends was found wanting;
and that not from dissent or opposition in opinion,
but from simple indifference and neglect. One of
them so far misconceived the situation as to con-

gratulate him on the publication of the first two
volumes as the completion of his task, kindly ex-
horting him to undertake another. This he mentioned in a letter to me, adding that, 'if he had not
known all that long ago, and digested all that it
implied,' he should have thought it discouraging!
'But,' he added, 'I have long been aware that to
ninety-nine hundredths of the reading public, including about nine-tenths of my own particular
friends, the most satisfactory intelligence with
regard to my immortal work would be that there is
no more to come, and that I might have made that
announcement at the end of my volume without
danger of detection. . . . In the vote on the question whether my idea of Bacon's character is the
right one, I have always expected a large majority
against me; and, indeed, for that matter, I care very
little how it goes. All I want is, that those who
would sympathize with me if they heard the story
rightly told should not be prevented by hearing it
told wrong.'"

Sir Henry Taylor relates how at one time Spedding's interest in his work seemed to decline. His
eyes and memory were, he said, no longer what they
had been, and both research and composition were
irksome to him. "But, after a year or so of rest,
there is found a revival of the old ardour, and the
eyes and the memory prove themselves not unequal
to twelve or thirteen years more of their long-en-
during and not easily exhaustible efforts. . . . The
labours of more than thirty years reached their com-

plction in 1874, and the *truth of fact*—fact developed
from Bacon's life, and fact throwing light upon it—
was presented to mankind in all its length and
breadth and height and depth, leaving it to the
justice of mankind to arrive at such *truth of inference*
as long-established prepossessions might permit."

During the long continuance of Spedding's
labours on Bacon, the episodes or intellectual diver-
sions in which he indulged sometimes partook of the
nature of hobbies. Though he was in political
opinion a steady Liberal, he felt but a slight and
occasional interest in ordinary political disputes ;
but in 1848 and 1849 he became a vehement partisan of Hungary, which was then engaged in its
gallant struggle against Austrian usurpation. He
was on the side of justice or historical right, but
there were before and after that time many contests
for just causes in which he took only a faint interest.
In later years he became a zealous and powerful
advocate of the theory that words should be written
in strict conformity to the actual or assumed pro-
nunciation of the day. He was always ready to
defend by forcible or plausible argument a doctrine
which for the present lies outside the range of practical controversy. It would seem that some persons
are destined by nature to lapse into the phonetic
heresy, while the rest of the world is beyond the
reach of proselytism. In some vigorous minds, and
to a certain extent in Spedding's, originality tends
to border on paradox. He found readier sympathy
in his literary predilections, which were for the most

part both earnest and just, though they were by choice or accident limited to a few authors. His study of philosophy or scientific method was, I think, confined to Bacon ; and his knowledge of the details of history extended in neither direction beyond the times of Elizabeth and James I. He took pleasure in displaying, and sometimes in exaggerating, his want of acquaintance with many things which are supposed to be universally known. He was in the habit of saying that he got undeserved credit for knowledge, because no one would believe that such a man could be so profoundly ignorant. His apparently simple desire for information not unfrequently resolved itself into a Socratic exposure of fallacies ; but it was true that he deliberately abstained from the study of subjects in which he felt no concern. The literature of fiction for the most part failed to attract him, but he had a minute and accurate knowledge of Miss Austen's novels. In the spirit of a thorough-going admirer and loyal champion, he formerly maintained that Miss Austen had never made a mistake ; and, when he was reminded that Emma ate strawberries in Mr. Knightley's garden under apple trees in blossom, he took much trouble to ascertain whether some apple blossoms are not very late, and some strawberries very early. At last he had the candour to admit that Miss Austen's perfect fidelity to nature had been in a single instance interrupted. His poetical tastes were more comprehensive. His appreciation of Wordsworth was neither enthusiastic nor indiscriminate ; and he admired Byron, who was less cordially liked by his contemporary friends. He thought with good reason that Keats would have become a poet of a very high order, and he was one of the earliest and steadiest votaries of the genius of Tennyson. It is well known that the touching little poem which bears his initials was addressed to Spedding. To the collected edition of Charles (Tennyson) Turner's beautiful sonnets he contributed an excellent critical essay. His knowledge of Shakespeare was extensive and profound, and his laborious and subtle criticism derived additional value from his love of the stage. In his collected essays on subjects unconnected with Bacon is included an instructive criticism on Miss Ellen Terry's representation of Portia, and on the character itself and the due place of Portia in the play. In his opinion Shylock had, through the histrionic capabilities of his part, usurped in popular estimation the protagonism which, as he thought, properly belonged to Portia. A generation has passed away since Spedding was induced to become an enthusiastic admirer of Mdlle. Jenny Lind by the combined charm of her voice and of her exquisite acting. His musical taste was as little diffusive as his political sympathy. Jenny Lind among singers, like Hungary among insurgent nations, had a monopoly of his devotion. He had a genuine love of art and a discriminating taste, and he took pleasure in the society of painters and sculptors. His knowledge of science was confined to his mathematical studies at Cambridge. He knew

little or nothing of the pursuits which seemed to
Bacon alone worthy of a philosopher.

His violent and sudden death caused a wide-
spread feeling of regret, as well as deep distress to
those who were nearest to him. On the 1st of
March, 1881, he was knocked down and severely
injured by a cab at the bottom of Hay Hill. The
occupant of the cab, instead of ascertaining his address, sent him to St. George's Hospital, from which
it was afterwards found impossible to remove him to
his home. The case was from the first hopeless, and
he died in the hospital on the 9th. While he was
still conscious, he was careful to assure those around
him that the driver was not to blame. The almost
paradoxical love of justice, whether or not his
opinion was well founded, was in the highest degree
characteristic.

The imperfect or deferred attainment of the chief
object of his life was, I think, in some degree
attributable to an original error in the plan of his
work. His vindication of the character of Bacon is,
as he intended, complete and conclusive, but only on
the condition that it is read. He insisted that his
readers should have before them all the proofs on
which his own convictions were founded. In his
great work the documentary evidence, consisting
mainly of Bacon's letters and occasional writings, is
inserted at proper intervals in the midst of the
biographer's argument and narrative. By an almost
perverse self-effacement, the extracts are given in large
print, and the far more interesting "Life of Bacon"

in small print. Spedding was never in a hurry, and
he knew that he was too late to convert his own
generation, but he determined, as he said, that all
persons who might be born in or after 1850 should
have the means of forming an accurate and independent judgment. Many of his expected proselytes
have now reached middle life without taking advantage of the opportunities which he provided.
It is the business of a literary artist, and especially
of an historian, while he collects raw materials only
for his own use, to supply finished products to his
readers. Spedding may boast of an illustrious
imitator, for the plan of Carlyle's history of Oliver
Cromwell was borrowed from the cumbrous arrangement of the "Life of Bacon." Even the irritating
distinction of type is transferred from the original
to the copy; for both biographers seem to have been
affected by the spirit of hero-worship which led
Assyrian sculptors to represent kings on a larger
scale than that which was assigned to themselves as
ordinary men. If the text of the "Life of Bacon"
had not been disfigured by incessant interpolations
it would not have been unreasonably voluminous. In
Spedding's own composition there is nothing superfluous or tedious; and the style is vigorous, pure,
and transparently clear. The "Evenings with a
Reviewer," written five and thirty years ago, and
now for the first time published, contain the substance
of the argument which was afterwards fortified by
detailed proofs and illustrations. The friends who
at the time received copies of the book regretted with

good reason Spedding's resolution to postpone the publication; and he seems, after a long interval, to have discovered his mistake in suppressing his more compendious vindication of Bacon's character. He had recently prepared the book for the press, with little change beyond the suppression of passages which might seem to be tinged with controversial acrimony.

Macaulay's "Essay on Bacon," written during his residence in India, has confirmed the vulgar belief on which it was founded more effectually than if it had been more elaborate in its details. Readers who are familiar with Macaulay's intellectual mannerism cannot but have observed that the essay is a mere amplification of Pope's hackneyed paradox about the greatest, wisest, and meanest of mankind. The almost hyperbolical language in which Bacon's genius is exalted prepares the way for indignation and contempt against the alleged baseness and servility of his practical career. Although the first gloss of Macaulay's popularity is worn off, it may be hoped that the essay is still sufficiently well known to excite an interest in the question whether the rhetorical antithesis which it propounds is either credible or true. Those who may be sufficiently curious to study Spedding's examination of Macaulay's elaborate libel will be surprised to find that the comment is at least as entertaining as the text, while it is infinitely more conclusive. On some points there may still be room for a difference of opinion, as for instance on the completeness of the exculpation of Bacon in his relations to Essex; but few students of Spedding's apology will recur to the moral standard by which Macaulay judges of the transaction. The biographical epigrammatist thinks it sufficient to compare the pecuniary benefits which had been respectively conferred on Bacon by Elizabeth and by Essex. The grave historian reminds the serious inquirer that, as Bacon owed loyal allegiance to the parsimonious queen, he was bound to vindicate her cause against his open-handed friend who had become a rebel. It was an easier task to expose the futility of the incessant sneers and misrepresentations which Macaulay directs against Bacon because he complied with the ceremonious usages of his time. For the fatal irregularities which caused Bacon's fall Spedding offers no defence, but he succeeds in extenuating errors which scarcely amounted to crimes. It is a matter of serious regret that Macaulay had not the opportunity of reading the "Evenings with a Reviewer." In other cases it was his habit to trust to his reputation, and to the comparative obscurity of his critics, even in cases where, according to every judgment but his own, they had clearly convicted him of error. In republishing the "Essay on Bacon," he boldly relied on the improbability that his readers should have consulted Mr. Jardine's treatise on the Law of Torture, which he slightly mentions. He justly calculated on the general indifference with which Mr. Impey's vindication of the character of his grandfather the Chief Justice was received; and

with less good fortune he underrated the demonstration of his mistakes which is contained in Mr.
Paget's "New Examen." He could scarcely have
afforded to treat the "Evenings with a Reviewer"
with equal levity. Spedding was his intellectual
equal, and he was not unknown in literary and
general society. Macaulay could scarcely have failed
to perceive that his own superficial acquaintance with
the history of Bacon was not to be compared with
the results of long and profound study. At a later
time Spedding was in the habit of suggesting a
conjectural excuse for Macaulay's occasional inaccuracy, and for his obstinacy in refusing to correct
his mistakes. Both peculiarities were with much
probability ascribed to habitual reliance on a mar-
vellous memory. The errors which could not always
be avoided during his youthful accumulation of
various knowledge became stereotyped in a recollection which probably reproduced with unfailing
fidelity the original impression. It might be excusable in a hasty student to accept and to exaggerate
the popular estimate of Bacon's character; and farther
study and reconsideration probably seemed superfluous. The proverbial warning, "Cave ab homine
unius libri," was naturally overlooked by the pos-
sessor of vast stores of miscellaneous erudition.

The most valuable part of Macaulay's "Essay on
Bacon" is his bold and ingenious reduction of
Bacon's philosophical doctrine to the simple rules
of common sense. In the "Evenings with a Reviewer" Spedding wholly abstains from dealing

with questions of which he never considered himself a thoroughly competent judge. His vindication of Bacon's character from the popular imputation of meanness could in no degree have been strengthened by arguments in support of the admission that he was also the greatest of mankind, but Spedding profoundly believed in the soundness of the general estimate of Bacon's services to the cause of knowledge. He justly deemed himself fortunate in securing the aid of the late Mr. R. Leslie Ellis as editor of Bacon's Philosophical Works. No commentator was more capable than Mr. Ellis of appreciating any relation which might be found to exist between the precepts contained in the "Novum Organon" and the scientific discoveries of later times. Writers of the rank of Sir John Herschel and Dr. Whewell have in recent times confirmed by their authority the long-established belief that the philosopher

> " Whom a wise king and Nature chose
> Lord Chancellor of both their laws "

had prepared the way for the conquests which he was not himself permitted to achieve—

> " And from the Pisgah-top of his exalted wit
> Beheld the promised land, and showed us it."

Mr. Ellis, in his learned and argumentative preface to the Philosophical Works, examined more severely the pretensions which have been advanced on behalf of the most eloquent commentator since Plato on the conditions of human knowledge. In his

conclusions Mr. Ellis will be found not to differ widely
from Lord Macaulay. He deduces from careful inquiry the proposition that Bacon contributed nothing
to the process of induction, and that his scientific
method would not have conduced to the advance of
knowledge, if it had ever been applied to the purpose
by any discoverer. For the general knowledge, for
the practical wisdom, and for the imaginative
eloquence of Bacon Mr. Ellis expresses cordial admiration ; but his rejection of Bacon's supposed
claims to the gratitude of mankind must have
disappointed his enthusiastic coadjutor. With characteristic honesty Spedding both published Mr.
Ellis's preface in his edition, and called attention
to his disparaging judgment of Bacon's services to
science. His own unshaken belief in the importance
of the " Novum Organon " was not inconsistent
with Mr. Ellis's assertion that Bacon's method had
never been tried by men of science. The zealous
biographer was inclined to suspect that their neglect
had obstructed the process of discovery, and he persuaded himself that the greater attention devoted in
the present day to the collection of physical facts
involved a tardy and wholesome approximation to
Bacon's neglected method. The issue was not
material to his life-long task. The historical and
biographical conclusions which he established depend on an exhaustive accumulation of evidence
arranged and interpreted by the clearest of intellects
with an honesty which is rarely known in controversial discussion. No more conscientious, no

more sagacious critic has employed on a not unworthy task the labour of a life. It will be well,
rather for students of history and of character than
for himself, if his just fame is rescued from the
neglect which he regarded with unaffected indifference.

G. S. V.

EVENING THE FIRST.

A.

Edinburgh Review, July 1837.—*Judex damnatur cum nocens absolvitur.*—Now, then, are you ready ?

" We return our hearty thanks—"

I suppose we need not trouble ourselves with the preliminary flourish. It is only the ceremony of shaking hands before the fight.

B.

No, no. I cannot let Macaulay go away with his first paragraph on that pretence. It is not a matter of compliment : it is the judgment of the Edinburgh Review upon the merits of the book.

A.

" We return our hearty thanks to Mr. Montagu, as well for his very valuable edition of Lord Bacon's works, as for the instructive Life of the immortal author contained in the last volume. We have much to say on the subject of this Life, and will often find ourselves obliged to dissent from the opinions of the biographer. But about his merits as a collector of the materials out of which opinions are formed there can be no dispute. And we readily acknowledge that we are in great measure indebted to his minute and accurate researches for the means of refuting what we cannot but consider as his errors."

B.

Stop. It is not worth while to enter upon the question as to the real merits of Mr. Montagu's well-meant book. But it *is* worth while to say that this critical estimate of it is so absurdly inapplicable that I can only suppose it to have been pronounced at mere hap-hazard. Ask anybody who has read the Life with attention, or attempted to *use* the edition, and he will tell you that no competent critic who cared whether he described the book correctly or not could possibly have described it so. For my own part I believe that the reviewer did in fact never trouble his head to consider what an edition of Bacon ought to be;—perhaps had not even turned over the leaves of half the fifteen volumes octavo upon which he was pronouncing judgment.

A.

Very likely. He was going to review Bacon himself, not his editor. It suited him to use Montagu's facts in order to overthrow his theory ; and a good round compliment like this was a striking position to start from ; besides that it made a show (however delusive) of candour. Whether the compliment were merited or not, I suppose he did not trouble himself to inquire. I told you it was only a flourish, —shaking hands before the fight.

B.

Yes; but remember, when I charge him presently with the same kind of recklessness in making round assertions, without caring whether he has any ground for them or not, you are not to say that he is incapable of it. Remember, that it will not be the first time he has been pulled up for that offence. *Judex damnatur cum nocens absolvitur.* The guilty has been acquitted in the first page : see now whether he will not attempt to mend the matter by condemning the innocent.

A.

Well, here are more compliments:—" Labour of love," " generous enthusiasm," " activity," " perseverance," " zeal which has perverted his judgment," &c. &c. Will you have all this ?

B.

No, I allow all that. And I have not much to say upon the next paragraph, in which the reviewer apologises on behalf of the rest of mankind for the weakness of treating their benefactors with tenderness. I am not myself concerned to advocate the practice ; and if he has any tendency that way himself (as he seems to confess), I think we must all acquit him in this case of the weakness of yielding to it. It may be as well to say however, by way of caution, that I think him quite wrong as to the fact. I never saw that posterity was reluctant to think ill of the personal characters of great *writers*. I was never taught, nor ever wished, to think of Sallust as a good man. Who has tried to prove that Fielding did not bilk landladies ? And as for Shakespeare's cudgelling of gamekeepers, if we are so reluctant to believe him capable of such a thing, why *do* we believe it ? There is no evidence of the fact except a popular rumour, which cannot be traced back within half a century of the time when it is supposed to have been committed. The truth is, it is not great *writers* whose faults are winked at by posterity, but great *sufferers*, where the suffering has been exhibited in picturesque and pathetic situations. But this is not our business at present. Let Cicero and Middleton pass. We will suppose if you will that " a great writer is the friend and benefactor of his readers, and they cannot but judge of him under the deluding influence of friendship and gratitude,"—(those are the words, I think)—and that Bacon owes the popular estimate of his personal character, " wisest, brightest, meanest," &c., to the prevalence of that affectionate delusion. Pass on to the bottom of page 4, where business begins.

A.

" Mr. Montagu's faith is sincere and implicit. He practises no trickery; he conceals nothing; he puts the facts before us in the full confidence that they will produce on our minds the effect they have produced on his own. It is not till he comes to reason from facts to motives that his partiality shows itself; and then he leaves Middleton himself far behind. His work proceeds on the assumption that Bacon was an eminently virtuous man. From the tree Mr. Montagu judges of the fruit——"

B.

Well, if a tree has to my knowledge borne apples for twenty years, I suppose I may suspect some mistake when I am told that it has borne crabs on the twenty-first.

A.

Stop a moment : we are not at the end of the sentence.

" He is forced to relate many actions which, if any man but Bacon had committed them, nobody would have dreamed of defending, which are readily and completely explained by supposing Bacon to have been a man whose principles were not strict and whose spirit was not high,—actions which can be explained in no other way without resorting to some grotesque hypothesis, for which there is not a tittle of evidence. But any hypothesis is in Mr. Montagu's opinion more probable than that his hero should ever have done anything very wrong. This mode of defending Bacon seems to us by no means Baconian. To take a man's character for granted, and then from his character to infer the moral quality of his actions, is surely a process the very reverse of that which is recommended in the *Novum Organum*. Nothing, we are sure, could have led Mr. Montagu to depart so far from his master's precepts except zeal for his master's honour."

B.

Stay a moment, and consider. Now, does all this sound to you like a fair exposition of Mr. Montagu's *modus operandi?* Do you think he really *began* his study of Bacon's actions by taking his character for granted ?

A.

Nay, how should I know? If he did not, the reviewer does him injustice.

B.

To be sure he does : and you will find that he does injustice to everybody in the same way. But does it not carry exaggeration and caricature on the face of it? I do not say that Mr. Montagu is not partial *for* Bacon, any more than that Macaulay is not partial *against* him. Both of them have a pleasure in making their periods round and their picture complete; and both try occasionally to effect it by supposing circumstances for which, though possible, they can produce no evidence. But the *method* is logical enough. Mr. Montagu had a general impression of Bacon's character, not pre-*assumed*, but pre-formed upon a *general* survey of his words and actions—of the context of his life. It is quite right that in interpreting each separate passage this general impression should be taken into account. Every man is entitled to the benefit of such an impression. No court of justice rejects as irrelevant evidence to the prisoner's general character where the direct evidence leaves room for doubt. Mr. Montagu started, not with a theory that a great writer must be a good man, but with a notion derived in the same way in which we all derive our notions of each other's character, that Bacon *was* a good man.

A.

Well, well. Never mind Mr. Montagu : our business is with Bacon. Whether the reviewer be right or wrong in charging this fault upon Mr. Montagu, it will be enough for me if he avoid it himself. Listen to this :—

" We shall pursue a different course. We shall attempt, with the valuable assistance which Mr. Montagu has afforded us, TO FRAME SUCH AN ACCOUNT OF BACON'S LIFE AS MAY ENABLE OUR READERS CORRECTLY TO ESTIMATE HIS CHARACTER."

Come, what can you desire better than that?

B.

Nothing. I am glad to hear you read the passage with such emphasis; for I may have occasion to remind you of it. I understand then that he is addressing himself not simply to overthrow Mr. Montagu's estimate, nor simply to make out a case for his own, but to present the facts in such a way that you and I (who are supposed to know nothing of the matter) may form a correct estimate for ourselves. This is the promise. Now mind;—if he confine himself only to the more questionable and less creditable parts of Bacon's history, however candidly he may discuss them—leaving unnoticed or lost in the background those parts which are unquestionable and certainly to his honour—I shall not think that promise fulfilled. If the temptations to which Bacon yielded are to be made the most of (and I would have nothing kept back), I must insist on having some account of those to which he did not yield.

A.

By all means. Here follow four or five pages upon the character of the statesmen of the generation preceding, who are introduced apparently by way of contrast. Shall I read them?

B.

Not for anything I have to say on the subject. I am not well enough acquainted with them to give an opinion. From what I do know indeed, I am not inclined to agree altogether with Macaulay. He draws a striking contrast between these two generations of statesmen; but I do not think he has taken the points of contrast truly. The difference was not so much, I think, in the men themselves as in the times and the personal character of the sovereigns. Francis Bacon bears a remarkably strong resemblance to his father in character and disposition. His temperament,— the fiery element which fed his genius,—probably came from his mother. And on the other side the character and fortunes of Raleigh and Essex are not without sufficiently near parallels among the generation of their fathers. But these matters have little or nothing to do with the sequel. Therefore let them pass.

A.

Together with the dissertation on female education, I suppose, which occupies ten pages more.

B.

Yes ; an account of the actual relation between Francis Bacon and his mother during the first forty years of his life, would have been more to the purpose. But none of his biographers have taken any notice of this; and probably Macaulay did not know that anything was to be known about it. His conduct both as a son and as a brother during his early manhood throws much light upon his personal character, and should certainly be taken along with us as we follow him through his career. But his mother's skill in the learned languages has but little bearing on the subject; therefore you may pass, if you will, to page 12.

A.

Does Mr. Montagu say nothing about it ?

B.

He gives a long list of eminent men who have had mothers. But he does not tell us what sort of woman Lady Ann Bacon was ; or how she was writing daily letters to her sons, full of affection, pride, passion, grief and dissatisfaction ; interfering in all their affairs, expostulating upon all their proceedings, quarrelling with all their friends, and treating them like children who could not take care of themselves :— a very singular and interesting person, who must have been extremely difficult to get on with ; the consideration of whose feelings and infirmities must, I think, have entered into and modified every act of her sons' lives. But (as 1 said) I have no reason to suppose that the reviewer knew anything about her more than her reputation for Greek and Latin. Therefore I infer nothing from his silence, except perhaps this,—I do not think he can have felt any intelligent curiosity about Bacon's personal character; for under a genuine and earnest desire to understand his character, so acute and book-learned a man would hardly have forgotten to look in that direction for indications of it. But let us hear how he tells those parts of the story which he *has* looked into.

A.

" Francis Bacon, the youngest son of Sir Nicholas, was born at York House, his father's residence in the Strand, on the 22nd of January 1561."

You do not dispute that, I suppose?

B.

1561 according to our way of reckoning. In those days it was called 1560. To avoid confusion, it is always better, in speaking of times when the civil year was reckoned as beginning on the 25th of March, to give the double date, 1560–1. But, well?

A.

" IIis health was very delicate, and to this circumstance may be partly attributed that gravity of carriage and that love of sedentary pursuits which distinguished him from other boys. Everybody knows how much his premature readiness of wit and sobriety of deportment amused the Queen, and how she used to call him her young Lord Keeper."

B.

It is a small matter, hardly worth stopping for, perhaps ; except that it shows the kind of licence these lively writers indulge in. I confess I should have preferred the un-varnished report of Dr. Rawley (which is the sole authority for this circumstance) without any pleasant turn given to it out of the writer's head for the entertainment of the reader.

Dr. Rawley only says that "the Queen delighted much then to confer with him and to prove him with questions; unto whom he delivered himself with that gravity and maturity above his years, that Her Majesty would often term him *her young Lord Keeper.*" Who can say from this whether the Queen questioned him for amusement or from a rational interest; whether his gravity was absurd, or only remarkable?

A.

Come, come; confess that he was something of a prig. One cannot imagine that he was ever a boy with a boy's heart in him. Look here—

"We are told that while still a mere child, he stole away from his playfellows to a vault in St. James's Fields, to investigate the cause of a singular echo which he had observed there."

B.

Ay, there again! That comes not from Dr. Rawley, but from Mr. Montagu. The *fact* is simply that in his old age he *described* this singular echo, and stated what he (being then above sixty) conceived to be the cause of it. For the fact of "stealing from his playfellows," and the purpose "to investigate the cause," we are indebted solely to Mr. Montagu. It is purely an inference, and (as it happens) a very bad inference. There was a brick conduit with a window in it, leading to a round-house of stone in which was a rift; and the phenomenon was, that if you cried out in the rift it made "a fearful roaring at the window." It may be probable (though it is not stated) that he made acquaintance with this fact when he was a child; but it must have been in the company of at least one of his playfellows. For there must clearly have been two,—one to cry at the rift and the other to listen at the window. Certainly if I were to draw any inference from his recollection of this echo, it would be that he had been used when a boy to play there *with* his companions. It must have been a delightful place for boys to play in. The "fearful roaring" is *boy*, all over. The young Lord Keeper listening to the fearful roaring would make a pretty picture in the hands of a good artist. Is there any more of this?

A.

Not much.

"It is certain that at only twelve he busied himself with very ingenious speculations on the art of legerdemain,—a subject which, as Professor Dugald Stewart has most justly observed, merits much more attention from philosophers than it has ever received."

B.

Bravo! I did not think he could have capped the last. This again comes from Mr. Montagu. But the Edinburgh reviewer, in compliment I suppose to the Edinburgh professor, has a little improved it. Mr. Montagu only says that "in his twelfth year he was meditating on the laws of the imagination." His grounds he gives in a footnote; so that in this instance the reviewer knew what he was talking about. And what do you think they amount to? In his twelfth year (or much earlier, or indeed two or three years later, for anything we know) Francis Bacon *saw* at his father's house a juggler who played tricks with cards. At some after-time (how long after we have no data whatever for determining) he met with "a pretended learned man, that was curious and vain enough" in speculations concerning the imagination, and *related to him* the tricks which the juggler had played, and the manner of it in detail;— upon which the learned man expounded to him an ingenious theory on the subject: a theory which, it is clear from his manner of telling the story, was at the time quite new to him; and which, "though" (he adds) "it did somewhat sink with me, yet I made it lighter than I thought, and said I thought it was confederacy between the juggler and the two servants," &c. And this is all. And upon no more than this Mr. Montagu tells us that "in his twelfth year

Bacon was meditating on the laws of the imagination:" and the reviewer announces it "as *certain* that at only twelve he busied himself with *very ingenious speculations* on the art of legerdemain." And this with the entire facts of the case lying legible (though in small print) under his nose !

A.

Well, but he builds nothing upon this. He goes on—

" These are trifles. But the eminence which Bacon afterwards attained renders them interesting."

B.

I do not accuse him of building anything upon it; nor of ascribing to these things undue value. I accuse him of stating them as if they were ascertained facts, when they are not so much as flying reports. The error, you may say, is trifling, as the things themselves are trifles. And so it is in these particular cases. But the habit which it implies is no trifle. It is a habit of inaccuracy; of carelessness in the use of words; of introducing essential variations into a story, not only without authority, but without notice; possibly without knowing it. And do not ask me to believe that a man who will do this in trifles upon no provocation, will not do it in serious things where there is provocation. If a boy under sixteen watching the tricks of a juggler is from inadvertency or for effect to be converted into a boy of twelve busying himself with very ingenious speculations on an important subject to this day neglected by philosophers, what security have I that a young man modestly applying for employment shall not be converted into the great philosopher meanly prostituting his genius and character for a place ? You will find as we go on that it is not in trifles only that the reviewer indulges in this kind of liberty. Remember that I do not impute to him wilful inaccuracy,—I have no doubt he believes all he says,—but inaccuracy so habitual that it has grown to be unconscious ; which (in a historian) is a worse thing. I accuse him of a readiness to believe anything that will heighten the effect of his description or sharpen the points of his argument.

Now let us see what he makes of Bacon at Cambridge.

A.

"In his thirteenth year he was entered at Trinity College, Cambridge. That celebrated school of learning enjoyed the peculiar favour of the Lord Treasurer and the Lord Keeper," &c.

Here follows an attack on the memory of Whitgift. Have you any objection to my considering him, on the authority of the reviewer, as at this time a chrysalis, "a kind of intermediate grub between sycophant and oppressor"? I begin to be prepared to modify my opinions in such matters.

B.

No; I know nothing about Whitgift, except that some years after he took a leading part in measures which Bacon did not approve. I shall keep my own opinion open until I know more. You can do as you like.

A.

I think we may as well let him rest for the present.

"It has often been said that Bacon, while still at college, planned that great intellectual revolution with which his name is inseparably connected. The evidence on this subject, however, is hardly sufficient to prove what is itself so improbable, as that any definite scheme of that kind should have been so early formed even by so powerful and active a mind. But it is certain that after a residence of three years at Cambridge, Bacon departed, carrying with him a profound contempt for the course of study pursued there; a fixed conviction that the systems of academic education in England were radically vicious; a just scorn for the trifles on which the followers of Aristotle had wasted their powers; and no great reverence for Aristotle himself."

B.

All this is certain, is it? I should like to know where the evidence is. For if it be true that Bacon felt at sixteen so much profound contempt, just scorn, and fixed conviction, I must materially alter my conception of his character. I know very well that in speaking of the Universities some fifteen or twenty years after, he pointed out certain grave errors and defects in the plan of education adopted there; also, that he had, some years earlier, come to the conclusion that the whole system of *philosophy* which was taught there was a progress in the wrong direction. But I know nothing of the contempt and scorn and spirit of sweeping condemnation which is here imputed to him at sixteen. Throughout his life he spoke of the Universities always with affection and respect, and treated them accordingly. The impression under which Macaulay wrote this sentence was suggested, I suppose, by Mr. Montagu's account of this period of Bacon's life; which is made up by gathering together everything he ever said about our own Universities, about the schoolmen of the middle ages, and about knowledge in general, and supposing that he felt it all while he was there. What we *know* of the matter is what Bacon himself told Dr. Rawley—which goes, by the way, rather to prove the point which the reviewer rejects as improbable, than those which he sets down as certain,—to wit:

"Whilst he was commorant at the University (as his Lordship hath been pleased to impart unto myself) he first fell into the dislike of the philosophy of Aristotle;—not for the worthlessness of the author, to whom he would ever ascribe all high attributes, but for the unfruitfulness of the way; being a philosophy, as his Lordship used to say, only strong for disputations and contentions, but barren of works for the benefit of the life of man; in which mind he continued till his dying day."

And certainly the title *Temporis partus maximus,* which he gave to a treatise composed about eight years after he left Cambridge,—of which nothing but the title remains,—does imply something like an idea of the Instauratio Magna, and a formed plan of the great intellectual revolution which the reviewer speaks of. And I do not know how it strikes you, but for my own part I can much more easily believe that he left the University at sixteen with such a plan in his head, than in the state of mind imputed to him.—Well?

A.

"In his sixteenth year he visited Paris, and resided there for some time under the care of Sir Amias Paulet, Elizabeth's minister at the French court, and one of the ablest and most upright of the many valuable servants whom she employed. France was at that time in a state of deplorable agitation. The Huguenots and the Catholics were mustering their forces for the fiercest and most protracted of their many struggles; while the prince, whose duty it was to protect and restrain both, had by his vices and follies degraded himself so deeply, that he had no authority over either. Bacon however made a tour through several provinces, and appears to have passed some time at Poitiers."

B.

How does he know (I wonder) that he made a tour through several provinces? Oh, I see. Mr. Montagu says, that " after the appointment of Sir Amias Paulet's successor, Bacon travelled into the French provinces, and spent some time at Poictiers." Well, I will admit that as a sufficient justification of the statement; though it happens to be wrong. Mr. Montagu knew that Bacon had been at Poictiers in his youth, and not knowing when or on what occasion, supplied the defect by a very fair conjecture. I have no fault to find with it, considered as a conjecture ; but I object to the statement of it as a fact. The fact is, that the French court was at Poictiers in the autumn of 1577, and Sir Amias Paulet (who had been moving about from place to place during the early part of the summer, that he might have an interview with the king upon some important and urgent matters of public business) remained there as ambassador from the latter end of July to the latter end of October; Bacon being no doubt in his suite; in which he continued certainly until his father's death, sixteen months after ; whether until the appointment of Sir Amias's successor (November 1st, 1579), we do not know.

A.

" We have abundant proof that during his stay on the Continent he did not neglect literary and scientific pursuits."

B.

Abundant proof? Unless he mean that his early proficiency is a proof,—and it is certainly a fair presumption,—I doubt whether we have any proof whatever. Mr. Montagu talks indeed of his contracting lasting friendships with men of letters, and making great impressions upon grave statesmen and learned philosophers; but he mentions no name and quotes no authority.

A.

But you do not deny the fact?

B.

By no means. The presumption is obvious and most reasonable; and I know of nothing whatever to contradict it. I am myself fully persuaded that he did not neglect literature or science. But I object to the assertion of it as a fact of which we have *abundant proof,* when there is in fact no proof, but only a natural presumption;—because I may be told presently that there is abundant proof of something of which I am by no means fully persuaded, however presumable it may be in the much-presuming eyes of the reviewer. Please therefore to remember that I checked you here; for I may have occasion, as you go on, to remind you that he is in the habit of using such words loosely.

A.

Very well, I'll remember. But do let us get on to the material points.

"But his attention seems to have been chiefly directed to statistics and diplomacy. It was at this time that he wrote those Notes on the State of Europe that are printed in his works."

B.

I beg your pardon. It is a small matter again, but you really must let me stop you. Here indeed our reviewer has taken some pains to be accurate; for he has materially modified the grossly inaccurate statement of Mr. Montagu.

But he has not quite succeeded. It is indeed most probable that Bacon was at this time *collecting the materials* for those Notes ; if they are really his, which is doubtful.* But the *composition* must have been as late as May 1582, as may be known from the allusion to the French levies in aid of Don Antonio, who "is *now* in France." † It is a small matter as I said ; but yet it is something to know whether such a work was composed at nineteen or at two and twenty.

A.

Yes.

" He studied the art of deciphering with great interest; and invented a cipher so ingenious, that many years later he thought it deserving a place in the *De Augmentis*."

B.

Yes, this (at last) is really correct. Mr. Montagu talks less correctly of his " preparing a work upon cyphers, which he afterwards published." The art of deciphering must necessarily have attracted his attention ; the most important diplomatic correspondence being then conducted in cipher.

A.

" In February 1580 "—

79–80, you would have him say—

B.

Not exactly. It is a good example of the inconvenience of not preserving the double date. Mr. Montagu tells us that Bacon returned to England "instantly," upon the death of his father " on the 20th of February 1579 ; " and then passes at once to the year 1580. The reviewer, supposing naturally enough that he used the old reckoning, reduces it without inquiry to the modern : thereby misdating the fact a whole year. Sir Nicholas Bacon died on the 20th of February 1578–9, as you may see either in Stow or Camden. Francis was then in Paris.

* For my reasons for doubting, see " Letters and Life of Francis Bacon," vol. i. pp. 15–17.
† Lansd. MSS. 35, f. 43.

A.

In February 1578-9, then,

"He received intelligence of the almost sudden death of his father, and instantly returned to England.

"His prospects were greatly overcast by this event. He was most desirous to obtain a provision which might enable him to devote himself to literature and politics. He applied to the government; and it seems strange that he should have applied in vain. His wishes were moderate; his hereditary claims upon the administration were great. He had himself been favourably noticed by the Queen. His uncle was prime minister. His own talents were such as any minister might have been eager to enlist in the public service. But his solicitations were unsuccessful."

B.

Unsuccessful, so far as the *provision* was concerned. But in other respects the answer to his first application (when he was in his twentieth year) was surely favourable. The Queen sent him some message so encouraging that he calls it "an appropriation of him to her service." * What it was in particular that he applied for, I cannot clearly make out. I should guess, however, that it was not for any independent provision or political appointment (as the reviewer seems to suppose), but for some employment, or for some advancement with a view to subsequent employment, in the public service, *as a lawyer.* Some provision to relieve him from the ordinary practice of the law may have been included in his suit, likely enough, though there is no hint of it in the letter; but service, and service as a lawyer, seems to be clearly indicated. "Although " (he says) " it must be confessed that the request is rare and unaccustomed, yet if it be observed how few there be which fall in with the study of the common laws, either being well left or friended, or at their own free election, or forsaking likely success in other studies of more delight and no less preferment, or setting hand thereunto early without waste of years;—upon such

* " Letters and Life," vol. i. p. 14.

survey made, it may be my *case* may not seem ordinary no more than my suit, and so more beseeming unto it." * That is to say, not many persons in my case would betake them to the study of the law at all; therefore if I ask for a favour out of the common way, remember that my course is out of the common way;—an argument in which, had he been applying to be *relieved* from the study of the law, there would have been no sense. If I were myself to hazard a guess on the subject it would be this : Bacon had been admitted *de societate magistrorum* of Gray's Inn in June 1576. As soon as he returned to England and had to work for his livelihood, he naturally betook himself to the law as his profession. But his hope and wish was, through his interest with Burghley and the Queen, to be relieved, by an early advancement to some place in the Queen's service, not from the *study*, but from the *ordinary practice*, of the law. It was an object to him therefore to rise as fast as might be through the successive degrees which all lawyers had to pass, that he might be called as soon as possible within the bar. His suit therefore at this time was probably for some facility or dispensation in being called to the bar ; and this, I take it, was granted ; for he became an *utter* barrister in 1582, after only three years' study. Afterwards, in 1586, he appears to have applied (in pursuance of the same object) for some "ease in being called *within* bars ; " † about which some difficulty was made at the time,‡ though it was ultimately granted, as we shall see probably as we go on. I do not know in what manner the Queen·could help him on in the first instance. But if she could and did, this explanation seems to satisfy all the other conditions.

    This however is all guess-work, and of no great con- sequence. But whatever the first application may have been for, I can hardly doubt that it was favourably received. It was made to Burghley on the 16th of September 1580 ; § and on the 18th of the following month it is that he writes

* "Letters and Life," vol. i. p. 13.   † Ibid., vol. i. p. 59.
‡ Letter to Anthony Bacon, Jan. 25, 1594 : Ibid., vol. i. p. 348.
§ Ibid., vol. i. p. 12.

again to him, in acknowledgment of "his comfortable
relation of Her Majesty's gracious opinion and meaning
towards him." He writes in the tone of a man who has
received at least as much encouragement as he had expected. He speaks of "her benignity being made good
and verified in his father so far forth as it extendeth to his
posterity; accepting them as commended by his service
during the non-age of their own deserts." He hopes that
God will supply the defects of those whom he has inspired
with zeal, and "see them appointed of sufficiency convenient
for the rank and standing where they shall be employed."
He can promise "for his endeavour that it shall not be in
fault; but that what diligence can entitle him to, that he
doubts not to recover:"—and "seeing that it hath pleased
Her Majesty to take knowledge of this his mind, and to
vouchsafe to *appropriate him unto her service,* preventing any
desert of his with her princely liberality," &c. &c.* Now
what can all this mean but that his solicitation (so far) had
been successful? It is not a letter of formal acknowledgment, but evidently written out of the fulness of his heart,—
a modest and bashful heart, overflowing and apparently a
little fluttered with encouragement. And we hear nothing
further in the way either of solicitation or acknowledgment
for the next six years.

You may think that the mistake (if it be one) is trifling.
I am not sure of that. Every man's career does in fact
depend upon the manner in which his prospects open. And
besides, you will see as you go on that upon this supposed
rebuff of a supposed application some serious insinuations
against the character both of Bacon, and of Burghley, and
of the Queen, do in fact rest.

A.

But you stopped me in the middle of a long paragraph.
Let us hear what more the reviewer has to say before we
decide upon this point.

"The truth is that the Cecils disliked him, and did all that
they decently could to keep him down."

* "Letters and Life," vol. i. p. 14.

I suppose you will ask for proof of this; for your story does not seem to imply any want of assistance, on the part of Burghley at least. And Robert Cecil must have been still a boy.

B.

Robert Cecil was about seventeen, and of course could have nothing to do with the matter. Of Burghley's behaviour all we know is, that Bacon's application had been made through him, and through him the encouraging answer had been received; which does not to me look like disliking or keeping down. I admit however that the charge is not of Macaulay's invention, but has some support from respectable contemporary authority, though I cannot make out that there is much colour for it; and what colour there is belongs to a much later period, which, as involving new circumstances, should be considered separately. For the present, therefore, we had better not enter into the question. Only you are to bear in mind that Bacon is not yet twenty; that Burghley has not yet shown any disposition to keep him down; and that whether he ever did, is a question which remains to be proved.

A.

Very well. I will bear in mind anything that is reasonable.

" It has never been alleged that Bacon had done anything to merit this dislike. Nor is it at all probable that a man whose temper was naturally mild, whose manners were courteous, who through life nursed his fortunes with the utmost care, who was fearful even to a fault of offending the powerful, would have given any just cause of displeasure to a kinsman who had the means of rendering him essential service and of doing him irreparable injury."

B.

All this speculation belongs of course to the general question whether any such supposed dislike existed, and may be put off till we come to consider that. But I may as well warn you in the mean time that I do not admit this as a true account of Bacon's character. " *Mild* " is not the word by which I should describe his temper; at least, it requires a good deal of qualification. His temper was very quick and sensitive. His mildness was the effect of the sweetness, thoughtfulness, nobleness, and modesty of his nature,—his sense of justice, and his self-command. Neither can I allow that he was a good nurser of his fortunes, otherwise than through a cultivation of his faculties so assiduous and effectual, that fortune could make him no offer which he was not qualified by merit, capacity, and preparation, to accept. But I suppose there was never any man who *got* so little in proportion to what he *gave*; and why? Because he did not understand *how* to make bargains with fortune? No: but from the necessity of a noble nature, which will not stoop to chaffer and take advantages. He could not but know that the way to get on in the world is, first by giving a taste of your services to make their value understood, and then, by holding them back, to make the want of them felt. But the principle upon which through his whole life he acted was the reverse. He always began by giving all he had to give, leaving the recompense to be settled afterwards by those who had already received the value. The consequence of which was, that during the best years of his life the government had the use of his best services for nothing. He was more than forty-six years old before he even obtained any lucrative office ; and I think (if we except a pension of 60*l.* which King James gave him when he was forty-three, and the clerkship of the Star-chamber which fell to him when he was about fifty, and which he held for five or six years) he was at least fifty-eight before he received sixpence from the government (and he did not ask for it then) beyond the ordinary salaries and fees of the very laborious places in which he served.*

However, these are points upon which people may

---

* I did not then know that in August 1601, he received (out of the fine imposed on Catesby for his share in the Earl of Essex's conspiracy) 1800*l.* See " Letters and Life," vol. iii. p. 14.

reasonably differ. And in the mean time I quite agree that he is very unlikely to have given just cause of offence to Burghley or any one else. What next?

A.

"The real explanation, we have no doubt, is this: Robert Cecil, the Treasurer's second son, was younger by a few months than Bacon."

B.

Younger by two years and a half, nearly, if we may trust Sir Theodore Mayerne, who has recorded both the day and the hour at which he was born.

A.

"He had been educated with the utmost care; had been initiated, whilst still a boy, in the mysteries of diplomacy and court intrigue; and was just at this time about to be produced on the stage of public life."

B.

Just at this time? And what time was this?

A.

Oh,—when Bacon made his application, I suppose.

B.

That was in September 1580, when Robert Cecil was only seventeen years and three months old.

A.

Well, never mind. Bacon's applications continued no doubt till Robert was old enough. He does not mean that Burghley refused Bacon once for all, but that he continued to neglect him.

"The wish nearest to Burghley's heart was that his own greatness might descend to this favourite child. But even Burghley's fatherly partiality could hardly prevent him from perceiving that Robert, with all his abilities and acquirements, was no match for his cousin Francis. This seems to us the only rational explanation of the Treasurer's conduct. Mr. Montagu is more charitable. He supposes that Burghley was influenced merely by affection for his nephew; and was 'little disposed to encourage him to rely on others rather than himself, and to venture on the quicksands of politics instead of the certain profession of the law.' If such were Burghley's feelings, it seems strange that he should have suffered his son to venture on those quicksands from which he so carefully preserved his nephew."

B.

That is one among many of Mr. Montagu's suggestions in which I do not concur; therefore it is not worth while to question the validity of the argument. But I hope you do not think it conclusive, or see anything strange in a man thinking that of two young men, very unlike each other though both of rare ability, one will do better in law, the other in politics. As it turned out indeed, the judgment would have been abundantly justified. To tread the "quicksands of politics" was precisely what Robert Cecil was made for; whereas Bacon, though under a sovereign that understood his value he would have made the greatest of all prime ministers, was ill qualified to work his way up through a court.

A.

That is a new doctrine, is it not?

B.

A strange one perhaps, like all true doctrine about Bacon, to these times. Not the less sound though. *Why* he was ill qualified it would be hopeless to explain now, when his writings are so little read and his character so totally misunderstood; and it will be needless to explain hereafter, if his life should ever come to be studied;—for the explanation will suggest itself. However, we have yet (you know) to prove that Burghley did not do his best to advance Bacon in the course which Bacon himself wished.

A.

Yes. And here, I think, we have it.

" But the truth is, that if Burghley had been so disposed he might easily have secured Bacon a comfortable provision which would have been exposed to no risk."

What do you say to that ?

B.

In the first place, I say, How do we know that ? Burghley, though the most powerful man in council, was not omnipotent. Elizabeth was mistress, and took good care that her counsellors should know it. And it is notorious that in matters of this kind she was anything but manageable. Moreover she was not profuse of gifts (except occasionally to personal favourites), and was always better pleased (partly out of policy perhaps, partly out of economy, and partly out of pride) to see her servants in hope and appetite for favours to come, than grateful and independent. *What* could Burghley have got for Bacon, and *when ?*

In the second place, I ask—If Burghley could have procured him a comfortable provision exposed to no risk (which I doubt), and if he did want to get him out of Robert Cecil's way (which there is no reason for believing), why did he not do it at once ? By *not* providing for him he left him *in* the way.

A.

No. By forcing Bacon into the law he threw him into a different line of competition.

B.

And by providing for him in that line he would have kept him in it. But by leaving him in a condition (for you have no right to say that he forced him into it) which, without diminishing either his necessities or his preference for political life, constrained him to add to his other qualifications those of a trained and grounded lawyer,—

what did he do but make him a more formidable rival than before?

A.

There is something in that, I confess. But here is more.

" And it is equally certain that he showed as little disposition to enable his nephew to live by a profession as to enable him to live without a profession."

B.

Alluding, I suppose, to the period when the places of attorney and solicitor-general were vacant. That was not till 1593, twelve years and more after the time we have hitherto been talking of. At least I am not aware that before that time Burghley had omitted any opportunity of advancing Bacon in his profession. Many things may happen in twelve years, and therefore we had better leave the discussion of his conduct on that occasion till we approach nearer to it. In the mean time you will understand that I do not admit that he acted an unfriendly part even then.

A.

But what do you say to Bacon's own testimony on the subject? Listen.

"That Bacon himself attributed the conduct of his relatives to jealousy of his superior talents we have not the smallest doubt. In a letter written many years after to Villiers, he expresses himself thus: ' Countenance, encourage, and advance able men in all kinds, degrees, and professions. For in the time of the Cecils, the father and the son, able men were by design and of purpose suppressed.'"

B.

Well, I dare say the censure was just in the general case; but it says nothing about his own in particular. If it was true of himself only, it was untrue as a general charge. If it was true of others, why suppose that he was thinking of himself?—I say to you now that the system of our own

public service at this day is bad, because it offers no adequate reward for industry and ability : do I therefore say
that any industry or ability of *my own* has been thrown
away upon the public ? Surely no man who has room in
his soul for anything besides himself will so interpret me.
I believe there is not a single sentence on record in which
Bacon betrays so much as a passing suspicion that *Burghley*
wished to keep him down; and I am sure there are several
in which he gratefully and affectionately acknowledges his
good offices in endeavouring to advance him.

A.

I understood you to say that there was contemporary
authority for the charge against the Cecils,

B.

Not against Burghley, that I know of. I was thinking
of what Dr. Rawley says of " the arts and policy of a great
statesman then, who laboured by all underhand and secret
means to suppress and keep him down, lest if he had risen
he might have obscured his glory." The allusion I think
is not to Burghley, but to Robert Cecil, and as against him
I dare say the imputation is just. It was certainly an
impression current among Bacon's friends at the time, and
shared more or less by Bacon himself. I see, indeed, that
Mr. Payne Collier,* on the authority of Cecil's correspondence preserved at Bridgewater House, discredits it. And
there were times no doubt when he showed himself really
friendly. But Robert Cecil was a great artist in dissembling
and double-dealing. He had just the constitution for
it ;—" *Temperamentum calidum, siccum, biliosum ; Cerebrum
frigidissimum, humidissimum.*" †—But go on.

A.

" Whatever Burghley's motives might be, his purpose was
unalterable. The supplications which Francis addressed to his
uncle and aunt were earnest, humble, and almost servile."

---

* Egerton Papers (Camden Society).
† Sir Theodore Mayerne's Memoranda.

B.

"His uncle *and aunt.*" We are still then in September 1580; Francis not yet twenty. There is no letter to his aunt later than that. The other letters to Burghley we shall hear more of, and I shall have something to say about them. In the mean time I wish you to mark that word "servile;" because the reviewer's notions of servility are peculiar, and very necessary to be understood by those who would understand the true value of those epithets, from the thick laying-on of which his reasoning sometimes acquires an appearance of force. Will you read those two letters, and tell me what one expression in either of them deserves any worse epithet than modest, respectful, and affectionate? You will find them in Volume xii.* there, with the red back, page 471.

A.

How old was Burghley at this time?

B.

Sixty. He had been Elizabeth's principal counsellor for twenty-two years.

A.

And Bacon not yet twenty?—Here it is.

"To my Lady Burghley.

"My singular good Lady,—I was as ready to show myself mindful of my duty by waiting on your Ladyship at your being in town, as now by my writing; had I not feared that your Ladyship's short stay and quick return might well spare one that came of no earnest errand. I am not yet greatly perfect in ceremonies of court, whereof I know your Ladyship knoweth both the right use and true value. My thankful and serviceable mind shall be always like itself, howsoever it vary from the common disguising. Your Ladyship is wise and of good nature to discern from what

* Montagu's Edition.

mind every action proceedeth, and to esteem of it accordingly. This is all the message which my letter hath at this time to deliver; unless it please your Ladyship further to give me leave to make this request unto you; that it would please your good Ladyship, in your letters wherewith you visit my good Lord, to vouchsafe the mention and recommendation of my suit; wherein your Ladyship shall bind me more to you than I can look ever to be able sufficiently to acknowledge. Thus in humble manner I take my leave of your Ladyship, committing you as daily in my prayers, so likewise at this present, to the merciful providence of the Almighty. From Gray's Inn, this 16th of September 1580. Your Ladyship's most dutiful and bounden nephew, B. FRA."

B.

So much for my Lady. Now for my Lord.

A.

"To Lord Burghley, to recommend him to the Queen.

" My singular good Lord,—My humble duty remembered, and my humble thanks presented for your Lordship's favour and countenance, which it pleased your Lordship at my being with you to vouchsafe me above my degree and desert ; my letter hath no further errand but to commend unto your Lordship the remembrance of my suit, which I then moved unto you; whereof it also pleased your Lordship to give me good hearing so far forth as to promise to tender it unto her Majesty;—and withal to add in the behalf of it that which I may better deliver by letter than by speech; which is, that, although it must be confessed that the request is rare and unaccustomed, yet if it be observed how few there be which fall in with the study of the Common Laws, either being well left or friended, or at their own free election, or forsaking likely success in other studies of more delight and no less preferment, or setting hand thereunto early, without waste of years,—upon such survey made, it may be my case may not seem ordinary, no more than my suit,—and so more beseeming unto it. As I force myself to say this in excuse of my motion, lest it should seem altogether undiscreet and unadvised, so my hope to obtain it resteth upon your Lordship's good affection towards me and grace with her Majesty; who methinks needeth never to call for the experience of the thing, where she hath so great and so good of the person which recommendeth it. According to which trust of mine, if it may please your Lordship both herein and elsewhere to be my patron, and to make account of me as one in whose well-doing your Lordship hath interest,—albeit indeed your Lordship hath had place to benefit many, and wisdom to make due choice of lighting-places for your goodness,—yet do I not fear any of your Lordship's former experiences for staying my thankfulness borne in heart, howsoever God's good pleasure shall enable me or disable me outwardly to make proof thereof."——

Stay, I don't understand that last sentence.

B.

No. There is something wrong in the text. The letter is preserved only in a copy, and some words have most likely dropped out. The meaning must have been—Though your goodness has lighted upon many worthy subjects, it has not lighted upon one more truly thankful than I shall prove so far as I may have opportunity.

A.

Yes, I see.—" For I cannot account your Lordship's service distinct from that which I owe to God and my prince ; the performance whereof to best proof and purpose is the meeting-place and rendezvous of all my thoughts. Thus I take my leave of your Lordship in humble manner, committing you as daily in my prayers, so likewise at this present, to the merciful protection of the Almighty. From Gray's Inn, this 16th of September 1580. Your most dutiful and bounden nephew, B. FRA."

Well, I expected something worse than this, I confess. To be sure it is not the kind of letter that the reviewer himself would have written in such a case. I suppose he cannot well imagine a youth of so great talents really *feeling* so much deference for mere age and dignity; therefore looks on it as false and affected,—a sacrifice of self-respect to the desire of self-advancement. I don't say that I think the supposition a fair one in this instance; but if I did—if I took the same view of it as I dare say he does—I should not object to his calling it " servile." I do not think he meant to misrepresent the character of the letter. I can well believe that he really felt some scorn to see a young philosopher taking off his hat to an old uncle.

B.

I do not dispute that. I only wish you to bear in mind that his *description* of these letters made you expect something very different from what you find. I can easily believe that he *felt* what you describe; but what are the opinions of a man good for who does feel so?

A.

They should, perhaps, be taken with some little allowance.—By the by, why does Bacon sign himself B. *Fra. ?*

B.

I cannot guess. These, and another dated 18th October, are the only instances I have met with. The letters are all transcripts, and transcribed in the same hand;—some fancy of the transcriber, I suppose. The full name, Fra. Bacon, is given in the docket, and they are no doubt his composition.

A.

Well; I agree to drop the "almost servile," and substitute "modest."

"The supplications"—[that, by the way, is a stronger word than the occasion calls for; but never mind]—"which Francis addressed to his uncle and aunt were earnest, humble, and modest. He was the most promising and accomplished young man of his time. His father had been the brother-in-law, the most useful colleague, the nearest friend of the minister. But all this availed poor Francis nothing. He was forced much against his will to betake himself to the study of the law. He was admitted at Gray's Inn, and during some years he laboured there in obscurity."

Do you admit any of this to be correct? For I will at once grant you that there is a good deal in it which is not correct.

B.

Yes, I admit that he was a very promising young man, with hereditary claims upon Burghley's favour. How large and how sure the promise appeared in the eyes of the elderly statesmen of the day, while it was yet only in blossom, it would not perhaps be very easy to determine. Elderly statesmen are apt to be cautious in their judgments of youthful promise; especially of youths who start with an announcement that their elders and teachers are all in the wrong. Neither would I undertake to say that even in the most discerning eyes Francis Bacon's promise of abilities for active service must have been greater than that of some others—Philip Sidney, for instance, or Walter Raleigh. Therefore had Burghley only held back that he might prove him before he used him, I do not see that he could be reasonably blamed. But I dispute the assertion that Burghley did hold back. I deny that Burghley's backwardness had anything to do with his admission at Gray's Inn. It was his father, not Burghley, who caused him to be *admitted* there. I deny that he betook himself to the study of the law against his will: for it is clear from the terms of his first application to Burghley, which you have just read, that he had already begun, and meant to go on with the *study* of the Common Law; however he might hope to be relieved at an early period from practising it for his livelihood. I deny that his claims on Burghley "availed him nothing;" for I am inclined to believe (for reasons which I will tell you presently) that he enjoyed through Burghley's influence some important dispensations and exemptions, which hastened his career through Gray's Inn. And finally I deny that "he laboured some years there *in obscurity*;" because his rise was unusually rapid.

But I think we have done enough for one evening. We have scarcely got to Bacon himself yet. We are now approaching the period of his life of which we know something, and had better enter upon it as upon a fresh chapter; which we will open if you please to-morrow. In the mean time I think you will do well to look through what you have read to-day, substituting as you go correct expressions for what you find incorrect, and then see how much remains. It is an exercise I shall frequently have to propose to you, and will throw great light upon this subject.

A.

I am afraid the residue will taste rather flat.

B.

By which you will learn how much was only fixed air. If I had to decide what should be done to the reviewer for writing this article, I would require nothing worse of him than that he should perform that office himself; discarding every sentence, epithet, expression, and assertion which he could not justify; putting "*I*" instead of "*We*," but without otherwise altering the form; and then print it with his name. It would look as forlorn as a plucked peacock, strutting and shouting without a tail to spread.

A.

I'll do it.

EVENING THE SECOND.

A.

Well, I have tried to correct and expurgate what we read yesterday; but I find it will not bear the process. By discarding epithets and superlatives and qualifying round statements, you not only diminish the force and liveliness of the composition, but destroy its logical coherency.

But we are only in the fifteenth page, and we have fifty more to get through before we come to the Philosophy; and (to judge by the marginalia which I see before me) our progress is not likely to be more rapid. Therefore if you please we will wander as little as possible from the text.

B.

Very well. I will not stop you to make comments of my own; but only to dispute statements of fact, and inferences which, if undisputed, are in danger of taking place as facts.

We left "poor Francis" labouring in obscurity (if we are to believe the last paragraph),—rising very rapidly into business and distinction (if we are to believe the next) —at Gray's Inn. We are now to hear what kind of lawyer he makes.

A.

"What the extent of his legal attainments may have been, it is difficult to say. It was not hard for a man of his powers to acquire that very moderate portion of technical knowledge which, when joined to quickness, tact, wit, ingenuity, eloquence, and knowledge of the world, is sufficient to raise an advocate to the highest professional eminence. The general opinion appears to have been that which was on one occasion expressed by Elizabeth. 'Bacon' (said she) 'had a great wit and much learning; but in law showeth to the uttermost of his knowledge, and is not deep.' The Cecils, we suspect, did their best to spread this opinion by whispers and insinuations. Coke openly proclaimed it with that rancorous insolence which was habitual to him. No reports are more readily believed than those which disparage genius and soothe the enmity of conscious mediocrity. It must have been inexpressibly consoling to a stupid serjeant —the forerunner of him who 150 years later 'shook his head at Murray as a wit'—to know that the most profound thinker and the most accomplished orator of his age was very imperfectly acquainted with the law touching *bastard eigné* and *mulier puisné*, and confounded the right of free fishery with that of common piscary.

"It is certain that no man in that age, or indeed during the century and a half which followed, was better acquainted with the philosophy of law. His technical knowledge was quite sufficient, with the help of his admirable talents and his insinuating address, to procure clients. He rose very rapidly into business, and soon entertained hopes of being called within the bar. He applied"——

B.

Stop a moment. Now what do you collect from all this to be Macaulay's opinion of Bacon's attainments as a lawyer?

A.

As a practical lawyer? It is clear enough, is it not? He thinks that he was superficial, and apt, perhaps, to make blunders; but that nevertheless he had as much law as a gentleman and a philosopher could want,—that is, as much as was necessary to gain clients. To judge from the tone of the paragraph, I should say he thinks rather the better of him for not knowing more.

B.

In short, that the opinion which the Cecils di l their best to spread by whispers and insinuations was in fact the truth. If so, does it not strike you as rather hard upon them that they should be censured for spreading it, as if their only motive had been jealousy?

A.

Certainly it would appear to have been their best justification, if it was so. For the Queen's service required, no doubt, real learning and practical skill, not philosophy and plausibility only. But was it so? Bacon surely was not the sort of man to be contented with superficial knowledge and plausibilities in anything that he had to deal with.

B.

The last man in the world. And therefore (though I can easily believe that his head was not a library of law-cases, as Coke's was, and that on that account Coke very honestly despised him), I should be slow to think that he was apt to confound any two things that were distinct, or that he was superficially acquainted with the law in any case which he was prepared to argue. I have not seen it stated that he ever gave an opinion on a point of law which was wrong, or ever attempted anything in his profession which he did not perform excellently well. His writings on legal subjects it is not fair to form a judgment by. They were none of them published by himself. They are all, or almost all, fragments, and very incorrectly printed; and yet they are so good that some learned judge has recorded his regret for the waste of such a mind upon other studies. This however is a point upon which it would be absurd in me to attempt to form an opinion of my own. Only until I hear of an instance in which his want of technical knowledge betrayed him into an error, I shall believe that he was a good technical lawyer.

But it was not for this that I stopped you here. I

wished only to remind you that when you hear a little
further on (or a little further back) the Cecils censured as
backbiters because they told the Queen that he was not a
deep and sound practical lawyer, but great only in *speculation ;*—the Queen censured for injustice so gross as to
cancel all obligations because she did not make him one of
her principal law-officers when he was only thirty-three ;—
and himself censured for servility because he did not, in
resentment of that neglect, plunge himself into the faction
and fortunes of a dangerous malcontent and rebel, but continued faithful to his original trust ;—you are to remember
that the Cecils said no more against him than the reviewer
now says,—that the Queen slighted no claims but such as
the reviewer now believes he did not possess,—and that
Bacon had nothing to resent except the not being advanced
to an office for which (if the reviewer's opinion be correct)
he was not eminently qualified.—Mind, I do not myself
agree that it was so. I cannot but believe that Bacon was,
by professional as well as by all other accomplishments,
eminently qualified for the highest offices ; and that the
Queen did herself no good service when she made Coke her
attorney-general instead of him. But I can well believe
that this was not the opinion of the world ; for when did the
world ever believe a man to be good at his own trade who
had shown that he was good for anything else? Why
should we suppose that Burghley and Cecil did not think
as the world thought? And how should the Queen know
better than they?

A.

Surely. I suppose that (now-a-days at least) the reputation of a *Temporis partus maximus* at twenty-four would be
quite fatal to the prospects of a lawyer, though he had law
accumulating in his head enough to furnish forth another
" Coke upon Littleton." The attorneys would certainly be
shy. And even when recommending him to the Prime
Minister for a commissionership, a judicious friend would
keep the progress of the *Instauratio Magna* in the back-

EVENINGS WITH A REVIEWER.

ground.—Yes; I can make allowance for the Cecils and the Queen. And if our young friend Francis can also make allowance for them and hold on his course unaltered, I shall think the better of him and not the worse.

B.

Then you will find yourself very much out with your favourite reviewer.

A.

We shall see.

"He rose very rapidly into business, and soon entertained hopes of being called within the bar. He applied to Lord Burghley for that purpose, but received a testy refusal. Of the grounds of that refusal we can in some measure judge from Bacon's answer, which is still extant. It seems that the old lord, whose temper, age and gout had by no means altered for the better, and who omitted no opportunity of marking his dislike of the showy quick-witted young men of the rising generation, took this opportunity to read Francis a very sharp lecture on his vanity and want of respect for his betters. Francis returned a most submissive reply, thanked the Treasurer for the admonition, and promised to profit by it."

Let me see. By this we are meant to understand that Francis showed some want of spirit in not telling his old uncle to make him a better answer. Was Burghley's rebuke so very unreasonable?

B.

That I really cannot pretend to say. The admonition does not appear to have been conveyed in a letter, but in a conversation; and we know nothing of the terms or spirit of it, any more than of the grounds, except as we may infer them from the terms and spirit of the letter which Francis wrote, after reflecting (I suppose) upon what Burghley had said. Burghley, it seems, had heard some insinuations to the disadvantage of Bacon, of which he thought it right to inform him; and in so doing he alluded to his recent application as in some degree bearing them out. But Bacon's

letter is not long. We had better read it; and then you
will know all that the reviewer knew of the matter, and can
judge for yourself. It is worth while to do it now; because
we shall meet with more than one sweeping clause in which
Bacon's habitual demeanour to his patrons is touched on in
passing as if it were notorious; the fact on which the description is founded being contained in this letter. Here it
is—6th of May 1586—Bacon being, as you will remember,
only twenty-five years and three months old.

" My very good Lord,—I take it as an undoubted sign of
your Lordship's favour unto me, that being hardly informed
of me, you took occasion rather of good advice than of evil
opinion thereby; which if your Lordship had grounded
only upon the said information of theirs, I might and would
truly have upholden that few of the matters were justly
objected; as the very circumstances do induce,—in that
they were delivered by men who did misaffect me, and
besides were to give colour to their own doings. But because
your Lordship did mingle therewith both a late motion of
mine own, and somewhat that you had otherwise heard, I
know it to be my duty (and so do I stand affected) rather to
prove your Lordship's admonition effectual in my doings
hereafter, than causeless by excusing what is past. And yet
(with your Lordship's pardon humbly asked) it may please
you to remember that I did endeavour to set forth that said
motion in such sort as it might breed no harder effect than a
denial. And I protest simply before God that I sought
therein an ease in coming within Bars, and not any extraordinary or singular note of favour.

" And for that your Lordship may otherwise have heard
of me, it shall make me more wary and circumspect in
carriage of myself. Indeed I find in my simple observation
that they who live as it were *in umbrâ* and not in public or
frequent action, how moderately and modestly soever they
behave themselves, yet *laborant invidiâ*. I find also that
such persons as are of nature bashful (as myself is), whereby
they want that plausible familiarity which others have, are
often mistaken for proud. But once I know well, and I

most humbly beseech your Lordship to believe, that arrogancy and overweening is so far from my nature, as if I think well of myself in anything it is in this, that I am free from that vice. And I hope upon this your Lordship's speech I have entered into those considerations as my behaviour shall no more deliver me for other than I am.

"And so wishing unto your Lordship all honour and to myself continuance of your good opinion with mind and means to deserve it, I humbly take my leave. Gray's Inn, this 6th of May 1586. Your Lordship's most bounden nephew,   FR. BACON."

A.

Is that all?

B.

Every word.

A.

And is nothing more known of the matter or manner of Burghley's speech?

B.

But for this letter we should not have known that any such application had been either made or refused,—any such admonition either needed or given.

A.

Then the *testiness* of the refusal; the *sharpness* of the lecture; the imputation of want of respect for his *betters;* are all out of the reviewer's own head?

B.

All. For you see the offence was not any want of respectfulness in his demeanour towards Burghley himself, or any of that generation; but apparently an overweening estimate of his own pretensions and abilities, as compared with the men of his own generation. These persons who " did misaffect him " were most likely his competitors for advancement and favour; who thought him a conceited young fellow, and wished to lower him in Burghley's opinion.

For anything I can gather from this letter, Burghley's admonition may have been the kindest thing possible in itself, and done in the kindest manner. Even the fact that Bacon's application had been refused is not certain. For we do not know exactly what it was that he asked for; or whether it was a thing that could be done immediately. And we do happen to know that Bacon was ultimately (though I cannot make out exactly at what time) admitted within the bar in some unusual manner.

A.

Well, I was right to stop. I wonder if all history is written in this way.

" Strangers meanwhile were less unjust to the young barrister than his nearest kinsmen had been."

B.

Kinsmen?—meaning, I suppose, Burghley and Robert Cecil;—Burghley, whose injustice to him had consisted at the very worst in not procuring him an independent provision when he was twenty, and not getting him called within the bar at twenty-five;—Cecil, who was as yet only twenty-three, and cannot be supposed to have had any influence independent of Burghley.—Well; what did the strangers do?

A.

" In his twenty-sixth year he became a Bencher of his Inn : and two years after he was appointed Lent Reader."

B.

True. But he had also received other distinctions of a special character, with which it seems probable that Burghley had something to do, though I cannot positively affirm it. There is preserved among the Lansdowne MSS. an extract from the Gray's Inn Register, with some memoranda upon it in Burghley's hand. The memoranda are written short, after Burghley's fashion, and not very legibly ; so that

I cannot be sure of all the words. But it is plain that they are an enumeration of certain special distinctions enjoyed by Francis Bacon at Gray's Inn. It seems that he was admitted "of the Grand Company" in some unusual manner so as to give him an advantage over others in point of *standing :* "whereby" (writes Burghley) " he hath won ancienty of 40." It also appears that he became an "Utter Barrister upon 3 years' study "—(I suppose unusually early) ;—that some of the regulations respecting attendance in Commons had been specially set aside in his favour; and finally that he was specially admitted to have place at the Reader's table on the 10th of February 1586, two years before he was himself a Reader. These memoranda being unquestionably in Burghley's hand, the natural inference is that Burghley had something to do with these distinctions and exemptions. But, however that be, they are enough to show that, through the influence either of his kinsmen or of strangers, Francis's interests had not hitherto been neglected. And he is now entering on his twenty-seventh year.—Go on.

A.

" At length, in 1590, he received for the first time show of favour from the court. He was sworn in Queen's Counsel extraordinary. But this mark of honour was not accompanied with any pecuniary emolument."

B.

This is the date assigned by Mr. Montagu,—I do not know on what authority. Some one else says 1588. Dr. Rawley only says "after a while." The fact I believe to be that he was employed by the Queen's command in business belonging properly to members of the Learned Counsel, *without* any regular appointment either by patent or in writing. But this was some years later. I have not yet found any ground for fixing the exact date. Moreover he was not sworn. But how can it be said that he had not received *show* of favour from the court before ? He had had the privilege of access to the Queen all this time ; which, coming from Queen Elizabeth, and being generally upon business of state, was no small *show of favour*. What he had not received was money.

A.

" He continued therefore to solicit his powerful relatives for some provision which might enable him to live without drudging at his profession. He bore with a patience and serenity which we fear bordered on meanness, the morose humours of his uncle and the sneering reflections which his cousin cast on speculative men lost in philosophical reveries and too wise to be capable of transacting public business."

B.

Is it worth while to stop you here that you may take in the full light which this sentence reflects on the character, not of Bacon, but of the reviewer?

A.

If you allude to the word " meanness " as characterising the letter you read just now, I noted that. And it is not more than I was prepared for, though much more than I can assent to. I told you he seemed to think Francis wanting in spirit for not making a sturdier answer.

B.

Yes. But that might be from misunderstanding the occasion and spirit of the letter. There is something more implied here. Here we get some light (and we shall get a good deal more presently) as to his *principles* of moral approbation and disapprobation. Take the fact exactly as he understands it. Suppose Burghley to have been " morose," and Francis to have been " patient and serene." What follows? " *Patience* " and " *serenity* " shown by a nephew of twenty-six in bearing the morose humours of an uncle of sixty—of an uncle whom he had been brought up to revere —a man full of years and honours—the most eminent man in the kingdom—his dead father's nearest friend and colleague—the husband of his living mother's own sister,—a

man, too, whose very moroseness was the effect of age and
sickness :—*patience* and *serenity* border on meanness !

A.

A thing to be remembered, I confess. I am afraid our
friend has not a clear notion of the difference between
magnanimity and magniloquence, and judges of the greatness of a man's heart by the bigness of his words.

But I am not so well satisfied about that young Robert.
With him, I think Bacon might have been angry and sinned
not.

B.

Why, so he was. The particular expressions indeed
which are here put into Robert's mouth, it would not be
fair to charge him with. Mr. Montagu thinks he has seen
them somewhere, but cannot remember where. But Bacon
certainly did once suspect him of having put the word
speculation into the Queen's ear in a disparaging sense, and
otherwise to have been working underhand against him ;
how truly I cannot say ; and what then ? His patience and
serenity quite failed him, and he was betrayed on the
moment into a tone of unreasonable irritation and almost
petulant remonstrance, which the reviewer might probably
think fine, but which in my opinion (and I think in his
own upon reflexion) it was easier to excuse than to justify.
And yet I am glad the record remains ; for it shows how
keenly he could feel an injury, and how much his habitual
serenity and patience were owing, not to want of sensibility,
but to self-controlling virtue. This also was characteristic
of him in the matter : he made his complaint against Robert
Cecil not *of* him, but *to* him.

A.

Come, I am glad he could be angry and unreasonable.
They told me he was made up of policy.

" At length the Cecils were generous enough to procure him
the reversion of the Registrarship of the Star-chamber. This

was a lucrative place; but as many years elapsed before it
fell in, he was still under the necessity of labouring for his
daily bread."

B.

My only exception to that sentence is upon the indefinite "at length"; which makes the period of application
and neglect seem longer than it really was. The date of
the grant was the 29th October 1589, Bacon's twenty-ninth
year. It was obtained for him by Burghley, and (as Bacon
himself declares) against great opposition.

A.

"In the parliament which was called in 1593 he sate as
member for Middlesex, and soon attained eminence as a
debater."

Here follows a discussion upon his style of oratory, with
the quotation from Ben Jonson. Unless you have some
exception to make, we may skip this; for it has no bearing
upon his personal character, which is what I want to see
cleared up.

B.

If you please. It would have been more to the purpose
if the reviewer had spent a few hours over D'Ewes's
Journals and endeavoured to trace, by the scattered foot-
prints which remain, Bacon's path in politics from the time
he first entered parliament in 1584. He would have come
better prepared to understand the single passage which, out
of a very prominent and active parliamentary career of
thirty years, he has selected as a sample; not a bad sample
if rightly reported; but, as he reports it, a mere contrast
and incongruity. Of this passage I shall have much to
say.

A.

"Bacon tried to play a very difficult game in politics. He
wished to be at once a favourite at Court and popular with the
multitude."

B.

Popular with the *multitude!* When in all his life did Bacon address himself to the *multitude?*

A.

The popular party in the House of Commons was popular (I suppose) with the people generally; and he seems to have wished to stand well with them.

B.

Yes, but the "multitude" was not then a party to the proceedings in the House of Commons. There were no strangers in the gallery. He spoke *for* his constituents, not *to* them. To establish a reputation out of doors as a patriot, it was not enough now and then in the House to support a popular measure, so long as he was known to be in the service and favour of the Court. The populace judge by broad facts. To win the reputation of a popular man, it would have been necessary to break with the Court. What he did wish was to be in favour at once with the Court and the *House of Commons,* by being faithful to both his trusts. My objection is to the use of the word *multitude.*

A.

Well, then, "with the popular party in the House of Commons," we'll say. It is not material.

"If any man could have succeeded in this attempt, a man of talents so rare, of judgment so prematurely ripe, of temper so calm, of manners so plausible—— "

B.

For "calm" read "well under command"; and for "plausible" read "simple, noble, and courteous."

A.

"—might have been expected to succeed. Nor did he wholly fail. Once, however, he indulged in a burst of patriotism—— "

B.

A *burst?*—But go on. I have a long story to tell you about this presently.

A.

" —which cost him a long and bitter remorse, and which he never ventured to repeat. The court asked for large subsidies and for speedy payment. The remains of Bacon's speech breathe all the spirit of the Long Parliament."

B.

Does he not say what the subsidies were wanted for? Were they wanted for national or only for court objects? for a popular or an unpopular cause? a sufficient or an insufficient one?

A.

No, he says nothing of that? But of course we are to understand him as condemning the proposition. Where there is a difference on any question either of policy or of fact between the government and anybody else, all our modern liberal historians assume as a matter of course that the government is in the wrong. With them all opposition is presumably patriotism. It is as superfluous to ask which party the reviewer thinks right in this case, as whether he is going to vote with Sir Robert or Lord John the next time they divide against each other. But let us see what Bacon has to say about it.

" The gentlemen (said he) must sell their plate, the farmers their brass pots, ere this will be paid : and for us, we are here to search the wounds of the realm, not to skin them over. The dangers are these :—First we shall breed discontent and endanger her Majesty's safety, which must consist more in the love of the people than in their wealth. Secondly, this being granted in this sort, other princes hereafter will look for the like; so that we shall put an evil precedent upon ourselves and our posterity: and in histories it is to be observed of all nations that the English are not to be subject, base, or taxable."

B.

Well this was his one burst of patriotism, I suppose.
Now for the " remorse."

A.

" The Queen and her ministers resented this outbreak of
spirit in the highest manner. Indeed, many an honest member
of the House of Commons had for a much smaller matter been
sent to the Tower by the proud and hot-blooded Tudors."

B.

There was some courage then at any rate in venturing it.

A.

Wait.

" The young patriot condescended to make the most abject
apologies. He adjured the Lord Treasurer to show some favour
to his poor servant and ally. He bemoaned himself to the Lord
Keeper in a letter which may keep in countenance the most
unmanly of the epistles which Cicero wrote during his banish-
ment."

I suppose we had better have a look at the letters themselves. An " almost servile supplication " turned. out just
now to be only a modest request. Perhaps the " abject
apology " may turn out to be only a respectful justification.

B.

Yes, we will have the letters now, while this character
of them is fresh in your ears. And then I will give you
a true history at large of this transaction, which is really a
very significant one. Here is the first letter to Burghley,
written upon the first official intimation of the Queen's
displeasure.

" It may please your Lordship,—I was sorry to find by
your Lordship's speech yesterday, that my last speech in
parliament, delivered in discharge of my conscience and
duty to God, her Majesty, and my country, was offensive.

If it were misreported, I would be glad to attend your Lordship to disavow anything I said not: if it were misconstrued, I would be glad to expound myself to exclude any sense I meant not. If my heart be misjudged by imputation of popularity or opposition, by any envious or malicious informer, I have great wrong;—and the greater, because the manner of my speech did most evidently show that I spake simply and only to satisfy my conscience, and not with any advantage or policy to sway the cause; and my terms carried all signification of duty and zeal towards her Majesty and her service. It is true that, from the beginning, whatsoever was above a double subsidy I did wish might for precedent's sake appear to be extraordinary, and for discontent's sake might not have been levied upon the poorer sort:—though otherwise I wished it as rising, as I think this will prove, and more. This was my mind; I confess it: and therefore I most humbly pray your good Lordship first to continue me in your own good opinion; and then to perform the part of an honourable friend towards your poor servant and alliance, in drawing her Majesty to accept of the sincerity and simplicity of my heart and to bear with the rest, and restore me to her Majesty's favour, which is to me dearer than my life.

"And so &c.,
"Your Lordship's most humble in all duty."

A.

I thought so. No apology at all, but a plain justification. Now for the other letter;—written, I suppose, about the same time.

B.

I think later; but I can find nothing to determine the exact date. However it is of no consequence.

"My Lord,"—[I believe by the way that the Lord to whom the letter is addressed was the Earl of Essex, not the Lord Keeper *],—"It is a great grief unto me joined with marvel,

* See "Letters and Life," vol. i. p. 239.

that her Majesty should retain an hard conceit of my speeches in parliament. It might please her sacred Majesty to think what might be my end in those speeches, if it were not duty, and duty alone. I am not so simple, but I know the common beaten way to please. And whereas popularity hath been objected, I muse what care I should take to please many, that take a course of life to deal with few. On the other side, her Majesty's grace and particular favour towards me hath been such, as I esteem no worldly thing above the comfort to enjoy it, except it be the conscience to deserve it. But if the not seconding some particular person's opinion shall be presumption, and to differ upon the manner shall be to impeach the end,—it shall teach my devotion not to exceed wishes, and those in silence. Yet, notwithstanding, to speak vainly as in grief, it may be her Majesty hath discouraged as good a heart as ever looked toward her service, and as void of self-love. And so in more grief than I can well express, and much more than I can well dissemble, I leave your Lordship; being, as ever, your Lordship's entirely devoted, etc."

A.

Why, this is better and better. ˙ This means, if it mean anything, that he *cannot* apologise for what he has done, and only regrets that it should be so ill taken. It means that he cannot serve the Queen at all, if service on these conditions is not accepted. But tell me ;—what after all was it that he had done?

B.

That is the very thing I was going to tell you. This one *burst of patriotism* in which he indulged—But I drew up a few weeks since an account of the whole affair. ˙I had better read it to you; and that will be enough for to-night.

In February 1592-3, Bacon's duty as a member of the House of Commons drew him into a course which deeply displeased the Queen, and materially damaged his prospects. The case is curious, and for its bearing upon his character as well as his fortunes, deserves to be carefully noticed.   To understand his position fully, it is necessary to go a little further back.

The parliament which met on the 4th February 1588-9 (the year after the Spanish Armada) had been summoned especially for supplies.   Francis Bacon was one of the committee to which the question of the supply was referred, and appears to have taken a prominent part in the deliberations; for when they had agreed to recommend an extraordinary provision in proportion to the extraordinary necessity, yet at the same time to provide by words inserted in the preamble of the bill against its being drawn into a precedent, it was he who "set down a note in writing" for that purpose, and was appointed to repair with it to the Queen's learned counsel, who were charged with the preparation of the bill.   On this occasion no further difference appears to have arisen ; the bill finally passed the Commons on the 10th of March and the Lords on the 17th.

The next House of Commons, which met on the 19th of February 1592-3, under circumstances very similar, appears to have been disposed to take this proceeding for a precedent.   The business was supplies, and the occasion the designs of Spain.

A debate (in which Francis Bacon took a leading part) * upon the dangers the country then stood in, was followed by the appointment of a committee of supply; which agreed to recommend the same provision that had been voted the last parliament (two subsidies and four fifteenths and tenths) coupled with the same precaution, viz. a reference in the preamble of the bill to the circumstances which made the case extraordinary.   With the proposed amount, however, it seems that the court was not satisfied ; for, while the bill was yet in preparation, the Lords desired a conference with the Commons, at which it was flatly declared in their name by Burghley, that " they might not nor they would not give

* The end of his speech (as we learn from D'Ewes, p. 471), was to enforce the necessity " of present consultation and provision of treasure to prevent the dangers intended against the realm by the King of Spain, the Pope, and other confederates of the Holy League."

their consents to less than a treble subsidy; and not to a treble nor a quadruple, unless qualified both in substance and in circumstance of time:" * "to what proportion of benevolence, or unto how much their Lordships *would* give their assents in that behalf, they would not then show," but desired another conference.

The substance of this communication being referred to the House by Sir Robert Cecil (apparently without any motion or opinion from himself), "Mr. Francis Bacon" (who had been himself present at the conference) "stood up, and made a motion."—And now what do you think he will say? The immediate question is not what amount of supply they shall yield to, but what answer they shall send to the Lords. The Lords (that is, the Court party) desire to confer with the Commons in order to set before them the case of the realm, and persuade them to vote a larger supply. Bacon is a young and aspiring lawyer with a good prospect of rapid advancement through court patronage, and without any prospect of advancement from any other quarter. Of course, you will say, he will go with the court party : his motion will be that the House agree to the conference as proposed by Burghley. And indeed why not? Whom can he offend by doing so? What credit can he lose? To what odium or reproach can it expose him? Obviously it is the safe and prudent course: apparently it is quite unobjectionable. But perhaps you think it may lose him credit, or the opportunity of gaining credit, in the House of Commons. To be prominent in support of the government (you think) may weaken his authority with the popular party. In that case he has only to hold his tongue. There is no call on him to take an active part. No inference can be drawn from his silence. No need, if the court is to be opposed, that *he* should lead the opposition.—But you are wrong. He will do neither the one nor the other. He thinks that for the Lower House to consent to a conference with the Upper for the avowed purpose of discussing the amount of contribution to be voted (and this was unquestionably Lord Burghley's proposal), will be to

* Hargr. 324, f. 21.

abandon one of their understood and ascertained privileges. He does not object to an increase of the grant, nor to the reconsidering of the question: he objects to admit the Lords as a party to the discussion of a money question. Accordingly he rises at once and advises the House to decline to accede to Burghley's proposition; in fact (to translate it into the modern phrase), he, though belonging to the government party, does on this occasion *lead the opposition against the government.*—" His motion was for yielding to the subsidies; but disliked that we should join with the Lords of the Higher House in the granting of it: for the custom and privilege of this House had always been to make offer of the subsidy from hence unto the Higher House. And reason it is that we should stand upon this our privilege. Seeing the burden resteth upon us as the greater number, no reason the thanks should be theirs. And in joining with them in this motion, we shall derogate from ourselves; for the thanks will be theirs and the blame ours, they being the first movers. Wherefore he could wish that in this action we should proceed as heretofore we had done, apart by ourselves, and not joining with them. And to satisfy their Lordships who expect an answer to-morrow, some answer would be made in all obsequious and dutiful manner."—(You see it was not the Queen and government only to whom he thought it right, even in opposing them, to be obsequious and dutiful. Indeed the answer which he proposes that the Commons should send to the Lords might perhaps by the reviewer be called an "abject apology." It has as much right to be so called as the letter to Burghley which we read just now. There is as much modesty and respect in it, and as little acquiescence.)

"And out of his bosom he drew an answer framed by himself, to this effect in brief: That we had considered their Lordships' motion, thought upon it as was fit, and in all willingness would address ourselves to do as so great a cause desired; but to join with their Lordships in this business we could not but with prejudice to the privileges of this House, wherefore desired as we were wont, so that now we might proceed therein by ourselves apart from their Lordships.

"Thus," (he added) "I think we may divide ourselves from their Lordships, and yet without dissension. For this is but an honourable emulation and division. To this he cited a precedent in Henry the Eighth's time. Four of the Lords came down into the Lower House and informed them what necessity there was of subsidy. Hereupon the House considered of it and granted a subsidy." *

His motion was "well liked by the House" (the government party being taken I suppose by surprise, and making no opposition), and the committee was appointed to frame an answer accordingly.

But before we follow the business forth to its issue, let us pause for a moment and consider it as it regards Bacon's character and ways. For as far as he is concerned it is already a complete act; a decision promptly, decidedly, and effectually taken; no *if* in the matter; no back-door open for retreat or explanation; no device reserved for giving it a different colour. What could be his motive? He could not be ignorant that he was doing a thing very unpalatable to Burghley, to Cecil, and to the Queen herself; and omitting to do a thing which would have been extremely palatable to them. Was it in pique then? Could he be in despair of any good to come from that quarter; or angry, as feeling that his interest and pretensions had been neglected? Surely no. It was but two years since he had received through Burghley's influence the reversion of a valuable office; this very year he had gone out of his way to write the most affectionate and eloquent vindication on record of the characters both of Burghley and Cecil; he was beginning to be employed in business of trust by the Queen; a vacancy in the law offices had just been made by the death of the Master of the Rolls; and it was but a few months after that he was one of the most likely candidates for the Attorney-Generalship. He could have had neither

* Hargr. MSS. 324.

end nor motive to make him seek an occasion for quarrelling. with Burghley. Or if you suppose that he was less careful to keep well with Burghley because he had now begun to depend upon Essex, through whom his other chance lay; you must remember that this other chance also lay through the Queen. To offend the Queen's party was as fatal to the one as to the other. For his own private fortunes in that direction, he could not but see that he was not pursuing a prudent course.

Was there then any other direction in which he could be beginning to look? any interest elsewhere, which he could have hoped by this show of popularity to improve? Could he be preparing to *rat,*—to become instead of the Queen's man the people's man? Surely this would have been the vainest of all projects. It is true there was a popular party in the country and in the House of Commons; and of that party he might easily have made himself the idol. But what could he have gained by that? Wealth or greatness it was not in their power to bestow; nor was there any chance of their having it for many years to come. Thirty years afterwards an ambitious young courtier with popular talents might well have *ratted* to the parliament as to the most powerful patron. But in Queen Elizabeth's time the popular party was a small minority which could only promote its leaders to the Tower. Or even now if Bacon had been a rich and powerful man, a man of lands and alliances, who wanted not fortune but greatness and political power, he might have allied himself to the popular party as a politic move. His ambition might have tempted him that way as the likeliest road to what he wanted. A man like Essex, might in taking such a course have been suspected of selfish objects. But this would not have done for Bacon. *His* want was the means of living and working, which the popular party could not have helped him to. Neither any lucrative office, nor success in the ordinary practice of his profession, nor importance that could in any way be turned into money, nor even a position that would have brought him helps for his studies, could have come to him through that channel. Not to add that his whole life had been laid out on another plan, which tended to withdraw him (except as an active member of Parliament) from all popular courses.

But, you will say, though he may not have been courting popularity, he may yet have been influenced by the fear of *un*popularity. And had the cause been a very unpopular one, he might perhaps not unreasonably have been suspected of such a motive. But this was by no means the case. The cause was contribution, the contribution was to sustain the war against Spain; than which nothing was more popular, either with the House of Commons or with the nation generally. Of the many prominent men who sided with the court on this occasion, and of the many more who held their tongues, it does not appear that any one was at all the less popular on that account.

Again, then, I ask, why did Francis Bacon,—the courtier, the aspiring lawyer, whose hope and object at this time was to obtain through court patronage some place under government which might relieve him from the necessity of drudging at the law for a livelihood—why did he on this occasion oppose the court? I can think but of one reason— a reason plain, simple, and sufficient, if people would but believe it. He thought it his duty. He sat in the House of Commons in a judicial capacity, as a representative of the Commons, as a guardian of their rights and interests, as a party to the making of laws and to the imposing of public burdens for the service of the commonwealth. As such, he believed it to be his duty to oppose what he thought injurious and to promote what he thought beneficial. The proposed conference with the Lords, though the proposal came from his own friends and patrons, he saw would be a dangerous precedent; and he advised the Commons not to agree to it. What can be plainer or more rational? Only it requires us to suppose that the public interests, not his own, were uppermost in his thoughts; that (to use his own words) "he loved his country more than was answerable to his fortune."

And now let us inquire how the matter was carried on,

and whether he did anything in the sequel that is inconsistent with this supposition.

The committee met, but could not agree. At length however, after a good deal of debate, they reported to the House, that a *majority* of their number was *for* the conference. But a debate arising upon the report (in which a fresh precedent *against* the conference,—which satisfied the greater part of the House, including Coke the Speaker,—was brought forward by Mr. Beale; but the privy counsellors and courtiers were still earnest *for* it), it was carried upon a division by 217 to 128, "that no such conference should be had with the said committee of the Lords by the said committee of this House." A grave and respectful answer was framed accordingly; and a committee appointed (in which it is to be observed that, if Sir S. D'Ewes's list be correct, Bacon was not included) to go up with it: the Chancellor of the Exchequer to declare it.

Such was the immediate result of Bacon's motion. But this was not the end. For the Lords were not satisfied with the answer, returned a message expressive of regret, and desired to "see the precedents by which the House seemed to refuse the said conference." Upon which, though the Commons resolved not to send the precedents, yet a general disposition appears to have arisen in the House to yield to the conference, upon the ground that the nature of the question had been misunderstood. Mr. Beale admitted that he had himself misunderstood it; that the precedent which he had cited was inapplicable (for in that case the Lords had proposed that the Commons should *confirm* what they had done, not confer about it), and that if he had conceived the question as it was meant, he would have been of another opinion. Others followed with retractations upon the same ground. Sir Robert Cecil (to smooth the way again) declared,—what, unless the reports are totally inaccurate, was not true,—that "it was never desired of the Lords to confer with the Commons *about a subsidy.*" And Sir Walter Raleigh, promptly taking the hint, proposed that it should be put to the House as a new question whether they should agree to a general conference with the Lords, without naming a subsidy; which question was put accordingly and carried *nem. con.* Whether Bacon took any part in this latter debate, or whether he was present, we cannot tell; for in the imperfect accounts which we have of the proceedings of the day, his name is not mentioned. But I suppose we may safely conclude that he was not among those who *retracted* their opinions, for such a circumstance could hardly have escaped mention.

The committee having been sent up to the Lords with this message and having heard what they had to say, returned to take fresh instructions as to their further answer; and upon this a general debate * arose concerning the dangers of the kingdom and the remedies. That three subsidies and six-fifteenths should be granted was generally agreed; the difference of opinion turned chiefly upon the time and manner of payment. " Some of the committees (says Sir S. D'Ewes) would have this propounded, whether the three subsidies should be raised in four years or in three : others dissented from it."

And now, once more, what line will Francis Bacon take ? If his first motion was made (which it is hardly possible to suppose) inconsiderately, without reflecting upon the consequences to his own standing in the good graces of the Queen, he could not at any rate be under any such mistake now. It was notorious that the court was much offended and annoyed at the opposition. It had been publicly talked of in the House as an offence which had been reported to the Queen and members "noted" for it; † and though he had omitted the opportunity which had been already offered, of retracting his opinion (as others had done) on the plea of having misunderstood the nature of the question, he might now at least make some amends by actively seconding the government proposition for the speedy collection of the increased contribution. This he could do without any apparent inconsistency, because he had from the first declared himself to be in favour of the proposed increase, and had

---

* Wednesday, March 7.   † Sir Henry Umpton's speech.

said nothing about the time or manner of collection. It was also evident that there was no strong feeling in the House against it; in fact, that there was a majority of voices in favour of it. What motive can he now have for opposing his party and so increasing the displeasure which he knew that his first opposition had drawn upon him?

Yet again we find him leading the opposition in a speech which it is plain (because all the leading members of the Court party addressed themselves to answer it) was a telling and effective one. After Mr. Heale had spoken on the Court side, recommending that " more than subsidies should be yielded," and if subsidies only, then that the commission should have power to "force men," Bacon got up, and assenting to the three subsidies (as he had done at first) objected to " the payment under six years," as making each subsidy in effect a double subsidy, which would entail a twofold danger ; one to the Queen, for the burden would be found so heavy that the collection would breed discontent dangerous to her safety ; the other to the country, for it would stand as a precedent which other parliaments would be expected to follow and other sovereigns would claim. He objected also to the manner of supply (though it had been intimated that morning by the Vice-Chamberlain, that " the Queen liked not such fineness of device and novel inventions, but liked rather to have the ancient usages offered "), and recommended a supply "by levy or imposition when need should most require " rather than by subsidy. He was answered by Sir Thomas Heneage (Vice-Chamberlain), by Sir Walter Raleigh, by Mr. Heale, and by Sir Robert Cecil, each of whom (as appears by such memoranda of their speeches as have been preserved) addressed himself directly to answer his arguments. And in the end it was carried against him without a division.

After this, we have no particulars of the debates upon this question ; we only know that a bill was framed according to this resolution, and going through the usual stages (though *difficultly* and not without the help of the Speaker,*

* Coke.

who is stated to have " overreached the House in the subtle putting of the question ") was passed on the 22nd of March.

I must confess that upon reviewing Bacon's conduct in this matter, I find some difficulty in accounting for it; though it is not the kind of difficulty which his conduct generally is supposed to involve. That he should have been rather shy in publicly opposing a proposition of this kind, even if it were one which he did not altogether approve, could not seem strange to any one in the year 1845. But that a young member, whose reputation was not yet fully made and whose fortune was all to make, should divide his own party upon a question of such deep interest to them, unless he were constrained to do it by some stronger motive than (in our present imperfect knowledge of the affairs of the time) we can discover,—does, according to our modern code of party morals, seem odd. The occasion for these subsidies was confessedly great, worthy, and popular. The difficulty might indeed be considerable ; the danger of discontent when they came to be collected probably was serious ; and it may be that the measure was on that account really impolitic, and that the Queen would have acted more wisely for her own interest had his suggestion been adopted. But it does not appear that there was any imminent or desperate danger. Such danger as there was he might have thought it his duty to point out; but this he might have done quietly in the committee, and then left it to the government and the House to settle it for themselves upon their own responsibility. He was not in such a position of authority with the House that his *silence* was to carry the question. He could hardly think therefore that he lay under any imperative duty to go out of his way for the purpose of obstructing a measure upon which his own party were so earnestly bent. It was such a point as a member of the cabinet might in these days dissent from his colleagues upon, and *in the cabinet* earnestly oppose them ; being nevertheless prepared to give up his opposition if outvoted, and go along with them when the matter came before the House. Perhaps the privacy of the House of Commons in those days (which was then really a deliberative assembly) may partly account for it. The matter was (as it were) within the walls of the Council Chamber, and every one might speak his thought. But I cannot help thinking that we must look further for the true secret of it,—in some peculiarity of his personal character. A year or two after, the Lord Keeper Puckering had taken offence at something which he had said or written, and Essex writing to pacify him says, " I told you before this manner of his was only *a natural freedom and plainness* which he hath used with me, and to my knowledge with some other of his best friends ; " and this, I suspect, contains the true key of his conduct on this occasion. It was the simplicity and earnestness of the man, and the careless confidence of a good intention, which prompted him to speak out what he thought and felt, presuming that what was uttered so candidly would meet with as candid a construction ; what was meant only for the good of all would surely be taken as well-meant. It was the advice which (had he had a right to advise) he would himself have given to the Queen ; and (having such a right in the House of Commons) he gave it by way of advice to them. As an approved friend, it was his privilege to give a free censure ; as a man who had no personal interest in the course he recommended, he could the better recommend it boldly. That a man of so singular a genius should have some singularity of character is but natural ; and this I suppose was his. For certainly though he could not but have known that such a course would not be acceptable to the Queen, he does not seem to have been prepared for the degree of displeasure which it brought upon him. And even when the extent of her displeasure was fully known to him, he could not bring himself to make any apology or retractation, or to explain away what he had said.

But this again should be considered apart, as a fresh case. His duty to the House of Commons and to the public has

been performed ; the offence to his party and to the Queen
has been given ; his fortunes are in jeopardy. How will he
set about to recover the favour which he has lost? The
Queen would not allow him access, as she had used to do ;
and caused the occasion, namely his late speeches in parliament, to be intimated to him through Burghley. As to the
real ground of her displeasure, there could be little doubt.
It could not be so much for the single act,—a solitary "burst
of patriotism," as Macaulay describes it,—as for the spirit
and temper which it manifested. Here was a young courtier
who could not be relied on for supporting the measures of
the Court; who, however zealous a royalist, nevertheless
acknowledged a divided duty ; and held himself bound, as a
member of parliament, to stand by his own opinion and
follow his own course in opposition to hers, if he could not
bring himself to approve it. To be restored to her confidence and favour was not only, from affection and loyalty,
a natural wish ; but with a view to his own fortunes, which
seemed to be then upon the point of being made or marred,
it was at that moment a prime object. The way to bring
about this object was obvious enough. It was to be sought,
not' by justifying his conduct as enjoined by duty ; that
would but aggravate the offence ;—but by acknowledging it
as an error ; by explaining it away ; by ascribing it to mis-
apprehension ; by pretending some secret design to win
thereby the confidence of the House, disarm suspicion, and
acquire authority there, that he might be the better able
to further her ends afterwards; in short, by putting some
colour upon it that might make her believe he would not
do so again, but might be depended upon as an obsequious
and manageable supporter. He could hardly have had
much difficulty in conveying such an impression, had he
really wished it ; he could certainly have no difficulty (conscience apart) in inventing a construction for his conduct
tending that way ; and ample time he had for working,
seeing that her displeasure lasted at least two years and
a half.

Now I do not find that he moved a single inch in this

direction. He stood frankly and firmly upon his justification ; refusing to understand upon what ground his conduct (rightly construed) could be considered offensive. His
tone and terms were, no doubt, modest and respectful; of
sorrow and discouragement rather than of haughtiness and
self-assertion; but the substance of his answer was remonstrance and expostulation, as of a man who feels that he is
injured; not submission or apology. Look back at the
letter to Burghley which we have just read. He is sorry to
find that his speech, delivered in discharge of his duty to
God, her Majesty and his country, was offensive. He thinks
it must have been misreported or misunderstood; and, if so,
would be glad of an opportunity to explain. If he were
suspected of " popularity or opposition " (*i.e.* of joining the
party then in opposition and turning demagogue) he had
great wrong, for there was nothing in his speech that
savoured of party opposition : " the manner of it did most
evidently show that he spake simply and only to satisfy his
conscience, and *not with any advantage or policy to sway the
cause ;* and his terms carried all signification of duty," &c. ;
all which was strictly true. But did he retract or explain
away anything ? Not a jot. It was true that " whatsoever
was above a double subsidy he did wish "—(just as he had
wished in 1588 when he himself drew up a clause in the
preamble for that purpose)—" for precedent's sake might
seem to be extraordinary, and for discontent's sake might not
have been levied upon the poorer sort; though otherwise he
wished it as rising," &c. (and though it is true that he says
nothing on this occasion about his opposition to the speedy
collection, which he alludes to in a letter on the same
subject of later date, yet he says nothing to explain away or
retract even that). " This was his mind : he confesses it ;
and *therefore* he hopes that Burghley will continue him in
his own good opinion, and endeavour to draw her Majesty to
accept of the simplicity and sincerity of his zeal, and to
hold him in her favour," &c. In other words,—It is true
that I opposed the government proposition; but I opposed
it not out of any ill-will to the government, but because I

thought it impolitic and dangerous ; therefore what could I
do but oppose it ?   And therefore the Queen ought to think
the better of me for what I did, seeing that I did only what
I thought right.

But this was a strain of public morals rather too high for
the Queen.   That was not the kind of service which would
do for her; and her displeasure showed no symptoms of
abating.

Seeing then that *she* would not think better of it, did he
begin to think better of it himself, and try to show that her
displeasure had had the effect of bringing him to a better
sense of his duty ?   There would have been good hope in
that, for your strong mind likes nothing so well as to see the
reluctant will brought into subjection.   But no such thing.
He could still be humble, dutiful, and affectionate ; but he
could not say that he had been in the wrong, or that he
could rightly have done anything other than what he did.
Look back again to the other letter, the last which we read,
addressed, I think, to the Earl of Essex.   "It was a great
grief to him, *joined with marvel,* that her Majesty should
retain an hard conceit, &c. &c.   It might please her gracious
Majesty to think what might be his end in those speeches
if it were not duty, and duty alone."   (Still not a word about
being sorry that he had made them ; he is only sorry that
she should take them so ill.)   "And whereas popularity had
been objected, he mused what care he should take to please
many, who took a course of life to deal with few."   (He had
nothing to look for from that quarter; his hopes were all
from the Queen.)   "Her Majesty's particular favour towards him had been such that he esteemed no worldly thing
above the comfort to enjoy it, except it were the conscience
to deserve it."   (What then would he give for it ?   He
knew the price well enough.)   "He was not so simple but he
knew the common beaten way to please."   But will he do
as he is bid ?   By no means ; the condition is too hard
for him.   "If the not seconding some particular person's
opinion shall be presumption, and to differ upon the manner
shall be to impeach the end, it shall teach him "—what? to

know better hereafter ? to trust her judgment rather than his own ? to advise nothing but what she wishes ? Not at all. " It shall teach his devotion not to exceed wishes, and those in silence." And this is the nearest approach to submission that he can bring himself to make. He must still *wish* to serve her ; but not being able to serve her on such conditions, he can do no more than wish. Nay, he cannot even admit that her jealousy is reasonable ; but must still maintain that she is doing injustice to him and injury to herself. " It may be her Majesty hath discouraged as good a heart as ever looked to her service, and as void of self-love."

Still the jealousy of the Queen was not mitigated ; for a year and a half later we find the same cause of offence still uppermost. Burghley, indeed, and Robert Cecil, having known Bacon since he was a boy, and being convinced therefore that his explanation was sincere, and that his opposition had been that of a free counsellor, not of an antagonist, appear to have been satisfied and to have wished the Queen to advance him—but she still objected (June 1595) that same " speech in parliament." So here he had one opportunity more of endeavouring to explain his conduct away if he had wished to do so. But still we have the old story—he had nothing to apologise for. " My hope is, that whereas your Lordship told me her Majesty was somewhat gravelled upon the offence she took at my speech in parliament, your Lordship's favourable and good word (who hath assured me that for your own part you construed that I spake to the best) will be as a good tide to remove her from that shelf. And it is not unknown to your Lordship that I was the first of the ordinary sort of the Lower House that spake for the subsidy ; and that which I after spake in difference was but in circumstance of time and manner ; which methinks should be no great matter, since there is variety allowed in counsel as a discord in music to make it more perfect." * Still, you see, it is in the spirit of justification, not of apology, that he writes. Not a hint that he would do differently another time upon a similar occasion.

* Letters and Life of Francis Bacon, vol. i. p. 362.

He cannot admit that he was himself in the wrong; his anxiety is that the Queen may be brought to understand that he was right. And this, so far as I can learn, is the last we hear of the matter.

Now let any man, setting aside any preconceptions he may have formed as to Bacon's character, and all modern notions of the indignity of treating queens with respect, endeavour to interpret naturally these words and actions, and then say whether they indicate anything but simplicity, sincerity, and integrity. Had he been the selfish, crafty, time-serving man that he is now commonly taken for, is it not clear that at each successive step throughout this whole action he would have taken a different course?

First, on the question of the conference, he would not have divided the House against his own party.

Secondly, he would at least have taken occasion to retract his opinion when he saw a disposition in the whole House to retract.

Thirdly, on the question of supply (which was the next stage in the business) he would have supported his party, instead of again opposing them.

Fourthly, when he found that the Queen (instead of thanking her stars that she had so able and so honest a man on her side) resented such independence and withdrew her favour, he would have tried to put it to the account of any motive rather than that of imperative duty which left him no other choice, and to give her assurance that hereafter he would be better advised and understand his duties differently.

Upon each and all of which occasions he took a course so directly opposite to that which would naturally have been taken by a time-serving politician, that one might better cite the story as an instance of a man knowing and deliberately sacrificing what he knew to be his private interest to what he conceived to be his public duty. This however would be going further than I mean to go myself. I think it possible enough that in this case he thought his

interest and his duty compatible. Out of his great reverence
for the character of the Queen, he may well have given her
credit for understanding her own interest better than she
seems to have done, and valuing a man all the more highly
for such independence. His precept addressed more than
twenty years after to Buckingham was, "Rather make able
and honest men yours than advance those that are otherwise
because they are yours;" and he may have hoped that the
Queen would act upon this principle. Be it so. Be it that
he thought the reputation of honesty a better means of
rising than sycophancy. All I contend is, that it was by
honesty and not by sycophancy that he was seeking to rise.

A.

Where does your story come from? It must be a
friend's statement,

B.

By no means. The facts all come from D'Ewes's Journals,
who was anything but an admirer of Bacon. But he was
not thinking of Bacon's character at all when he made the
collection. He was merely gathering together all the
records he could find of the proceedings in parliament
during the reign of Elizabeth. His opinion of Bacon's
character is worth nothing, for he was but a boy at the
time of his fall, and when a man was no great conjuror;
and probably neither had any means nor took any pains to
understand what sort of person Bacon really was. He would
naturally believe what the Puritan party said of him,—who
would of course think the worst of a disgraced royalist.
But, as a collector, I believe there is no reason to doubt his
fidelity,—any more than his dulness and prosiness, which
no man can doubt.   ·

A.

I should like to read it again. It seems to suggest an
entirely new view of Bacon's character, and of his relation
to the powers that were. And accustomed as one is to the

rules of modern parliamentary tactics, it is difficult at first to take it in.

B.

Take it home with you, and if you can find any other meaning in it, or solution of it, I shall be glad to hear it. Even if it should appear that he was all this while trying to second and to ingratiate himself with the government (which seems to me quite impossible), I should not on that account think the worse of him. There was never occasion when opposition for the purpose of obstruction could have been less justifiable:—never time when a man who "loved his country more than his fortune" might more reasonably have desired to be in the favour and service of the Crown. But this is a virtue of which now-a-days the very tradition appears to be lost among men. We have many a man who is ready enough to sacrifice his fortunes to his credit or his party, but no man who will (except in crises of great danger) sacrifice either his party or his credit to the public interests.

A.

I do not know that I can go the whole length of that proposition with you. But it is too late to dispute about it now; and besides it would lead us astray from our present business. I can well believe for my own part that a genuine patriotism might have found more to do *under* Queen Elizabeth than *against* her. If other sovereigns had been like her, we should have believed in divine right still. I will take your paper home with me.

EVENING THE THIRD.

A.

Well, I have read your story carefully, and I confess that
Bacon's conduct does look very unlike that of a man seeking
his own ends; and of that we have so many instances among
us now-a-days, that I feel as if I knew its face well. That
it is very *like* the conduct of a man whose uppermost wish is
the general good of the State, is not so easy to affirm,—the
examples are so few of that virtue. But it is very like what
one would imagine it to be.

B.

Suppose him to have believed in *both*,—both the Queen
and the Constitution; to have believed that the common
good was to be looked for from the combined and harmonious
operation of the three powers, not from the ascendency of
this or that; that their business was (especially at that time
of danger, internal and external), not to be struggling to
carry points against each other, but each to bear itself so
that the common good of all might be carried in common;—
and surely there could be no difficulty in believing this; for
whatever matters of dispute there might be between them,
they were all for Protestantism as against Popery, and for
England as against Spain;—suppose him to have believed
this, and we may surely account both for his speeches and
his apologies on this occasion, without considering the one
as an unguarded " burst of patriotism," a bid for " popularity

with the multitude," or the other as a servile desertion of his post,—a sale of his conscience for court-favour. Never was there a position in which a true patriot could do better service than that of mediator between two such parties as the Crown and the Commons in those days; never was there a man so fitted by nature, by rank, by talents, by principles, and by wishes, to do best service in such a position, as Francis Bacon. It was the very part which through his whole career he was striving to play; the only office, I think, into which he endeavoured on all occasions to *thrust* himself. It was the Queen's weakness,—her pride of will,— that prevented her from understanding or accepting such services rightly. It was Bacon's virtue—a virtue at once characteristic and honourable—in the first place not to suppose the existence of such weakness in her; and in the next place, when he could not but see it, to do what he could to save her from the bad effects of it. But let us have some more. We shall never get through, if we stay to discuss at this length.

We left off, I think, at the "abject apology;" which was the reviewer's expression for an offer to explain anything that had been misreported or misunderstood.

A.

" The lesson was not thrown away. Bacon never offended in the same manner again."

B.

Perhaps not. But what of that? Did a similar occasion ever arise again? Did the Lords ever propose again to confer with the Commons for the purpose of dictating to them the amount of supply which they should vote? Was an amount of supply ever proposed again in the House of Commons which he thought unnecessary or unwise? Larger supplies were voted afterwards I know. But, as they passed without difficulty, I conclude that according to the general sense of the House they were not larger than the occasion demanded, or the people could conveniently bear. It was no part surely of his duty to oppose a measure which he approved, merely for the sake of showing that he durst offend the Queen. To make good a charge of servility it is surely necessary to show that he did something which was bad for the State, or omitted to do something which the good of the State required. I am not prepared positively to deny that there are any grounds for such a charge, but I never heard of any; and I am sure it is the reviewer's business to state them.

A.

It is a business however which he does not undertake; for we are at the end of the paragraph ; and the next, I see, opens a new subject.

B.

Then I say that the charges in the former part of that paragraph are proved to be groundless; and that the last is no charge at all ; for it implies no fault. Now for the new subject.

A.

" He was now satisfied that he had little to hope from the patronage of those powerful kinsmen whom he had solicited during twelve years with such meek pertinacity; and he began to look towards a different quarter. Among the courtiers of Elizabeth had lately appeared— "

B.

Stop, stop, stop. Now you shall see how this carelessness as to small facts panders to serious misrepresentations; and how circumstances, true in themselves, by being artificially arranged in a false order of succession, can be made to tell a false tale.—But tell me first what is the tale which these sentences tell *you*. I would not take advantage of a careless expression. What do they seem to you to imply?

A.

It is plain enough, is it not ? The reviewer is going to explain the origin of Bacon's attachment to the Earl of

Essex. He had applied himself, he tells us, to Burghley, as the most powerful man in whom he had any interest, as long as he hoped to get anything from him. Having now fallen under his displeasure by this opposition in parliament, he could hope for no more; and therefore applied himself to his young rival.

B.

Just so. That no doubt was the impression which he intended to convey. What should you say if Bacon's attachment to Essex had commenced two or three years before; had commenced at a time when he had least reason to despair of favour from Burghley; at (or not long after) the time when he obtained through him the reversion of the Clerkship of the Star Chamber; and near about the time which Macaulay himself assigns (though I believe wrongly) as the date of his appointment as Queen's Counsel?

A.

I could only say that he is mistaken as to his facts, and that his inference therefore falls to the ground.

B.

Well then, we do happen to know that Bacon had attached himself to Essex,—had in a singular manner devoted himself to the service of Essex,—some time before February 1591–2. The date of the grant of the Clerkship was (as you remember) October 1589. His appointment as Queen's Counsel was (according to the reviewer) in 1590. The present occasion was in the spring of 1593.

A.

Then this point drops like the rest. And I suppose we may pass the next two pages, which relate to the character of the Court factions, and have nothing to do with Bacon.

B.

Pass this, if you will. But I had something more to say upon the last sentence. What was it that he had been doing during the last twelve years?

A.

Soliciting his powerful kinsmen with meek pertinacity.

B.

Ay. I only wanted to remind you that there are but five letters extant written to his powerful kinsmen during those twelve years. Two of them were written in 1580 (which we have read)—one a modest application to Lady Burghley to stand his friend; the other an equally modest recommendation of himself to Lord Burghley. The third, written about a month later, was a letter of thanks, not of solicitation. The fourth was in 1586,—the "patient and serene" answer to the "testy refusal" and the lecture on vanity,—which we have also read. A fifth was written in 1591, in which he speaks of his "vast contemplative ends" and his "moderate civil ends;" aspires only to serve her Majesty "in some middle place," which may enable him to devote the rest of his time to those studies; and (if this may not be) talks of "selling his inheritance and purchasing some lease of quick revenue," &c., and turning book-maker. Letters of solicitation therefore in these twelve years we know of only three; to which add one other application of the kind, either by word or by letter, which we know passed—but know no more about it. More *may* have passed; probably did. But these are all we hear of; all that remain for evidence of this course of solicitation pursued "during twelve years with such meek pertinacity."

A.

I do not feel bound to defend that expression.—In the next page I see it stated, that "Robert Cecil sickened with fear and envy as he contemplated the rising fame and in-

fluence of Essex." Is there any ground for this imputation
besides the fact that they were rivals? I have often
observed that among contemporaries feelings of this kind
are imputed as a matter of course to persons whose interests
clash, without any evidence whatever; and I suppose
historians do the same.

B.

Robert Cecil and Essex were rivals for the Queen's
favour, and each wished to keep the other down. For fear
and envy, I do not suppose there was much to choose
between them. Essex, though open and declared, was not
candid or generous, in his enmities. Robert Cecil, though
somewhat given to secret scheming and undermining, has
not been charged (so far as I know) with any act of palpable
injustice towards Essex. Essex would not have lost an
opportunity to overbear Robert Cecil; Robert Cecil would
no doubt have used occasions to undermine Essex. But for
my own part I never infer anything whatever from these
sweeping imputations of feelings and motives without evidence;—unless perhaps that the writer himself would
under such circumstances have felt so. And in this particular case I take them to be merely devices of rhetoric—
a point of art in composition.

But it is of no consequence. Pass on to the bottom of
the next page, in which he draws an estimate of Essex's
character. For that is important for the light it gives to
what follows.

A.

"Nothing in the public conduct of Essex entitles him to
esteem; and the pity with which we regard his early and
terrible end is diminished by the consideration that he put
to hazard the lives and fortunes.of his most attached friends,
and endeavoured to throw the whole country into confusion for
objects purely personal."

B.

Yes. I want you especially to remark and remember
that sentence. I was going to say that in this (for once)

the fact is not overstated. But the word "*endeavoured*" is too strong. It implies a worse *intention* than Essex can be justly charged with. He would have been glad, and I dare say did hope, to accomplish his ends without throwing the country into confusion. But say he was *prepared* to do it, or *did not shrink from* doing it,—which is strictly true,—and the case is bad enough. It is of prime importance to bear this in mind when we come to judge of Bacon's conduct towards him; which is commonly judged as if the question had merely been between his friend and his interest, and not at all between a bad cause and a good one. But of that presently. Only remember the reviewer's own judgment here pronounced upon Essex's cause.

A.

It is a damning judgment upon his *cause*. But if the man had so much good in him, I do not see why it should diminish our *pity* for him.

B.

Nor I. Pity him as much as you will. Pity him for ever—and all the more because his cause *was* so bad. But the question is not of pitying him, but of the propriety of excusing or defending him. The reviewer seems to think that though he is the less to be pitied now, he ought not the less to have been defended then.

A.

"Still it is impossible not to be deeply interested for a man so brave, high-spirited, and generous; for a man who, while he conducted himself towards his sovereign with a boldness which was then found in no other subject—"

B.

There the secret comes out! He was not (in the reviewer's opinion) a good patriot; not even a good friend; his objects were purely personal, and for such objects he was ready to sacrifice both friends and country. *But* he had the magnanimity to treat the Queen with *boldness*.

And what kind of boldness? The boldness of a faithful counsellor? No. He was never checked for that. But with the boldness of a man who could not endure to be reproved or slighted, or to see another man more powerful or more favoured than himself. As if there were any virtue in boldness where the ends are not virtuous which a man seeks to carry by it! But this is our reviewer's morality. To be overbearing and violent in the pursuit of personal power and wealth is honourable and interesting. To be meek, submissive, and affectionate, in going without them, is "abject," and "borders on meanness."

A.

No, no. You are unjust to Macaulay there. What he admires in Essex is his conduct towards his inferiors.

"—for a man who, while he conducted himself towards his sovereign with a boldness which was then found in no other subject, conducted himself towards his dependents with a delicacy such as has rarely been found in any other patron. Unlike the vulgar herd of benefactors, he desired to inspire not gratitude but affection. He tried to make those whom he befriended feel towards him as towards an equal. His mind— ardent, susceptible, naturally disposed to admiration of all that is great and beautiful—was fascinated by the genius and accomplishments of Bacon. A close friendship was soon formed between them; a friendship destined to have a dark, a mournful, a shameful end."

B.

Setting aside the epithet "shameful" to be discussed when we come to the particulars of the case, I subscribe to the rest of this. Essex's bearing towards his dependents deserves all the admiration which the reviewer bestows upon it. It was very noble and beautiful; and the only exception I have to take to it is this:—Though he wished to treat his dependents as friends, yet he wished his friends to *be* dependent. I wish it could be shown that he ever patronized genius or virtue which was not enlisted in his own service.

However, I am far from wishing to depreciate Essex's

many noble qualities. Indeed I think more highly of him than Macaulay does. For I believe that he did love his country, and would have done great things for it and for mankind, if he had had calm weather and his own way. He was only not great enough, or wise enough, or virtuous enough, to be content with serving where he could not command. When his ambition and his duty clashed, he forgot his duty. But though I admit that in this instance the reviewer shows a sense of his good qualities, it is not the less clear to me that he admires him also (if not still more) for his faults.

A.

It does look rather like it.

"In 1594 the office of Attorney-General became vacant, and Bacon hoped to obtain it."

B.

Say rather that early in February 1593, immediately before the parliament business, the Mastership of the Rolls became vacant, and was generally expected to be bestowed upon Sir Thomas Egerton, who was then Attorney-General. Bacon's friends hoped in that case that he would be made Attorney-General.

A.

"Essex made his friend's cause his own;—sued, expostulated, promised, threatened, but all in vain. It is probable that the dislike felt by the Cecils for Bacon had been increased by the connexion he had lately formed with the Earl."

B.

It is likely enough that, if not his connexion with Essex —which was no new matter—yet the manner in which Essex took up his cause may have inclined the Cecils against him. For as to any previous *dislike* of him, as here assumed, there is no evidence of any such matter. It is not even certain that in the first instance they opposed the appointment. I found in the British Museum a letter from Sir *Thomas* Cecil to Burghley,—Sir Thomas was his eldest son,—recommending Bacon for the place of Attorney in terms which rather exclude than imply any notion that the suit would be distasteful. And Sir Robert Cecil intimated to him, as early as 16th April 1593, his " good opinion, good affection, and readiness " to deal for him, in some cause which can hardly have been any but this. And though I find no proof that Burghley himself ever encouraged his suit for the *Attorneyship,* yet for the *Solicitorship* he certainly did; and to endeavour to make a man of thirty-two Solicitor-General, can hardly be called an unfriendly office. And as for his opposing or not encouraging his pretensions to the higher office, we must remember that the manner in which Essex took up the cause somewhat altered the nature of it; making the question to be, not whether Bacon or Coke should be Attorney, but whether Burghley or Essex should be the greater man. As Essex handled it, the appointment if made must have been taken for his act. And it is possible enough that Burghley was jealous of such an addition as this must have been to Essex's greatness. All men would have been for following the man whose influence at Court was great enough to procure such an appointment for so young a person as Bacon.

A.

" Robert was then on the point of being made Secretary of State. He happened one day to be in the same coach with Essex, and a remarkable conversation took place between them. ' My Lord,' said Sir Robert, ' the Queen has determined to appoint an Attorney-General without more delay. I pray your Lordship to tell me whom you will favour.' ' I wonder at your question,' replied the Earl. ' You cannot but know that resolutely against all the world I stand for your cousin, Francis Bacon.' ' Good Lord ! ' cried Cecil, unable to bridle his temper; ' I wonder your Lordship should spend your strength upon so unlikely a matter. Can you name one precedent of so raw a youth promoted to so great a place ? ' This objection came with a singularly bad grace from a man who, though younger than Bacon, was in daily expectation of being made Secretary of State. The blot was too obvious to be missed by Essex, who seldom forebore to speak his mind. 'I have made no search,' said he, 'for precedents of young men who have filled the office of Attorney-General. But I could name to you, Sir Robert, a younger man than Francis, less learned and equally inexperienced, who is suing and striving with all his might for an office of far greater weight.' Sir Robert had nothing to say but that he thought his own abilities equal to the place he hoped to obtain; and that his father's long services deserved such a mark of gratitude from the Queen;—as if his abilities were comparable to his cousin's, or as if Sir Nicholas Bacon had done no service to the State."

B.

There again—a small piece of injustice done in passing to Cecil. It is true that he pleaded his own competency for the place (and there is no doubt that he was competent), and his father's long services (which were in one respect at least distinguished above those of Sir Nicholas, inasmuch as they had lasted fifteen years longer), but this was neither all nor the principal part of what he had to say in favour of his pretensions, and as distinguishing his case from Bacon's. The main points which he urged, according to the report from which the narrative is drawn (which is the report of an opponent, coming as it does from Essex himself through a friend of the Bacons, and follower of the Earl), were *the school he had studied in*, the great wisdom and learning of his *schoolmaster*, and *the pains and observations he daily passed in that school*. He had in fact from his earliest youth been in special training under his father's eye for this very place; his capacity for it had been actually tried and proved; and his whole mind was devoted to the business and duties of it. No such points could be alleged in favour of Bacon. Bacon had not had the advantage of any special training for Attorney-General, or of any such experienced schoolmaster. He had not had opportunities either of practising or of proving his qualifications for it. His head was known to be full of other things. His qualifications as a lawyer were held cheap by the most learned lawyer of the time, and were indeed fairly questionable. The general opinion was (according to the reviewer himself) that they were superficial. Now if this had been true (and it was very natural that Cecil should believe it, though I do not), there would really have been no analogy between the two cases. Bacon's case would have come nearer to Cecil's if Sir Nicholas had been Attorney-General for the twelve years preceding, and he had been Sir Nicholas's devil.

I am still carping at small things, you see. But it is the small contributions that make the great sums.—Well?

A.

" Cecil then hinted, that if Bacon would be satisfied with the Solicitorship, that might be of easier digestion to the Queen. ' Digest me no digestions,' said the generous and ardent Earl: ' the Attorneyship for Francis is what I must have. And in that I will spend all my might, power, authority and amity; and with tooth and nail procure the same for him against whomsoever. And whosoever getteth this office out of my hands for any other, before he have it, it shall cost him the coming by. And this be you assured of, Sir Robert, for now I will fully declare myself. As for my own part, Sir Robert, I think strange both of my Lord Treasurer and you that can have the mind to seek the preference of a stranger before so near a kinsman; for if you weigh in a balance the parts every way of his competitor and him, only excepting five poor years of admitting to a house of court before Francis, you shall find in all other respects no comparison whatever between them.' "

B.

Yes.—Remember that though I do not think it strange that the Cecils should have thought Coke's claims on the Attorneyship higher than Bacon's, and though I can easily believe that it would have been more prudent in him to waive those claims and aspire only to the Solicitorship (and if so the Cecils were in fact his better friends,) yet I am far from thinking that his *obligations* to Essex were the less on that account. That Essex did in fact stand in the way of his fortunes, while he was injudiciously endeavouring to help them on, I am fully persuaded. But his gratitude was due for the endeavour, not for the issue; and Bacon himself never dreamed of making any deduction on account of the ill-success. But why not allow Essex the credit of superior sagacity in discerning and estimating Bacon's claims, as well as of eagerness in pressing them? The more inexcusable you make out the Cecils to be in not taking up his cause, the less praise to Essex for taking it up so warmly.

A.

"When the office of Attorney-General was filled up—"
By the by, who after all was appointed?

B.

No less a man than Edward Coke. He became Attorney-General on the 10th of April 1594.

A.

Had he any particular connexions with the Cecils?

B.

Not that I ever heard of. I do not even know that the Cecils favoured him. I fancy the Queen chose him, as being the most distinguished lawyer of his time; which I believe he was even then. He was in his forty-third year; was at the time Solicitor-General; had been Speaker of the House of Commons; and had in that capacity done some good court-service by giving the subsidy-bill a lift through the "subtle putting of the question,"—by which according to Sir Simonds D'Ewes another division was avoided;—a service likely enough to be remembered and to present itself to the Queen's mind in contrast with the part taken by Bacon upon the earlier stages of the same bill. Another motive probably was the wish to show Essex that he was not master. And a third, perhaps, that she could not quite depend upon Bacon for going her way; his conduct in the last parliament being still fresh in her memory. The appointment was a very natural one; why go so far out of the way to prove that everybody acted unnaturally? It was natural and laudable in Essex to desire the advancement of Bacon; but there was no romantic generosity in it. He was under great obligations to Bacon, though not for money. Bacon was his ablest, honestest, most industrious, and most affectionate counsellor; and was daily spending in his service hours more precious than landed estates. By advancing him he was not going to lose him, but to strengthen him for his own help. In fact it would have been very strange in Essex if he had *not* done what he could for him. The more than common generosity apparent in the *manner* of doing it, was only his way; it belonged to the natural impetuosity and intemperance of his character. On the other hand, that Burghley should think the Solicitorship a point high enough for him to aim at in the first instance and more likely to be attained, cannot surely be taken as a proof that he desired to keep him down. And if the Queen did choose for her Attorney-General the man who was popularly reputed the deepest and soundest lawyer among the candidates, why should we infer that she was governed by some malignant influence?—Well? "When the office of Attorney-General was filled up—"

A.

"When the office of Attorney-General was filled up, the Earl pressed the Queen to make Bacon her Solicitor-General; and on this occasion the old Lord Treasurer professed himself not unfavourable to his nephew's pretensions."

B.

" *Professed himself* not unfavourable!" Surely he both professed himself to be, and was, favourable. On the 27th of August 1593 he wrote to Bacon—"I have attempted to place you. But her Majesty hath required the Lord Keeper to give to her the names of divers lawyers to be preferred, wherewith he made me acquainted; and I did name you as a meet man; whom his Lordship allowed in way of friendship for your father's sake; but he made scruple to equal you with certain whom he named," &c. " *But I will continue the remembrance of you to her Majesty, and implore my Lord of Essex's help.*"—Robert Cecil wrote the same day—"To satisfy your request of making my Lord know how recommended your desires are to me, I have spoken with his Lordship, who answereth *he hath done and will do his best.*" Such was his profession. Is there any reason to doubt the sincerity of it? Quite the contrary. That he did recommend him to the Queen we have the most unquestionable evidence,—the Queen's own words upon Essex's relation. "She said (28th March 1594) none thought you fit for the place but *my Lord Treasurer* and myself. Marry, the others must some of them say so before us for fear or flattery." And again (18th May 1594), "She answered that the greatness of your friends, as of *my Lord Treasurer* and myself, made men give a more favourable testimony than else they would do, *thinking thereby they pleased us.*" And in the many letters written by Bacon himself during his suit for this office, there is not a syllable to be found which implies any doubt of Burghley's good-will. The difficulty here clearly lay with the Queen herself. And *she* certainly did use Bacon ill on this occasion.

A.

She was a frugal Queen. She knew that she was sure of his services, whether she advanced him or not.

B.

Yes. And I admire *him* for it, but not her. She should have known better than to keep such a mind as his waiting upon fortune. There are very few minds that would not have been ruined by it.

A.

"But after a contest which lasted more than a year and a half, and in which Essex, to use his own words, 'spent all his power, might, authority, and amity,' the place was given to another. Essex felt the disappointment keenly, but found consolation in the most munificent and delicate liberality. He presented Bacon with an estate, worth near £2000, situated at

Twickenham; and this, as Bacon owned many years after,
'with so kind and noble circumstances as the manner was more
than the matter.' "

B.

True : whatever Essex did was done nobly. He was a
thorough gentleman. For the thing itself, however. I
must confess it appears to me to have been made more of
than it deserves. During the last five or six years, Bacon
and his brother had been performing for Essex a kind of
services for which a thousand a year would not, now-a-days,
be thought very high pay; and for which he had as yet
received, in money or money's worth, nothing whatever.
Such services were in those days paid for by great men not
in salaries but in patronage. They used their influence to
get their adherents good places. This Essex had indeed
most faithfully endeavoured to do for Bacon; who complained of nothing, asked for nothing, and perhaps wished
for nothing. But he had not succeeded. On the contrary
he himself believed (and whether he believed it or not it
was certainly a fact) that he had stood in the way of Bacon's
fortunes. Bacon lost the Solicitorship *because* Essex urged his
claims so intemperately. In such a case, what more natural
than to feel that he *owed* him something? All this time
the bounty of the Queen had been showered most plentifully
upon himself. How much he had received up to this exact
date I cannot say; but only five years after he was reckoned
to have had from the Queen (besides the fees of his offices
and the disposition of great sums in her armies) not less
than £300,000,—" in pure gift for his only use." Now if he
believed that Bacon's services had deserved so well of the
State that not to reward him with a lucrative office like that
of Attorney-General was a great injustice ;—if he had himself received so large a share of these services; and had at
the same time, for his own services, received so large a
reward out of the State-coffers ;—was it anything so very
extraordinary that he should think Bacon had a *right* to
some share in that reward ? If I perform, with the help of

my friend, a service for which I receive a hundred pounds and he receives nothing ; and if I fail to obtain for him an *additional* fee proportionable to his labours in the service,— I can at least give him a share out of mine. Out of every hundred pounds Essex made Bacon a present of six shillings. It may have been an unusual piece of generosity, but surely it was not an extravagant one.

A.

Did Bacon himself put it on that ground ?

B.

By no means. He never (so far as I know) asked Essex for sixpence. He, as I told you, always *gave* his services, never bargained for them or thought of appraising them. But what he had too much liberality to remember, Essex had too much liberality to forget. And it is our business to remember it for him.

But, before we go further, let me call your attention to a circumstance which I shall have occasion to remind you of hereafter. This piece of liberality on the part of Essex we shall hear a good deal more of. It is the substance which has been made to throw a shadow over Bacon's whole character; and is, I believe, the ground upon which the popular dislike of him chiefly rests. "The man who had given him an estate worth nearly £2000,—how could he ever after say a word against him?" Now for my own part I meet this question by another. When a friend of mine makes me a valuable present, am I to consider it as a bribe to buy off my opposition, or fee to retain me as his advocate in all cases hereafter, how deeply soever I may disapprove of his future conduct? He may be impeached for embezzling the public money, or for selling the public interests; I may be in parliament. Am I, because I once received a present from him, to defend him in parliament, or even to abstain from speaking against him? Surely no man will say so. It is not necessary that I should *expressly* warn him before I accept the favour, that it is not to be considered as pledging me to follow him, support him, or shelter him, in courses which I do not approve. All friendships and all mutual duties of friendship are (as a matter of course) subject to an implied understanding to that effect. If indeed I accept the favour, knowing or having reason to suspect that he is about to fall into any such courses, I am to be blamed for accepting it. But I am not to be excused even then for countenancing him when he does actually fall into them. I shall not mend the first fault by making the second. My duty to truth and the public good was prior,—was and is superior,—to any duty I may have subsequently contracted on account of a private benefit.

A.

Certainly, the second duty must give way to the first. But was Essex's case one of the character you describe?

B.

Of that we will speak when we come to it. Essex had not as yet done anything which could make it wrong in the most virtuous man to lay himself under an obligation to him. Yet Bacon does seem even then to have feared that such a thing *might* happen. In a letter to Essex, written as I conjecture upon the final decision of the Queen to make Sergeant Fleming her Solicitor,—whether after or before Essex had given him the Twickenham estate, I cannot say; possibly on that very occasion;—I find these remarkable words:—"For your Lordship, I do think myself more beholden to you than to any man. And I say I reckon myself as a common; not popular, but common: and *as much as is lawful to be enclosed of a common*, so much your Lordship shall be sure to have:"—clearly intimating that he could not bind himself to any man for services incompatible with his public duty. I could quote other passages in his letters to Essex, written about or soon after this time, which point to the possibility of such a case arising. But what I want especially to call your attention to at this point is the express warning which Bacon gave to Essex upon the occasion of this very present of the Twickenham estate,—which he has fortunately recorded.

A.

Did he record it at the time, or afterwards?

B.

Afterwards, and from recollection. And therefore some people may suspect his testimony as that of a man telling his own story. Therefore it was that I quoted the letter first, which was written long before he had anything to explain or excuse, and has been preserved by accident,—not by any care of his own. I think you will see that there is a natural coincidence between the two, which is the best evidence of the accuracy of the story, to which I want you now to listen. In his "Apology," after mentioning his own labours in Essex's service, he says, " And on the other hand, I must and will ever acknowledge my Lord's love, trust, and favour towards me; and last of all his liberality; having enfeoffed me of land which I sold for £1800 to Mr. Reynold Nicholas, and I think was more worth; and that at such a time and with so kind and noble circumstances, as the manner was as much as the matter; which, though it be but an idle digression, yet because I am not willing to be short in commemoration of his benefits, I will presume to trouble your Lordship with relating to you the manner of it. After the Queen had denied me the Solicitor's place, for the which his Lordship had been a long and earnest suitor on my behalf, it pleased him to come to me from Richmond to Twickenham Park; and brake with me and said :—' Mr. Bacon, the Queen hath denied me yon place for you and hath placed another; I know you are the least part of your own matter; but you fare ill because you have chosen me for your mean and dependence; you have spent your time and thoughts in my matters: I die (these were his very words) if I do not somewhat towards your fortune: you shall not deny to

accept a piece of land which I will bestow upon you.'. My
answer, I remember, was that for my fortune it was no great
matter; but his Lordship's offer made me call to mind what
was wont to be said when I was in France of the Duke of
Guise, that he was the greatest usurer in France, because
he had turned all his estate into obligations; meaning that
he had left himself nothing, but only had bound numbers
of persons to him. 'Now, my Lord,' said I, 'I would not
have you imitate his course, nor turn your estate thus by
great gifts into obligations, for you will find many bad
debtors.' He bade me take no care for that, and pressed
it: whereupon I said, 'My Lord, I see I must be your
homager and hold land of your gift. But do you know the
manner of doing homage in the law? Always it is with
a saving of his faith to the King and his other Lords. And
therefore, my Lord,' said I, 'I can be no more yours than
I was: and it must be with the ancient savings: and if I
grow to be a rich man, you will give me leave to give it
back to some of your unrewarded followers.' "

Now if he did say this—of which I have myself no
doubt, for I have not yet been able to detect him in a single
inaccurate statement, and it is in perfect harmony with all
that we otherwise know to have passed between them—I do
not see how it was possible to make the conditions upon
which the gift was accepted more clearly and expressly
understood, or how he could have more effectually absolved
himself from any supposable obligation to follow Essex
where he could not follow him without sacrificing what he
not only held but professed to hold a prior and superior
duty. Whether such a dilemma actually arose or not, I am
not now inquiring. The particular case we will consider
when it comes before us; but in the mean time we may as
well agree as to the principle. What say you?

A.

What, whether the receiving of a favour from a friend
binds you to him for evil as well as for good? Of course

not. Is not there a story somewhere in the "Spectator" of a young man whose duty it was to defend his father in a bad case?

B.

Yes. He blushed or burst into tears, I think, and so threw the case up; the severest thing he could have done: and he is always quoted as an example for other young men to follow. Well, that is a case very much in point. And if you and I agree so far, I can hardly doubt that we shall agree further. But for the present we may as well stop here; it being the close of one of the most tiresome chapters in Bacon's actual life, and one which you must have found very tiresome in the discussion.

A.

You said, I think, that he attached himself to Essex, before he had any reason to doubt the favour of Burghley?

B.

Undoubtedly.

A.

And that he warned Essex in a pointed manner of the limits to which his attachment could go; as if he feared even then that he might get into mischief?

B.

At this time, the autumn of 1595, he certainly did. The letter which I quoted is enough to prove that, even if you doubt the truth of the narrative which I have just read. How soon he began to entertain such an apprehension I cannot say. Most likely it came upon him gradually, as he observed the growing impetuosity, ambition, imprudence, and inconstancy of Essex's character, and saw that, though he listened patiently and freely to advice, he did not mend by it.

A.

Then when he first knew him, he foresaw only his rising influence and greatness, I suppose ; and attached himself to him as the most powerful patron.

B.

Rather, I should think, as the man with whom he had naturally the greatest sympathy, and whom he thought most likely, should he attain great power (which he had a fair path open for), to make a great use of it. Essex was then only two or three and twenty. He had all the rudiments of a truly great character, and his faults were, or seemed to be, only the faults of youth. But as a *patron*, as an advancer of other men's fortunes, he was not at all likely to supersede Burghley. He was the prime personal favourite at Court, and *personal* favours and honours were likely to be lavished upon him : but it was well known (and to nobody better than to Bacon) that Elizabeth, whatever else she allowed her favourites to do, never allowed them to govern her, or to govern for her. Whomsoever she kept about her for amusement, pleasure, or affection, she always recurred to Burghley for advice. That Bacon thought his personal fortunes would grow faster under Essex's patronage than under Burghley's it is very hard to believe.

A.

You do not mean that in transferring himself to Essex, he was consciously and deliberately making a sacrifice of them ?

B.

I do not say that :—though I believe he was capable of such a thing. But there was no occasion for it here. He was not called upon, in devoting himself to Essex, to sacrifice his interest with Burghley. He never quarrelled with Burghley : and though he could not but know that in attaching himself so affectionately to a young and formidable rival he was not likely to improve his relations with him, he never considered himself as detached from him. All I say is, that if Bacon's sole object of ambition had been the advancement of his own personal fortunes, he would have had the wit to stick to Burghley. But on the other hand, for that which really was the object of his ambition,—for the realization of his great visions of reform in Philosophy, in Letters, in Church, in State,—Essex, when he first appeared in court, must have seemed like an instrument sent from heaven. With a heart for all that was great, noble, and generous; an ear open to all freest and faithfullest counsel; an understanding to apprehend and appreciate all wisdom; an imagination great enough to entertain new hopes for the human race; without any shadow of bigotry or narrowness; without any fault as yet apparent except a chivalrous impetuosity of character,—the very grace of youth, and the very element out of which, when tempered by time and experience, all moral greatness and all extra-ordinary and enterprising virtue derive their vital energy;—he must have seemed in the eyes of Bacon like the Hope of the World. Burghley was but the experienced pilot who thoroughly understood the navigation of the narrow seas; Essex was, or seemed to be, a commissioned genius for the discovery of new regions. What Burghley had in him was known, and no more could be expected from him. It must have seemed impossible to say what might *not* be expected of Essex. The proffered friendship and confidence of such a man,—what could Bacon do but embrace it as frankly as it was offered? Such a friend and counsellor seemed to be the one thing which such a spirit stood in need of. If Essex seemed like a man expressly made to realise the hopes of a new world; so Bacon may seem to have been expressly made for the guardian genius of such a man as Essex.

A.

Well, it sounds all very fine. And I cannot oppose to your doctrine anything better than the inertia of a sus-

pended judgment.   Macaulay had it all his own way before ;
now *you* have it all your own way.   So my only chance is to
be resolutely sceptical.

B.

Be so by all means as long as you can.   I shall have you
on my side presently.   In the mean time I ask neither credit
nor favour.   Your ear and your understanding are all I
stipulate for.

A.

They will both be at your service to-morrow.   Just now
they are both inclined to sleep.

EVENING THE FOURTH.

A.

As we seem to have come to a landing-place, we had better perhaps, before we go further, look back a little and see where we are.

We left off, I think, in the autumn of 1595; Bacon being in his thirty-fifth year; rising in reputation every way; a Bencher of Gray's Inn for the last nine years,—

B.

Yes, and a Reader too. He was appointed Reader in 1588;—and during the last three or four years he had distinguished himself as a Pleader in two or three important causes—

A.

—Highly recommended to the Queen by Burghley, Essex, and Sir Thomas Egerton, and by the general opinion of the Bar, as a fit candidate for one of the most important places in his profession;—by the Queen herself trusted, employed, and distinguished;—knight of the shire for Middlesex and eminent as a speaker in Parliament;—but still very much embarrassed in his circumstances; as yet without any lucrative office; and just relieved by a final disappointment from a most wearisome suit, in which he has been tempted on by continual delusive encouragement for two years and a half—

B.

—A suit (you may add) which he has been prevented by an express prohibition from the Queen herself from forsaking nearly a year ago, and settling himself to more congenial pursuits upon a scanty independence. For it is clear that this was his deliberate intention in January 1594–5, as imparted not only to the Earl of Essex but to his own brother, in a letter which is evidently confidential.

A.

And he is still on good terms with Burghley, and receiving great favours from Essex, and repaying them with services of the most important character,—services (you say) undertaken as much with a view to the public good as from interest or affection; and not extravagantly rewarded by a piece of land worth more than £1800.

B.

Certainly. Without at all undervaluing Essex's generosity, I hold that it left Bacon (especially as accompanied with that express and prophetic warning) perfectly free to do whatever he believed his public duty required.

A.

Anything else?

B.

You cannot understand his position fully, without taking into account his views and feelings with regard to Politics and Philosophy; the interests of his country and the interests of his kind. Because (however strange it may seem now-a-days that a man should devote himself to the public service from any other motive than private interest) I am convinced that if you could have seen into his mind during these years, you would have found that in the secret aspirations of his heart these things were to those but as the

means to the end;—the advancement of his private fortune
and name, the means; his end, the advancement of his
kind among the creatures and his country among the
nations.

For in the first place with regard to his country, you are
to remember that both Church and State were still among
the breakers; the Protestant religion exposed to the attacks
of a formidable league from without, under the disadvantage
of dissensions within; the civil government beginning to
shake under the rising spirit of discontent and innovation,
which in less than fifty years after did actually overthrow
it; each in danger from whatever endangered the other;—
and that too with the present prospect of a struggle for
ascendency among the court factions during Elizabeth's life,
(for Burghley could not live long,)—and a disputed succession and struggle for the crown itself upon her death,
which could not now be far off;—and if a man would be
ready to take the command in case of danger, he must be
prepared for it (you know) by rank as well as by ability :—

And in the next place with regard to the advancement
of the human race among the creatures, you must not
forget that the " Instauration " which Bacon looked forward
to, was anything rather than a matter of talk and speculation that might be delivered as well as conceived in a
private man's study. The *Temporis Partus Maximus*—the
design with which he had been labouring from his youth—
was a thing, as even then he conceived it, not to be brought
about by the labours of a single man, much less of a needy,
obscure, and friendless man; but one that required the
world for an audience, nations for fellow-labourers, princes
for patrons and paymasters. For this, as for all purposes
of honourable ambition—but especially for this, which from
first to last was his great ambition of all,—civil greatness,—
the power of speaking from a far-seen and commanding
position,—was an important, almost an indispensable, condition. And it fortunately happens that fragments of his
actual labours during these years have been preserved
(though for the most part not by his own care) sufficient

to show that in these things he was no idle dreamer or wisher, but an assiduous labourer and a diligent watcher for opportunities to give affairs an impulse in the right direction.

For his great enterprise upon the kingdoms of Nature,—an enterprise for no less an object than the recovery to Man of what he believed to be his lost birthright,—it was necessary not only to conceive the plan of operations but to muster the forces. And accordingly we find him at the age of twenty-four composing the *Temporis Partus Maximus;* a composition of which (though it be lost, or rather absorbed in the works of his maturer age) we know thus much, that it was a rudiment or first sketch of the great design. And not many years after we find him looking about for means to set the work on foot. "I have taken" (he writes to Burghley in 1591) "all knowledge to be my province. And if I could purge it of two sorts of rovers, whereof the one with frivolous disputations, confutations and verbosities, —the other with auricular traditions, and blind experiments and impostures,—hath committed so many spoils; I hope I should bring in industrious observations, grounded conclusions, and profitable inventions and discoveries;—the best state of that province. This, whether it be curiosity, or vain-glory, or nature, or, if one take it favourably, *philanthropia,* is so fixed in me as it cannot be removed. And I do easily see that place of any reasonable countenance doth bring commandment of more wits than of a man's own, which is the thing I greatly affect." And indeed what other chance had he of obtaining the requisite co-operation? For who was young Francis Bacon that he should undertake to set right the world? Long after, when he had made himself known through all Europe as the ablest man living, the popular impression with regard to his philosophical speculations was only that he had "a feather in his head." So his designs for the good of mankind were not a pretence or a dream, but a thing which he was really about.

Then for the services which he could in those days

render to the State,—they must have been for the most
part done in Parliament, the records of which are scanty,
imperfect, and inaccurate; or in private advices and memorials, of which few have been preserved; or in personal
conferences with the Queen, of which we know nothing but
that she was in the habit of consulting him. Some foot-
prints, however, remain from which we may gather the
spirit in which he worked, the manner in which he watched
for and used opportunities, and the general character of
the policy which he advocated and would have carried into
operation had he had the power to direct.

The great political problem of the time was to keep the
several orders of the State in harmonious co-operation with
each other; the nation at unity with itself; to reconcile the
authority of the Crown with the liberty of the subject. And
accordingly we find him always acting not as a partisan but
as a mediator; always forward in advocating a course which
should prevent any too curious inquiry into the exact limits
of the power of either party; persuading the Commons on
the one hand to abstain from anything which should seem
to pretend a limitation of the regal prerogative; the Crown
on the other from anything which should provoke the
Commons to try the extent of their privileges. Were there
grievances? Turning to the Commons he said,—Petition
for the redress of them as a favour, do not demand it as a
right. Turning to the Crown he said,—Remove the grievance, and the question of the right will not be raised.
Were reforms called for? Let the Crown itself be the
reformer. Take away the strength of the popular party
by doing their work for them. Re-compile the laws. Remove abuses. Do justice. Reward merit. Advance honesty
and ability.

Another difficult problem of the time was how to deal
with the then formidable body of Roman Catholics. And
on this point (if I am right in ascribing to Bacon a tract
which has been very improbably ascribed to Burghley) we
are fortunate in having a record of his sentiments at a very
early period. This tract was written at a time when the

life of the Queen was in continual danger from the plots of that party. And what was his advice? This, in sum:— Remove as much as possible all reasonable occasions of discontent: Take away their weapons of offence; but avoid troubling their fortunes or their consciences so long as their consciences do not require them to trouble the State: Relax the rigour of the oath; let them swear that they will resist a foreign invader; do not ask them whether the Pope has a *right* to invade; it is enough if they are true subjects in practice, do not insist upon points merely theoretical: Let no man have the credit of martyrdom or of suffering for conscience-sake: Seek to diminish their numbers by setting on foot a better system of education, and by encouraging zealous and persuasive preachers.

A third difficulty, closely connected with the last, was how to counteract the impression produced upon the discontented party both at home and abroad, by the many libels and false statements which were in circulation, charging the Government with oppression and injustice. In what manner he proposed to deal with these, we know from his "Observations on a Libel published in 1592," and from Walsingham's "Letter to Critoy," which was drawn up and probably suggested by him. His method was simply to set forth in semi-official style, plain, unvarnished, historical statements of the course which had really been pursued, with the grounds of it;—confronting the falsehood with the truth; a service for which in all cases his pen appears to have been ready: and I am not aware that in any of his many writings of this kind, a single false statement has as yet been detected.

A fourth problem of the time, which he appears to have had deeply at heart, was the reconcilement of Church controversies. And upon this we have an exposition of his views at large about the year 1589; in which he marches up so directly to the seat of the disorder,—points out the sources, mischiefs, and remedies of all party dissension, and urges the duty of mutual justice, tenderness, public spirit, self-review, and self-reformation on either side, with a reason so unanswerable and in a spirit so modest, earnest, serious, and persuasive,—that if every man were to read it through before he took up his pen or opened his mouth upon a party question of any description, I believe the face of Christendom would visibly change for the better. And in this no one can pretend to say that he had any personal interest, in the vulgar sense of the word ; for it was out of the line of his own profession, therefore could not lead to the advancement of his private fortunes ; he was not called upon to say a word about it either way ; and what he did say was (as he well knew) not likely to ingratiate him either with the Bishops or the Puritans,—to promote either his favour with the Court or his popularity with the multitude : only he trusted that it " might find a correspondency in their minds which were not embarked in partiality, and which loved the whole better than a part; wherefore he was not out of hope that it might do good; at the least he should not repent himself of the meditation."

But perhaps of all the particular reforms then under consideration, that which he had most at heart was a reform in the state of the Law. And in this also we have proof that he was a diligent labourer according to his means and opportunities. At the opening of the Parliament which met in February 1592-3, the Lord Keeper had declared, as from the Queen, that " it was not called for the making of new laws or statutes ; for that there was already a sufficient number both of ecclesiastical and temporal : and so many were there, that rather than burthen the subject with more to their grievance, it were fitting *an abridgment were made of those there were already.*" Of this declaration (though it may seem to have been intended rather to discourage the Commons from meddling than to intimate any real design of the kind) Bacon immediately took advantage to enlarge upon the importance of such a proceeding. Nothing is preserved of his speech but the first few sentences, and they are inaccurately reported. But from the tenor of these it is easy to see that his aim was to present the subject in the same light in which all through his life he continued, as opportunities offered, to urge it upon the attention of the legislature; the same in which thirty years after he pressed it upon the King; proposing in the leisure of his fallen fortunes to undertake the task himself, and only laying it aside because he could not, in those deserted days, obtain the countenance and assistance requisite for the completion of it. An abridgment and digest of the Law, however, must necessarily have been the work of many hands, and he could at this time do no more than urge the undertaking and offer his own help. This he did, not only in the speech to which I have alluded, but shortly afterwards in a letter to the Queen herself (8th of January 1596-7), in which he says:—" But I am an unworthy witness to your Majesty of an higher intention and project, both by that which was published by your Chancellor in full Parliament in the 35th year of your happy reign, and much more by that I have been vouchsafed to understand from your Majesty, importing a purpose for these many years infused in your Majesty's sacred breast, to enter into a general amendment of the state of your laws and to reduce them to more brevity and certainty, that the great hollowness and unsafety in the assurances of lands may be strengthened; the snaring penalties that lie upon many subjects removed; the execution of many profitable laws revived; the judge better directed in his sentence, the counsellor better warranted in his counsel; the student eased in his reading; the contentious suitor that seeketh but vexation disarmed, and the honest suitor that seeketh but to obtain his right relieved; —which purpose and intention, as it did strike me with great admiration when I heard it, so it must be acknowledged to be one of the most chosen works, of highest merit and beneficence towards the subject, that ever entered into the mind of any King. . . . . And though there be rare precedents of it in Government, as it cometh to pass in things so excellent, there being no precedent full in view but that of Justinian, yet I must say as Cicero said to Cæsar, *Nil vulgare te dignum videri potest;* and as it is no doubt a precious seed sown in your Majesty's heart by the hand of

God's Divine Majesty, so I hope in the maturity of your
Majesty's own times it will come up and bear fruit."—But
though towards a work of this nature he could not of himself
do more than urge the undertaking of it, something towards
the improvement of the Law he could do without help.
And it was on this occasion that he composed that specimen
of a collection of "Maxims of Law," *i.e.* "the rules and
grounds dispersed through the body of the laws," which was
printed after his death. This is in fact an essay towards
that very "Treatise *de Regulis Juris,*" which twenty years
after he pointed out as a desideratum,—a thing "the most
important to the health and good institutions of any laws"—
which he was himself then going on with, and which he
hoped, when completed, (which however it never was,) would
make it a question with posterity whether he or Sir Edward
Coke were the greater lawyer. For what reason, or by what
mischance, a work of which he thought so highly, both as to
its object and its execution, was not more carefully preserved
among his papers and bequeathed to the care of a competent
editor, I cannot guess. It was not published till four or five
years after his death, and was then sent into the world without so much as a publisher's preface to say how the printer
came by the manuscript, or in what condition it was left.
It may be that what we have is more than that which he
presented to Elizabeth in 1596 ; it may be all that he ever
completed of it, and in the shape in which he ultimately left
it. From a passage in the preface to the paper as originally
drawn up, it would seem that the *expositions* of the "Maxims"
were then written in Law-French, which they are not in the
tract as we have it ; and he says himself in 1616 that it was
a work in which he had himself travelled "at first more
cursorily—*since more diligently."* So it may be that the
publisher had it in its latest shape. One cannot tell. But
for our present argument the question is not material.
Anyhow, the "letter dedicatory" and the preface remain as
a sufficient proof that at this time he was actually labouring
in this field. He had collected three hundred maxims, and
had set forth a few of them in such form and with such ex-

positions as might serve for a sample of the work which he
meditated and recommended. It is possible that the opinions
of those persons to whom the sample was submitted discouraged him from proceeding at that time: for I suppose
lawyers were always lawyers: the Queen may have asked
her Attorney-General what he thought of it. And even the
worth of it as it stands, and the value of the design, our
modern authorities may possibly hold cheap. All I wish
you to bear in mind at present is, that in this as in all other
departments he was working hard to supply by his own
industry whatever he thought his country stood most in
need of.

How far he succeeded in furthering these various views
and objects, I cannot say. But if he failed, it was only for
want of that vantage-ground of power and reputation to
which he aspired. Whatever he went out of his path to do
or to advise tended that way; and nothing that he did
tended any other way. Therefore when he professes to desire advancement that he may be able to do his country
service, you cannot treat it as a mere colour and pretence on
his part; nor is it a gratuitous and groundless assumption
on mine when I say that this was the primary motive of his
ambition. I do not say that he had not other motives,
besides, supplementary and collateral. To be able to pay
his debts without sacrificing his leisure or selling his inheritance, was one motive. To have the pleasure of seeing
his talents and industry bear their proper fruit was another.
And so on. Every advantage which his course led to was
in some sense a motive,—that is, he foresaw it and wished
for it. But when I see that a man cannot serve his country
without rank and power, and that what rank and power he
has he does use for the good of his country, I give him
credit for desiring the rank in order that he may do the
good.

A.

But where do you find all this? for the reviewer says
nothing about it.

B.

You will find it in the Parliamentary Journals, and the tracts which I have mentioned;—scanty and imperfect records, I grant; where the intention and the purport must sometimes be gathered by inference and presumption. But the foot-prints (as I call them), though few and scattered, lie all in one direction. Not one that I can find or hear of points any other way. Therefore I presume that was the direction in which he was going.

A.

Well, at any rate one cannot reasonably quarrel with a man for desiring to rise in his profession, so long as he uses no unfair means; or for seeking place and power so long as he makes no ill use of them.

But now let us see what more the reviewer has to say.

"It was soon after these events that Bacon first appeared before the public as a writer. Early in 1597 he published a small volume of Essays, which was afterwards enlarged by successive editions to many times its original bulk. This little work was, as it well deserved to be, exceedingly popular. It was reprinted in a few months. It was translated into Latin, French and Italian; and it seems at once to have established the literary reputation of its author."

B.

Yes; it was popular in England from the first, and may possibly have "established his literary reputation;" though in an age when there were no reviews and no circulating libraries, it was not so easy to say whose literary reputation was established, and whose not. The *translations* were not made till long after his reputation had been established on quite other grounds. The earliest was the French, in 1618,— long after the publication of the "Advancement of Learning," the "Wisdom of the Ancients," and the second edition of the "Essays" themselves;—after he had become celebrated both in Parliament and in the Courts and in the Star Chamber as the greatest orator of his time; after he had been successively Solicitor-General, Attorney-General, Privy Councillor, Lord Keeper, and Lord Chancellor;—after the "*Cogitata et Visa*" and other rudiments of the *Instauratio Magna* had been, though not published, yet circulated privately among the learned men both in England and abroad. The translation into Italian was published in the year following; and the translation into Latin (which had been prepared under his own direction a year or two before his death) was not published during his life. So that you see even in a trifle like this, your friend cannot state the case with real fairness; but must still be putting distant things together in order to produce a false show of vigour.

A.

Well, never mind all that. No doubt the "Essays" contributed to increase Bacon's reputation.

" But though Bacon's reputation rose, his fortunes were still depressed; he was in great pecuniary difficulties; and on one occasion was arrested in the street at the suit of a goldsmith for a debt of 300*l.*, and was carried to a sponging-house in Coleman Street."

B.

True. And it will be as well to remember this, if the question should arise whether advancement in his profession was an object of real importance to him or not. Even a philosopher, when he is in debt, must be allowed to work for money. This, by the way, was in 1598.

A.

" The kindness of Essex was in the mean time indefatigable. In 1596 he sailed on his memorable expedition to the coast of Spain. At the very moment of his embarkation he wrote to several of his friends, commending to them during his own absence the interests of Bacon."

B.

True again. This was in contemplation of a vacancy in the Mastership of the Rolls, Sir Thomas Egerton, who then

held it, having been newly advanced to be Lord Keeper.
Bacon's friends hoped to procure this office for him ; and a
great pity it was that they did not succeed. But Egerton
continued to hold both. Bacon, it is to be observed, did not
make any application for it on his own behalf.

A.

Is it known that he did not, or merely not known that
he did?

B.

As far as a negative can be proved in such a case, I think
one may say it is known that he did not.

A.

And why not?

B.

I suppose he thought that, as his circumstances and
qualifications were known to all the parties concerned, it
would be *offered* to him if he were thought fit to hold it.
He had nothing to say for himself except what they all
knew.

A.

"He returned after performing the most brilliant military
exploit that was achieved by English arms during the long
interval which elapsed between the battle of Agincourt and that
of Blenheim. His valour, his talents, his humane and generous
disposition had made him the idol of his countrymen, and had
extorted praise even from the enemies whom he had conquered.
He had always been proud and headstrong, and his splendid
success seems to have rendered his faults more offensive than
ever. But to his friend Francis he was still the same. Bacon
had some thoughts of making his fortune by marriage; and
had begun to pay court to a widow of the name of Hatton.
The eccentric manners and violent temper of this woman made
her a disgrace and torment to her connexions. But Bacon was
not aware of her faults, or was disposed to overlook them for
the sake of her ample fortune. Essex pleaded his friend's
cause with his usual ardour. The letters which the Earl ad-

dressed to Lady Hatton and her mother are still extant, and are highly honourable to him. ' If (he wrote) she were my sister or my daughter, I protest I would as confidently resolve to further it, as I now persuade you.' And again, ' If my faith be anything, I protest, if I had one as near me as she is to you, I had rather match her with him than with men of far greater titles.' The suit, happily for Bacon, was unsuccessful. The Lady was indeed kind to him in more ways than one. She rejected him, and she accepted his enemy. She married that narrow-minded, bad-hearted pedant, Sir Edward Coke, and did her best to make him as miserable as he deserved to be."

Have you any objection to any of this ?

B.

No. I never interfere with matrimonial arrangements, or with quarrels between man and wife. Sir Edward Coke and Lady Hatton were a rough, wrangling couple. But one does not know what either of them might have turned out had they been differently matched. Each of them required a mate with good temper for two. Lady Hatton was a woman of talent, and I believe of beauty ; and might for anything one can tell have been no bad wife for Bacon, whose characteristic weakness it was to be an over-indulgent master, that could never find it in his heart to be strict or angry with a servant. If he could have kept her temper in order for her, she would have kept his household and finances in order for him. But this is an idle speculation. There is no doubt that Essex's letters on this occasion to her father and mother (for there is none addressed to herself) were in the highest degree honourable both to himself and his friend.

A.

" The fortunes of Essex had now reached their height and began to decline. He possessed indeed all the qualities that raise men to greatness rapidly ; but he had neither the virtues nor the vices which enable men to retain greatness long. His frankness, his keen sensibility to insult and injustice, were by no means agreeable to a sovereign naturally impatient of opposition, and accustomed during forty years to the most extra-

vagant flattery and the most abject submission. The daring
and contemptuous manner in which he bade defiance to his
enemies excited their deadly hatred. His administration in
Ireland was unfortunate, and in many respects highly blamable.
Though his brilliant courage and his impetuous activity fitted
him admirably for such enterprises as that of Cadiz, he did
not possess the caution, patience, and resolution necessary for
the conduct of a protracted war,—in which difficulties were to
be gradually surmounted, in which much discomfort was to be
endured, and in which few splendid exploits could be achieved.
For the civil duties of his high place he was still less qualified.
Though eloquent and accomplished, he was in no sense a statesman. The multitude, indeed, still continued to regard even his
faults with fondness. But the Court had ceased to give him
credit even for the merit which he really possessed. The person
on whom during the decline of his influence—"

B.

Wait a moment. For though much of this is true, and
none of it directly false, yet it is put together so—skilfully
shall I say, or unskilfully?—that I am convinced it would
convey a wrong impression as to the occasion and process of
Essex's fall. The last words especially—" during the decline of his influence "—do not properly describe his case.
His influence did not *decline,* but fell flat. When he went
out to Ireland, his influence was at its height. He had
stipulated for larger powers than had ever been given to
any one in such a case; and all he stipulated for had been
granted. And though the continual delay from month to
month of the enterprise for which he was specially sent
out must no doubt have diminished the Queen's confidence
—(she is said to have exclaimed in anger that "she was
allowing him a thousand pounds a month to go a progress ")
—yet his *influence* can hardly be said to have declined, till
after the termination of that enterprise in a treaty so dis-
advantageous that it might almost be termed a victory for
the rebels. For it was as late as the middle of July that
he had authority granted him to raise 2000 men in Ireland
in addition to the large force (upwards of 14,000) that had
been sent out with him from England. Upon the failure

of the enterprise, which was in September, he received from the Queen a severe reprimand and an injunction not to leave his post without leave. By the end of that month he was over in England in direct disobedience to that injunction, and committed to his chamber for contempt. This was the end of his *influence.* And the period which the reviewer is going to speak of should properly be described, not as the decline of his influence, but as the time of his disgrace.—Well? " The person on whom," from the time when he returned in disgrace,—that is to say, the end of September 1599,—what of this person ?

A.

" The person on whom he chiefly depended, to whom he confided his perplexities, whose advice he solicited, whose intercession he employed,—was his friend Bacon."

B.

Stop once more. Here again our dates are all in confusion. But this is a more serious matter. There *had been* a time when all this was true ; when Essex did, in the many troubles and reverses which checkered his prosperity, depend chiefly upon Bacon; when he confided to him his perplexities and solicited his advice; and would probably have employed his intercession had he needed it. But we happen to know that this kind of confidence had ceased between them for nearly two years. "For some year and a half before his Lordship's going into Ireland," Bacon had not (as he himself expressly declares) " been called nor advised with as in former times." Shortly before his going, Essex did indeed *solicit* his advice, but altogether neglected to take it; and there are no traces of any further communication between them until his return. Upon the news of his return,—sudden, against orders, and with the objects of his mission all unaccomplished,—Bacon desired to speak with him ; and again advised him as earnestly and as wisely, but as ineffectually, as before, how to bear himself in this new conjuncture. Immediately after this interview followed

his restraint (first to his own chamber at Court, then to the
Lord Keeper's, and afterwards to his own house), which
lasted from the beginning of October to the latter end of
July following; during which time no communication can
well have taken place between them; for Essex (though he
seems to have been in secret communication with his disloyal and violent advisers) did not openly converse with
anybody. When at length he was set at liberty Bacon once
more offered his services, and they were accepted. This
was on the 20th July 1600. From this time Bacon did
indeed consult with him, advise him, draw up letters for
him, and do his utmost to bring him again into favour with
the Queen. But did Essex on his part open his heart and
confide his perplexities to Bacon? Far indeed from it!
When he ceased (now some three years ago) to consult with
Bacon, he had begun to open his heart to a very different
set of counsellors, and to meditate designs altogether in-
communicable to an ear like his. What purposes he was
revolving when he *undertook* his mission into Ireland, it
would perhaps be rash to pronounce. But there can be no
doubt as to those which he had learned, if not to intend, at
least to entertain, before he came away. There can be no
doubt that, at as early a period as that, he had deliberately
contemplated the alternative of making his peace with the
Queen by force of arms, if he could not do it by force of
argument. He had in fact gone so far as to communicate
to his two most intimate friends (the Earl of Southampton
and Sir Christopher Blunt) a formed intention to land in
Wales with 2000 men and march up to London, gathering
force by the way. That particular intention he did indeed
by their advice abandon; but he did not abandon the
general design of using force to regain favour; and though
he left the companies behind, he took with him the cap-
tains. During the long interval of his restraint in free
custody, with continual hope of being restored to favour, it
is true that he did not attempt any violence. But even
during all that time he appears to have been engaged in
intrigues with a view to some such issue. He even went

so far as to enter into negotiations with the King of Scotland for the joining of some Scotch forces with 8000 men of the Irish army,—to be landed by the help of Lord Mountjoy in Wales,—with the professed object of compelling Elizabeth to nominate James as her successor; a project which was abandoned, not upon his own better consideration, but because Mountjoy, after being appointed to the charge in Ireland and finding what was to be done there, would no longer listen to it. And thus by good luck, though so much combustible matter was lying about, no fire broke out while he continued under restraint. After his liberation he seems indeed to have been willing to take the *chance* of what Bacon's good offices might be able to effect; but it was only with the view of keeping both issues of the game in his hands, so that either way he might be a winner. For he never shut his ear to his other counsellors, or abandoned the thought of using force in case he could not get what he wanted without it. There is very good evidence to show that he was engaged in practices for that purpose as early as August 1600, which was the next month after he was finally discharged from custody. At this time therefore, though I admit that he solicited Bacon's advice and employed his intercession, I utterly deny that he trusted him, depended upon him, or confided his perplexities to him. He never confided to him either what he had done, or what he was then meditating to do. To Bacon, almost as much as to the Queen, he was playing a part. To Bacon he was the submissive, devout, secluded penitent, desiring only restoration to the Queen's favour. To Southampton, Mountjoy, Blunt, Davers, Cuffe, he was the aspiring malcontent meditating his reinstatement by some act of violence. And good reason he had for his dissimulation. Knowing Bacon as he did and remembering the constant tenor of his counsels, he must have felt that to confide to him such "perplexities" as these, would be to break off all intercourse between them at once. He could not have uttered them for shame. Bacon could not have listened to them for horror.

A.

You are ready to produce your authorities for all these statements?

B.

Quite ready. I rely for all of them upon the evidence of contemporary documents. But go on now. We shall probably have to discuss them more in detail presently.

A.

"The lamentable truth must be told. The friend,—so loved, so trusted,—bore a principal part in ruining the Earl's fortunes, in shedding his blood, and in blackening his memory."

B.

This also we shall have to discuss presently in detail. Therefore I will let it pass now,—only with an emphatic contradiction of every proposition which the sentence contains. So far from admitting that Bacon bore a principal part either in ruining the Earl's fortunes, or in shedding his blood, or in blackening his memory,—I deny most positively that Essex suffered any one thing either in purse, person, or fame, which he would not have suffered had Bacon never been born, or even had he joined his party and shared his guilt.

A.

This might be so, and yet Bacon might be said to have borne a principal part in the proceedings which had all these results.

B.

As the hangman may be said to bear a principal part in an execution, though if he threw his part up the execution would nevertheless proceed. The qualification is surely a material one; and even in that sense I should be disposed to deny that Bacon bore a *principal* part in the ruin of Essex.—But go on now; we will talk of that presently.

A.

" But let us be just to Bacon. We believe that to the last
he had no wish to injure Essex. Nay, we believe that he sincerely exerted himself to serve Essex so long as he thought he
could serve Essex without injuring himself."

B.

He served him much longer than that. But go on.

A.

" The advice which he gave to his noble benefactor was
generally most judicious. He did all in his power to dissuade
the Earl from accepting the government of Ireland. 'For,'
says he, ' I did as plainly see his overthrow chained as it were
by destiny to that journey, as it is possible for a man to ground
a judgment upon future contingents.' The prediction was
accomplished. Essex returned in disgrace. Bacon attempted
to mediate between his friend and the Queen; and we believe
honestly employed all his address for that purpose. But the
task which he had undertaken was too difficult, delicate, and
perilous, even for so wary and dexterous an agent. He had to
manage two spirits equally proud, resentful, and ungovernable.
At Essex House he had to calm the rage of a young hero incensed by multiplied wrongs and humiliations— "

B.

What wrongs? Only the loss of favour and influence,
and the restraint of his person (in no harsh or unusual
manner),—consequent not upon the neglect merely of his
instructions and miscarriage of his undertaking, but upon
the abandonment of his post in direct disobedience to a
positive command.

A.

"—And then to pass to Whitehall for the purpose of soothing
the peevishness of a sovereign, whose temper, never very gentle,
had been rendered morbidly irritable by age, by declining
health, and by the long habit of listening to flattery and exacting implicit obedience. It is hard to serve two masters."

B.

Bacon had only one master. To serve both the Queen and the Earl truly and faithfully, was not hard; for that which would have been best for each would have been best for both. It was hard only to obtain *acceptance* from both as a true servant.

A.

"Situated as Bacon was, it was scarcely possible for him to shape his course so as not to give one or both of his employers reason to complain. For a time he acted as fairly as in circumstances so embarrassing could reasonably be expected."

B.

For a time? I wish he had stated how long.

A.

"At length he found that while he was trying to prop the fortunes of another, he was in danger of shaking his own."

B.

At length? I wish he had said how soon. For there can be no doubt that he saw that danger from the beginning.

A.

"He had disobliged both the parties whom he wished to reconcile. Essex thought him wanting in zeal as a friend;—"

B.

Did he indeed? I never heard that before. On what ground could he possibly think him wanting in zeal, unless he thought it the duty of a friend to join him in his conspiracy? And though one is obliged to believe many things of Essex in this unhappy business which one would gladly think incredible, I still hope that one need not believe this.

A.

"—Essex thought him wanting in zeal as a friend; Elizabeth thought him wanting in duty as a subject. The Earl looked upon him as a spy of the Queen—"

B.

Did he? That again is quite a new suggestion, and, so far as I can discover, totally without foundation. No such suspicion is hinted at anywhere in the correspondence; and indeed it seems totally incompatible with the relation which at the time we are speaking of subsisted between them. The Earl knew him to be a *good* *subject* of the Queen; therefore could not confide to him his own bad thoughts and purposes. But he could not for a moment doubt the earnestness of his desire to effect a reconciliation between the Queen and him.

A.

" The Earl looked on him as a spy of the Queen,—the Queen as a creature of the Earl."

B.

No, no. Not a *creature*. Such a thought never entered her head. She thought him too devoted in his attachment. Put it thus,—" The Earl knew that he would be true to the Queen,—the Queen that he would be tender to the Earl."

A.

" The reconciliation which he had laboured to effect appeared utterly hopeless. A thousand signs, legible to eyes far less keen than his, announced that the fall of his patron was at hand."

B.

I must trouble you again with dates. *When* did it first become clear that Essex's fall was at hand? I doubt whether there was any time before the last fatal outbreak (which overthrew all at once), when Essex had it not in his own power to recover his favour with the Queen. It was only to *be* what he was trying to *seem,*—a loyal subject, really sorry for what he had done ill, and really desirous of doing better. To be this, and to be quiet, was all the art he needed. It is true that some three months before his final outbreak, it had become but too evident that he was not in a temper to try this plan. And it may be that Bacon at that time began to despair of effecting the reconciliation for which he was still labouring. But it is certain that he did not begin to despair of it earlier than *October* 1600. Therefore if I consent to let the last sentence pass, it must be as qualified by the addition of this date.

A.

We will date it by all means, if you are sure your date is accurate.

" He shaped his course accordingly."

B.

That is to say,—after he saw that the fall of his patron was at hand (whose fortunes he had hitherto been trying to prop), " he shaped his course accordingly "—meaning that he *altered* his course. Now I wonder in what respect he altered his course in or about October 1600.

A.

" When Essex was brought before the Council to answer for his conduct in Ireland, Bacon, after a faint attempt to excuse himself from taking part against his friend, submitted to the Queen's pleasure, and appeared at the Bar in support of the charges."

B.

Hollo! Where are we now? Why that was at least four months ago. That was on the 5th of June 1600,—while Essex was still in restraint,—six weeks and more before his liberation ;—a time when, so far from thinking his case desperate, Bacon thought the prospect of a reconciliation more hopeful than ever ; a time when, so far from having failed in his endeavours to bring such reconciliation about, he had not yet had an opportunity of commencing them; when, so far from forsaking Essex's cause, he was just going to enter upon that course of mediation which the reviewer has been describing—"honestly employing all his address" alternately to calm the rage of the young hero and soothe the peevishness of the old Queen,—and getting looked on for his pains by the one as a spy, by the other as a creature.

A.

Well, but he did appear in support of the charges against Essex. You cannot dispute that. And what matters it whether the act of treachery was committed in June or in October?

B.

If you are sure that it *was* an act of treachery,—nothing. But if there be any doubt as to the nature of the act, it may matter very much. Why do you call it an act of treachery? Because the reviewer tells you that it was done upon a resolution to new-shape his course when he found that his friend's fortunes were desperate and his own in danger. But if I can show to the contrary that it was done at a time when he was not only most in hope of his friend's fortunes, but actually using his best endeavours, at the hazard of his own, to re-establish them,—I suppose you will allow me to doubt whether it was done with a treacherous intention. Bacon himself says that he hoped that proceeding before the Council would be an end of the quarrel between the Queen and the Earl; that he consented to take a part in it, not only because it was his duty to do so if required; but because, the better odour he kept in with the Queen, the more effectually would he be able to perform the office of a mediator between them; and that this office he did actually set about the very next day. The reviewer on the other hand supposes that he consented to appear on that occasion against the Earl, not as hoping to serve his cause the better afterwards, but as having made up his mind to abandon it for desperate. Now though we cannot know Bacon's *motives* except from himself, we do know that for three months immediately following he was in fact endeavouring all he could to reinstate the Earl in the Queen's favour, and was in that endeavour risking his own fortunes. Which of the two will you believe? Surely you can have no hesitation in accepting the story with which all the dates, and all the recorded facts otherwise ascertainable, agree—which is Bacon's; and in rejecting that with which they all disagree,—which is Macaulay's.

A.

You are sure that it was *after* the proceeding before the Council that Bacon's attempts at mediation were made?

B.

Not all of them. He had been making such attempts according to his opportunities all along. But that the principal of them were made after, there can be no doubt. The proceeding before the Council was on the 5th of June, before Essex was discharged from custody.

A.

And you are sure that his endeavours at mediation were sincere?

B.

Essex thought so; for he employed him as an intercessor. The reviewer thinks so; for he says they were such as made the Queen take him for a creature of the Earl. But the best evidence is the tenor of the letters which he drew up. The intention with which they were drawn up speaks for itself and cannot be mistaken. There can be no doubt whatever that his endeavours were sincere. Indeed what else but a desire not only sincere, but anxious and eager, to bring about a reconciliation, could have induced him to meddle in such a matter at all?

A.

Then how after all did these endeavours miscarry? When and why did Bacon turn against the Earl?

B.

How the reconciliation came to miscarry, I am not sure that Bacon himself could have told you,—more than that it was by no fault of his. And as for turning against the Earl, —the Earl, by taking a course which it was utterly impossible to defend or excuse, left him no choice. This we shall come to presently. In the mean time I will trouble you with one more date, which happens to be preserved and throws some light on the history of Essex's miscarriage;— the date, I mean, of that visible change in the Queen's feelings towards Essex when his restoration to favour began to seem hopeless, and Bacon's friendly intercessions in his behalf began to be looked on with dislike and suspicion. Bacon's own account of the matter is as follows:—" The truth is, that the issue of all his dealing grew to this, that the Queen, by some slackness of my Lord's, as I imagine, liked him worse and worse, and grew more and more incensed towards him. Then she, remembering belike the continual and incessant and confident speeches and courses that I had held on my Lord's side, became utterly alienated from me ; and for the space of at least three months which was between Michaelmas and New Year's tide following, would not so much as look on me, but turned away from me with express and purpose-like discountenance whensoever she saw me ; and at such time as I desired to speak with her about law-business, even sent me forth with very slight refusals ; insomuch as it is most true that immediately after New Year's tide I desired to speak with her," &c. &c.—The date then of the decided and visible change that I speak of was Michaelmas 1600. Now it so happens that from independent sources we know of some things that may help to explain the causes of this change. Essex had been his own master since the latter end of July. But to be his own master was not enough for him. He could not bear to be without his former power and favour. For the recovery of these, his violent counsellors (to whom and not to Bacon his confidence was now given) had urged him to take some decisive step. But while his restoration in the natural course of things (for which he continued to implore the Queen in letter after letter of most dejected and passionate supplication) seemed probable, he put off the resolution from day to day. Wearied at length with the delay, he had resolved to take the issue of his suit for the renewal of his monopoly of sweet wines (the lease of which was to expire at Michaelmas) as an earnest of what he might expect. If it were granted, he might hope for returning favour; if rejected, he would then decide upon some more vigorous course. Soon after Michaelmas it was finally granted to another. And before the end of the month it appears that a project for surprising the Court and forcibly removing the principal counsellors was—if not resolved upon—at least formally discussed and deliberated. "It is three months or more" (said Southampton at the consultation at Drury House, 3rd February 1600–1) "*since we undertook this.*" * Such then being the real state of Essex's mind and intentions at this time, can it be wondered at that the Queen began to like both him and his friend worse and worse? And as for Bacon's "shaping his course accordingly,"—what means had he of "shaping a course" at all? He could not shape his course so as to help Essex, because Essex was shaping a new course for himself, which he could not even disclose to Bacon, much less use his assistance in furthering it. He could not shape his course so as to mitigate the Queen's displeasure, for the Queen would not listen to him. Between Michaelmas and the day of Essex's insurrection, he had only one interview with her, which was in the beginning of January. On this occasion he frankly expostulated with her upon her treatment of himself; and was received (for himself) graciously; but could draw forth no word about the Earl. Then it was that he at last resolved to meddle no more in the matter;

* Sir F. Gorge's Confession (State Pap. Off.).

and the very next month the Earl was up in arms against her, and the whole face of the matter was changed.

These are all the data we have for judging of the spirit in which he acted and the part he took after the Earl's case began to seem hopeless; and I should like to know what pretence there is for assuming that up to this period he had in any way changed his course, or had determined to save himself at the expense of his friend.

A.

Then you mean to say that Bacon's appearance before the Council in support of the charges against Essex was in fact a friendly proceeding; that his motive was to clear himself in the first instance of all imputation of partiality, that he might afterwards plead his cause with the less suspicion.

B.

I do not say that that was his only motive. There is hardly an action in any man's life which can be ascribed to a single motive. Who can say what his motive for dining is? to satisfy his appetite, to keep up his health and strength, to gratify his palate, to do as other people do,— or merely to do as he has been accustomed. For not refusing to discharge on this occasion the ordinary duties of his place, Bacon had every motive but one. The single consideration that might have deterred him was the fear of unpopularity,—of a false imputation of ingratitude. Of his many concurring motives, which was the strongest, and which would have given way in a conflict with the rest, it is idle to inquire. There was here no conflict. Whether his desire to serve Essex was or was not stronger than his reluctance to lose his influence with the Queen, there is no doubt that he did desire to serve him, and there is as little doubt that the only chance of serving him was to *keep* his influence with the Queen. Had it been otherwise,—had he (for instance) been in possession of some secret which his duty to the Queen required him to disclose, and the disclosure of which would have ruined Essex—then there would have been a conflict; and I do not pretend to say what he would have done in such a case: probably he did not know himself. As it was, he could not have done Essex a worse service than to throw away in an idle ostentation of magnanimity his opportunities of access and audience at Court; these being in fact the only handles by which he could help him through.

A.

Well, I suppose I must let this go. For certainly upon your showing I cannot say what better he could have done.

His exertions then went on (you say) all that summer; and he continued to speak in favour of Essex as long as the Queen would allow him to speak at all. And there is no symptom of any change either in his feelings or in his conduct towards his benefactor, until now that we are on the eve of the insurrection. Let us see what the reviewer has to say of that.

"But a darker scene was behind. The unhappy young nobleman, made reckless by despair, ventured on a rash and criminal enterprise, which rendered him liable to the highest penalties of the law. What course was Bacon to take? This was one of those conjunctures which show what men are. To a high-minded man, wealth, power, Court-favour, even personal safety, would have appeared of no account when opposed to friendship, gratitude and honour. Such a man would have stood by the side of Essex at the trial,—would have spent 'all his power, might, amity, and authority' in soliciting a mitigation of the sentence,—would have been a daily visitor at the cell,— would have received the last injunctions, and the last embrace upon the scaffold,—would have employed all the powers of his intellect to guard from insult the fame of his generous though erring friend. An ordinary man would neither have incurred the danger of succouring Essex nor the disgrace of assailing him. Bacon did not even preserve neutrality. He appeared as counsel for the prosecution. In that situation he did not confine himself to what would have been amply sufficient to procure a verdict. He employed all his wit, his rhetoric and his learning—not to ensure a conviction, for the circumstances of the case were such that a conviction was inevitable—but to deprive the unhappy prisoner of all those excuses, which, though legally of no value, yet tended to diminish the moral guilt of the crime; and which therefore, though they could not justify the peers in pronouncing an acquittal, might incline the Queen to grant a pardon."

B.

I let you go on through this tissue of loose misrepresentation, because I hoped every moment to hear something about the real nature of Essex's crime; and how it was *right* (not how it was "high-minded," but how it was *right*) that it should be dealt with according to justice and policy. The law against treason was made, I suppose, not merely to gratify vindictive sovereigns with the death of their enemies, but for the good of the commonwealth, for the protection of the State against violence. A true patriotism enjoins us surely not only to keep the law ourselves, but to assist in carrying the laws into execution. And though this is a duty from which those who are suspected of a bias in favour of the offender are commonly relieved, yet that is not because it is not their duty, but because they cannot be trusted to do their duty. How can you tell what a high-minded man, standing in Bacon's position with regard to Essex, would have done, until you know what it was that Essex had done? Suppose he had been engaged in a gunpowder plot;—would a high-minded man have thrown up his office rather than assist in the examination and prosecution? Suppose he had poisoned his friend;—would a high-minded man have stood by his side at the trial, and spent all his strength in soliciting a mitigation of the sentence? It is true that Essex's offence was not so black as either of these; but it was something much worse than the reviewer would give you to understand. From his way of talking you would suppose it was a mere burst of impatience under circumstances of extreme provocation. "The unhappy young nobleman, made reckless by despair, ventured on a rash and criminal enterprise." Why was Essex unhappy? He had liberty, leisure, the society of

his friends, the love of his countrymen, all the accomplishments of mind and body, and all the tastes which give
sweetness and dignity to private life; and if he wanted
wealth, it was only because he had been so wasteful. Why
unhappy? Simply because he was no longer a Court-
favourite.—" Made reckless by despair!" Despair of what?
Not of life, liberty, fortune, reputation: all these were safe
in his own hands. His despair was only of being restored
to his former greatness at Court.—" A rash and criminal
enterprise!" Rash enough, no doubt; and criminal enough.
But was that all? Surely it deserved some worse epithets
than these. Rash as it was, it was not entitled to any of
the excuses of rashness. It was an enterprise long pre-
meditated; not undertaken in heat, on the sudden; an
enterprise which, after cooling in his mind for a whole year,
had been revived three months before upon no greater
occasion than the loss of his monopoly, and during those
three months had been diligently thought on, discussed, and
prepared.—Then as for its criminality and its " rendering
him liable to the highest penalties of the law," surely that
is very little to say of an enterprise which the reviewer
himself described just now as " an endeavour to throw the
whole country into confusion for objects purely personal,"
and which was in fact very likely to lead to a civil war.
Think of the popularity of Essex and his interest with
military men; think of the power, the resolution, the vigi-
lant policy of Elizabeth, and the zealous and affectionate
loyalty which she had always at command; think of the
discontented body of Catholics at home and abroad;—and
then imagine the issue of an attempt to master her person
and force her to change the Government! It is true that
popular opinion has made very light of this rebellion; but
that is owing merely to the characteristic levity and
thoughtlessness of popular opinion, which never takes due
account of dangers escaped. We think Essex's insurrection
a small matter, because it was so suddenly and effectually
extinguished; just as we think little of a spark when we
have trod it out, which might have set the house on fire.

But had Essex been a few hours sooner in striking, or the Court a few hours later in preparing, the whole country would have probably been in a flame.

And now let us consider how Bacon stood. For no less a crime than this, Essex was to be tried before his peers. To Bacon's part, as one of the Queen's Learned Counsel, it fell in the ordinary course of things to set forth a portion of the case against him. It was as grave, as impartial, as temperate, as truly judicial a proceeding, as the records of that time contain. What pretence could he allege for refusing to take his part in it? We are agreed (you and I, at least) that his obligations to Essex were not such as to make it his duty to defend him in a bad cause. His obligation to the Crown did unquestionably (so long as he held that office) bind him to assist in the prosecution of all offences against the State. Upon what pretext could he decline? He could not say that it was an offence which ought not to be proceeded against. He could not say that the proposed proceeding was in any way unjust, unfair, or harsh. He could not say that Essex, if guilty, ought not to be declared guilty. Did he think there were palliating circumstances in the case? He could not deny that the proper time for bringing them forward was at the trial. Did he think those circumstances were such as might properly induce a pardon? He could not deny that it was after the trial, not before, that that question ought to be considered. Clearly, the first thing to be done was to discover the *truth*; and what he had to do was no more than to set forth truly that portion of the case which was assigned to him.

A.

I cannot think that there was any occasion for him to meddle with the matter at all. He might easily have got excused: at any rate he might have *asked* to be excused.

B.

Upon what ground should he have asked?

A.

As from a proceeding which involved the life of his benefactor, and in which his help could not possibly be needed. There must have been plenty of people to pursue the case against Essex.

B,

There being no hope for his benefactor, he might have left him, you think, to his enemies. Why yes, if nothing had been wanted but to get up a case against Essex, there were others no doubt who were willing and competent to make the worst of that. But the legal conviction of Essex was but a small and incidental part of the business which lay upon the Government. Care was to be taken for the safety of the State, which was threatened with a danger of which no one could guess the extent or imminence. It is all very well for us, after everything has been found out, to say there was no danger at all; but if you want to understand Bacon's position, you must imagine the aspect which the affair presented on Sunday evening the 8th of February 1600–1. Imagine an enterprise so aspiring and audacious suddenly bursting forth without any note of warning or preparation; an enterprise in which more than a hundred noblemen or gentlemen of birth and character were engaged; in which the authorities of the city, if not actually implicated, were at least so dealt with and appealed to by the insurgents that it was plain they were by them supposed to be ready to join;—what could such a thing mean? what had been the beginning of it, what was to be the end? how far had it spread? what secret mines were ready to burst under their feet? what secret treason was there in the heart of the Court upon which the conspirators relied for aid? These are the questions which must have agitated the Council; for who could have supposed that it would turn out to be a piece of mere madness, without plan, bottom, or hope? Not the conviction of the traitor, but the discovery of the treason, was the first thing needful;

not the punishment of the incendiary, but the extinction of the fire.

It was on Wednesday the 11th of February, while the whole affair was an inexplicable and alarming mystery, that Bacon, along with the rest of that small body of practised and confidential servants whom Elizabeth kept about her, received a commission from the Council to examine witnesses with a view to the discovery of the plot.* Upon what pretence should he have declined to act ?

A.

Were there not plenty of examiners without him ? He was not Attorney or Solicitor; though one of the Learned Counsel, he was the least and lowest among them.

B.

He was the least in official rank; but in investigations of this kind he was, with one or two exceptions, the most practised hand among them; probably without any exception whatever the most skilful and sagacious. At any rate he could not have excused himself on account of the superfluity of examiners; for the very letter from the Council which contained the commission contained likewise a direction to the commissioners to divide themselves (on account of the number of examinations to be taken) into parties of not more than three. It was not a time therefore when the best hand could be conveniently spared. The object of the inquiry was to discover the truth. Upon what pretence, I repeat, could Bacon have asked to be excused? It was a service which came strictly within the duty of his place. And though I do not mean that a man ought to consider the duties of his place as absolutely overruling all other considerations,—though I admit that there may be cases in which he ought to resign his place rather than perform the duties of it,—yet I cannot think that he is at liberty to do so without a very strong reason, especially if the season be one of emergency and danger, in which all

* See the Letter; Add^l. MSS. (Brit. Mus.) No. 12497.

hands are wanted. It is in truth this point of emergency and danger which lies in the way of a true understanding of this question. Living as we do in such profound security,—the Crown as safe from all traitorous attempts (and for the same reason) as a beggar is safe from robbers,—we cannot think of treason as dangerous. If a man shoots at the Queen, we think it right that he should be whipped or sent to Bedlam, but we feel that there is no hurry; justice may proceed as leisurely as she likes; it is but the act of a fool or a madman, and the only question is, as to the best way of preventing the example from spreading. Now you must really endeavour to remember that it was not so in Queen Elizabeth's time. Upon the continuance of her life and authority great things depended. The temptation to assail them, and the danger of assault, were great in proportion. Conspiracies against her life were things of annual occurrence. For protection against them she relied not so much on her military guard as on the vigilance of her councillors and lawyers in detecting the treasons and bringing the traitors to justice. And no doubt their loyal zeal was kept by such services in a state of continual excitement, so that hesitation to act was as much out of the question with them as with a soldier. Now suppose Bacon instead of being a law-officer had been an officer of the guard; and when Essex was coming in strength down Ludgate-hill had been ordered to charge. Would you have had him say—"No, he is my benefactor; he gave me a piece of land; you have plenty of people to fight him; I resign my commission, and will be only a looker-on"?

A.

Why no. A *soldier* could not have said so.

B.

Of course he could not. Nor would any true soldier have paused to ask himself which side he must take, or whether he might stand neutral. Now I say that in tur-

bulent times, which teemed with conspiracies open and
secret; being nevertheless times of peace, when the Law
was the weapon by which they were to be met; times too
when the divine right of kings was universally believed in,
and loyalty was felt as a *religious* obligation; a sworn law-
officer of the Crown must have felt his charge to be as
definite, as imperative, as paramount, as that of a soldier
upon duty. An order to examine witnesses or to prepare
an indictment was to the one what an order to charge was
to the other. Not to be *with* the Crown in such a case
would have been to be *against* it. Nay, setting all that aside,
I doubt whether even as a friend of Essex who would not
willingly believe him guilty of the worst, Bacon would
naturally have *wished* to decline the duty. So long as
Essex's plans and motives were unknown, it must have been
possible to hope that his case was not so bad as it appeared.
A seasonable question to a witness might have brought out
a palliating circumstance, which an unfriendly examiner,
not looking or wishing for, would have missed. Moreover
the personal relations between the two Bacons and Essex
made it very desirable that somebody in their interest
should have a part in the examinations. A large part of
Essex's correspondence had for some years passed through
the hands of Anthony Bacon, and he must inevitably have
fallen under suspicion of being more or less implicated in
the present business. His name *was* brought in question on
that ground.

A.

I do not know that I should object to Bacon's consenting
to take part in the examinations, so long as the object was
to discover the true nature of the conspiracy and make all
things secure. But when all that was over,—when they
had got to the bottom of the business,—when they knew
that there was no further danger, and nothing remained but
to punish the delinquents,—I think he might have withdrawn himself. They might surely have got some one else
to discharge his part of the pleading against Essex's life.

B.

Not so easily perhaps as you think. How long do you suppose it was before the mystery was all cleared up? Are you aware that they did not get to the bottom of it till the tenth day? For ten days the examinations had been going on incessantly with very unsatisfactory results, when at last some of the principal conspirators were induced to confess the truth. It is true that their confessions, taken separately yet agreeing in all material points, made the case clear enough. But as the trial came on the next day, there was not so much time as you suppose to cram a new man for Bacon's part. And I still think that even then it would have been difficult for him to find a reasonable pretext for begging off. Nay, I must be allowed to doubt whether (even then,—even as a friend) he should have wished it. For though it be true that the confessions had now made the case against Essex so clear that there could be hardly any doubt of his guilt; yet you are to remember that nobody as yet knew what Essex had to say for himself, or what line of defence he would adopt. 'It was not only necessary, with a view to a just conclusion of the trial, that the counsel for the prosecution should be perfect masters of the case; but for the interest of Essex himself (who though he could not have escaped a verdict of guilty, might nevertheless by his demeanour have deserved mercy), it was most desirable that the prosecution should not be left entirely in the hands of the most illiberal and merciless and passionate of all prosecutors—Edward Coke. A tender, temperate, and skilful speaker, though his office were to urge the charge home, might nevertheless have done much to temper and soften it, and moderate the behaviour of the prisoner. If Bacon had not cared about his duty at all,— if his entire sympathy had been with Essex, and his sole object to befriend him as far as his case admitted,—I do not think he could have wished to be released from his share in the prosecution. Not that I believe that *was* his motive. I believe he was a true soldier, prepared to defend his position against whomsoever, friend or enemy. But I have no doubt that he wished Essex to come as handsomely out of the scrape as he could, consistently with truth and justice; and on both accounts,—both as a lover of justice and as a lover of Essex,—he must have wished to have the opportunity of speaking. As for standing by the side of the prisoner at the trial and soliciting a mitigation of the sentence, visiting his cell, and all that, it is a mere idle flourish. And I wonder that the reviewer had not too much respect for his own reputation as a historian to indulge in it. He knows perfectly well that Bacon would not have been permitted to hold any communication with the prisoner, or to open his mouth in his behalf.

A.

Yes, that is all foolish enough. And upon your showing I do not know that his consenting to take his part in the prosecution can be justly objected to. But what do you say to the *manner* in which he did it? You do not mean to say that his duty to the Crown required him to make the case worse than it was?

B.

Undoubtedly not.

A.

Then how do you justify him in urging the case beyond what was necessary to ensure a conviction, and pleading away excuses which diminished the moral guilt of the crime?

B.

That he pleaded away any *true* excuses, I deny. The excuses against which he argued were false; and were moreover such, that to have admitted them must have involved an admission that the crime had not been committed.—But of this presently.

As for pressing the case further than might have been necessary to ensure a conviction,—if you mean that he

should have been contented with making out just enough
to bring the offence within the law of treason,—just enough
to avoid the chance of an acquittal,—and should have kept
clear of all those points which indicated the real nature
and magnitude of it ;—I must say that I cannot conceive
a more preposterous position. I can conceive a man disliking the office of assisting in the prosecution of a friend ;
I can conceive him thinking it his duty to decline it. But,
once undertaken, he is surely bound to discharge it (to use
Bacon's own words) "honestly and without prevarication."
And what kind of honesty would it be in a public prosecutor
of a public offence to blink all the circumstances of aggra-
vation? Not a man who followed Essex on that day but
was, according to the letter of the law, guilty of treason ;
but was every man as guilty as he ? or was it fit that, in a
proceeding upon so grave a matter in the highest court of
justice, no distinction should be made between the leader
and the follower, or between a crime of malice and a crime
of madness ?—But let us go on, for as yet we have had
nothing but general assertion. I want to know what these
extenuating circumstances were—these excuses tending to
diminish the moral guilt of the crime—of the benefit of
which Bacon laboured to deprive the prisoner.

A.

" The Earl urged as a palliation of his frantic acts that he
was surrounded by powerful and inveterate enemies, that they
had ruined his fortunes, that they sought his life, and that their
persecutions had driven him to despair. This was true, and
Bacon well knew it to be true. But he affected to treat it as
an idle pretence. He compared Essex to Pisistratus, who by
pretending to be in imminent danger of his life, and by ex-
hibiting self-inflicted wounds, succeeded in establishing tyranny
at Athens. This was too much for the prisoner to bear. He
interrupted his ungrateful friend, by calling upon him to quit
the part of an advocate—to come forward as a witness—and tell
the Lords whether in old times he, Francis Bacon, had not,
under his own hand, repeatedly asserted the truth of what he
now represented as idle pretexts. It is painful to go on with
this lamentable story."

B.

Then let us pause awhile, and see if we cannot obtain a little relief by telling it more truly ; for a more monstrous misrepresentation I never heard.

In the first place, Essex pleaded the persecutions of his enemies, not in palliation of a frantic action, but in justification of a deliberate action which he came prepared to avow and defend. Had he acknowledged his guilt and excused it as a short madness brought on by despair of the Queen's favour (for this after all was the only kind of persecution which he was suffering), the whole trial would probably have taken a different turn; and Bacon would undoubtedly have made a very different speech from that which he did make.* But he took the opposite course. He boldly pleaded not guilty ; came prepared to justify the whole action as an act of self-defence against a plot laid by his private enemies to assassinate him. And this ground (in the opening of the case, when he thought the Government knew of nothing beyond the armed assembly and tumult) he did actually and explicitly take up. It is true that when he found that they had ferreted out the whole story—that they knew all the particulars of the previous preparations and consultations,—and how (many days before) the expediency of raising a party in the city had been talked over, the project of seizing the Tower formally discussed, and a plan for surprising and mastering the Court considered in detail and all but matured ;—and moreover when the Earl of Southampton, standing by his side at the bar and answering on the sudden to these unexpected charges, had by his answer virtually admitted the facts ;—it is true, I say, that he then shifted his position, and (being compelled in his extremity to put another colour upon his proceedings) pretended, or admitted, (call it which you will) that he had a further object, which was

---

* " I did not expect that matter of *defence* would have been pleaded this day ; and therefore *I must alter my speech from that I intended.*"—*Report of the Trial.*

to force his way to the Queen and induce her to remove his enemies from her councils. But his mention of these "enemies" in the first instance was distinctly as of persons from whom he stood in fear of a personal attack; and his motive for mentioning them was to account for the armed assembly on Sunday morning at Essex House, and for locking up the Lord Keeper, Lord Chief Justice, and other officers sent from the Council to command them to lay down their arms. It was indeed the pretence which he had devised and meditated from the beginning, and which he always intended to rest upon. For a day or two before the insurrection, he had industriously scattered about the city and elsewhere, rumours of a pretended plot against his life. On the morning of the insurrection he declared to the Lord Keeper, as accounting for the concourse of so many armed friends, that his life was sought, that he should have been murdered in his bed, that he and his friends were assembled there to defend their lives. When he went into the city to seek help there, he repeated the same story with some variations to the people in the streets. Upon his trial he again alleged the same apprehension in justification of his proceeding on that day. "Having had certain advertisement (he said) on Saturday at night that *my private enemies were in arms against me*, and the same news being seconded on Sunday morning by persons worthy the believing, I resolved to stand upon my guard." And again—" As for locking up the Lords sent from the Council, it was done in charity and without disloyalty, and intended only to safeguard them lest they should have taken hurt: for when the people in the streets shouted with a great and sudden outcry, they said, 'We shall all be slain'—at which time I and my friends thought *our enemies had been come to beset the house.*" —You see therefore that Essex's plea was not that the persecutions of his enemies had " *driven him to despair* "—but that they had driven him to take up arms in defence of his life. And this was the plea against which Bacon's answer was directed. And so much for the first principal proposition in the last paragraph.

In the second place, the reviewer tells us that the plea " was true, and Bacon well knew it to be true ; " both which assertions I flatly contradict. It was false ; and Essex well knew it to be false. There were no enemies of the kind. Enemies who sought his life (the only kind of enemies in question) there were certainly none. *Rivals* there were no doubt, who were doing what they could to keep his fortunes down ; but the worst they could do was to keep him out of Court, and the worst of his despair was but a farewell to Court-favour.

But though Essex's plea was totally false, it was necessary that it should be answered. For had he been able to make it good ;—had he been able to show that his original design in gathering a number of armed men at Essex House was no more than to resist an attack by armed enemies, which he really apprehended ; and that the rest of the action followed upon this, one thing drawing on another in the hurry and distraction of the time;—it would have amounted not only to a palliation, but very nearly to a justification. At any rate it would have discharged him of all imputation of a treasonable *intention.* It seems also to have been a line of defence which the Government had not anticipated : and in the desultory progress of the trial (during which, in consequence of the prisoners being allowed to make their remarks upon the several points of the charge and evidence as it proceeded, the argument was continually shifting from one thing to another), there was some danger of its being left unanswered. And therefore it was that Bacon (whose eye was always upon the material points of the case in hand) rising in his turn and " altering his speech from that he had intended," recalled this point of the defence, and showed how ill it hung together, and what a mere pretence it was, and an artifice as old as the days of Pisistratus. The illustration was certainly fair and apt, and what harm there was in quoting it, I confess I cannot see. The comparison was not in any way degrading. It was not as if he had compared him to Nero or Catiline, or any of the infamous characters of history. And so much for the second principal proposition in the paragraph.

In the third place, the reviewer gives us to understand that Bacon had himself " in old times, under his own hand, repeatedly asserted the truth of what he now represented as idle pretexts;" which again I deny. Bacon had never asserted any such thing as that Essex had any enemies against whom it was necessary that he should stand upon armed guard ; or that there was any machination against him which could be resisted by force. "Under his own hand" (if by that be meant *in his own person*), Bacon had said nothing about the existence of enemies of any kind. It was only in a letter drawn up by him in Essex's name, and which was to be taken for Essex's own composition, that he had (not "repeatedly " but once; not "in old times" but lately ; not " under his own hand" but under Essex's ;) attributed the depression of his fortunes to the power of certain persons about the Queen, who, having access to her ear, abused it with false information. To say that this amounted to an admission on the part of Bacon that the story about the plot against Essex's life was true, is merely absurd.   It does not even prove that the depression of his fortunes was *believed* by Bacon to be the work of Court enemies.   It only proves that he could think of nothing so likely to make the Queen restore him to favour as the suggestion that his exclusion from favour was not her own doing, but the work of others who were abusing her.   Anyhow, the matter was totally irrelevant.   The letter was a dramatic work ; a device got up between Bacon and Essex for the purpose of working upon the Queen's humour.   And this public reference to it was no less idle, considered as an argument upon the point in question, than unjustifiable considered as a violation of confidence.   If there be anything lamentable in the story, it is the light in which it exhibits such a man as Essex ; who did still worse things of the same kind afterwards, in bearing witness (and unfortunately not always true witness) against his friends.   One can only account for them as the random plunges of a drowning man catching at straws.

A.

Well, now that you have contradicted every proposition in the paragraph we last read, I suppose you are satisfied. I want to hear the reviewer out before I make up my mind. He goes on—

"Bacon returned a shuffling answer to the Earl's question.—"

B.

" Shuffling " is an epithet; and from epithets we agreed, I think, that the reviewer was to be interdicted. Bacon's answer was—"Since you have stirred up this matter, my Lord, I dare warrant you that for anything these letters contain I shall not blush in the clearest light. For I did but perform the part of an honest man, and ever laboured to have done you good, if it might have been. For what I intended for your good was wished from the heart." Essex had no more to say.

A.

"—And as if the allusion to Pisistratus were not sufficiently offensive, made another allusion still more unjustifiable. He compared Essex to Henry Duke of Guise, and the rash attempt in the city to the day of the barricades at Paris. Why Bacon had recourse to such a topic it is difficult to say. It was quite unnecessary for the purpose of obtaining a verdict. It was quite certain to produce a strong impression on the mind of the haughty and jealous princess on whose pleasure the Earl's fate depended.—"

B.

And whose fate perhaps, and the fate of the whole kingdom, depended upon the issue of this proceeding against the Earl.

A.

" The faintest allusion to the degrading tutelage in which the last Valois was held by the House of Lorraine, was sufficient to harden her heart against a man who in rank, in military reputation, in popularity among the citizens of the capital, bore some resemblance to the Captain of the League."

B.

Here again, the reviewer seems to be talking as if the object of a criminal trial were to obtain a bare verdict,—not to discover the offence; and moreover as if a public prosecutor in a court of justice ought to be thinking, not of his business, which is to "show the face of Truth to the face of Justice,"—but of the means of working on his sovereign's humour. Elizabeth, you may depend upon it, knew all about the day of the barricades without being reminded of it by Bacon. It was as superfluous to remind *her* of the true nature of this business as it would have been vain to attempt to conceal it from her. But there *was* a party whom it was not superfluous to remind of these things,— who were but too likely to overlook them,—and to whom it was of great national importance to present them in a just light;—I mean the public at large. Whatever might be the result of the trial, whatever punishment might be awarded to the offenders, it was most important that the justice of it should be made out to the satisfaction not only of the judges, but of the people. Substantiated as the charge against Essex was—fully substantiated in every point—we know that the people did in fact murmur against the sentence. How much more and how much more dangerously would they have murmured, if the case had been left by the counsel for the prosecution only half made out! How unjust would it have been, not only to the State, the safety of which depended upon the right dealing with it, but to the prisoner himself! Such an attempt by so popular a man as Essex was really a very serious thing. The advantage of a few hours might (as I said before) have turned it into the first stroke of a civil war. The punishment of it was a momentous question of state; and the question was what it really *deserved*, therefore what it really *was;*—not whether a capital sentence was justified by the bare letter of the law, but whether the execution of that

sentence was demanded by justice and State policy. For
this purpose, to present the case in its true colours was
surely the imperative duty of all persons charged with the
prosecution. To let the Queen and the people believe that
Essex's real object was only to defend himself against assassination, would have been most unjust to them. To explain
to the Queen privately, or to the people extra-judicially,
the falsehood and frivolity of that plea,—without having
publicly challenged it at the bar,—would have been most
unjust to him. The first would have betrayed the State in
concealing the truth; the second would have betrayed
Essex in cheating him of his opportunity of defence.

Now as to this fresh allusion which the reviewer says
was "more unjustifiable" than the other—this topic which
he "cannot understand why Bacon had recourse to";—take
it as it comes in the course of the trial, and surely nothing
is more natural and pertinent. Essex's first story was that
he was merely acting in self-defence against private enemies
from whom he had reason to apprehend an attack. In
answer to this it was shown that there was no ground for
any such apprehension, and that it was in fact a mere pretext like that of Pisistratus. But this excuse, even if true,
would have accounted only for the muster of friends and
the restraint of the councillors. How was he to account for
his projected attempt upon the Court and for his endeavour
to raise help in the city? To this question he replied that
his object was only to secure access to the Queen that he
might "unfold to her his griefs against his private enemies."
Bacon answered,—" Grant that you meant only to go as a
suppliant, shall petitions be presented by armed petitioners? This must needs bring loss of liberty to the Prince.
Neither is it any point of law (as my Lord of Southampton
would have it believed) that condemns them of treason, but
it is apparent in common sense. To take secret counsel, to
execute it, to run together in numbers, armed with weapons,
—what can be the excuse? Warned by the Lord Keeper—
by a herald—and yet persist; will any simple man take
this to be less than treason?" Upon this Essex argued

that "if he had purposed anything against others than those his private enemies, he would not have stirred with so slender a company." "Whereunto Mr. Bacon answered" (continues the Report), "It was not the company you carried with you, but the assistance you hoped for in the city, which you trusted unto. The Duke of Guise thrust himself into Paris on the day of the barricades, in his doublet and hose, attended only with eight gentlemen, and found that help in the city which (thanks be to God) you failed of here. And what followed? The King was forced to put himself into a pilgrim's weeds, and in that disguise to steal away and scape their fury. Even such was my Lord's confidence too; and his pretence the same; an all-hail and a kiss to the city; but the end was treason, as hath been sufficiently proved."

This is all the passage. Can you see anything strange in the introduction of such a topic? Surely it was necessary to meet Essex's argument, which was in fact a very plausible one. For if he could have proved that his purpose was merely to present himself to the Queen *in formâ supplicantis*, without any force to back him—I do not say without meaning to *use* force, for his meaning would have been no guarantee for his actions; he could not himself know what he would have been led to do when he once found himself in that position—but if he could have shown that he had taken no measures nor made any endeavour to provide himself with force more than for his personal protection—then, although the act might still perhaps have been treason in law, yet the aspect of his offence, politically as well as morally considered, would have been totally altered. Now the fact that he went into the city with a slender company, armed only with pistols, rapiers, and daggers, seemed to keep this story in countenance. It was necessary to reconcile that fact with the more criminal intention imputed to him, or the case against him would have been left incomplete in a material part. And the example of the Duke of Guise was so directly in point and lay so obviously in the way, that one does not see how Bacon could have passed it by. And none of the reports of the trial represent him as having wandered into any declamations or aggravations in the matter. He appears to have confined himself strictly and exactly to what was material.

A.

Then you really believe that Essex's ends were *bonâ fide* treasonable; that he went out into the city in the hope of gathering a force there strong enough to make head against the Government?

B.

I do not see how any one who has read the confessions and depositions can have a doubt of it. It may be true that Essex's *ultimate* objects (so far as he himself knew them) were limited to what we should now-a-days call a change of ministry. But his *immediate* object was to make himself by force of arms master of the then established and lawful Government. How can you doubt this, when you know that the preparatory conferences had turned upon the means not only of surprising the Court, but of gaining possession of the Tower and of raising a party in the city? He did, I dare say, mean to assume the attitude of a suppliant; but being well aware that his supplication would not be freely granted, he meant to provide against that accident by coming with a power strong enough if necessary to enforce it.

A.

Then I confess that in these circumstances it would not have been easy for Bacon to say less than he did. For I quite agree with you that, having undertaken the part of a counsel for the prosecution, it was his duty to make the charge out in all its parts, so far at least as he believed it to be true.

B.

And I would not hold him justified in going an inch further. But I have yet to learn that he ever did urge an unjust charge against anybody.

A.

We shall see. I agree to acquit him of censure for all that he has done up to this time, so far as by the reviewer's help and yours I know what it was. But I see many more charges coming in the remaining part of this paragraph, which we are not yet nearly through.

B.

Out with them then. It would be an agreeable variety to meet with something not grossly inaccurate.

A.

"The Earl was convicted. Bacon made no effort to save him; though the Queen's feelings were such that he might have pleaded his friend's cause, possibly with success, certainly without any serious danger to himself."

B.

That is all mere guessing. For first, how does the reviewer know what the state of the Queen's feelings was? Secondly, how does he know that Bacon had any opportunity of pleading his benefactor's cause? Thirdly, how does he know that if he had any such opportunity, he did not use it for the purpose of working upon her feelings in his favour? What he did, and what he had the means of doing, could be known only to two persons—himself and the Queen. The Queen has told nothing of what passed between them. Bacon has told something. What he tells us is of course to be taken with caution, being his own story told in his own defence when nobody could contradict him. But when a man is charged with a grave offence, it is usual at least to hear what he has to say in answer, and to give him the benefit of his explanation so far as it goes, and so long as there is no evidence to throw discredit upon it. Now Bacon expressly says,—"For the time which passed, I mean between the arraignment and my Lord's suffering, I well remember that I was but once with the Queen; at what time, though I durst not deal directly for him as things then stood, yet generally I did both commend her Majesty's mercy, terming it to her as an excellent balm that did continually distil from her sovereign hands and made an excellent odour in the senses of her people; and not only so, but I took hardiness to extenuate, not the fact, for that I durst not, but the danger; telling her that if some base or cruel-minded persons had entered into such an action, it might have caused much blood and combustion; but it appeared well they were such as knew not how to play the malefactors; and some other words which I now omit." And in another place he distinctly says, that after the Earl's " last fatal impatience, *there was not time to work for him.*" All this is told under the most solemn asseveration that a man can make of its truth; nor has a shadow of evidence ever been produced to contradict it, or any part of it. What business then has this reviewer,—I do not say to doubt it,— but to assert, as an undisputed fact, the exact contrary ? Who can now say what was the most judicious way of deal- ing with Elizabeth in such a matter ? Who can say what obstacles there may have been to dealing directly for the Earl, "as things then stood ? " One obstacle suggests itself at once. The disclosures to which the trial led were every day altering the aspect of Essex's offence. He was con- victed on the 19th of February. He began to make his own confessions on the 20th. And considering that in these confessions he accused many persons of being privy to the conspiracy who had not been suspected before; and among them persons no less important than Lord Mountjoy, commander of the army in Ireland, and Sir Henry Neville, our ambassador in France, it must have been growing daily more doubtful how far it had spread and what was the bottom of it. His practices with the King of Scotland came to light about the same time, and there Bacon himself must have been under some suspicion ; for the greater part of Essex's correspondence with Scotland passed through the hands of *Anthony* Bacon,—though it would seem that he was not made privy to this part of it. Easy therefore it is to imagine that an attempt by a man in Bacon's position to "deal directly for Essex *as things then stood*," would have been absurd and impertinent, and would have done more harm than good.

But this is mere guessing. All I am concerned to make out at present is that the reviewer has no shadow of right to say that Bacon, even at this conjuncture, omitted any opportunity of befriending Essex so far as it was possible to befriend him without violating a prior and superior duty.

A.

Well; but here's more.

"The unhappy nobleman was executed. His fate excited strong, perhaps unreasonable, feelings of compassion and indignation."

B.

Perhaps unreasonable! Certainly most unreasonable.

A.

"The Queen was received by the citizens of London with gloomy looks and faint acclamations. She thought it expedient to publish a vindication of her late proceedings. The faithless friend who had assisted in taking the Earl's life was now employed to murder the Earl's fame."

B.

As for "assisting in taking the Earl's life," you remember that we acquitted Bacon of any fault in taking the part he did at the trial. And now be on your guard against admitting such an expression as "murdering the Earl's fame." One might think the writer had taken his pattern of historical composition from the speeches of counsel in crim. con. cases. Five lines back it was but a "vindication" of proceedings which had been "perhaps unreasonably" condemned. Now it is a murder of the fame of the person proceeded against. If the sentence was not a murder of the man, why should we suppose that the vindication of that sentence must be a murder of his fame?

A.

That would depend upon the fidelity with which it was drawn up.

B.

True. Then suspend your opinion till the reviewer produces some proof of want of fidelity. Assertions he will produce in plenty; but he seems to think it superfluous even to pretend to bring proofs.

A.

" The Queen had seen some of Bacon's writings and had been pleased with them. He was accordingly selected to write a 'Declaration of the Practices and Treasons attempted and committed by Robert Earl of Essex;' which was printed by authority. In the succeeding reign Bacon had not a word to say in defence of this performance—"

B.

Not a word to say in defence of it?

A.

"—a performance abounding in expressions which no generous enemy would have employed respecting a man who had so dearly expiated his offences. His only excuse was that he wrote it by command,—that he considered himself as a mere secretary,—that he had particular instructions as to the way he was to treat every part of the subject,—and that in fact he had furnished only the arrangement and the style."

B.

Do you happen to have read this Declaration?

A.

No; I think not.

B.

Then I can only offer you my own opinion. I have read it carefully many times over, and have endeavoured to examine and weigh the authority for every statement in it. And I must aver that the further I have proceeded in this examination, the more I have been convinced that it is a statement judicially and historically accurate; and though it is true that there is here and there an expression which a friend writing in his own person and character would hardly have used, I doubt whether there is even an expression in it, to the introduction of which in an official declaration professedly proceeding from "authority" any reasonable exception could be taken. This however is a point with which I am not properly concerned. My business is with Bacon's part in the transaction, not with that of Elizabeth and her councillors. And here again I must say, that our reviewer has either strangely overlooked, or still more strangely omitted, that part of Bacon's exculpation which is more material than all the rest. You had better hear it all together in Bacon's own words:—"It is very true also that her Majesty . . . . . . commanded me to pen that book which was published for the better satisfaction of the world; which I did; but so as never secretary had more particular or express directions and instructions in every point how to guide my hand in it:—" so far the reviewer goes; giving the substance with (for him) tolerable accuracy. But there he leaves off, as if that were all; as if Bacon, having been told beforehand what he was to do, had gone and done it, and *this were it;* as if therefore he had deliberately consented beforehand to the introduction of every expression which the printed · paper contains. But, by his leave, Bacon's excuse is not half done yet; we have not even got to a full stop:—"And not only so" (he goes on), "but *after* I *had made a first draught thereof,* and propounded it to certain principal councillors by her Majesty's command, it was perused, weighed, censured, *altered,* and *made almost a new writing,* according to"—What? my own suggestions? No; but according to—"*their Lordships' better consideration.*"—Now surely this is a very material part of the case. For though he were to be held personally answerable for every word in his own first draught, on the ground that if he disapproved of the plan proposed he ought not to have consented to draw it at all, (and even that would be rather hard measure,) he is not at any rate to be held answerable for the *alterations* which the Council thought fit to make in a paper which was to be published by their authority and as their own manifesto. But here is still more :—Did not the reviewer say just now that Bacon had not a word to say in defence of this performance? Listen to this :—" Wherein their Lordships and myself both were as religious and curious of *truth* as desirous of satisfaction."—Surely to say of a composition that it was drawn up with a religious adherence to truth is to say a word in defence of it.—" And myself indeed gave only words and form of style in pursuing their direction."—Nay, we are not done yet. Here are yet more alterations, and those precisely of the kind which are most pertinent to the present argument. " And after it had passed their allowance, it was again exactly perused by the Queen herself, and *some alterations made again* by her appointment; nay, and after it was set to print, the Queen, who, as your Lordship knoweth, as she was excellent in great matters, so she was exquisite in small, and noted that I could not forget my ancient respect to my Lord of Essex, in terming him ever *my Lord of Essex, my Lord of Essex*, almost in every page of the book, which she thought not fit, but would have it *Essex* or *the late Earl of Essex ;* whereupon of force it was printed *de novo*, and the first copies suppressed by her peremptory commandment."

Now, you know, when a Queen's counsel refuses to do what a Queen commands, he must do it at some particular time and for some assignable reason. Can you suggest at what particular stage of this transaction Bacon could have objected to undertake the proposed task, or what pretence he could have put forward? Essex had been tried, condemned, and executed. That the execution was unjust no man could say who knew the particulars of the crime. Yet the people, being ignorant of those particulars or deaf to them, were agitated by unreasonable feelings of compassion and indignation. The Queen, naturally anxious to relieve her Government of this unjust odium, determined to put forth a declaration of the facts of the case from the beginning ; and for this purpose applied to the man who, of all the men in her dominions, could tell a story most truly, most concisely, and most perspicuously. Him she instructed

in what manner she wished the subject to be handled ; that
is, she told him—(so at least I conjecture)—that it was not
to be merely a narrative of the insurrection and the trial;
for though this included the specific act of treason for
which Essex suffered, it did not include all or nearly all the
matters which the Queen had to take into consideration in
order to determine whether or not it were a fit case for
mercy ; but that it was to contain an exposition of all the
precedent practices which had now come to light, and which
proved Essex to be a man whose life was dangerous to the
State. This task the Queen commanded Bacon to execute.
Upon what pretence could he possibly decline ? He was
not called upon to justify a case which he believed to be a
bad one; however sorry he might be for Essex, he could not
but believe that both sentence and execution were just and
inevitable. He was not asked to assist in a needless and
superfluous attack upon the memory of a dead man ; he
could not but believe that to relieve the Government from
a popular imputation of unjust severity executed upon a
popular idol, was necessary for the security of the State
and the peace of the nation. He was not called upon to
say a word that he believed to be untrue, or to countenance
an imputation which he believed to be unjust. Part of the
very scheme of the proposed declaration was to print as an
appendix the very words of the evidence from which the
statements in the narrative part were drawn.—Well, he
undertook the task, as what else could he do ? He prepared
a draught and laid it before the Council.

A.

That draught, as originally prepared by himself, I suppose has not been preserved.

B.

No. If it had, we should have been able in some degree
to judge, from its tone and manner, of the *spirit* in which
he worked. But all we know about it is that the shape in
which he drew it was very different from the shape in which

we have it; and so far as we know anything of the particulars of the alterations, we know that the effect of them was to make the tone of the writing more cold and severe towards the memory of Essex than it was originally. Therefore unless we believe that the whole transaction was discreditable, and such as a man of honour and delicacy should rather have thrown up his office than engage in, we are really without any means of judging of the propriety or impropriety of Bacon's part in it;—for we do not know what his part was. When the paper was once laid before those principal councillors and submitted to their censures and alterations, it ceased to be his; he had no further command over it. He could not say to the Lord Keeper, or the Archbishop, or the Secretary of State, or the Attorney-General,—"I cannot consent to this or that omission or addition; the passage must stand as I wrote it, or I will withdraw the paper altogether." The paper was not his to withdraw. He might as well be held responsible for the alterations which the Queen made after it was printed, as for those which the councillors made after it was laid before them. Nor could he reasonably have claimed a right to object to the introduction of alterations. The declaration was to be printed by authority, not of Bacon, but of the Queen and her councillors; the responsibility being theirs, it was fitting that the work should be theirs also.

At the same time you are to remember that I say this, only that Bacon may have to bear no blame but what belongs to him. I am far from thinking that, had he been personally responsible for every syllable in the Declaration as it stands, the blame would have been much. There are a few harsh and stern expressions which it would not have become him to use, in his own person, and which even in a State paper he would naturally have wished to avoid. But it is the manner only of the expression, not the matter, that can be objected to. It was to be a *judicial* statement, and I doubt whether there is a single phrase in it which would have misbecome a judge in passing sentence.

A.

Well, all this I can only listen to and wonder at; being matter of moral taste which does not admit of direct proof or disproof. I must confess that your story taken by itself would seem the more credible, because there is nothing monstrous in it. But while it removes one kind of difficulty it creates another. For if *your* account of the matter be true, what am I to make of the reviewer's? What motive could he have for misrepresenting it so grossly? Or if the misrepresentation was unintentional, how could he fall into such a series of mistakes?

B.

We had better put off that question to another night. The author of this review is reputed to have read an immense number of books; and if you ask how he found time to read so many, you will be told (I believe) that he had the faculty of reading not by sentences, but by pages. Now I can myself, in one sense, read a book by pages; that is, I can see by a glance at each page whether there is anything in it *which I want to find*. I fancy he ran through this Declaration in that way,—seeing only what he wanted to find.

EVENING THE FIFTH.

A.

I have been looking forward; and I see that the reviewer goes on to vindicate at large his views of Bacon's conduct towards Essex, and lays it on thicker and thicker. Therefore we will hear him out first, before we sit in judgment upon him; for he has a great deal more to say.

B.

Grant him his own historical facts and his own principles of moral judgment, and he may go on vindicating his own views for ever. But I join issue with him on both.

First, I deny that a present, even a present of money, made to me as an acknowledgment for honest services, binds me either to take part with, or not to take part against, the giver, when he takes to dishonest courses. This is a question of principle. And upon this it seems that I am at issue with the reviewer.

Secondly, I deny that Bacon ceased to stand by Essex until Essex had ceased to deal sincerely with him. Thirdly, I deny that he took any part against him, so long as it was possible to befriend him without violating a superior duty. Fourthly, I deny that even then he took any stronger part against him than the strict duty of his place required. And finally, I deny that even if he had thrown all obligations to his country overboard, and had thought of nothing but his obligations to his friend, he could have done him any good whatever. He might have sinned with him and perished with him; or without sinning (further than by defending the wrong cause instead of the right), he might have sacrificed his fortunes for him; but he could not have saved him.

These are all questions of fact, and on these also I am at issue with the reviewer. If he can show that I am wrong on any one of these points, I shall be willing to admit that he has done something to vindicate his position. But you will find that he will only (as you say) "lay it on thicker and thicker"—that is, will repeat his former mis-statements with greater emphasis and grosser exaggeration. But we shall see.

A.

I see he addresses himself to answer Mr. Montagu's arguments, which I suppose are not the same as yours.

B.

No; I do not undertake to make common cause with Mr. Montagu. There are many of his arguments that may be easily triumphed over. But whatever Macaulay has to say, let us hear it. It will at any rate supply some fresh texts, and some fresh illustrations of his way of writing history.

A.

" We regret to say that the whole conduct of Bacon through the course of these transactions appears to Mr. Montagu not merely excusable, but deserving of high admiration. The integrity and benevolence of this gentleman are so well known that our readers will probably be at a loss to conceive by what steps he can have arrived at so extraordinary a conclusion ; and we are half afraid that they will suspect us of practising some artifice upon them when we report the principal arguments which he employs.

"In order to get rid of the charge of ingratitude, Mr. Montagu attempts to show that Bacon lay under greater obligations to the Queen than to Essex."

B.

Here we come to the question of principle. Please to watch carefully the use of the word "*obligation.*"

A.

" What these obligations were it is not easy to discover. The situation of Queen's Counsel, and a remote reversion, were surely favours very far below Bacon's personal and hereditary claims. They were favours which had not cost the Queen a groat, nor had they put a groat into Bacon's purse."

B.

Mark that!

A.

" It was necessary to rest Elizabeth's claims to gratitude on some other ground; and this Mr. Montagu felt."

B.

Claims to *gratitude!* We were speaking of *obligation.* Gratitude is only one kind of obligation. The question is of duty, service, fidelity. These are obligations which may hold good where there is no question of gratitude.—But go on.

A.

" ' What perhaps was her greatest kindness,' says he, ' instead of having hastily advanced Bacon, she had, with a continuance of her friendship, made him bear the yoke in his youth. Such were his obligations to Elizabeth.' "

B.

A suggestion, with which I have nothing to do. It is hardly worth while to inquire whether it is fairly stated.

A.

" Such indeed they were. Being the son of one of her oldest and most faithful ministers; being himself the ablest and most accomplished young man of his time,—he had been condemned by her to drudgery, to obscurity, to poverty."

B.

That is, she had not *raised him above the necessity of working for his livelihood.* The rest is gross rhetoric. Above *obscurity* she *had* raised him. For she had distinguished him by unusual access, employed him in the business of the Learned Counsel, and used him in State affairs. What next ?

A.

"She had depreciated his acquirements."

B.

That is, she had shared what the reviewer himself admits to have been "the general opinion" with regard to his acquirements as a lawyer. She had said, "He had a great wit, and an excellent gift of speech, and much other good learning; but *in law* thought he could rather show to the uttermost of his knowledge, than that he was deep."—Well?

A.

" She had checked him in the most imperious manner, when in Parliament he ventured to act an independent part."

B.

Not him more than others.

A.

"She had refused to him the professional advancement to which he had a just claim."

B.

Nay, hardly a *claim.* She had preferred Coke before him to be Attorney-General; and Fleming to be Solicitor-General. They were both of older standing. Coke was nine years his elder, and had a much higher professional reputation. Fleming was, according to Bacon himself, "an able man." "If I see her Majesty (he said) settle her choice upon an able man, *such an one as Mr. Sergeant Fleming,* I will make no means to alter it."—More ?

A.

" To her it was owing that while younger men—not superior to him in extraction, and far inferior to him in every kind of personal merit—were filling the highest offices of the State, adding manor to manor, rearing palace after palace,—"

B.

It is a pity to strip that sentence of its feathers; but it must be done. Read instead (*meo periculo*), "While his cousin Robert Cecil had been for two years Secretary of State." The manors and palaces, I think, came after.

A.

" —he was lying at a spunging-house for a debt of three hundred pounds."

B.

That was a pity, certainly. Yet I cannot think that even that injury was enough to cancel his duty as a subject to the State. *He*, at least, could not have pleaded it as a valid excuse.

A.

" Assuredly if Bacon owed gratitude to Elizabeth, he owed none to Essex. If the Queen really was his best friend, the Earl was his worst enemy. We wonder that Mr. Montagu did not press his argument a little further. He might have maintained that Bacon was fully justified in revenging himself upon a man who had attempted to rescue his youth from the salutary yoke imposed upon it by the Queen;—who had wished to advance him hastily;—who, not content with attempting to inflict the Attorney-Generalship upon him, had been so cruel as to present him with a landed estate."

B.

All this gaiety is aimed at Mr. Montagu, whom it is not my business to shield. As far however as the matter itself, apart from Mr. Montagu's way of handling it, is concerned, I need only say that the argument at best only goes to show that Bacon did not *owe* gratitude to the Queen,—that

is, he *ought not* to have felt gratitude. But the fact is
that, whether he ought or not, he did feel it; and felt it
deeply. Whatever may have been the nature of the
obligations conferred by her, there can be no doubt as to
the nature of the emotion with which they had inspired
him:—an earnest, grateful, affectionate, disinterested devotion; an ambition, not to be paid for serving, but to
serve; a sentiment of reverence and duty, which neglect
and injustice could never shake; which the fear of obloquy
could never make him betray; which the pursuit of fortune
could never make him forget; which Death could not
cancel,—for it attached itself to her memory when it could
no longer avail herself. However base and unworthy of a
father of philosophy the reviewer may hold such a feeling
to be,—even he can hardly doubt the sincerity of it. It
lives to this day in the words which flowed fresh from his
heart at various times and in various circumstances,—in
times when he felt most elated by the gracious acceptance
of his services; in times when he felt most depressed by
the ill requital of them;—in times when he had everything
to hope from her favour; in times when he had nothing
to hope;—in times when all men were emulous to flatter
her; in times when it was thought by many men that the
most acceptable way of flattering her successor was by
disparaging her.

But do you not see that the reviewer is speaking all this
time of gratitude and obligation as if they were merely
matters for a money bargain? So much money you have
had from me; so much zeal and fidelity I expect from you.
How, says he, could Bacon lie under greater obligations to
the Queen than to Essex, when the Queen had not put
a groat into his purse, and Essex had given him land?
You might as well ask how a man can lie under greater
obligations to his religion or his conscience than to his
patron,—when his religion and conscience have always stood
in the way of his fortunes, and his patron has offered him
large bribes to betray them. If the reviewer really thinks
that the laws of duty are like the laws of an auction; that

there are no "obligations" that a man can lie under, but such as may be bought up by a higher bidder; if he thinks that offices of friendship and loyalty belong as a matter of course to the party that pays the largest fee ;—only let him say so. We shall then know how to argue with him ; if we think it worth while to argue with him at all. Yet even on this ground he might, if it were necessary, be met. Bacon could have alleged as an excuse that he was already *retained* on the Queen's side, and was not permitted by the etiquette of his profession to transfer himself for a double fee to the other party. His duty to the Queen and State was indefeasible ; any subsequent engagement incompatible with it was *ipso facto* void.

A.

The reviewer may reply that in that case he should not have *taken* the fee.

B.

Yes ; and I may reply again that the fee was not given for any such object, or at any rate was not taken with any such understanding. Bacon, at the time he took it, expressly said, "I can be no more yours than I was." But if I speak of it as a *fee*, it is only that I may bring it within the compass of the reviewer's argument. It was not in fact any fee for services to come, but a fair and honourable acknowledgment (though by no means an extravagant one) of services past. The simple and sufficient explanation of the unpopularity which Bacon incurred on account of his conduct to Essex,—of the " solitude and want of comfort " in which his course involved him,—is most shortly expressed in his own words addressed to the Queen in December 1599—(the time when he was threatened with assassination) —" which I judge to be (he says) because *I take Duty too exactly and not according to the dregs of this age.*" I am afraid the ages have not mended us in this respect. We seem to be deeper than ever in these dregs.

A.

You need not press this further on my account. For assuming that you are correct in saying that he took no further part against Essex than the duty of his place required, I quite agree with you that there is no just ground for censure; especially as he had attached himself to the Queen's service before he saw Essex's face. And this point being settled, the next appears superfluous. But we may as well have it.

" Again, we can hardly think Mr. Montagu serious when he tells us that Bacon was bound for the sake of the public, not to destroy his own hopes of advancement; and that he took part against Essex from a wish to obtain power which might enable him to be useful to his country. We really do not know how to refute such arguments except by stating them. Nothing is impossible which does not involve a contradiction. It is barely possible that Bacon's motives for acting as he did on this occasion may have been gratitude to the Queen for keeping him poor, and a desire to benefit his fellow-creatures in some high situation. And there is a possibility that Bonner may have been a good Protestant, who being convinced that the blood of martyrs is the seed of the Church, heroically went through all the drudgery and infamy of persecution that he might inspire the English people with an intense and lasting hatred of Popery.—"

B.

To make that an analogous case, we must suppose Mr. Montagu to have argued that Bacon's object in taking part against Essex was to inspire the people with a hatred of the Government; which is not Mr. Montagu's argument.

A.

Yes.

" —There is a possibility that Jeffreys may have been an ardent lover of liberty, and that he may have beheaded Algernon Sydney and burned Elizabeth Gaunt, only in order to produce a reaction which might lead to a limitation of the prerogative."—

Your last remark applies still more exactly to this case.

—" There is a possibility that Thurtell may have killed

Weare only in order to give the youth of England an impressive warning against gaming and bad company. There is a possibility that Fauntleroy may have forged powers of attorney only in order that his fate might turn the attention of the public to the defects of the penal law."

B.

Here he should have cited (if he wanted a case truly analogous), not Thurtell and Fauntleroy, but some one among the counsel for the prosecution who had formerly received money from them:—and told us that it was " barely possible" that these counsel might have taken their part in the prosecution in the hope of advancing in their profession, and so serving their country or their party in parliament. I suppose most people would agree that such a thing was not only " possible" but probable.

A.

" These things, we say, are possible; but they are so extravagantly improbable, that a man who should act on such a supposition would be fit only for St. Luke's. And we do not see why suppositions upon which no man would act in ordinary life should be admitted into history.—"

It is odd. I swallowed all this without straining when I read the article first. I must confess now that it appears intolerable trifling with a serious subject. You will of course answer that all these pretended analogies are cases in which notorious crimes are supposed to be committed upon a pretence merely absurd and extravagant: whereas in Bacon's case the act itself was no crime, and at any rate lay in the direct road to the supposed object.

B.

Unquestionably I should say that. For since we are debating possibilities,—it is surely *possible* that Bacon, knowing the Queen's cause to be a good one and Essex's cause to be a very bad one, may have thought it no crime to stand by the good cause even if he should die the day after. And setting aside the question of duty altogether, it is quite certain that by throwing up his office on such an occasion he would have greatly diminished his opportunities of doing service to his country. So that assuming the motive to be a possible one in itself, there is no absurdity in supposing that it had its influence here. If it impelled him to do anything, it must have impelled him to do what he did.—But I should say much more than this. I should say that this glimpse into the reviewer's breast through the window which he here inadvertently opens, presents a spectacle which is to me almost awful; and a spectacle of no good omen for mankind. Here is a young aspirant for political power and distinction in the year of grace 1837 who sets it down as "extravagantly improbable" that a man should wish for power in order to benefit his fellow-creatures.

A.

Hardly that, perhaps. He thinks it extravagant to suppose that this was *Bacon's* motive.

B.

That point I may have a word to say upon presently. But I will not consent to qualify what I said just now. I maintain that his argument implies an opinion—(I say, "his argument implies the opinion;" for I do not undertake to say that he *thinks* as he talks, in any true sense of the verb "to think;")—his argument, I say, implies an opinion, independently of Bacon's case, that the supposition itself is extravagant. Grant him for a moment that Bacon's conduct was indefensible in itself,—a sacrifice of the duty of gratitude to the desire of power. Still the prospect of power was before him, and through that power lay his chance of doing good. Why is it extravagant to suppose that in desiring the power he desired the ability to do good which it must confer? To say that a man who is capable of doing a base action in order to obtain a commanding position, is not capable of *desiring* that position in order that he may do great and good actions, is to contradict all daily as well as all historical experience. My only hope is that the reviewer did not *think* about the matter; that the words embody no opinion of his whatever, and express nothing more than the pride and pleasure which he feels in turning a good sentence.

A.

That is the true reading of them, I dare say.—But here is more.

" Mr. Montagu's notion that Bacon desired power only in order to do good to mankind, appears somewhat strange to us, when we consider how Bacon afterwards used power, and how he lost it."

B.

"How Bacon *afterwards* used power" is a question on which very much may be said, and on which the reviewer will give us very little light. The use which he had endeavoured *hitherto* to make of the little power he had, I have already spoken of. And I think it would puzzle the reviewer himself to explain away the appearances which it exhibits of a desire to do good. The uses to which he directed his influence in later life I shall probably have to employ some evening in explaining; for the present I shall content myself with denying altogether the relevancy of the question. Suppose it true that Bacon after attaining to power did no good with it,—what then? Does it follow that he intended none? Whether he was honest enough to *do* noble things or not, surely he was capable of *desiring* to do them. It is possible enough that a man who in his silent meditations and resolutions was always intending the largest benefits to mankind, might be perpetually turned aside from his purposes by the fears or flatteries of the time. But that a man who had the heart to dedicate himself from his earliest years to the service of mankind in the highest and largest sense,—to devote his whole leisure to the building up of a work which was to bring (as *he* at least believed) infinite benefit to mankind through all their generations, but to himself no present reward except the consciousness of that service,—that such a man should in his daily dealings with the world have been incapable not only of noble actions, but even of noble *wishes*,—should have given up that heart to objects purely sordid and selfish, —is it not a monstrous and incredible supposition?

A.

Quite incredible; but unfortunately too much in keeping with the reviewer's doctrine of "extravagant improbability," upon which I thought just now you were too severe. —But wait; we are coming to particulars.

"Surely the service which he rendered to mankind by taking Lady Wharton's broad pieces, and Sir John Kennedy's cabinet,—"

B.

—those being the only services he ever rendered to mankind.

A.

Yes; I see.

—"was not of such vast importance as to sanctify all the means that might conduce to that end."

Monstrous! to think that this man was one of my historical authorities!

"If the case were fairly stated, it would, we much fear, stand thus:—Bacon was a servile advocate that he might be a corrupt judge."

B.

Fairly! As if it could be fairly presumed that in endeavouring to rise in his profession he was only speculating on becoming Chancellor and receiving the profits of corruption!

A.

Say no more. I wonder if the reviewer was a reader of books that he might be a writer of slanders.

Now we come to a new point.

"Mr. Montagu conceives that none but the ignorant and unreflecting can think Bacon censurable for anything that he did as counsel for the Crown; and maintains that no advocate can justifiably use any discretion as to the party for whom he appears."

B.

The validity of that argument must depend upon the meaning which we attach to the word "discretion;" the use of which in what follows I beg you to watch narrowly.

A.

There may be some difficulty perhaps in deciding what kind of discretion is permitted in particular cases; but none surely as to the general principle. The end of the whole proceeding is to do justice; and the means is to know the truth. The business of the counsel for the prosecution is to set forth the evidence *against* the defendant; that is, the evidence which tends to show that he is guilty of the crime imputed to him. His discretion is to be exercised in setting forth that evidence *fairly;*—in such a manner (I mean) that it shall have upon the minds of the judges its true and proper value,—that it shall weigh with them for exactly so much, and only so much, as it would weigh in the judgment of a just and understanding man, balancing in his own mind the arguments for and against. He is not to attempt to strike the balance himself; because that would be to assume the office of Judge; which (besides that it is not *his* office) cannot be exercised until the other side has been heard. He is only to take care that all the true weights and that no false ones are put into the scale of which he has the charge. This surely is the *principle* upon which it is his duty to act. And I thought it had been (as a *principle*) universally recognized. For even the monstrous practices of our modern Courts of Law are justified—(or I should rather say, an attempt is made to justify them)—on the plea that they do, in fact and upon the whole, tend to produce this result. So many false weights must be put in on one side to balance so many false weights on the other.

B.

I agree with you entirely. You could not have described more exactly the extent and the limit of the discretion with which I conceive the counsel for the Crown were in those times charged. It was their duty to present to the judges in its *true* light, *all* the evidence *against* the prisoner. I am curious to hear in what respect the reviewer can maintain that Bacon in this instance either exceeded or fell short of it.

A.

" We will not at present inquire whether the doctrine which is held on this subject by English lawyers be or be not agreeable to reason and morality: whether it be right that a man should, with a wig on his head and a band round his neck, do for a guinea what, without those appendages, he would think it wicked and infamous to do for an empire : whether it be right that, not merely believing but knowing a statement to be true, he should do all that can be done by sophistry, by rhetoric, by solemn asseveration, by indignant exclamation, by gesture, by play of features, by terrifying one honest witness, by perplexing another, to cause a jury to think that statement false. It is not necessary on the present occasion to decide these questions. The professional rules, be they good or bad, are rules to which many wise and virtuous men have conformed and are daily conforming. If therefore Bacon did no more than these rules required of him, we shall readily admit that he was blameless."

B.

Will you indeed ? If he did half as much as is here implied, *I* should hold him unpardonable.

However, I have no objection to make to all this. Only I want you to mark and remember it with reference to an argument which we shall meet further on. Here are practices which in the year 1837 the reviewer admits to be not only general, but conformed to daily by many wise and virtuous men ; and yet this is the description he gives of them. I shall want to refer to it hereafter, as showing in a good modern illustration that a practice which is not only immoral, but is thus publicly denounced as immoral,—which is not only indefensible, but undefended,—may continue nevertheless to prevail and to be countenanced by the universal Respectability of England. If any occasion should arise presenting this practice in an odious and unpopular light, especially if in the person of an eminent and unpopular man, I am convinced that the excuse which the reviewer here makes for it would be of no avail for him whatever; he and his excuse would be swept away in a flood of popular indignation. But this, as I said, has reference to a period which is yet a long way before us.—Well; and what did Bacon do more than professional rules required of him?

A.

"But we conceive that his conduct was not justifiable according to any professional rules that now exist, or that ever existed in England. It has always been held that in criminal cases, in which the prisoner was denied the help of counsel, and above all in capital cases, the advocate for the prosecution was both entitled and bound to exercise a discretion."

B.

A discretion, undoubtedly. But what kind of discretion? within what limits? Was he bound, or was he entitled even, to become the *advocate* of any accused party from whom he happened to have received in former times a present in money or in land? For to let the prisoner go away with the benefit of an excuse which he, the counsel for the prosecution, knew and could prove to be false,—what were it but to become his advocate? No; he was bound to use his discretion in rejecting all unfair arguments against the prisoner,—in presenting the evidence to the jury with such explanation, qualification, or reservation as might be necessary to prevent its having undue weight with them;— presenting it, in short, so as not to deceive them. But he was not at liberty to use it in concealing important facts, or in allowing a false colour to be put on the case the other way.

A.

Certainly; but let us hear him out.

"It is true that after the Revolution, when the Parliament began to make inquisition for the innocent blood which had been shed by the last Stuarts, a feeble attempt was made to

defend the lawyers who had been accomplices in the murder of
Sir Thomas Armstrong, on the ground that they had only acted
professionally.   The wretched sophism was silenced by the
execrations of the House of Commons.   ' Things will never be
well done,' said Mr. Foley, ' till some of that profession be made
examples.'   ' We have a new sort of monsters in the world,' said
the younger Hampden, 'haranguing a man to death.   These I
call bloodhounds.   Sawyer is very criminal and guilty of this
murder.'   ' I speak to discharge my conscience,' said Mr. Gar-
roway: 'I will not have the blood of this man at my door.
Sawyer demanded judgment against him and execution.   I
believe him guilty of the death of this man.'   ' If the profession
of the law,' said the elder Hampden, ' gives a man authority to
murder at this rate, it is the interest of all men to rise and
exterminate that profession.'   Nor was this language held only
by unlearned country gentlemen.   Sir William Williams, one of
the ablest and most unscrupulous lawyers of his age, took the
same view of the case.   He had not hesitated, he said, to take
part in the prosecution of the Bishops, because they were allowed
counsel.   But he maintained that where the prisoner was not
allowed counsel, the counsel for the Crown was bound to exercise
a discretion ; and that every lawyer who neglected this distinction was a betrayer of the law."

B.

There again. *A discretion.* Still I ask what kind of
discretion ? Not surely to make, or allow any one to make,
a bad cause seem a good one. In a trial for murder, for
instance, is a prosecutor bound, in the exercise of this " discretion," to sink all facts which prove malice and cold
blood ; and to leave Iago the benefit of all Othello's
excuses ? If not in a case of murder, why in a case of
treason ?

A.

Wait one moment more.—

" But it is unnecessary to cite authority. It is known to
everybody who has ever looked into a Court of Quarter Sessions,
that lawyers do exercise a discretion in criminal cases; and it
is plain to every man of common sense that, if they did not

exercise this discretion they would be a more hateful body of men than those bravoes who used to hire out their stilettoes in Italy."

Now fire away, for we are at the end of the paragraph.

B.

I have discharged myself already. I have nothing to say of the historical example, because I know nothing of the case. Only I protest in general against an appeal to the "execrations of the House of Commons" by way of settling any question either of justice or of fact. The House of Commons is at best a mob of gentlemen assembled to discuss matters which they have neither been trained to understand nor chosen for their aptness to understand. When they begin to "execrate," you may safely conclude that they are in no humour either to judge or to give evidence.—However, I am not concerned to dispute their sentence on this occasion. They were unquestionably right in rejecting the plea (if this was the plea which they did reject) that an advocate in a criminal case has a right to resort to the tricks of advocacy for the sake of obtaining a sentence against the prisoner. Any advocate who conducted his pleading against Sir Thomas Armstrong as unfairly as the reviewer has in this article conducted his pleading against Bacon, was (I admit) guilty of his blood, and well deserved the execrations both of the lawyers and of the country gentlemen.—Now for the proof that Bacon brought himself within the range of this censure.

A.

I once read that debate upon the case of Sir Thomas Armstrong. But I think the word "discretion" was not used in it from beginning to end ;—and (between ourselves) it is a case not at all in point. The charge against Sir Robert Sawyer was not that he *conducted the prosecution* against Sir Thomas ; but that he *demanded execution of judgment* in the face of a demand put forward by the prisoner (which he knew to be just) for *arrest* of judgment. Sir Thomas had a right of appeal from the judgment of that Court. When the Court refused to acknowledge it, he demanded that the statute under which he claimed the right should be read ; upon which Sawyer, the Attorney-General, only answered, "Your statute will do you no good ;" and without hearing it read, proceeded to demand execution ; thus making himself a party (as it was argued, and I suppose justly) to an act which he knew to be illegal. Instead of demanding execution of judgment, it was his duty to advise the Court to suspend judgment. By taking the opposite course he became a party to the *illegal* execution ; therefore an accomplice in the murder. For this,—not for pressing against him the evidence such as it was,—he was expelled from the House by a large majority.

B.

Then the decision of the House in that case would have applied to Sir Edward Coke at the trial of Sir Walter Raleigh in 1603 ; if it be true (for that is a clause never to be omitted in such matters) that, believing it to be illegal to condemn a man upon the evidence of one witness, he did what he could to get that plea overruled : and if by any accident an execrating House of Commons had seen his conduct in that light, he might have found it no easy matter to defend himself against a charge of murder. But in the trial of Essex nothing of this kind occurred. It has not even been asserted that anything was done contrary to law, either by judges or by counsel.—But let us hear how the reviewer attempts to apply his principles to the case.

A.

"Bacon appeared against a man who was indeed guilty of a great offence, but who had been his benefactor and friend."

B.

Most true : but not in any suit of his own, nor in any unjust cause.

A.

No. We have already discussed that point and acquitted

Bacon. He certainly had no ground for refusing to appear in his place against Essex.

" He did more than this. Nay, he did more than a person who had never seen Essex would have been justified in doing. He employed all the art of an advocate to make the prisoner's conduct appear more inexcusable and more dangerous to the State than it really had been."

B.

That is the general charge over again; which in the absence of all particulars I can only meet as before by a general contradiction. I assert confidently that he did nothing of the kind.

A.

" All that professional duty could in any case have required of him would have been to conduct the cause so as to ensure a conviction."

B.

There we have over again Macaulay's doctrine as to the duty of the counsel for prosecution, upon which, as before, I join issue with him. To make out the case sufficiently to ensure a conviction, was *not* enough. It was necessary to make out the case so as to show *what it was*.

A.

" But from the nature of the circumstances, there could not be the smallest doubt that the Earl would be found guilty. The character of the crime was unequivocal."

B.

That again I take leave to deny. That the crime amounted to treason in law, was indeed unquestionable. But treason in what degree? of what character? What *animus* did it imply? Was it an act of self-defence, as Essex pretended? Was he urged into it by great provocation, as the reviewer pretends?—by fear,—by strong temptation? Was it done in hot blood or in cold blood? Was he under any delusion? How far (in short) did it

imply a disloyal will in him, and danger in its consequences
to the State ?—How idle to talk of "the character of the
crime being unequivocal" while all these questions remained doubtful !

A.

Idle indeed !—

" It had been committed recently—in broad daylight—in
the streets of the capital—in the presence of thousands."

B.

What was " *it* " ?

A.

" If ever there was an occasion on which an advocate had
no temptation to resort to extraneous topics for the purpose of
blinding the judgment and inflaming the passions of a tribunal,
this was that occasion."

B.

Blinding the judgment and inflaming the passions !   I
suppose it is too much to ask for an instance in which he
either did or attempted to do either the one or the other.

A.

Our reviewer is not prolific of " instances " in this article.
But such as they are, they are coming :—

" Why then resort to arguments which, while they could add
nothing to the strength of the case considered in a legal point
of view— "

B.

It was a question of state as well as of law: not to add
that, even " in a legal point of view," there is a difference
between a crime provoked and a crime unprovoked.—Well ?

A.

"—tended to aggravate the moral guilt of the fatal enterprise ;
and to excite fear and apprehension in that quarter from which
alone the Earl could now hope for mercy ? "

B.

Nay, the "moral guilt" was surely an essential point to ascertain. Was he or was he not a *dangerous* man? So far from exaggerating his guilt beyond what it really was, Bacon's speech conveys no notion of its real magnitude. And as for " exciting fear and apprehension " in Elizabeth, I would ask this simple question: was there, or was there not, before Bacon opened his mouth, any danger of her feeling less apprehension than the case justified? If there was, then I say it was the part of a faithful servant to *awaken* her apprehensions. If there was not, then I say it was the part of a faithful servant to justify publicly to the prisoner's face the apprehensions which she in private justly enter- tained.

A.

" Why remind the audience of the arts of the ancient tyrants ? "

B.

Because Essex had endeavoured by arts resembling those of one of those "ancient tyrants,"—(if you choose to call him so,)—to impose upon the people. Bacon (by the way) *avoided* the word "tyrant"—for the same reason, I suppose, that the reviewer introduces it; it makes the parallel *sound* harsher than it really is. The precaution is characteristic of them both. Bacon knew that the word "tyrant" had grown odious since the time of Pisistratus; therefore, though Pisistratus *was* a tyrant in the ancient sense, he did not call him so, lest the term should convey a false impression. The reviewer, on the contrary, feels that to a modern reader, a charge of practising " the artifice of Pisistratus " will not seem to contain any very horrible imputation,—whereas a charge of practising "the arts of the ancient tyrants " will be at once understood as a gross calumny and insult. Therefore, though Pisistratus—

A.

Stop ; I see what you are going to say ; but do not say it. Keep your temper. Your case is growing quite strong enough without wandering from the text.

" Why deny what everybody knew to be the truth, that a powerful faction at Court had long sought to effect the ruin of the prisoner ? "

B.

Bacon did not deny that. He denied only that there was any such plot against him as made it necessary for him to take up arms in defence of his life. And this he denied, because many persons believed it on the credit of Essex's declaration to be true, though Essex himself knew very well that it was false.

A.

" Why above all institute a parallel between the un- happy culprit and the most wicked and successful rebel of the age ? "

B.

The most wicked, I suppose, *because* the most successful. Bacon, however, does not seem to have thought him par- ticularly wicked,—except in so far as ambition was a wickedness. He mentions him honourably in the " Ad- vancement of Learning " as " that *noble* prince, Henry Duke of Guise,—howsoever transported with ambition." Had Essex been as successful, there might perhaps have grown a question which was the most wicked.—But this is not to the purpose. It was not between the culprits but between the *enterprises* that Bacon instituted a comparison. He confined himself strictly to the argument respecting the *danger* of Essex's attempt. From the actual issue of a similar enterprise which had succeeded, might be understood the possible issue of that which had not succeeded.

A.

"Was it absolutely impossible to do all that professional duty required, without reminding a jealous sovereign of the League, of the Barricades, and of all the humiliations which a too powerful subject had heaped on Henry the Third ? "

B.

Bacon dwelt upon none of these things. He confined himself strictly to the substantial and material points of resemblance which the two cases presented. But I would meet the last question more directly. I would answer boldly, that without showing that the prisoner had done something more than take necessary precautions against assassination,—(he having been in fact engaged in an unprovoked, a long-premeditated, a deliberate attempt to master the Queen by force of arms,)—it *was* absolutely impossible to do all that professional duty required. We have read the whole passage to which the reviewer refers, so you can judge for yourself whether I understate the intention and effect of Bacon's argument.

A.

I remember, and I am clearly with you on that point. Now, we come to the Declaration of Treasons again.

B.

Ay : let us see what new shape that has taken since we last parted from it.

A.

" But if we admit the plea which Mr. Montagu urges in defence of what Bacon did as an advocate, what shall we say of the 'Declaration of the Treasons of Robert Earl of Essex '? Here at least there was no pretence of professional obligation."

B.

Put a query to that. It was not an obligation under which he lay *as a lawyer*. But Bacon's profession was to be a true subject and servant to the Queen and State. If it were for the good of the State that he should draw up a Declaration of Essex's treasons, he did lie under a professional obligation to do it.

A.

"Even those who may think it the duty of a lawyer to hang, draw, and quarter his benefactors, for a proper consideration—"

B.

—As Bacon hung, drew, and quartered Essex. I am afraid we are beginning to "blind the judgment and inflame the passions" of our readers. We must substitute for this —"Those who think it the duty of a Crown lawyer to assist in the prosecution of a traitor, even though that traitor be his benefactor—" Well?

A.

"—will hardly say that it is his duty to write abusive pamphlets against them after they are in their graves."

B.

Ah! There we have it. First it was a "vindication" of a proceeding which had been "perhaps unreasonably" condemned. Next it was a "murder of the fame" of the person proceeded against. Now it is an "abusive pamphlet." And all this without a single instance quoted of false statement, unfair insinuation, or even exaggerated censure! You say you have not read this Declaration. You cannot therefore appreciate the true character of this last expression. I do hope that the reviewer has not read it himself. In spite of all that has gone before, I will still hope that if he had read this Declaration, he would not have described it for the information of those who have not read it, as an "abusive pamphlet," gratuitously written for the purpose of defaming a dead benefactor.—Only remember the occasion which called for it. A popular idol and a dangerous rebel,—a man who (to use the reviewer's own words) has "endeavoured to throw the whole country into confusion for objects purely personal "—is executed for most just and urgent cause. After his execution fresh matter comes out which proves that his case was even worse than it had appeared to be,—his execution therefore still ·more amply justified. Meanwhile rumours and pamphlets are actively circulated among the people, giving false accounts of the causes of his execution—false accounts of the act for which he had been condemned ; awakening dangerous disaffection to the Government at a time when it seemed to be on the point of being assailed by three dangers coming upon it at once—foreign levy, domestic malice, and the present prospect of a disputed succession. In such a case, who that had a spark of patriotism in him could shrink from assisting in an· endeavour to place the conduct of the Government in its true light, by drawing up an account judicially and historically accurate of the real grounds of the late proceeding? In speaking of such a case, who but the fool in the Proverbs that scatters firebrands and says he is in sport, could describe such an account written for such an object as an "abusive pamphlet"?

A.

Certainly if your statement of the case be correct, Macaulay's best excuse must be that he misunderstood it. But he has more to say yet. Perhaps he will come to particulars after all. Let us hear him out.

"Bacon excused himself by saying that he was not answerable for the matter of the book, and that he furnished only the language."

B.

Pardon me. That excuse related to the manner rather than to the matter. The *matter* he excused by declaring that it was drawn up with a religious adherence to truth.

A.

I remember.

"But why did he endow such purposes with words?"

B.

Because he believed the purposes to be just and for the good of the state.

A.

" Could no hack-writer, without virtue or shame, be found to exaggerate the errors, already so dearly expiated, of a gentle and noble spirit ? "

B.

I deny the exaggerations. And if I content myself with a general denial, it is only because the reviewer has not given so much as a hint of the particular exaggerations to which he alludes. And I much doubt whether he was even thinking of anything in particular. He has long ceased to look at the original, and is finishing the picture after his own fancy.

A.

" Every age produces those links between the man and the baboon. Every age is fertile of Concanens, of Gildons, of Anthony Pasquins. But was it for Bacon so to prostitute his intellect? Could he not feel that while he rounded and pointed some period dictated by the envy of Cecil— "

B.

Which of the periods does he mean ?

A.

" —or gave a plausible form to some slander invented by the dastardly malignity of Cobham— "

B.

What slander ?

A.

Nay, don't ask me. Perhaps he thought himself entitled to infer from Bacon's own excuse that the Declaration

contained such things. In eagerly disclaiming all responsibility for the *matter* of the alterations made by the
Council, he may be supposed to admit that it was (in some
respects at least) such as he could not justify.

B.

How can he be supposed to admit that the alterations
contained *slanders*, when he expressly says that in framing
them " their Lordships were as religious and curious of
truth as desirous of satisfaction ? "—Prove that the alterations contained anything slanderous, or anything dictated
by envy—(the charge of envy against Cecil is itself I
believe a slander)—and I will admit that *in saying that*
Bacon was not justified. For the slander itself he might
not be to blame ; but if he knew that slanderous matter had
been inserted, I will admit that he ought not to have
answered for the veracity of the insertors. But remember
that we have no hint of such proof as yet.—Well, what
could he not feel ?

A.

Could he not feel " that he was not merely sinning against
his friend's honour and his own? Could he not feel that
letters, eloquence, philosophy, were all degraded in his de-
gradation ? "

B.

Is that all ?—The substance then of all this is,—that
Bacon, being commanded to draw up a *true* report of Essex's
case (for in the absence of all proof that it contains a single
lie, and in the presence of his express declaration that truth
was the object of all the parties concerned in drawing it up
I must still assume that it was to be a *true* report), ought
to have declined the task, and discharged it, because for-
sooth Essex was his *friend*, upon some " hack-writer without
virtue or shame." As if a " hack-writer without virtue or
shame " were a fit person to draw up an historical document ;
or as if it were a *friend's* part to consign one's fame to such
hands !

A.

Of course the reviewer must be understood as saying this on the assumption (an unjust one, I dare say; certainly an unsupported one) that the object of the document was merely to slander and defame the character of Essex. Had it been so, I do think it would have been Bacon's duty to refuse to soil his own hands with it, even at the risk of its falling into worse. But assume the case to have been (as I suppose it was) one in which the vindication of the Government required, not perhaps a slanderous or unjust, but a harsh and severe construction of the sufferer's conduct;—was it a friend's part to undertake it? Suppose you were yourself called on to perform a task which could not be performed properly without putting your friend's character in the worst light,—would you not feel disposed to decline it, as a task which would better become some one who was *not* his friend?

B.

If I did, would my friend have any reason to thank me? I will put you a fair case. Your best friend and benefactor shall do something for which he deserves to be hanged; yet he shall not be a bad man, but generous, gentle, noble, beloved; he shall also "dearly expiate his offences" by being hanged as he deserves. Well; for some reason or other (I will not even insist upon its being a good reason), it shall be determined by the party that ran him down— (for to avoid preconceptions, it shall be the act of a party, not of a King or Queen; neither will we say which party; nay, it shall be the whole House of Commons, if you like)— it shall be determined, I say, by this party to publish in vindication of their proceedings a statement of the case,— an account of the acts for which they impeached him, and for which he suffered. I will not even suppose that such a vindication is, in your opinion, called for. I release you from all considerations of *public* duty in the case; you shall think only of your friend and his reputation. All I stipulate for is, that you believe the prosecution and the sentence

to have been just. And now comes the point. This party,
—knowing that he was your friend and benefactor, yet
knowing you to be a man of sense, justice, and veracity,—
propose that you should draw up this statement. There is
no want of persons who can do it; there are plenty of
" hack-writers without virtue or shame " belonging to the
party, whose pens are sharp enough, and who will be only
too glad of an opportunity to write themselves and their
party up by writing your friend down. Written by somebody it is to be. And, in short, if you will not undertake
it, the reviewer will. Now what will you do ?

A.

M-m-m-m! To leave one's friend's fame in this reviewer's hands when one might take it out of them, would
be a serious responsibility. But then on the other hand—
Tell me honestly, what would you do yourself?

B.

You know the rule. What would you have your friend
do for you in such a case ? But every man can answer best
for himself; and for me, I can only say that if I should be
that unhappy friend of yours, I hope you will not hesitate.
If my character as well as my body becomes public
property, let it be dissected handsomely and scientifically;
not thrown like offal to a bear.

A.

I suppose you are right. I suppose in refusing such an
office in such circumstances, a man would after all be acting
out of regard to his own reputation, not to his friend's. We
dare not be true for fear of being thought false.—Yes; I
give up.

B.

And remember that the case I put is one specially discharged of all considerations except that of regard to your
friend's memory. Bacon's case was different. He had to

consider his duty not only to the memory of Essex, but to his country ; which had in fact an older as well as a stronger claim upon him ; for he was an English subject, before he was the friend of Essex.

You see therefore that, upon my view of the matter, everything is plain and natural. There is nothing strange to account for. According to Bacon's scale of duties, the degrees were,—first, your God ; next, your King and country ; then your friend ; last yourself. For a long time all these duties drew in a line. Essex, when they first became acquainted, seemed the likeliest instrument for the service of religion and the state. While he was moving in that direction, Bacon strengthened him for the service with the full force of his own counsel and industry. When he began to look aside from the path, Bacon laboured to keep him in it. When he swerved, Bacon laboured to win him back. When he got fatally astray, Bacon laboured to arrest his course and to keep him quiet, if he could not keep him right. When this too was hopeless, and his fortunes became dangerously involved, Bacon still laboured to save them from becoming desperate. When at last he turned quite round and was coming headlong in a direction exactly opposite to that along which they had both begun, and one still continued, to travel, Bacon withstood him to the face. When the act of so withstanding him raised against the Government discontent and disaffection, Bacon stood forward to take his own share of the odium, and would not (for fear of what men might say) shrink from justifying the cause which he knew to be just.

So far the question had still been between his friend and his country ; never, except collaterally and by accident, between his friend and himself. But one trial more remained. Upon the accession of a new King, supposed favourable to Essex, the stream of popular indignation, no longer setting against the state, was left to spend itself upon individuals. Among these Bacon was most conspicuous. Most ignorantly and unjustly was he accused of having taken part against the friend whom he had been doing all he could to serve ; of

having been faithless to his private, when he had only been
true (and *because* he had been true) to his public obligations;
of having calumniated his benefactor for the sake of defending public injustice, when he had in fact been only defending
public justice against popular calumny. Most ignorantly
were these charges made; for they were made at a time when
nothing could be known of what he had really been doing;
upon the credit only of such vain rumours as fly abroad
when rumours are most vain—rumours bred out of that
" pity in the common people, which if it run in a strong
stream doth ever cast up scandal and envy." Most unjustly
were they made; for those who made them were in a humour
to disbelieve everything that told against Essex, and to believe anything that told against those who were reputed to
have been his enemies. Now therefore, at last, the struggle
for Bacon was solely between regard for his own reputation
and tenderness for the memory of his friend. The inculpa-
tion of Essex could now serve no public object; yet without
it, his own exculpation (as you may judge from my answer
to this invective) could not be made complete. The heavier
we make the fault of Essex, the lighter we must of necessity
make the charge against Bacon. Yet about the faults of
Essex, Bacon is from this time forth tenderly and nobly
silent. Not a word more of censure passes his lips. He
vindicates himself from the charge of ingratitude to his
friend by showing that he had laboured from first to last to
serve him; that he had given him counsel, which if he had
followed in his best fortunes, they would never have declined; if in his worst, they might still have been recovered;
that he had not desisted from interfering in his behalf until
interference became not only dangerous but useless. In
commemorating his virtues and acknowledging his benefits,
he is large and warm. But in justification of the trial, the
sentence, and the execution, he says scarcely a word. And
why? Certainly not because he had nothing to say; he
might have said at least all that I have said in his behalf;
but because he would not, out of regard for his own reputation and credit, keep alive for one day more the memory of

his benefactor's guilt. To any one who has generosity
enough in himself to sympathize with generosity in another,
and who remembers the circumstances under which it was
written, Bacon's " Apology," in its unstudied simplicity and
subdued earnestness, is one of the most affecting compo-
sitions that can be. Its sincerity can be doubted only, I
think, by the insincere. The very style bears witness to it,
—faltering, hurrying, breaking,—as a man's voice falters
when it speaks out of too full a heart. To me at least, there
is something in the reserve with which he touches upon the
last act of Essex's tragedy, inexpressibly affecting. The
earlier movements of disloyalty, and especially the preparations which were making for the insurrection three months
before it took place, are not alluded to, or lightly hinted at,
as " some slackness " in his demeanour towards the Queen.
The insurrection itself is only a "fatal impatience." The
8th of February is " the day of my Lord of Essex his misfortune." That most ungenerous and unjustifiable attack
upon himself at the trial (on the subject of the letters) is
only a thing " which it pleased my Lord *very strangely* to
mention at the bar." These are the strongest expressions of
censure which the paper contains. And in fact, so tenderly
has he dealt with his friend's crime, that this very
"Apology" has had the effect of depriving him in the popular
judgment of the benefit of his best excuse. I suppose this
may have been in his thoughts when he said that he " must
reserve much which made for him, upon many respects of
duty, which he esteemed above his credit." But however
that may be, it is certain that his chariness in throwing
blame on Essex has helped mankind to forget how much
Essex was to blame. And yet it was a reserve which one
can perfectly understand and approve ; for even at this
day one would be sorry to bring to light the faults of a
character so noble, if this review had not made it necessary
in order to vindicate one so much nobler.

But you have had my reading of the story. We are
now to hear one of our reviewer's recapitulations—one of his
masterpieces of composition—the greatest amount of false
effect conveyed in the smallest number of words.

A.

" The real explanation of all this is perfectly obvious, and nothing but a partiality amounting to a ruling passion could cause anybody to miss it. The moral qualities of Bacon were not of a high order. We do not say that he was a bad man. He was not inhuman or tyrannical. He bore with meekness his high civil honours, and the far higher honours gained by his intellect. He was very seldom, if ever, provoked into treating any person with malignity and insolence. No man more readily held up the left cheek to those who had smitten the right. No man was more expert at the soft answer which turneth away wrath. He was never accused of intemperance in his pleasures. His even temper, his flowing courtesy, the general respectability of his demeanour, made a favourable impression on those who saw him in situations which do not severely try the principles. His faults were—we write it with pain—coldness of heart and meanness of spirit."

B.

To that proposition I shall only ask you to suspend your assent, until you come to some instance in proof of it. To any one familiar with Bacon's writings, I would confidently protest against it as utterly untenable. There was never yet cold heart which could utter words so feeling and so touching; never yet mean spirit the natural movements of which were at once so simple and so majestic. But it is useless to debate where we are not agreed either upon principle or facts. Bacon's faults were coldness of heart and meanness of spirit! And the reviewer writes it with pain!!—Well?

A.

" He seems to have been incapable of feeling strong affection, of facing great dangers, of making great sacrifices."

B.

I wait to hear of the particular dangers and the particular sacrifices from which he shrank. Hitherto he has not met with anything that has either deterred or seduced him from doing what he conceived to be his duty.

A.

You do not mean that moral courage was one of his conspicuous virtues, do you?

B.

I don't know. He was not often in situations where moral courage was conspicuously required. A man who is not quarrelsome may be brave enough, but has rarely occasion to prove it. But I cannot at present recal any instance in which he showed a want of courage. And as for making great sacrifices, I rather think his whole life was a sacrifice of objects which most people would have thought great, though they may not have seemed great to him.

A.

How do you mean?

B.

I mean that he passed the greater part of his life in subordinate positions, above which he might no doubt have risen, if he had been willing to use the means which other men much inferior to himself were using daily with success.

A.

" His desires were set on things below."

B.

Put two notes of admiration to that,—Bacon's desires set on things below ! !

A.

" Wealth, precedence, titles, patronage,—the mace, the seals, the coronet,—large houses, fair gardens, rich manors, massy services of plate, gay hangings, curious cabinets,—had as great attractions for him as for any of the courtiers who dropped on their knees in the dirt when Elizabeth passed by, and then hastened home to write to the King of Scots that her Grace seemed to be breaking fast."

B.

Indeed! If so, he was, for a man of his talents, the most unsuccessful courtier on record, and for a man of his activity, the idlest. But you are so familiar by this time with the trick of the reviewer's style, that I need hardly draw your attention to the construction of this last sentence. The kind of composition is not difficult. If I had a bill for upholstery before me, I could easily— But that would draw me into personalities; and the case needs no illustration. You see the trick of it. It is only to enumerate each good thing with a sounding name that a man has ever been in possession of,—to add a plural termination,—and then to assume that because he had them while he lived, they were the things he lived for,—and the thing is done. Now only look at this formidable array of objects, which are represented as having such peculiar "attractions" for Bacon; not merely as having attractions for him;—(attractions no doubt they had, being things for the most part of real value; all contributory, though not all essential, to the substantial powers, dignities, comforts, or elegances of life;)—but as having "*as great* attractions;"—only think of that;—having for Francis Bacon "*as great* attractions,"—"as for *any* of the courtiers," &c. Look through the list once more, and tell me which of them he went out of his way for. They all lay in the direct line of that career which he entered upon merely for the sake of an honest livelihood in his nineteenth summer. And for the manner of pursuing them—the only difference in this respect between him and other diligent and successful lawyers was, that he was longer in gaining wealth and freer in throwing it away. He spent too much of it in laying out "fair gardens," and too little in buying "rich manors." It is true that for some thirteen or fourteen years in the latter part of his life he had a large income; but he was all the time working hard for it in the sweat of his brow. No man is blamed for taking the gifts which his industry earns or his fortune brings. But when it is laid to his charge that they have peculiar *attractions* for him, it is but reasonable

to ask for some instances of their attractive force.   What
did he do, which but for them he would have left undone; or
what leave undone, which but for them he would have done ?

A.

That is a question which Macaulay seems very well
prepared to answer :—

" For these objects," (he goes on,) " he had stooped to everything and endured everything."

B.

I have yet to learn that he had stooped to a single
unworthy action.   But tell us of *something* which he had
endured or to which he had stooped.   Everything means
nothing.

A.

" For these he had sued in the humblest manner, and when
unjustly and ungraciously repulsed, he had thanked those who
had repulsed him, and had begun to sue again."

B.

Ay ; I thought we should catch him out when he condescended to particulars.   Do you recognize our old friend
under this new disguise ?

A.

You do not mean that he alludes to the old application
to Burghley to be called within the Bar, when he was five-
and-twenty ?

B.

To be sure he does.   The " testy refusal " and the
" patience and serenity bordering on meanness."   I told
you we should have some large descriptions of Bacon's
habitual demeanour drawn from that passage.

A.

Then we may strike out that, without more words.   Let
us try the next.

"For these objects, as soon as he found that the smallest show of independence in Parliament was offensive to the Queen, he had abased himself to the dust before her, and implored forgiveness in terms better suited to a convicted thief than to a knight of the shire."

B.

Number two. Do you remember the "abject apology" and the debate on the money bill, which we discussed at large at our third sitting?

A.

Very well. Strike out number two.

" For these he joined, and for these he forsook Lord Essex."

B.

For these he *joined?*

A.

Yes; that is the word. You know the reviewer represented him as joining Essex because he despaired of advancement through Burghley. I remember you showed that the dates were incompatible with that supposition. I agree to strike out number three.

"He continued to plead his patron's cause with the Queen as long as he thought that by pleading that cause he could serve himself."

That is a new insinuation. His advocacy of Essex's cause during his disgrace had credit, according to the reviewer's own former statement, at least for disinterestedness as far as it went.

"Nay, he went further; for his feelings, though not warm, were kind; he pleaded that cause so long as he thought that he could plead it without injury to himself."

B.

Longer than that;—as long in fact as he could plead it with any advantage to Essex.

A.

Yes.

" But when it became evident that Essex was going head long to his ruin,— "

B.

Say rather (for the words are the reviewer's own),—" was endeavouring to throw the whole country into confusion for objects purely personal."

A.

"—Bacon began to tremble for his own fortunes."

B.

And why not for the fortunes of the country ?

A.

" What he had to fear would not indeed have been very alarming to a man of lofty character   It was not death.   It was not imprisonment.   It was the loss of Court-favour.   It was the being left behind by others in the career of ambition. It was the having leisure to finish the *Instauratio Magna.*   The Queen looked coldly upon him.   The courtiers began to consider him as a marked man.   He determined to change his line of conduct, and to proceed in a new course, with so much vigour as to make up for lost time."

B.

Here again we have the old story repeated ; still, as before, without any reference whatever to the *nature of the cause.*   As if an "endeavour to throw the whole country into confusion," were not a thing dangerous to the best interests of the country,—a thing which it was the duty of every man who loved his country to take part against. It is said too as if Bacon had *changed* his course.   He did not change an inch.   It was Essex that changed.

A.

True.   When Essex took the wrong side, Bacon continued to stand by the right.   That point, I think, you have clearly made out. Therefore we may strike out number four.

"When once he had determined to act against his friend, knowing himself to be suspected, he acted with more zeal than would have been necessary or justifiable if he had been employed against a stranger."

B.

Number five. You agreed, I think, to acquit him of that charge.

A.

Yes. He seems to have done nothing but what was necessary to make out the case fully and fairly. By all means let us keep one place in the land sacred to the discovery of Truth. Out with number five.

"He exerted his professional talents to shed the Earl's blood,—"

B.

Only to show that he had done more than defend himself against assassination.

A.

"—and his literary talents to blacken the Earl's memory."

B.

Only to state truly what he *had* done. Out therefore must go number six and seven.—Is there any more?

A.

No. I must confess that paragraph is effectually plucked. It would be no bad deed to set up the skeleton as a scarecrow. But stay,—here is still the tail left.

"It is certain that his conduct excited at the time great and general disapprobation."

B.

That I dare say is true. But what is it to the purpose, unless we know who the disapprovers were, what the value of their judgment, and what their means of knowing? The conduct of Bacon has excited since July 1837 great and general disapprobation; because this article has been since that time generally read and greatly admired, and not at all inquired into. Having shown you how baseless the assertions and how worthless the judgments of the writer are, I need scarcely remind you that the general disapprobation of the British public for the last seven or eight years cannot be pleaded as evidence, because it rests entirely upon a false foundation. In the same way I decline to admit as evidence the general disapprobation of the year 1601, until I know whether those who disapproved had either the means of knowing or the faculty of judging. Let some one man be named who, living in those times and knowing what Bacon's conduct had really been, condemned it. When I can hear of such a man, I will do my best to ascertain the value of his opinion. But hitherto I have not heard any such so much as named. Of one such man who thought it quite right, I have heard; and that was Bacon himself.

A.

The challenge I think is but fair. As far however as I am concerned, it is unnecessary. Popular censures in such cases are never worth a straw as evidence in courts of morality.

" While Elizabeth lived, indeed, this disapprobation, though deeply felt, was not loudly expressed."

B.

Was it ever more loudly expressed, during Bacon's lifetime, than it was in the reign of Elizabeth? As far as my information goes, the time when it was most loud and violent was at the close of 1599; at the time when he was actually doing all he could to serve Essex, and offending the Queen by interceding for him. It was then that he was threatened with assassination.

A.

What part of his conduct was it then that excited so much disapprobation?

B.

No part of *his* conduct; but a false rumour that had gone abroad, which said that he had been advising the Queen to bring Essex's case into the Star-Chamber; a proceeding from which he had in fact been using all his influence in vain to dissuade her. Why should we suppose that the disapprobation which was expressed afterwards rested on any better grounds?

A.

It will be the reviewer's business to show that.—In the mean time I suppose we may as well shut up for to-night; for I see he is going to tell us of a great change at hand.

B.

Very well. Remember that we have now accompanied Bacon up to his fortieth year; and that you have not as yet been able to sustain any one of Macaulay's charges against him. I may still claim for him the benefit of general good character.

EVENING THE SIXTH.

A.

Before we go on with our article, I want you to satisfy me on one point which I forgot to mention at our last sitting. If I recollect it right, it goes against your account of the part which Bacon took and the spirit in which he acted with regard to the "Declaration of Treasons." You said that part of the scheme was to print as an appendix the very words of the confessions and depositions upon which the statements in the narrative part rested. Now I am sure I have heard of the discovery not long ago of some manuscript, from which it appeared, on the evidence of Bacon's own handwriting, that he had himself *garbled* these confessions and depositions, for the purpose of strengthening the case against Essex. I am sure "garbled" was the word.

B.

Oh yes. I can tell you all about that. And I am glad you have reminded me of it; for the story is instructive in many ways.

Mr. David Jardine published in the "Library of Entertaining Knowledge" an account of some criminal trials, including that of Essex and Southampton. He appears to have bestowed some pains upon them, and to have wished to execute his task in a fair and judicial spirit. Among other things, he searched, or employed somebody to search, the State Paper Office; and there he found many of the depositions which were read at the trial, in their original condition, with Sir Edward Coke's memoranda and directions as to what parts should be read, still legible in the margin. In several places, however, he observed in another hand, which he says is Bacon's, the letters *om.* written; and upon looking at the printed "Declaration" for the passages so marked, he found that they were all omitted. Upon this he concludes that the passages in question, though they had been read and proved in Court, were struck out after the trial by Bacon himself, to suit the purposes of the Declaration; and then sets himself to guess what those purposes might be. His conclusion is that the passages were omitted because they tended to soften the case against Essex, and to contradict or qualify in some of its material features the story of the transaction which the Government thought fit to circulate. And he represents it as "a flagrant instance of partiality," and a "garbling of the depositions," of which Bacon is thus proved to have been personally guilty.

A.

Yes; that is what I was thinking of. What do you say to it?

B.

I might ask first to see the passages. One thing however I may say at once without seeing them. Even taking Mr. Jardine's own view of the effect and intention of the omissions in question, still since we know that material alterations were made in Bacon's draught by "certain principal councillors,"—and that he "only gave style and form of words in pursuing their Lordships' direction,"—it by no means follows, because the directions to omit were written by him, that he is answerable for the act of omission. He was attending "certain principal councillors" with his pen in his hand. One of them may have said to him, "We had better not print that passage; mark it for omission." Upon what pretence could he, in the preparation of a State document, not one word of which he had a right to publish without authority from the Council, have objected to the striking out of passages which the Council thought it expedient to

suppress? If this was the real history of the transaction
(and it is quite as likely as any other), it is clear that he
was no more responsible for the act than the goose-quill
which he guided.

Moreover, to any one who looks carefully at the papers
in question, it will appear very doubtful whether these
marks of omission were originally made with any reference
to the proposed "Declaration." For though it is true that
none of the passages so marked for omission are inserted in
the appendix to the Declaration, yet it is also true that
several passages which are *not* so marked are nevertheless
omitted in the appendix to the Declaration; and that
similar marks are found in other papers of which no part is
printed there. And when we remember how many persons,
each of whom had borne a different share in the rebellion,—
whose several cases therefore required each a separate proof,
—were to be tried upon the evidence contained in these
same confessions and depositions, we may easily suppose that
these marks were made with a view, not to the general
Declaration, but to the preparation of the cases against
some of these several delinquents; the object of the omissions being to clear the evidence in those cases of irrelevant
matter.

These are guesses;—I mention them only to show how
questionable such imputations are; and how far the mere
turning over of papers which nobody else has turned over,
is from entitling a man to be received as an authority upon
the matters to which they relate. In the case before us,
however, there is fortunately no occasion to encounter one
guess by another, or to rest anything upon questionable pre-
sumptions. For it happens that whoever was responsible
for the act of writing these *om.*'s, and whatever the object
may have been, the act itself was perfectly harmless. Mr.
Jardine's statement of the *effect* of the omissions is, upon the
very face of the paper itself, manifestly and absurdly wrong;
and therefore his speculation upon the *intention* may be
safely dismissed. Would you believe that the very facts
which he gathers from these suppressed passages, and for

the purpose of concealing which he supposes the passages
to have been suppressed, are told as distinctly as possible in
the narrative itself?—that the story which he charges the
Government with circulating is *not* the story told in this
their own especial manifesto,—and that the story to conceal
which he charges them with garbling the evidence,—*is?*
" In Gorge's deposition," says he—

A.

Stay; who was Gorge? You forget that I know none of
the particulars of the evidence.

B.

Let me see then, where shall I begin?—You know—(or
if you don't, you are now to know)—that five days before
the insurrection there was a meeting of some of the principal conspirators at Drury House, where Sir Charles Davers
lodged. Essex was not present himself; but it was con-
vened by his direction for the express purpose of deliberating
upon certain definite projects; and the better to assist the
deliberation, a schedule was provided of the names of the
friends on whom he principally relied; of whom there were
one hundred and twenty. What these projects were, and
what passed at this consultation, it was at the time a matter
of much consequence to ascertain; and it is still a matter
upon which it behoves every one to inform himself who would
form a judgment on Essex's case. Upon this point Elizabeth's ministers contrived to extract from three of the persons
present very ample confessions; and Sir Ferdinando Gorge's
was the first. The three projects discussed were the seizing
of the Tower, the surprising of the Court, and the stirring of
the City. Now Mr. Jardine's notion is that the Government wished to have it believed that the *insurrection in the
city* was planned and resolved upon at that consultation; and
that that part of Sir Ferdinando's deposition which goes to
prove the contrary, was struck out of the extracts appended
to the "Declaration of Treasons," on that account. But you
shall have his own words:—

" In Gorge's deposition, after stating that 'the projects at Drury House were, whether they should stir in London first, or surprise the Court and Tower at the same instant,' the original goes on to state, that ' the most resolved to attempt the Court and Tower.' Can any man doubt" (he proceeds) " that these latter words were omitted by Bacon because they contradicted the story published by the Government, not only to the people of England by the preachers and other means, but to all the world by the despatches of the foreign ambassadors,—namely, that the insurrection in the city was planned and determined on at Drury House? So also in the passage which immediately follows, the words 'they thought' and 'began to' must have been struck out because they seemed to denote, not a settled design, but merely a vague proposal."

A.

What was the passage in which those words occurred ?

B.

" I prayed them first to set down the manner how *they thought* it might be done. Then Sir John Davis took ink and paper, and *began to* assign to divers principal men their several places."

A.

What was he speaking. of ?—the insurrection in the city ?

B.

No ; the surprising of the Court.

A.

Was that all that was suppressed ?

B.

No. The whole concluding part of the deposition was omitted; from which it appears that Gorge was against the attempting of the Court or Tower ; and recommended rather that the stirring of Essex's friends in the city should be tried first :—

" —which recommendation was so evil liked of, that they brake up, and resolved of nothing; but referred all to my Lord of Essex himself."

A.

Well. And what was the version of the story which the preachers and foreign ambassadors had published to the world?

B.

Why even in the directions given to *them* I have not been able to find any such statement as Mr. Jardine charges the Government with. But what have these to do with the matter? They were of an earlier date than the Declaration; and Bacon had nothing to do with them. The first question surely is, what is the version of the story given in the body of the Declaration itself,—the story in attestation of which these "garbled" depositions are appealed to? You shall have it in its own words :—

"For the action itself, there was proposition made of two principal articles; the one of possessing the Tower of London, the other of surprising her Majesty's person and the Court; in which also deliberation was had what course to hold with the city, either towards the effecting of the surprise or after it was effected."

So far at least you will admit that there is no misrepresentation of the facts, nor any insinuation that the insurrection in the city was planned and determined on at that consultation. He then states the reasons for which the first of the two principal articles—the possessing of the Tower— was " by the opinion of all rejected ; " and proceeds :—

"But the latter—which was the ancient plot, as was well known to Southampton,—was by the general opinion of them all insisted and rested upon."

The story therefore plainly is, that what " was planned and determined on" was not the insurrection in the city, but the surprise of the Court. And he afterwards explains that the resolutions were " to be reported to Essex, who ever kept in himself the binding and deciding voice."

A.

But did he not say that there was also some deliberation about the course to be taken with the city ? What became of that?

B.

Yes; as if to prevent the possibility of any misconception on that head, he adds, after detailing the manner in which they proposed to manage the surprise of the Court,— (and adds it in a paragraph professedly parenthetical):—

"There passed *a speech* also in this conspiracy of possessing the city of London, which Essex himself in his own particular and secret inclination had ever a special mind unto."

But instead of saying that the "speech" ended in any resolution, he merely suggests the probable grounds and motives of Essex's opinion, and quits the subject with "But to return: these were the resolutions"—and so on. If therefore the suppressed passages seemed to denote (as Mr. Jardine says), "not a settled design, but merely a vague proposal," I do not know how the true import of them could be more accurately conveyed.

.A.

Certainly it would seem that Mr. Jardine had not read that part of the Declaration. But if the story which Bacon tells agrees with the passages thus omitted from the depositions, what reason could there be for striking them out?

B.

There may have been twenty good reasons which we cannot now know of. Many eminent and honourable persons were implicated either personally or through their friends, many important interests were affected and many angry and dangerous feelings irritated, by that conspiracy. Of the persons who had been actually engaged in the rebellion, there were only a few against whom it was thought necessary to proceed with severity. Those whose lives were to be spared, it was desirable also to spare in their reputation, and not needlessly to exhibit them to the public as engaged in an undertaking which was in all ways so discreditable. Mr. Jardine has restored a few of the omitted passages—(why he did not either restore them all when he was about it, or explain his reason for not restoring them all,—why, at the very least, he has not warned us of the fact that others are omitted besides those which he has restored,—I cannot guess; but so it is) —and these he has distinguished by italics; and in almost every one of these some motive of the kind is immediately visible. In that which we have just been speaking of, Southampton is represented not only as taking a leading part in the consultation, but as declaring that he had been engaged in the undertaking for more than three months; a fact which has been allowed to sleep ever since the trial, until Mr. Jardine thus disinterred it. And Sir Ferdinando Gorge himself (who was already an object of popular odium from an unjust imputation of treachery) admits, what could not have been gathered from the narrative, that he personally advised the stirring of the city. Now both Southampton and Gorge were marked for pardon.

Again: references are made in the body of the paper to a declaration made by Sir Henry Neville, who was in fact implicated slightly, and had been accused by Essex of being further implicated than he really was,—and this declaration is not printed. Now we happen to know that it was withheld by his own particular desire. A letter of his to Cecil, or a memorandum of the contents of a letter, to that effect is still extant. His declaration itself, all written in his own hand, may be still seen at the State Paper Office; and there is nothing in it that mends Essex's case.

Again: in the Earl of Rutland's confession there were clauses stating that the " Earl of Southampton had shown himself discontented long before;" *—that (about six weeks before) he had sent one of the Earl of Rutland's servants " into France for saddles, pistols, and other things; "—that " *Sir John Heydon* cried out divers times, ' For the Queen,

---

* Mr. Jardine prints this first sentence in italics (as being omitted in the Declaration), but for some unexplained reason says nothing about the rest.

for the Queen!'"—and that Essex had, on the morning of
the insurrection, told the Earl of Rutland "and other his
company, that *The Earl of Sussex* would be with them presently." These passages are all omitted in the appendix to
the Declaration—(no marks of *om.*, by the way, in the MS.)
—why? Out of consideration, no doubt, for the reputation
of the persons whom they implicate : namely, of the Earl of
Southampton; a very young man, who had been misled and
was sorry for what he had done, and whose offences it was
not necessary to bring again upon the stage, as they were not
to be further punished;—of Sir John Heydon, whose name
does not appear at all, I think, in the report of the proceedings;—and of the Earl of Sussex, whose name was probably
used by Essex merely for countenance, and without any
authority.

Again : a portion of the examination of Edward Bushell
appears to have been read at the trial, which represents
Essex as having said, that "if a certain black purse he had
about his neck were found, it should appear *how he was betrayed in the city.*" This does not appear among the evidence appended to the Declaration ; for it would have been
understood as referring to Sheriff Smith, who had been
falsely represented as a favourer of the conspiracy.

Again : an examination of Lord Monteagle is omitted
entirely; I suppose because it brings him needlessly on
the stage as implicated in the attempt to stir the city.

Again : Sir Walter Raleigh's deposition represents Sir
Ferdinando Gorge as recommending him (on the morning
of the insurrection) to get back to the Court with speed, for
"the Earl of Essex had put himself into a strong guard at
Essex House, *and you are like to have a bloody day of it.*"
This deposition, though a rather important one, is not given,
—out of consideration no doubt for Sir Ferdinando.

Again : the entire examination of Henry Widdrington,
though it tells strongly against Essex, is omitted; I do
not know why, unless it be because Essex in his reply urged
good reasons to take off the weight of his testimony.

Again : a sentence is omitted from Sir Christopher

Blunt's confession, in which, being asked whether it were against the *Queen's forces* that they meant to secure the Earl by aid of the city, he says, " That must have been judged afterwards ; *for the forces might be such as came by direction of such of his enemies* " [the Earl's enemies] " *as might have had authority to command in the Queen's name, and would have done that without the Queen's privity* ; "—an admission which (though Mr. Jardine says that it " qualifies the preceding statement ") does in fact make the case worse for Essex. For it clearly admits that the defence contemplated was not (as Essex pretended) against private enemies, but against the *Queen's forces* ; the only question being whether their lawful commander might not be exceeding his commission ; —an absurd distinction, under plea of which (if it were allowed) any rebel might take up arms against any constituted authority. Why then was it omitted ? As pointing (I fancy) at Raleigh, who was then Captain of the Guard ; and conveying an insinuation which, though quite false and groundless, was likely enough to be believed by the people and to inflame their hatred against him ; the rather, too, because Sir Christopher Blunt had asked of Sir Walter Raleigh forgiveness " for the wrong he had done him," [viz. shooting at him on the river,] " and for his particular ill intent towards him ; " and they had exchanged forgiveness just before his death. The omission of such an insinuation as this may have been prompted as much by consideration for what Sir Christopher would have wished, as for what was due to Raleigh.

These of course are only guesses ; and there are one or two other (unimportant) omissions the causes of which I cannot even guess. But this I may say in general :—I have carefully examined all these suppressed passages ; both the single sentences which Mr. Jardine has restored and distinguished by italics ; and the other single sentences which he has (in his hurry I suppose) overlooked altogether ; and the entire depositions, the suppression of which he has not noticed ; and I have found nothing in any of them which tends to extenuate the offence of Essex, or to contradict the story of the Declaration; but something in almost every one of them which tends to inculpate (either needlessly or unjustly) somebody else. Whether therefore the act of suppressing them be attributable to the Council, or to the Queen, or to Bacon himself, is a question which I am not concerned to settle. Whoever did it, it was certainly harmless, for it tended in no degree to pervert the truth; and, as far as one can guess, it was suggested by a feeling of just and considerate mercy. But whatever the motives may have been, they have long since expired. And when I come myself to edit this Declaration, I shall think it right (not only for the sake of showing that they are not inconsistent with it, but really for the sake of better illustrating and confirming it) to print within brackets *all* the passages thus omitted, in their proper places.*

A.

Well, if this be all that is meant by that black word *" garbling,"* one need not be much moved by it.

B.

No. And I may as well warn you that this is the sense in which Mr. Jardine commonly uses the word. Tell him that a word has been left out or altered, he does not stop to ask whether it alters the sense or not, but sets it down at once as " garbling." According to which use of the word, the garbling of State-papers has with us become a recognized and authorized practice. When a member of parliament moves for the production of an official correspondence, he moves not for *copies*, but for *copies or extracts*. Now an " extract of a despatch " is, in our modern official phraseology, exactly what Mr. Jardine would call a " garbled " despatch. It is understood to be a copy with no words inserted which are not in the original, but with as many omitted as the Government think expedient. Neither are the places where omissions occur indicated by *marks* of

* This has been done in the " Letters and Life," Vol. ii., p. 292-385.

omission (which I think they ought always to be), but the faith of the Government is supposed to be discharged if words are not omitted in such a manner as to pervert the meaning of the sentence.

A.

The Government being themselves the judges.

B.

Yes ; there is no help for that. But this is from our business. Do you agree to acquit Bacon of Mr. Jardine's charge ?

A.

Willingly. I will bear witness that he has borne a good character hitherto to the best of *my* knowledge.

Let me see, where did we leave off? Oh, page 31. Do you know that we are not yet half through the first division of the article?

"But a great change was at hand. The health of the Queen had long been decaying, and the operation of age and disease was now assisted by acute mental suffering. The pitiable melancholy of her last days has generally been ascribed to her fond regret for Essex. But we are disposed to attribute her dejection partly to physical causes, and partly to the conduct of her courtiers and ministers. They did all in their power to conceal from her the intrigues which they were carrying on at the Court of Scotland. But her keen sagacity was not to be so deceived. She did not know the whole. But she knew that she was surrounded by men who were impatient for that new world which was to begin at her death—"

B.

Were they indeed ? Her *people* might perhaps be impatient for a new world, as people always do look forward with hope and pleasure to a change ; but surely not her *ministers*. By all politicians the greatest apprehensions were entertained of trouble and confusion likely to arise at her death. No successor declared. Many rival interests both at home and abroad watching their opportunity. No man knowing what the other thought. Much worth the striking for by many who were *out* of office ; much therefore to be lost by those who were *in.* If they were impatient, it could only be as men are impatient to be relieved from anxiety,— as men over whom a danger impends are impatient to have the crisis over, one way or another. If it had been possible to make Elizabeth immortal, the men " by whom she was surrounded " would have done it at the cost of half their substance.

A.

" —who had never been attached to her by affection—"

B.

What ! Elizabeth's ministers never attached to her by affection !

A.

" —and who were now very slightly attached to her by interest."

B.

If so, it could only be because their interest in her had so short a time to run.

A.

"Prostration and flattery could not conceal from her the cruel truth, that those whom she had trusted and promoted had never loved her, and were fast ceasing to fear her. Unable to avenge herself, and too proud to complain, she suffered sorrow and resentment to prey on her heart, till after a long career of power, prosperity, and glory, she died sick and weary of the world."

B.

All which will, I suppose, be set down in the next history of England as part of the narrative. As yet we have the advantage of knowing that it is only what the reviewer is "inclined " to suppose. And surely it is a most idle and extravagant display of originality. What Prince

was ever served for love, if not Elizabeth? What Prince's
death was ever deprecated, if hers was not? What colour
is there for such a notion, more than the bare fact that her
ministers had been secretly negotiating with James? And
yet how did that argue any want of affection for her? The
motive for those negotiations was obvious and natural; the
occasion in fact urgent. It had been part of her policy,—a
weakness if you will,—to forbid during her life all speech of
a successor. But die she must; and a successor must be
thought of. Since she would not allow any arrangements
to be made for her, it was merely necessary that they should
make arrangements for themselves. It is true that everything did in fact come round peaceably and prosperously,
and without any difficulty. But that it did so was a matter
of astonishment to the whole nation.

A.

I dare say you are right. But let us get on with our
proper business.

"James mounted the throne; and Bacon employed all his
address to obtain for himself a share of the favour of his new
master. This was no difficult task. The faults of James both
as a man and as a Prince were numerous: but insensibility to
the claims of learning and genius was not among them. He
was indeed made up of two men,—a witty, well-read scholar,
who wrote, disputed and harangued,—and a nervous drivelling
idiot, who acted. If he had been a Canon of Christ Church or
a Prebendary of Westminster, it is not improbable that he
would have left a highly respectable name to posterity,—that
he would have distinguished himself among the translators of
the Bible, and among the Divines who attended the Synod of
Dort,—that he would have been regarded by the literary world
as no contemptible rival of Vossius and Casaubon. But fortune
placed him in a situation in which his weakness covered him
with disgrace, and in which his accomplishments brought him
no honour. In a college much eccentricity and childishness
would have been readily pardoned in so learned a man. But
all that learning could do for him on the throne was to make
people think him a pedant as well as a fool."

B.

I suppose you will not think it worth while to stop and examine this character of James. But if I let it pass, you are not therefore to set me down as assenting even to the accuracy of it as far as it goes; much less to the completeness of it. It is true that James's character was ill-fitted to deal with the critical times on which he fell. But it is not at all true that his actions (except possibly in the few last years of his reign) were those of a drivelling idiot. It is not even true that, at the time, they were generally thought so. His popular reputation as a pedant and a fool is of much later growth. His subjects never doubted his wisdom; and though they did not fear him, they never despised him. The truth is, that he was remarkable not only among kings, but among men, for the absence of all affectation and reserve, and was sadly wanting in the great gift of holding his tongue; and (as mankind always measure a man's ability by his success) when we look back upon his reign and see that the broad result was failure, we infer that he was a fool; when we remember how quick he was in learning and how much he knew, we add learning to folly and call him pedant; and being prepossessed with this idea of his character, we find in the perpetual droppings of that fertile brain and loose tongue, abundant and amusing illustrations of it. But I must confess, for my own part, that the more I become acquainted with him, the more I feel not only a great personal kindness for him, but a conviction that, as a governor, he was both wise and patriotic; —wise in his views, patriotic in his desires and purposes. But then he had three great failings;—so great, that they were sufficient of themselves to make his whole life a failure. He could not command or reserve his affections; he could not disappoint his inclinations; and he could not hold his tongue. The first made him continually submit his own judgment to the will of his favourites; the second kept him in continual poverty; the third, by provoking him to measure his own single wit against a whole House of

Commons, and thereby to set his reputation upon the hazard of the vote of a popular assembly, lost him all majesty in the eyes of his people. But if he had not talked so much, I question whether, even now, his *acts* would have been thought foolish.

However it is premature to discuss the character of his reign at the very entrance of it. There is at least no doubt of this,—that he ascended the throne amid general acclamations of joy, with great reputation, and full of promise. Had he been blown up on the 5th of November, 1605, it would have been universally lamented as the blasting of one of the fairest hopes that a nation was ever flattered with in the personal character of a King.

A.

I fancy I shall want some further satisfaction on these points before I have done. But we will go on now with Bacon.

" Bacon was favourably received at Court, and soon found that his chance of promotion was not diminished by the death of the Queen. He was solicitous to be knighted, for two reasons, which are somewhat amusing. The King had already dubbed half London, and Bacon found himself the only untitled person in his mess at Gray's Inn. This was not very agreeable to him. He had also 'found an alderman's daughter, a handsome maiden, to his liking.' On both these grounds he begged his cousin Robert Cecil, 'if it might please his good Lordship,' to use his interest in his behalf. The application was successful. Bacon was one of three hundred gentlemen, who on the Coronation-day received the honour, if it is to be so called, of knighthood. The handsome maiden, the daughter of Alderman Barnham, soon after consented to become Sir Francis's Lady."

B.

This would be too trifling a matter to stop for, were it not told with a kind of contemptuous chuckle, as if an absurd pride in vain and conventional distinctions, and a sycophantic habit of plastering great persons with their titles, had been characteristic of the man. And such tones and gestures (as one may call them) of style produce more effect than you would think. Every reader who is not continually on his guard will naturally fall into such a sympathy with his writer, as to receive impressions almost unconsciously from indirect and impalpable insinuations of this kind. They take him at unawares, and bespeak his judgment without its own consent. In this instance I beg leave to protest against any such insinuation. I utterly deny that an undue value for titular distinctions was at all characteristic of Bacon,—that he desired them for himself further than as they were the ordinary decorations and the recognized stamp of honour and rank; or that he 'obtruded them upon others more than the manners of the time required. But this you will say is my partiality. Then let us apply the test, which I think you will admit has never failed me yet. Let us have the matter in Bacon's own words, not in the reviewer's version of them. The words, I should premise, occur at the close of a rather long letter full of other matters,—a letter not written for the purpose of asking Cecil's interest in obtaining a knighthood for him, but in answer to some communication from Cecil himself, who had at this time been taking a very friendly interest in Bacon's fortunes, had been lending him money, and assisting to extricate him from some "disgrace" (the particulars of which we do not know, but probably some arrest for debt while employed in the King's service, like that affair of the goldsmith four or five years before), and had (as I guess, though I cannot positively affirm) *offered* to use his interest in getting him knighted. I should also tell you that Bacon, far from being absorbed at this time in the pursuit of vanities, was diligently occupied in clearing his estate from embarrassments by the sale of his lands, with the professed intention of withdrawing from State-business and sitting down to his profession and his studies. The death of the Queen had set him free so far as old attachment and obligation were concerned ; the death of his brother (two years before) had left him what remained of his paternal estate, which was not large, and was much encumbered with debt. This therefore was the time to recover himself from pecuniary embarrassments, to place his finances upon a sound footing, and to new-shape his course for the future.

It was in these circumstances that he wrote to Cecil (after speaking of some money-matter then pressing) in those words :—

"For my estate, because your Lordship hath care of it, it is thus : I shall be able, with selling the skirts of my living in Hertfordshire, to preserve the body; and to leave myself, being clearly out of debt, and having some money in my pocket, 300*l.* land per annum,—with a fair house and the ground woll-timbered. This is now my labour.

"For my purpose or course, I desire to meddle as little as I can in the King's causes, his Majesty now abounding in counsel; and to follow my private thrift and practice, and to marry with some convenient advancement. For as for any ambition, I do assure your Honour mine is quenched. In the Queen's, my excellent mistress's, time, the quorum was small ; her service was a kind of freehold; and it was a more solemn time. All those points agreed with my nature and judgment. My ambition now I shall only put upon my pen, whereby I shall be able to maintain memory and merit of the times succeeding."

I may mention, by the way, that Bacon had received no rebuff that we know of; and it was but two months since the King's arrival in London ; so there had been no time for the grapes to grow sour. And now for the knighthood :—

"Lastly, for this divulged and almost prostituted title of knighthood, I could,—without charge, by your Honour's mean, —be content to have it ; both because of this late disgrace, and because I have three new knights in my mess in Gray's Inn commons; and because I have found out an alderman's daughter, a handsome maiden, to my liking. So as if your Honour will find the time, I will come to the Court from Gorhambury upon any warning."

And again, about a fortnight after, (and also at the close of a letter about other business,) he writes :—

"For my knighthood, I wish the manner might be such as

might grace me, since the matter will not: I mean, that I
might not be merely gregarious in a troop. The Coronation is
at hand. It may please your Lordship to let me hear from you
speedily."

A.

Are these letters some of your own recent discoveries?

B.

Oh no. They were first printed by Birch about eighty
years since, and are in all the editions of the works. They
were found among Cecil's papers at Hatfield. The reviewer
knew it all; and it was in fact all he knew. And now, what
is there in it to chuckle at? Knighthood, unbought, and
bestowed with judgment and selection upon worthy objects
(as till then it had always been), was in those times a very
honourable distinction; not less honourable, I fancy, than
the Order of the Bath is now. True, it was soon to lose this
dignity by being made venal and promiscuous. But it had
not lost it yet; and even if it had begun already to fade,
what then? It may be a slight *not* to receive what it may
be no great honour to receive. Lord Cecil asks Bacon
(surely a fit object) whether he would not like to be
knighted. Bacon answers, Yes, provided it be "without
charge," that is, given, not bought; and " by your Honour's
mean," that is, given, not upon his own application, but
upon the recommendation of a principal Counsellor: and
provided also that it be conferred in such a manner as to
give it a character of selectness and distinction. An honour
of this kind, proceeding from the fountain of honour, was
at that time a thing of substance, not vain show. It was
looked upon, not by lackeys only, but by all the world,
as the outward sign of inward worth, conferred by those
who could best judge of that worth as an evidence to those
who could not. " Sir Francis Bacon " was in the year 1603
to " Master Francis Bacon " just what in the year 1844
" Lord Metcalfe " was to " Sir Charles Metcalfe ": the
" Sir " in the first case, as the ' Lord ' in the second, being
simply a mark of distinction for services well-done.

And as for the other point by which the reviewer seems "somewhat amused," I need hardly remind you, that "it may please your Lordship," meant no more then than "my dear Lord" means now. It was the ordinary phrase with which every letter addressed to a Lord, or even to an ambassador, by a person of inferior rank, began; no matter how near or how distant the acquaintance. Bacon never wrote to his mother but he began, "it may please your good Ladyship." The thing was a matter of course. But, as introduced here, it contributes not the less to the general effect, and I suppose to the general purpose of the passage, namely that of holding up Bacon to contempt, as a man with the soul of a courtier and the tongue of a sycophant.

A.

Yes, you were right to stop for this. And between ourselves, these smaller kinds of misrepresentation are what I like worse than all the rest. When a man inveighs against another (however unjustly) as guilty of a great crime, it is often a just hatred of the crime that misleads him. He sees the crime in the criminal, and is in fact inveighing against *it*. I never yet met with a *very* honest man who could be really just to a man charged with dishonesty. Your *very* honest man is so shocked at the notion of apologizing for dishonesty, that he overleaps the previous question, whether the dishonest thing has been really done, or whether the culprit before him be really the man who did it. But in matters of this kind, in which at the very worst there is nothing to put the moral sense in a passion, that a man should be always exaggerating, miscolouring, and traducing,—it seems to argue a tone of feeling habitually un . . . .—However, we must not both take part against the reviewer, or we shall be falling into the honest man's error ourselves. You may depend upon my taking no impression from the last paragraph.

" The death of Elizabeth, though on the whole it improved Bacon's prospects, was in one respect an unfortunate event for him. The new King had always felt kindly towards Lord Essex, who had been zealous for the Scotch succession; and as soon as he came to the throne began to show favour to the house of Devereux, and to those who had stood by that house in its adversity. Everybody was now at liberty to speak out respecting those lamentable events in which Bacon had borne so large a share."

B.

Yes, to speak *out :* but to speak out *what?*—lies or truth? There were some important parts of the truth with regard to Essex, which, after James's accession, it must have been very awkward to meddle with.

A.

" Elizabeth was scarcely cold, when the public feeling began to manifest itself by marks of respect to Lord Southampton. That accomplished nobleman, who will be remembered to the latest ages as the generous and discerning patron of Shakespeare, was held in honour by his contemporaries chiefly on account of the devoted affection which he had borne to Essex. He had been tried and convicted together with his friend; but the Queen had spared his life, and at the time of her death he was still a prisoner. A crowd of visitors hastened to the Tower to congratulate him upon his approaching deliverance. With that crowd Bacon could not venture to mingle. The multitude loudly condemned him; and his own conscience told him that the multitude had but too much reason."

B.

That can be only as the reviewer guesses, upon his own assumption that the multitude were in the right. Bacon himself never for a moment admitted this; but, on the contrary, expressly declared " that for any action of his towards the Earl of Essex, there was nothing that passed him in his lifetime which came to his remembrance with more clearness and less check of conscience." Beware therefore how you take an impression from this passage that Bacon's own conscience can be cited as one of the witnesses against him.

A.

Oh yes, I understand all that. The reviewer tells the story according to his own reading of it. But he is going, I think, to tell us something new in confirmation of this assumption.

" He excused himself to Southampton by letter, in terms which, if he had, as Mr. Montagu conceives, done only what as a subject and an advocate he was bound to do, must be considered as shamefully servile.   He owns his fear that his attendance would give offence, and that his professions of regard would obtain no credit. ' Yet,' says he, ' it is as true as a thing that God knoweth, that this great change hath wrought in me no other change towards your Lordship than this, that I may safely be that to you now which I was truly before.' "

I move that this letter be produced.   There is nothing so likely to detect a man who has done anything wrong, as a comparison of the excuses he makes to different people on the same occasion.   His case must be very good, or his honesty very great, if he is not betrayed into some inconsistency.   But first let me hear how his case did really stand with Southampton.   For I do not remember that he has been charged with having done Southampton any ill office, beyond maintaining at the trial that the offence for which he was arraigned was apparent treason.   And since (whatever may be thought of his obligations to Essex) he certainly stood under no such obligation to Southampton as could have made it his duty to quarrel with the Queen rather than appear against *him* on such an occasion, I do not so well see what it was that he had to excuse.   Has he been supposed to have taken any part against Southampton *after* the trial ?

B.

Not that I ever heard of.   And since it is not pretended that the arraignment was in itself unjust,—since not a single harsh word has been reported as uttered by him personally against Southampton,—since the name of Southampton is in the Declaration of Treasons handled as tenderly and lightly as possible,—it seems to be quite clear that he had nothing to excuse.   For myself at least, I have little doubt that Bacon had not only done nothing against him except what as a subject he was bound to do; but that he had shared the anxiety which was felt, not by the public alone, but also by the Queen's ministers (at least by two of them, Nottingham and Cecil), for his preservation. There is a letter from Cecil to Sir George Carew, in which, after detailing the particulars of the conspiracy and the trial, he proceeds :—

"It remaineth now that I let you know what is like to become of the poor young Earl of Southampton, who merely for the love of the Earl hath been drawn into this action ; who in respect that most of the conspiracies were at Drury House, where he was always chief, and where Sir Charles Davers lay, those that would deal for him (of which number I protest to God I am one as far as I dare) are much disadvantaged of arguments to save him. And yet when I consider how penitent he is, and how merciful the Queen is, and that never in thought or deed but in this conspiracy he offended,—as I cannot write in despair, so I dare not flatter myself with hope."

And Nottingham, sending to Lord Mountjoy a few days later an account of Essex's confession, adds in a postscript :—

"There hath been executed, the Earl of Essex, Sir Charles Davers, Sir Christopher Blunt, Sir Gilly Mericke, and Cuffe. And I trust they shall be all. For the Earl of Southampton, though he be condemned, yet I hope well for his life ; for Mr. Secretary and myself use all our wits and power for it."

This seems to be conclusive as to the feeling of these two ministers ; why should we suppose that Bacon took a different part ? What part he actually took after the trial is not known except from his own account, and from the general handling of the subject in the " Declaration." But so far as that evidence goes, it goes to show that he did (as from his character and position one would have anticipated) work in the same spirit with Cecil and Nottingham. And though he does not in the " Apology " mention Southampton's name, there is a passage in which I always fancy that the allusion must be to Southampton. Having said that after Essex's last " fatal impatience," " there was not time to work for *him*," he goes on : " though the same my affection when it could not work upon the subject proper, went *to the next,* with no ill effect towards some others *who I think do rather*

not know it than not acknowledge it." Now the Apology was
written some time after the liberation of Southampton (the
date of the writing is not known, but it was printed in 1604) ;
we have only to suppose therefore that this letter of Bacon's
met with a cold reception, and the allusion fits the case
exactly, and is very characteristic of the man.

However, I do not want to rest anything upon a guess.
Bacon, as you say, had nothing to excuse in his conduct to
Southampton. He had never wished him ill; never done
him any ill office, but the contrary. He was now glad of his
approaching liberation. Still, knowing that his conduct had
been much misrepresented, and loudly though unjustly condemned, by Essex's and Southampton's friends, he could not
reasonably expect to find Southampton himself untinctured
with the same prejudice. In such a case, what was the
course which a mind of true delicacy would naturally take ?
He might easily commit an error in either of two different
ways. Was Southampton disposed to take a true view of
his case, and to be friends? To stand aloof would in that
case have seemed churlish and unfriendly, and might be
supposed to argue an ashamed conscience. Did Southampton (on the contrary) regard him as the ungrateful and
ungenerous enemy of his friend and himself? In that case,
to present himself would at the best have seemed indelicate
and unfeeling ; at the worst it would have shown like an act
of vulgar and shameless sycophancy. What could he do
then better than write, to excuse his *non*-attendance and explain the reasons of it ?

A.

Yes, but let us have the letter. Let me hear the tone in
which a man asks pardon, and I will tell you whether he has
been doing anything to ask pardon for. All you say may be
true, and yet the letter may be " shamefully servile," and all
the more servile because all you say *is* true.

B.

Here then the letter is,—word for word. Your mind is
in an excellent frame for judging ; which is what I wanted.

I should really like to know what fault can be found with it; or how it could be improved.

"It may please your Lordship,—I would have been very glad to have presented my humble service to your Lordship by my attendance, if I could have foreseen that it should not have been unpleasing unto you. And therefore because I would commit no error, I choose to write; assuring your Lordship (how credible soever it may seem to you at first), yet it is as true as a thing that God knoweth, that this great change hath wrought in me no other change towards your Lordship than this, that I may safely be now that which I was truly before. And so, craving no other pardon than for troubling you with this letter, I do not now begin but continue to be your Lordship's most humble and much devoted Servant,— FR. BACON."

There is the whole letter. Must you pronounce it " shamefully servile " ?

A.

On the contrary, a model of manliness and delicacy well mixed. What kind of spirit is the reviewer possessed with that he cannot get through a single paragraph without some monstrous error either of fact, of judgment, or of feeling?

B.

No worse spirit, I dare say, than vanity. Much desire of feeling and displaying his own power; little desire of doing justice or of understanding the truth. But let us have some more.

A.

" How Southampton received those apologies we are not informed."

B.

There he goes again! What *apologies*, I should like to know. He did not say that he was sorry for anything he had done. He asked pardon for nothing but for troubling him with the letter.

Yes, yes.   It is all of a piece.

" But it is certain that the general opinion was pronounced against Bacon in a manner not to be misunderstood."

B.

True ; the general opinion of people who did not know what he had done.

A.

" Soon after his marriage he put forth a defence of his conduct, in the form of a letter to the Earl of Devon. This tract seems to us only to prove the exceeding badness of a cause for which such talents could do so little."

B.

Ay, there it is. "Could *do* so little ! "   But since this is the only notice which the reviewer deigns to take of that composition ; simply dismissing it as a thing which has not altered *his* opinion (a feat to which I well believe Bacon's talents were unequal),—without explaining either what the tenour of the defence is, or what the points are in which it fails,—it is impossible to answer him otherwise than by saying generally that to *me*, on the contrary, it seems to prove the exceeding *goodness* of a cause, which a simple statement, without any special pleading whatever, was sufficient to vindicate.   How much such a statement could " *do* " for the cause, you must have seen from the fact that it has supplied me with the means of convicting the reviewer of (I think) some half-dozen material misstatements.   Why it was not pitched in a bolder key, and made so complete as to answer by anticipation such an attack as this, and set 'the whole question at rest for ever, is intelligible enough to anyone who understands Bacon's character.   He could not have done it without bringing the worst of Essex's case again upon the stage, when it could have served no purpose higher than that of vindicating his own reputation.   To show *what* the Apology " did for the case," would be to go through the

whole story again. But it may be as well to remind you of
the general purpose and spirit of it. The imputation which
Bacon sustained "in common speech," was that he had
been "false and ungrateful" to Essex. The grounds of this
imputation were of two kinds ; the part which he had actually
taken against Essex in public ; and the part which he was
supposed to have taken against him in private. Upon the
first he touches briefly and generally, not entering into any
argument, but simply appealing to the "true rules and
habits of duties and moralities," as "they which shall decide
the matter."

" Wherein (he says) my defence needeth to be but simple
and brief ; namely, that whatsoever I did concerning that
action and proceeding was done in my duty and service to the
Queen and the State ; in which I would not show myself false-
hearted nor fainthearted for any man's sake living. For every
honest man that hath his heart well planted will forsake his
King rather than forsake his God, and forsake his friend rather
than forsake his King, and yet will forsake any earthly com-
modity, yea, and his own life in some cases, rather than forsake
his friend. I hope the world hath not forgotten these degrees ;
else the heathen saying *amicus usque ad aras* shall judge them."

And this is the whole of his defence upon the first point.
What he had done was known. He had nothing to explain ;
and he could not, for the reason I have mentioned, enter
into a more particular application of the principle to the
case. And indeed, if the *principle* be admitted, I hardly
see how the objection can be sustained, or what further
justification was needed. And it was a principle (you are to
remember) which did not in those days need to be further
enforced ; being well recognized, and scarcely disputed by
anybody. In our times it is true that the notion of forsaking
a friend rather than forsaking a *king* seems extravagant ;
because the king is no longer the real governor and chief
magistrate of the country ; and the observance owing to him
from his subjects is a matter of form and ceremony rather
than of substance. The *State* has in fact very little interest
in him. If however I say that a man should forsake his

friend rather than forsake his *party* (which comes a little
nearer to the case, though not quite up to it), I think many
people would at once assent, though I am not clear that I
should assent myself. But if I say that a man should forsake
his friend rather than forsake his *country*, meaning the true
interests and legitimate authorities of the State, I suppose
the proposition will hardly be disputed by anybody. Now
in Bacon's time, when the theory of a responsible ministry
had not yet been developed, this is what " the King " really
was. I conceive therefore that if we do but substitute the
thing for the name, we shall all agree that he has laid down
his *principles* of duty truly ; and that, if we do but substitute
the facts as they were for the facts as the reviewer tells them,
we must all agree that he did not misapply them. At all
events, whether we adopt the principle or not, there can be
no doubt that Bacon believed it to be the true one. Therefore, if he must be condemned, let him be condemned for
believing it, not for acting upon it.

A.

This then, you say, is his defence of what he did in
public at the trial. How did he meet the other part of the
charge?

B.

The other part of the charge he meets by a simple narrative, from which it appears that the imputation was wholly
without foundation. The charge was that he had acted
against his friend. The answer is that he had acted *for*
him. Admit the fact to be made good, and I do not know
what more the greatest talents could " do for a case," or
wish to do for it.

But to make out *a* case was not his object. His object
was to present *the* case as it truly was. The judgment upon
it he left to friends and enemies.

" And this, my Lord," (he concludes) " to my furthest remembrance is all that passed wherein I had part; which I have
set down as near as I could in the very words and speeches that

were used,—not because they are worthy the repetition—I mean those of my own,—but to the end your Lordship may lively and plainly discern *between the face of truth and a smooth tale.*"

If he had told a smooth tale instead of presenting the face of truth, the reviewer would have thought the cause not so bad; because then his talents would have " done something for it."

But, seriously, can it be shown that the truth is in any single feature either distorted or miscoloured? I have not yet heard of any attempt to do so. And if not, was he not justified in adding,—

" Wherein I report myself to your honourable judgment, whether you do not see the traces of an honest man; and had I been as well believed either by the Queen or by my Lord as I was well heard by them both, both my Lord had been fortunate and so had myself in his fortune."

Whether the reviewer disbelieves Bacon's account of what he did,—or, believing it, does not see in it " the traces of an honest man,"—he does not inform us. Therefore I do not know how to meet him more directly than. by saying that, until I hear of some argument for the one or the other, I shall hold my present opinion, that in the whole of his relation to Essex, Bacon acted quite rightly.

A.

And as I cannot invent any argument myself for either, I must hold you justified in doing so.

" It is not probable that Bacon's defence had much effect upon his contemporaries."

B.

And pray why not? Is it a thing so improbable in itself, that the defence of a man who has been condemned unheard should produce an effect in his favour? or is there any evidence that his unpopularity continued afterwards undiminished? The old slander was indeed revived after his fall, when any slander against the character of a disgraced royalist was sure to find plenty of believers, and when there was no one to contradict it. But by what *contemporary* of name and repute was his conduct to Essex censured *after* the appearance of the "Apology"? He was frequently in places where he was most likely to hear of it;—exposed continually to the whispers of the Court and the invectives of the House of Commons. Surely if the condemnation had been general, he would have been now and then taunted with it by his enemies or his antagonists. Yet I do not think I have met anywhere with so much as an allusion, from which one might infer that such a charge had been so much as whispered during the twelve or thirteen years that followed the printing of the "Apology." Of course the reviewer will not favour us with an instance.

A.

Rather the contrary. He seems to admit that the censure, if not withdrawn, was forgotten.

"But the unfavourable impression which his conduct had made appears to have been gradually effaced. Indeed it must be some very peculiar cause that can make a man like him long unpopular. His talents secured him from contempt; his temper and his manners from hatred. There is scarcely any story so black that it may not be got over by a man of great abilities, whose abilities are united with caution, good-humour, patience, and affability; who pays daily sacrifices to Nemesis; who is a delightful companion, a serviceable though not an ardent friend, and a dangerous yet a placable enemy."

B.

The drift of all which is apparently to account for the fact that he was not so unpopular with those who knew him as he ought to have been. My version of the story does not stand in need of any such explanations. But I am glad of this admission of the fact; because it shows that Macaulay's reading could supply no expression or anecdote which his ingenuity could distort into a semblance of proof that anybody condemned Bacon's conduct after he had once heard it explained.

A.

"Waller in the next age was an eminent instance of this. Indeed, Waller had much more than may at first sight appear in common with Bacon. To the higher intellectual qualities of the great English philosopher,—to the genius which has made an immortal epoch in the history of science,—Waller had indeed no pretensions. But the mind of Waller, so far as it extended, coincided with that of Bacon; and might, so to speak, have been cut out of that of Bacon. In the qualities which make a man an object of interest and veneration to posterity, there was no comparison between them. But in the qualities by which chiefly a man is known to his contemporaries, there was a striking similarity. Considered as men of the world, as courtiers, as politicians, as associates, as allies, as enemies, they had nearly the same merits and the same defects. They were not malignant. They were not tyrannical. But they wanted warmth of affection and elevation of sentiment. There were many things which they loved better than virtue, and which they feared more than guilt. Yet after they had stooped to acts of which it is impossible to read the account in the most partial narrative, without strong disapprobation and contempt—"

B.

The most partial narratives! I know nothing about that. When I speak of Bacon's conduct it is not as reported in a partial narrative, but in a true one. And I still wait to hear of some one act of his of which we cannot read without disapprobation and contempt.

A.

" —the public still continued to regard them with a feeling not easily to be distinguished from esteem. The hyperbole of Juliet seemed to be verified with respect to them—' Upon their brows shame was ashamed to sit.' Everybody seemed as desirous to throw a veil over their misconduct as if it had been his own. Clarendon, who felt and had reason to feel strong personal dislike towards Waller, speaks of him thus :—' There needs no more to be said to extol the excellence and power of his wit and pleasantness of his conversation, than that it was of magnitude enough to cover a world of very great faults,—that is, so to cover them that they were not taken notice of to his reproach,—viz. a narrowness in his nature to the lowest degree,—an abjectness and want of courage to support him in any virtuous undertaking,—an insinuation and servile flattery to the height tho vainest and most imperious nature could be contented with. . . . It had power to reconcile him to those whom he had most offended and provoked, and continued to his age with that rare felicity that his company was acceptable where his spirit was odious, and he was at least pitied where he was most detested.' Much of this, with some softening, might, we fear, be applied to Bacon."

B.

Wait a moment. Whether all or any of this be true of Waller I do not pretend to say; for I know nothing about him. If it is, I need hardly observe that the parallel is absurd. But what I want to say is, that the respect which Bacon's character commanded during his life was quite different in *kind* from that which Clarendon describes. Where is the evidence that any human being who despised Bacon, liked him? Of those who detested him, which pitied him? It is common enough for a man to be popular and agreeable who is at the same time despised; nor does it argue any extraordinary power of pleasing. A man will always be popular in that sense who can make time pass agreeably. And this he can do all the better for *not* being too much respected. The poorer kind of men, who will always be the greater number, do not like a man whom they have to look up to, whose greatness or goodness makes them sensible of their own mediocrity or unworthiness. But the impression which Bacon is described as producing upon those who conversed with him was not that of pity, or good-nature, or merely social kindness, but of " an awful reverence." That is the phrase used by Osborne (a writer whose fault is a tendency to depreciate and detract), and he ascribes the impression not only to his reputation for universal knowledge, but to that " majestical carriage which he was known to own." Ben Jonson again—(a still better witness, for ho

knew him well in both his fortunes, and was by nature an
extremely fine observer)—tells us, not that he *liked* him
for the "pleasantness of his conversation," but that he
"*reverenced*" him ; and for what?—"for the greatness which
was only proper to himself,"—a greatness which place and
honours could not enhance, and a "virtue" which made it
impossible to condole with him on his misfortunes, because
they seemed only like "accidents," which served to make
the virtue manifest, but could not harm it. Is this the
description of a man whose "company was acceptable where
his spirit was odious ;" whose manners procured pity from
those by whom his character was "detested"? Surely no
two pictures can be more unlike. Indeed, in the case of
Bacon, it would probably be found—(if the witnesses could
still be called up)—that those who thought ill of him and
those to whom his company was acceptable were two distinct
sets of persons. By those who knew him he was "reverenced"
for his greatness and goodness ; by those who did not know
him, or could not understand him, he may (for anything I
know) have been thought ill of and disliked. But I have
yet to learn that his character was ever ill-spoken of by a
man of a great spirit who had had opportunities of knowing
him. Aubrey tells us (and his information was derived
chiefly from two persons who knew Bacon well,—Hobbes
and Sir John Danvers), that "all who were great and good
loved and honoured him." If so, it cannot possibly have
been for such qualities as Clarendon ascribes to Waller. For
what qualities it was, no one can be at a loss to understand
who is acquainted with his writings ; especially those which
are most familiar, unstudied, and unreserved.

A.

No; *if* so. And yet indeed why not? It is a friend's
account, to be sure. But a friend's is at least as likely
to be true as an enemy's. And Sir John Danvers, I think,
was one of the friends of his adversity. Well.

"The influence of Waller's talents, manners, and accomplishments died with him ; and the world has pronounced an
unbiassed sentence upon his character."

Q

B.

That is to say, Clarendon has written down his own opinion of his character in a readable book; and "the world," knowing nothing whatever about the matter, has just taken it for granted. If Clarendon had pronounced him ·a martyr, the world would have believed that just as readily.

A.

"A few flowing lines are not bribe sufficient to pervert the judgment of posterity. But the influence of Bacon is felt and will long be felt over the whole of the civilized world. Leniently as he was treated by his contemporaries—"

B.

Leniently! That must refer then to this period which we have been speaking of, when as yet he had done nothing wrong. It surely cannot be said that he was treated leniently at the time of his fall, or after it.

A.

"Leniently as he was treated by his contemporaries, posterity has treated him more leniently still."

B.

Posterity treated him leniently! Why, what is the popular opinion of him which is now current? How comes it that in contending that he was not a cold-hearted, mean-spirited, selfish, perfidious, and servile sycophant, I feel that I am maintaining what will seem to half the world a preposterous paradox? It is true that a few individual writers here and there have treated him with respect, possibly with lenity. But have their views been adopted into the popular opinion? If you want to know how *posterity* has treated Bacon, look into any of the anonymous notices of his life prefixed to the popular editions of his works. Look into our modern Encyclopædias, Biographical Dictionaries, British Plutarchs, or British Neposes. Look

into our histories of England.* Look at the first thought
which occurs to a respectable and dispassionate man like
Mr. Jardine, upon discovering that Bacon had struck a
sentence out of a deposition. What (thinks he) could his
object be? Some *bad* one of course! And so prepossessed
is he with this notion, that he sets down the first bad one
he can think of, without even turning to the book which
lay before him, to see whether such an object was compatible with the rest of the story! Surely the judgment
of posterity upon Bacon's *moral* character is as harsh and
rigorous as it well can be,—the greatest of intellects united
with the smallest of hearts. If there be anything wearing
the appearance of lenity and indulgence, it is only a tendency in the better sort of natures (arising out of a secret
aversion from the contemplation of so monstrous and re-
volting a combination) to keep the two parts of his character separate, and not to let their minds dwell at all upon
the moral part. It is not that they see it with indulgent
eyes; they turn their eyes away and try to forget it
altogether.

A.

That is true enough. I cannot say that I have myself
been in the habit of judging Bacon *leniently*. And certainly people in general are ready to believe the worst of
him; as may appear (among other things) by the appetite
with which they have swallowed this article.

"Turn where we may, the trophies of that mighty intellect
are full in view. We are judging Manlius in sight of the
Capitol."

B.

And we pronounce him the meanest of mankind.

A.

True. I wonder whether it occurred to the reviewer,
while he was declaiming against the scandal of blackening

* This was written in October, 1845. Of late, a considerable change may
be observed.

the fame of benefactors and writing abusive pamphlets against them when they are dead, to consider what he was doing himself all the time.—I suppose not.

But we had better break off here. For the next paragraph relates apparently to the progress of his. books and studies.

B.

Very well. Only remember that Bacon is now in his forty-third year; that he has been placed in many situations which try the character severely; and that you have been compelled to own that, in every one of these, he has acquitted himself with fidelity, with sincerity, with disinterestedness, and with honour. The worst that can be said of him is, that he was desirous of advancement in his profession; that he endeavoured to obtain such advancement by pre-eminently deserving it; and that in a conflict between two duties, he preferred the course which he knew to be right before that which he knew would be popular. Neither can it be said that, if we know nothing worse of him, it is only because we know so little. There are very few men of whose private affairs and proceedings so much is known that was never intended to see the light.

Now I do not want to bespeak your judgment upon what is coming. But I want you to remember that in cases of *doubtful* interpretation, the *presumption* is not with you or me, whatever it may be with the reviewer, against him. If the reviewer thinks himself entitled, from the fact that Bacon did afterwards abuse power, to infer that from the beginning he desired power only for the sake of abusing it, —much more may you and I, from the fact that he has actually behaved well for forty-three years, infer that he is likely to behave well hereafter.

A.

I don't know. He has not yet been tried with prosperity. But of course there is always a presumption in favour of a man who has hitherto borne a good character. And to this I agree that Bacon is fully entitled.

EVENING THE SEVENTH.

—◦◦◦—

A.

Shall we go on at once with the review, or have you anything to say by way of preparation ?

B.

Let me see. We are on the threshold of a new world.— Yes, I think I shall have a good deal to say before we go much further. But let us see what Macaulay makes of it first.

A.

"Under the reign of James, Bacon grew rapidly in fortune and favour. In 1604 he was appointed King's Counsel with a fee of £40 a-year, and a pension of £60 a-year was settled upon him. In 1607 he became Solicitor-General, and in 1612 Attorney-General. He continued to distinguish himself in Parliament, particularly by his exertions in favour of one excellent measure on which the King's heart was set,—the union of England and Scotland. It was not difficult for such an intellect to discover many irresistible arguments in favour of such a scheme. He conducted the great cause of the *Post-nati* in the Exchequer Chamber. And the decision of the Judges,—a decision the legality of which may be questioned, but the beneficial effects of which must be acknowledged,—was in a great measure attributed to his dexterous management. While actively engaged in the House of Commons and in the Courts of Law, he still found leisure for letters and philosophy. The noble treatise on the Advancement of Learning, which at a later period was augmented into the *De Augmentis*, appeared

in 1605. The 'Wisdom of the Ancients,'—a work which if it
had proceeded from any other writer, would have been considered a master-piece of wit and learning, but which adds little
to the fame of Bacon,—was printed in 1609. In the mean time
the *Novum Organum* was slowly proceeding. Several distinguished men of learning had been permitted to see sketches
or detached portions of that extraordinary book; and though
they were not generally disposed to admit the soundness of the
author's views, they spoke with the greatest admiration of his
genius. Sir Thomas Bodley, the founder of the most magnificent of English libraries, was among those stubborn conserva-
tives who considered the hopes with which Bacon looked
forward to the future destinies of the human race as utterly
chimerical; and who regarded with distrust and aversion the
innovating spirit of the new schismatics in Philosophy. Yet
even Bodley, after perusing the *Cogitata et Visa*,—one of the
most precious of those scattered leaves out of which the great
oracular volume was afterwards made up,—acknowledged that
in 'those very parts and in all proposals and plots of that book
Bacon showed himself a master-workman,'—and that 'it could
not be gainsaid but all the treatise over did abound with choice
conceits of the present state of learning and with worthy contemplations of the means to procure it.' In 1612 a new edition
of the Essays appeared, with additions surpassing the original
Collection both in bulk and quality. Nor did these pursuits
distract Bacon's attention from a work the most arduous, the
most glorious, and the most useful, that even his mighty powers
could have achieved, 'the reducing and recompiling' (to use
his own phrase) of the Laws of England.

"Unhappily he was at that very time employed in perverting those laws to the worst purposes of tyranny. When Oliver
St. John—"

B.

Stay, that will do. That was ten years and more further
on; and I want to know a great deal more about the positions
he has occupied in the mean time;—what opportunities he
has had of working out the great purposes of his life as he
originally laid them down, and how he has used them.

He entered upon life, you remember, now about twenty
years since, under the attraction of two principal objects,
with a view to which he endeavoured to shape his course.

The first,—as that which first revealed itself to his opening imagination, and for which he felt more peculiarly adapted by nature,—was the advancement of the fortunes of the human race by extending the bounds of human knowledge, clearing it from error, and directing it to right ends. The other was the advancement of the fortunes of his country by faithful service of the State.

To these two objects he was, during the whole of Elizabeth's reign, very true and constant. But he had little external furtherance for either; none at all for the first; but little for the second. Elizabeth was above fifty years old, and her hands were so full of the immediate cares of state, that even if she had had genius she had scarcely leisure to set about legislating for the human race. Burghley does not seem to have had any aspirations of the kind in him. Essex might have done something, being young, capable, aspiring, and imaginative; but not being proof against the intoxicating effects of precocious greatness, his ambition soon fell away to vulgar and personal ends; and Bacon was left to carry on that enterprize by himself without assistance, encouragement, or sympathy. For his other object he was not altogether without external advantages; for his service was used. But it was service without means, place, or authority to give it effect. Such as it was, he made the most of it by giving the best direction he could to such matters as he had to deal with. But the price he had to pay was a heavy one; for being without either lucrative office or independent fortune, he could not hold on in that career without plying his private practice at the Bar; and this (as he said) "drank too much time," which he wanted for better things. For some years he was trained on, as it were, by a single thread, which he was more than once on the point of breaking. What he wanted to do, when he found that his Court-service instead of yielding him the means of working out the great purposes of his life, was consuming his life in work of no permanent value, was to shake himself free at once, turn his fortune into an annuity, and for a while to go abroad.

A.

Was not that a feint, think you,—to quicken the Queen's movements?

B.

No, I think not. I should have thought that possible, but for a confidential letter to his brother (not preserved by himself), in which he says, "And to be plain with you"— [this was in January, 1594-5, when he was just thirty-four] —"I mean even to make the best of those small things I have, with as much expedition as may be without loss, and so sing a mass of requiem I hope abroad. For I know her Majesty's nature that *she neither careth though the whole surname of the Bacons travelled, nor of the Cecils neither.*" In this however he was mistaken; for when a rumour of his intention reached the Queen's ear, she was offended, and showed a dislike to it, which (with him) was as much as a prohibition. And I am half inclined to think—for there are some other things that countenance the supposition— that it was at this time, and not in 1588 as has been asserted, that by way of keeping him in her service she began to employ him in the business of her Learned Counsel. This, I suppose, fixed him; and he sat down quietly to make the best he could of that career. All hope of the Solicitor-ship seemed for the present at an end. And he betook himself (as I gather from some loose papers in his hand-writing which are preserved in the British Museum) vigo-rously to his private studies. Among these papers I find the rudiments of that little treatise upon the "Colours of Good and Evil," which was printed with his Essays in 1597, and afterwards incorporated into the *De Augmentis.* Traces are there too of the "*Meditationes Sacræ,*" which formed part of the same volume. And several sheets of notes, which look like hints of essays towards the supply of some of the desiderata afterwards pointed out in the "Advancement of Learning," bear witness to the activity with which his studies were now setting in the direction of his great work. The "Maxims of Law," too, must have been composed about this time. And he appears to have had a design of writing a History of England from the beginning of Henry the Eighth's reign; a commencement of which (unquestionably of his composition and written during Elizabeth's reign) is to be found in the Cabala.*

Nor did he remit his diligence in matters of State, but worked according to his opportunities. He presented the Queen with a discourse (a fragment of which is preserved) on the best means of defeating the conspiracies against her life, which were perpetually hatching among the fugitives abroad; was active in collecting and examining evidence against detected conspirators at home, and in drawing up for public satisfaction statements of the cases prosecuted; as those (for instance) of Dr. Lopez and of Edmund Squire, which are preserved; the first published after his death by Dr. Rawley; the other printed by authority at the time, and afterwards republished in Carleton's "Thankful Remembrance," where I lighted upon it for the first time not many months ago. It does not bear his name indeed, nor has it ever been ascribed to him so far as I know; but if I were to find the rough draught of it in his own handwriting, I could hardly be more certain that it is his. He continued also to give the Earl of Essex his best advice and assistance in all affairs political and personal as long as it was desired. And in Parliament he was more busy and important than ever.

A.

No more opposition to money-bills, I suppose?

B.

No more occasions that I can hear of, which would have justified opposition. The supplies that were wanted, were wanted for purposes strictly national, and the Upper House did not again interfere with the privilege of the Lower. No doubt he was strong on the Queen's side in both her last Parliaments; but I do not find that he was at all the less on the side of the people than he had been in 1593.

* See "Works," vol. vi. p. 17.

A.

Is there not some charge against him for defending monopolies?

B.

Some idle writer — (Lord Campbell, I think, in the biographical romance which he calls a life of Bacon)—has said that in the Parliament of 1601 he "took a very discreditable part" in the discussions about monopolies. But it is only one instance more of the carelessness with which such epithets are used. It is true that he opposed a bill which had for its object the abolition of monopolies; but he did not say a word in vindication of the monopolies themselves, or in deprecation of any constitutional course for getting rid of them. The case is not a bad illustration of his principles and policy in dealing with such questions; and I may as well tell you what it was.

These monopolies, you know, were licenses granted by the Crown to individuals for the sole importing or sole selling of certain articles: very bad things no doubt, except where granted, as our modern patents are, only to inventors, in order to secure them a reasonable interest in the fruits of their own labour and ingenuity. But in those days, when the voting of supplies by the Commons was not a matter of course, when the ordinary expenses of Government were expected to be supported by the fixed revenue of the Crown, and when those expenses (owing not only to the troubles of the times, but to the rapid growth of the nation in numbers, wealth, and commercial enterprise) were increasing much more rapidly than that revenue,—they were a valuable and very tempting resource. They enabled the Queen to reward servants, whose claims would otherwise have drawn hard upon the privy purse, in a very economical manner; (economical for herself, I mean, not for the public';)—for I take it most of these patentees had to pay something for their privilege, and were thus made at once thankful and profitable. Accordingly these monopolies grew fast, as ill weeds will, and began to be felt as a great grievance. Some stir had been made about them in the preceding Parliament of 1597, and the Queen had promised to inquire into the subject and remove such as were found to be abusive. But though some steps had been actually taken with that view, the troubles of Ireland and the insurrection of the Earl of Essex had suspended or diverted them, so that when the new Parliament met in the autumn of 1601, nothing had in fact been accomplished. Meanwhile the complaints of the people had grown more loud and clamorous, and the reception of the Queen by the Commons when she opened Parliament in person, and "very few said 'God save your Majesty,'" seems to show that the representatives shared the general discontent. Share it at any rate they did. And before the subsidy bill had reached a third reading, the question of monopolies was formally brought forward in the House. But it was brought forward in the shape, not of a petition, but of a "Bill *for the explanation of the Common Law* in certain cases of letters patent." Of this bill nothing remains except the title: but the object of it (as may be clearly enough inferred from the turn of the debate) was to declare these patents illegal by the Common Law. Now since they had been granted in virtue of a prerogative which was at that time confidently assumed, asserted, and exercised as indisputably belonging to the Crown, which, though not perhaps wholly undisputed was freely allowed by a large body of respectable opinion, and which had not yet been disallowed by any authority that could claim to be decisive, it was now no longer the monopolies, but the prerogative itself that was in question. Therefore to say that those who opposed the bill on that ground were defending monopolies, is as absurd as to say that the Commons themselves, when they demanded the release of a member arrested for debt, were conspiring to defraud his creditor. The arrest of a debtor, though by a process strictly legal, became in that case a breach of privilege ; the taking away of patents by act of parliament became in this case an invasion of prerogative. The passage of such a bill could only have issued in that kind of collision between the Commons and the Crown which was especially to be deprecated, and, whichever way it ended, must have created a precedent full of uncertain and dangerous consequences. This bill therefore Bacon did no doubt strenuously oppose. But did he defend the monopolies at which it was aimed? Did he maintain that the prerogative had in this instance been rightly used? Did he say that the House ought not to meddle? Far from it. "This is no stranger (he said, pointing to the bill) in this *place;* but a stranger in this *vestment.* The usual course has been to proceed by petition." Nay, he went further; for he gave his decided and emphatic support to a motion not only for petitioning the Queen to revoke such patents as were grievous, but for following it up immediately by a second petition for leave to pass a law making these patents to be "hereafter of no more force than they were by the Common Law *without the strength of her prerogative;*"—which motion, it seems, was assented to. In what respect then was the part he took discreditable? Is not this the course which at this very day (given an analogous case) any discreet reformer would follow? For example:—One prerogative still remains to the Crown,—the power of choosing its ministers. Suppose the Queen to choose for her prime minister some odious man; and suppose that in order to get rid of him, a bill were introduced in the Commons declaring the appointment void:—what would you do if you were a member?

A.

I should be for an address to the Queen, praying her to remove him.

B.

Of course you would. That is, you would do exactly what Bacon did on this occasion. But you would do it, let me tell you, at the peril of your reputation with the next ages for patriotism. For some hundred years or so hereafter, when this remnant of the royal prerogative shall have been shorn away like the rest, and a direct voice in the appoint-

ment of the minister shall be one of the constitutional
privileges of the House of Commons,—if your speech on
the supposed question should cross the path of some constitutional gentleman—

A.

Well, never mind my reputation for patriotism. I do
not mean to be famous enough to be worth gibbeting a
hundred years hence. But tell me about the monopolies.
Did the Commons get leave to pass their law.

B.

No, the Queen knew better than to let it come to that.
While the House was still hot in the debate (of which she
of course knew nothing), it so happened that she was
touched with gratitude for their forwardness with the subsidy
bill, which had luckily had precedence; whereupon sending
for the Speaker to tell the House how sensible she was of
their affection, she took occasion by the way to inform him
that complaints having reached her from various quarters of
abused and oppressive patents (which indeed her officers had
been ordered many months before to investigate, but had
been interrupted by well-known accidents of State), she had
now taken effectual steps for redress of all such grievances ;
that some should be immediately revoked, and all should be
suspended until their validity were tried by the course of
Common Law. The Speaker delivered the message to the
House. Sir Robert Cecil followed it up by a speech full of
wit and graceful raillery in the manner, but of substantial
satisfaction in the matter ; concluding with an intimation
that the Queen would receive no thanks for the promise
until it were effectually performed. The House was overcome with delight ; insisted on sending a message of thanks
immediately ; prayed that all might have access to deliver
it ; was received with that grace and majesty which was
indeed a prerogative inseparable, if not from the Crown, at
least from Queen Elizabeth; and was dismissed with a speech
which, if Shakespeare had but turned it into blank verse, we

should all know by heart. And so the clouds severed and dispersed, leaving her and her faithful Commons to part in a general sunshine. If this result were in any measure owing to Bacon, I do not see why it should be mentioned to his discredit.

A.

Nor I. And this, I think, was her last Parliament.

B.

Yes, she died about fifteen months after. But Bacon found one more opportunity before she died of doing, or trying to do, the State a service. Within a week or two after the dissolution of the Parliament came news that the Spanish forces in Ireland had been utterly defeated at Kinsale, and had left the country. This seemed to Bacon a critical juncture, and an opportunity which, if lost, might be lost for ever. And therefore, though it did not concern him otherwise than as everything concerned him in which the well-being of the State was interested, he made an effort to put the right handle of it into Sir Robert Cecil's hand, who had now the chief sway of affairs. His suggestions were conveyed in that little paper, entitled "Considerations touching the Queen's service in Ireland," which has been preserved, and the interest of which is far from obsolete. His object was to urge the importance of seizing the occasion of that decisive victory for a change of policy,—for an endeavour to make it believed and felt that the end of the Government was not simply to subdue, but to civilize. Rebellion had been effectually chastised. Now was the time,—first by a liberal proclamation of grace and pardon, then by active measures for establishing justice and order ;— as by sending a peaceable commission *ad res inspiciendas et componendas;* by appointing governors and judges with power to administer justice, summarily so as to save delays and costs, and yet as nearly as might be according to the laws of England ;—by removing all particular causes of complaint ;—by treating the English residents and the native Irish indifferently, as if they were one people ;—by counte-

nancing the Irish nobility both in Ireland and in England ;—
by tolerating ("for a time, not definite") the exercise of the
Roman Catholic religion, and trusting for the advancement
of Protestantism to the sending over of zealous and persuasive preachers and the education of the youth ;—by re-
pressing as much as possible all barbarous customs and laws';
—by a more careful selection of undertakers for the English
plantations there, and more effectual measures for keeping
the settlements together and in a condition for self-defence;
—in short, by undertaking in all their branches the true
offices of protection and government,—to enter upon a course
for the recovery of the hearts of the people.

The care of this business Bacon recommended to Cecil,
—in the summer (as I take it) of 1602,—as the most
honourable and meritorious action, "without ventosity or
popularity, that the riches of any occasion or the tide of any
opportunity could possibly minister or offer;" with what
effect I do not know. This was rather less than a year before the death of Elizabeth, and rather more than a year
after the death of his brother Anthony; when (as I have
already said) he was busily employed in paying his own and
his brother's debts, and clearing his estate from the embarrassments which during that long term of unrequited
service had been growing upon him. And so ends the old
world and begins the new.

Upon the accession of James we find him standing on the
watch, ready to lend any help which that new and anxious
crisis might call for. But everything came round quietly
and prosperously. The King had no dangers to combat, no
great alterations to make, and counsellors only too many.
And Bacon found that in the ordinary business and routine
of government, his help was not wanted.

At this point therefore he was free to readjust his
position according to the occasions and exigencies of the
time; which presented some new aspects. His two principal
ends,—the service of his country and the service of his kind,
—had still their old hold upon him; as strongly as when he

took his original direction twenty-three years before. But his outward conditions were changed in two main features. On the one hand, instead of nineteen he was now forty-two years old; and though competency of fortune, civil station, and relief from time-absorbing drudgery, were not less important than before to the furtherance of his work, yet he could not so well afford to waste more years in waiting for them. His day was far spent; it was time to make the best of such means as he had without further delay, and to set about it. On the other hand, the character of the new King seemed to promise more sympathy with that work than he had hitherto found in high places, and thereby encouraged him to prompt exertion. He might well hope that a word well-spoken in that auspicious season,—the spring-time of a monarch still in the prime of life, devoted to peace, sympathising largely with the interests of mankind, and eminent even among learned men in a learned age for proficiency in all kinds of learning,—would turn James's ambition into this direction, and give him a king for a fellow-labourer. Under this impression no doubt it was that he now made it his aim to "meddle as little as might be in the King's causes,"—to engage himself in public business no further than his professional and parliamentary duties required,—and (by way of giving an early foretaste and announcement of what he was about) a little to change the course and order of his work, and bring it forward in a shape more popular and rather less complete than that which he had originally contemplated, and in which he still intended that it should ultimately stand. The "Advancement of Learning," which was published in 1605, less than three years after James's accession, was begun, as I conjecture (for I cannot positively affirm it), about this time.

A.

What makes you think so?

B.

Several reasons concur; but perhaps the one which comes nearest to a proof is this. In sending a copy of the

"Advancement" to his friend Tobie Matthew, he says, "I have now taught that child to go, *at the swaddling whereof you were.*" And it appears from the same letter that Matthew had seen the first book only, not the second. Now Tobie Matthew sat in the Parliament of 1604, and was employed on so many committees together with Bacon, that they must have met nearly every day. But in the beginning of the following April he left England, and did not return till after the work was published. These circumstances therefore would exactly suit my conjecture. Bacon's incessant occupation during the whole of 1604 sufficiently accounts for his not having finished more than the first book that year; while his comparative leisure during the spring, summer, and autumn of 1605 might very well enable him to finish the rest before winter. Moreover from the statement in the "Novum Organum" sixteen years after, that the first part of the "Instauratio" (which is the part handled in the "Advancement") was still *wanting,* it is clear that the English treatise did not form part of the original design, but was a kind of interloper. And upon the whole I am persuaded that he hurried it into the world in its present shape that he might lose no time in awakening James's interest in the subject, and if possible obtaining his co-operation; which if he had succeeded in doing, I do not know why a greater movement for the recovery of man's dominion over nature than the world has yet seen,—a more successful enterprise than the world has yet learned to believe possible,—should not have begun 200 years ago. But (not to wander into a speculation of this kind, which indeed I am not qualified to handle) it will hardly be denied that this deviation from his general plan (if deviation it was) was a judicious one; and that this treatise forms of itself (even if he had had nothing else to show) a sufficient and indeed a splendid account of his employment during those three years. And yet so far was this from being the case,—so many and so important were his other labours during those years,—that they might fairly claim to have the same thing said of them; for had there been no "Advancement of Learning" to boot, they

would have made up by themselves an ample account of
work well done or endeavours well aimed.

For if you believe with me that he lived under the constant attraction of two distinct purposes,—distinct though
not discordant,—you must believe that throughout his life
they were perpetually crossing one another; and never more
so than at this opening of a new reign, which was far too
critical and too favourable a time to be let pass without an
attempt to set many other things in the right way besides
the study of Nature. The union of the two kingdoms : the
pacification of church controversies; the right direction of
affairs in Ireland ; the harmonious adjustment of the relation between the Crown and the Commons ; were matters
now of urgent consideration, which, if they lost the advantage
of this tide, might be (as in fact they for the most part were)
stranded for generations. And upon a careful examination
of their history, I suspect it would appear that if any of
them were not taken up at the right time and by the right
handle, it was not Bacon's fault.

A.

I am afraid I must trouble you for particulars.

B.

By all means, if you do not grudge the time.

First then for the Union. Bacon's observation upon his
first interview with the King was, that he seemed to be
"hastening to a mixture of both kingdoms and nations
faster perhaps than policy would conveniently bear." And
the first thing with which he greeted the King at his
entrance (using with a discreet boldness the privilege of a
scholar, for he had not then the privilege of speaking in
any other capacity) was, a " Brief Discourse of the happy
Union between England and Scotland." This paper was
written indeed (as he says himself) "scholastically and
speculatively, not actively or politicly, as he held it fit for
him at that time," when the King's desire had not yet been
declared, and he had not himself been used or trusted in

the service. It is however aimed nearly enough at the
particular case to suggest the principles which ought to
govern the attempt, and the cautions to be observed in
entering upon it; especially in these two main points: 1st,
that the object to be sought was not simply the putting the
two kingdoms together, but the making the two into one,—
the true mingling and uniting of them under a new form;
and 2ndly, that perfect mixture can only take place under
two conditions;—it must be left to time and nature, for
hurrying would but hinder and disturb it; and the greater
must draw the less, or the union would not be permanent.
And by way of historical examples, he holds up the Roman
unions, particularly the union between the Romans and the
Sabines, as the examples to imitate; and the union of
Arragon with Castile and of Judah with Israel as the
examples to avoid.

A.

Suggestions of that kind would be valuable enough, I
dare say; but you are surely not going to hold up the
proceedings with regard to the Union in James's reign as
a specimen of successful statesmanship?

B.

No; nor am I going to inquire how far these suggestions
were attended to, or how far the tardy accomplishment of
the Union was owing to some such error in the first intention as this discourse was meant to preclude. Such an
inquiry would be interesting, but it would hold us too long,
and to say the truth, I am not well enough read in the
actual history of the Union between England and Scotland
to attempt it. I mention the thing at present only as
showing how constantly Bacon's eye was fixed upon the
largest interests of the times, and how the services which
he *went out of his way* to perform or to offer were always for
ends truly public and patriotic. In this instance his offer
was as well accepted as it was well intended; for in all the
proceedings which took place on this subject in the House

of Commons, in all their conferences with the Lords and audiences of the King, he appears to have been by common consent elected as the chief speaker. In the selection of Commissioners to treat of a Union and prepare a measure for the next Parliament, the choice of the Commons fell upon him first of all the Commoners; and in the labours of that Commission he appears to have sustained a principal (if not *the* principal) part. And if you like to know how far this was from being a mere exercise of the speculative understanding, as the reviewer seems to consider it,—the mere "discovery of many irresistible arguments in favour of such a scheme,"—you must first read Bacon's own analysis (in the paper which he drew up for the King immediately after the close of the session) of the questions which had to be considered and the difficulties which had to be overcome;—you must then try and imagine to yourself what kind of task it really was, to devise, prepare, mature, and propose an arrangement for such a union between England and Scotland as should unite the hearts and affections of the two people,—to propose it, I say, in such a manner that it should have any chance of passing the judgments and prejudices of a Parliament of Englishmen on one side and a Parliament of Scotchmen on the other;— you must next run your eye through the Journals of our own House of Commons, observing the sort of obstructions through which it had actually to make its way; the number of meetings of the Committee of the House of Commons, of reports from the Committee of the House of Commons, of debates upon the report from the Committee of the House of Commons;—of messages from the Lords desiring conference, of debates whether they should confer, what points they should confer about, what instructions they should give;—of conferences, of reports of conferences, &c., &c., from "Sir Francis Bacon's report (13th April, 1604) of the thirteen objections against the Union in name," to his "finishing of a very long report" (2nd March, 1606-7)— too long to be got through in one day—" of the conference with the Lords on the point of general naturalization;" at which time, by the way, his health had suffered so much from his work that he was forced to "pray the House that at other times they would use some other and not *oppress* him with their favours;"—and finally you must bear in mind, that besides the business of working such a measure as this through the Houses of Parliament (a task which indeed proved after all too hard to be accomplished), the preliminary task of guiding the labours of the Commissioners to a successful termination (itself no easy one), which was accomplished with remarkable unanimity and despatch by the close of the year 1604, rested principally upon his industry and address.

A.

Well, but what was the use of it all? No great matter came of it.

B.

True. But we are considering, not the results of his life to other people,—I could give a fair account of them too,—but the life itself as illustrative of his character and purposes. The fig-tree was cursed because it bore no fruit, not because men threw the fruit away. If you would form to yourself a true image of the man and his life, you must not pass such a work as this over as if it were nothing, merely because nothing came of it, but must endeavour to let the labour and the endeavour have their due impression and importance. Not however that I claim for him any special and peculiar merit on account of this service, beyond that of diligence, judgment, and an eye to the larger interests of the State. I do not say that there was any extraordinary virtue in doing what he ought to do on this occasion; I only say that it *was* what he ought to do,—a worthy object well aimed at and strenuously endeavoured after; something much more than making a brilliant speech in the House of Commons;—and in that respect of a piece with the rest of his life, according to my view of it,—so far as we have gone.

A.

Nobody finds any fault with him for this that I know of. But you are to remember that if it was good public service, it was good court-service too. There must have been prospect of a vacancy in the Solicitorship, and it was a good road to that.

B.

No doubt, no doubt. There must have been a prospect, more or less remote, when he began; nay, before he got half-through, there was an actual vacancy. But if that was what his service aimed at, he was disappointed. His biographers do not mention it; but it is true that on the 28th of October (the day before the Commissioners of the Union began their labours) Sir Thomas Fleming, the then Solicitor, was advanced to the office of Chief Baron, and the vacant Solicitorship was bestowed on Serjeant Dodderidge.

A.

And what did Bacon say to that?

B.

I never heard that he said anything. Not a word, I think, is on record from which it can be inferred that he either asked for the place for himself, (he was probably too intent upon his business to be attending to his fortunes,) or uttered a syllable of complaint upon being passed over. And from the records which remain of the course he was pursuing both before and after, no one, I am sure, would guess that anything had occurred between to discontent him. Secretly disappointed he may very well have been. He was now ten years older than when the world had voted him worthy of a higher place; and the labours and distinctions of the last session must have both tested his ability and raised his reputation to the height. To judge from the continual recurrence of his name in the Journals as selected for all the most delicate and important services, he must have been generally recognized as the foremost man in the House of Commons. He was forty-four years old; and though his debts were now cleared off, his income, as we have seen, was still a very narrow one for a man in his position, with objects so vast and pretensions so undeniable. Disappointed, therefore, I dare say he was. But according to his estimate of life and its duties, no private disappointment could be a worthy motive to him for slackening. his endeavours to promote what he conceived to be a great public object. You will find therefore that whatever he may have felt, he continued to act as if nothing had happened.

But all this is from our present purpose. I tell you that I cite his conduct in this matter of the Union, not as evincing any extraordinary virtue; it involved no sacrifice except of health and leisure, and it was, as you suggest, the road to preferment, though it was not undertaken upon any bargain for preferment, and though it did not at present lead to any; I cite it only as showing that he still continued constant to the greater interests of his country, not to be wearied in pursuing them, and—though I will not say not looking for a reward (which he might surely do without blame)—yet not to be turned aside, slackened, or disgusted, when the natural reward did not come. And what more do you ask of a man? It is not in going unrewarded that the virtue consists, but in going *right* whether rewarded or not.

I have not half done yet. The union of the kingdoms was only one of the great interests which were now calling upon him for help. The next was the state of the Church, which had now a fresh chance of being recovered from its distractions and restored to a sounder condition. And upon this subject also he addressed a discourse to the King on his first coming in, which (like almost all his writings), though addressed to the immediate exigencies of his day, is scarcely less applicable to our own.

A.

Which side was he on ?

B.

On the side of true religion and good government, which included the interests of all sides,—therefore flattered the prejudices of none. It may seem strange, perhaps, that he should intermeddle at all in these religious differences, seeing that they were out of his province, and that the part he took was so little fitted to ingratiate him with either party. But the circumstances under which he entered life must naturally have led him to take a deep interest in the subject. From his earliest youth he must have heard a great deal of the rising body of Nonconformists. Cambridge, during his residence there, was agitated by the controversy between them and the High-Churchmen. When he returned from France he found them rising rapidly into importance. They had among them many of the most diligent, zealous, pious, and learned members of the Church, and had obtained a strong interest in the House of Commons. The abuses they complained of were many of them real and grave, the removal of which would have been a great public benefit. The rest were for the most part matters of outward form and ceremony, not worth quarreling about; yet the cause of a quarrel which was fast leading to a serious rupture. The Parliament in which he first sat, being then only twenty-four years old, was much occupied with a petition for the reformation of abuses in Church government (famous as the "sixteen-fold petition"), in which the Commons wanted the Lords to join, and which led to a great deal of discussion. The particulars of the debates we do not know, and he was too young a member probably to take any active part in them, but he was on that account all the more likely to be an attentive and anxious listener. There he must have heard the particulars of these abuses amply set forth and vehemently disputed. He must have heard of parishes served by ministers unlearned and incompetent, or not served at all;—of men of the greatest learning and the purest lives suspended from their ministry for objecting to wear a surplice, or for refusing to subscribe

articles newly devised, not imposed by the statutes of the
realm, not touching any vital or essential points of doctrine;
—of the gravest functions of the Bishops delegated to
officials and commissaries; — of ministers compelled to
answer on oath to any questions which the Bishops might
think fit to ask, either out of their own vague suspicions or
out of the suggestions of common rumour;—of excommunication abused into an ordinary instrument for enforcing
slight points of discipline or exacting fees;—of the suppression by authority of those conferences and exercises
among the clergy which were best fitted to instruct and
practise them in the duties of their calling;—of non-residents
and pluralists;—and much else of the kind. He must also
have heard measures for the redress of these defects and
abuses proposed and argued in no immoderate or unreasonable spirit; must have seen the grounds upon which the
authorities resisted them; must have formed his own opinion
upon the merits of the controversy and the issue to which it
was inevitably leading. What that issue must be it was not
difficult to foretell. The principal demands of the main
body of reformers were as yet indeed moderate and just and
involved no violent alteration; but the extremes were already
beginning to assail the very constitution of the Church, and
to erect within it a government by synods,—that is to say,
a government essentially democratical *within* a government
essentially monarchical;—a most perilous proceeding, because
as the two could never have gone at the same pace, one
must before long have overthrown the other ;—and it must
have been clear enough to such a judgment as his, that
unless the Church could distinguish and detach the moderate
from the immoderate, they would be continually drawing
closer together and making a common cause of it. All this
he must have seen upon his first entrance into public life.
It is not strange therefore if to his watching and understanding eyes these Church controversies seemed (as the
events of the next century proved that they indeed were)
the gravest and most critical question of the times. It was
in fact the infancy of the memorable struggle between the

High Church and the Puritans ; and upon the wise handling of it at this time hung the question whether the nation should proceed peaceably through stages of progressive reform or be shaken to its centre by a struggle between the opposing principles.

The authorities of the Church, seeing no further than authorities commonly do, saw nothing in the Puritans except a turbulent faction, which was to be suppressed in its beginnings ; on that old English principle,—which though continually compelled to shift its ground, could never yet in England be taught to understand its error, and had not then been taught even to understand its helplessness,—that concession would only embolden them to make further demands. But Bacon knew better. His own mother was a Puritan, sympathising with the cause from the bottom of her noble old soul; and well he must have known that, however poor and narrow the creed, there burned at the centre of that cause a fire of authentic faith, which an attempt to suppress by denying it vent might raise into a conflagration, but could never put out. The one chance for the Church was to understand this herself, and to understand it in time ; and thereupon to seek, by casting out all that was evil in herself, to assimilate and draw into her system all that was good in them ;—a course which, had it been commenced soon enough and judiciously followed out, would probably have converted the stream that not many years after burst in upon her like a torrent and flooded all her chambers, into a source of continual supply, health, and refreshment.

If these were Bacon's views in 1584, the events of the years immediately following must have strongly confirmed them. The resolution of the Government to alter nothing was followed by fiercer agitations, bolder demands, more settled disaffection, and a breach growing every day wider. It was then (about the year 1589) that he stepped out of his way to volunteer that advice upon this subject which I have already mentioned, and if possible to turn the thoughts of the contending parties into the proper channel.

" Ye are brethren," he said; " why strive ye? . . . . . Our

controversies we all know and confess are not of the highest nature; they do not touch the high mysteries of the faith or the great parts of the worship of God. .... We contend about ceremonies and things indifferent; about the extern policy and government of the Church; in which kind if we would but remember that the ancient and true bonds of unity are *one faith, one baptism,* and not *one ceremony, one policy;* if we would but observe the league that is penned by our Saviour, *He that is not against us is with us;* if we could but comprehend that saying, *Differentiæ rituum commendant unitatem doctrinæ,*—the diversities of ceremonies do set forth the unity of doctrine; and that *Habet Religio quæ sunt æternitatis, habet quæ sunt temporis,*— Religion hath parts which belong to eternity, and parts which pertain to time; and if we did but know the virtue of silence and slowness to speak, commended by St. James;—our controversies would of themselves close up and grow together."

He implored both parties, but especially the Church party as being then the stronger, to consider how far they had been carried away in the heat of controversy from their first position, and how many things there were unsound and untenable in their case as it now stood.

" Again, to my Lords the Bishops I say that it is hard for them to avoid blame in the opinion of an indifferent person, in standing so precisely upon altering nothing. *Leges novis legibus non recreatæ acescunt,*—Laws not refreshed with new laws wax sour. *Qui mala non permutat in bonis non perseverat,*—Without changing the ill a man cannot continue the good. To take away many abuses supplanteth not good orders but establisheth them. *Morosa moris retentio res turbulenta est æque ac novitas,*—A contentious retaining of custom is a turbulent thing as well as innovation. A good husbandman is ever pruning in his vineyard; not unseasonably, not unskilfully, but lightly he ever findeth somewhat to do. We have heard of no offers from the Bishops of bills in Parliament, which no doubt, proceeding from them to whom it properly belongeth, would have everywhere received acceptation. Their own constitutions and orders have reformed little. Is nothing amiss? Can any man defend the use of excommunication as a base process to lacquey up and down for fees,— it being a precursory judgment of the latter day? Is there no mean to train and nurse up ministers (for the yield of the Universities will not serve though they were never so well governed)

—to train them, I say, not to preach, (for that every man confidently adventureth to do,) but to preach soundly and to handle the Scriptures with wisdom and judgment ? .... Other things might be spoken of. I pray God to inspire the Bishops with fervent love and care of his people, and that they may not so much urge things in controversy as things out of controversy, which all men confess to be gracious and good."

This and much more in the same strain he had pressed upon the attention of the Church at that time ; fifteen years before the time we are now speaking of. But the city was not yet in such jeopardy as to bethink itself of the poor wise man who by his wisdom might have delivered it. The poor man's wisdom was despised and his words were not heard.

A new reign offered a new chance. "The first impression continueth long, and when men's minds are most in expectation and suspense, then are they best wrought and managed." Now was the time, or never. Another stroke of the clock and the time would never be. And now once more he tried the chance of his words. After rapidly running over some of the principal arguments, which he had formerly urged more at large, in favour of a reformation within the Church (for in all Bacon's proposals and ideas of reform there is a latent condition that the reform shall be from within), he proceeds to recommend certain particular points for consideration. The substance of his recommendations I cannot give in much smaller compass than the work itself. Like all his writings on business, it is all substance. But I should like to give you some notion of the scope, at least, and tendency of them ; because I think it will convince you that a man who saw the question in that light must have been really anxious to see things put in that train ; must have felt it a kind of duty to do what he could himself to that end ; and (how much soever he may have been longing, as I have no doubt he was, to be at his Novum Organum and his experiments) could not have felt justified in indulging the inclination, and sitting down to show the next ages how they might improve their fortunes, while he saw the most precious part of the inheritance which they were to derive from the present age going to the dogs before his eyes. A true apprehension of this will make a most important difference in your estimate of his character, and will reconcile many seeming inconsistencies by showing that they were in fact only the natural branches and developments of one consistent purpose. Do not lightly believe that the hours which he spent in efforts to serve the State were hours of weakness in which the temptations of vulgar ambition triumphed over his better nature and wiser judgment. The time employed by a prime minister in ordering the affairs of his family—you do not consider it mis-spent because it might have been employed in improving the public fortunes. Why should you suppose that the days which a philosopher devotes to the immediate concerns of his own generation are misemployed, because the interests of one generation are small compared with those of the human race? It may sound very heroical to sit apart and despise what the rest of mankind are fighting for; but it is not really so. It is only your amateur hero who is above the business of his day; your true hero sets his hand to the work.

A.

Well, well; let me first hear what he did for his own generation, and then we will consider whether it was worthy of him.

B.

What he did,—or what he tried to do. A man who would *do* all he can must *aim* at much that he can not.

Well, this paper (which is entitled "Certain Considerations touching the better Pacification and Edification of the Church of England") is not so much a treatise as a memorial of business;—a collection of the several points which required consideration with a view to practical reform : small points therefore as well as great; and taken in the order best suited for that purpose; consequently not the best for ours. For what concerns us, it will be better to break the matter into different divisions.

Now I gather from it that the troubles and dangers of the Church in that day grew in Bacon's opinion from defects in four principal departments : from defects in the constitution of its government; from want of adequate resources; from imperfect or injudicious methods of providing for its greater and more essential objects; and from needless strictness and pertinacity in insisting upon points indifferent or not essential.

For the first: the Bishops were in the habit of exercising their authority *alone ;* whereas he conceived that according to the primitive and true constitution of the Church, the Dean and Chapter were the Bishop's *council ;* and that the Bishop ought, in all his more important functions, to act with their advice, as a king with the advice of his privy council ;—a change which would have gone far to satisfy one important clause in the Petition of 1584; with this great advantage over the suggestion of the petitioners,—that it would have fitted better into the existing framework of the constitution, and might have been introduced at once, silently and without disturbance.

They were also in the habit of exercising their authority *by deputy ;* which (as in an office of trust and confidence) he considered unallowable; thinking that in all causes that "required a spiritual science and discretion in respect of their nature or of the scandal,"—(tithe and testamentary causes he set apart as being in their nature temporal)—no audience should be given but by the Bishop himself in council.

Moreover, the forms of ecclesiastical proceeding gave the Bishops a larger power in examining parties upon their oath than was allowed by the Common Law; and this (which had been abused into a great practical grievance and a kind of Protestant Inquisition) he thought ought to be limited.

These, together with some plan not explained in detail, for adding strength to the general Council of the Clergy,

were the principal reforms which he wished in what may bo
called the Constitution of the Church ;—reforms which seem
simple and obvious enough, but which would have had
practical consequences perhaps more important than any
man can guess.

For the second point. The insufficiency of the resources
of the Church he speaks of as a thing generally felt and
admitted :—

"That the case of this Church *de facto*" (he says) "is such
that there is a want in the Church patrimony, is confessed.
For the principal places, namely the Bishops' livings, are in
some particulars insufficient, and therefore enforced to be supplied by toleration of *Commendams*, things in themselves unfit
and ever held of no good repute. But as for the benefices and
pastors' places, it is too manifest that very many of them are
very weak and penurious."

The cause of this insufficiency was the number of impro-
priations (to the value, he says, of more than ten subsidies)
given away from the Church in Henry the Eighth's time,
and so given away that it was utterly impossible for the
Church to claim them back again. The remedy, he hints,
but without entering into particulars, was to be looked for
from Parliament. For as he holds Henry the Eighth's
Parliaments responsible for the deficiency, so he holds all
succeeding Parliaments bound in some sort to make it good,
and to restore the patrimony of the Church to a competency.

Thirdly, with regard to the internal regulations of the
Church, the cardinal defect (and one which was also urged
in the Petition of 1584) was the want of a good system for
training up competent preachers and excluding incompetent
ones. The first he proposes to remedy, in accordance with
the prayer of that petition, by a revival of the disused
exercise of " prophesying."

A.

What might that be? The defect still flourishes, and
we are still in want of the revival, or the discovery, of something to correct it. I should like to hear Bacon's ideas on
that point.

B.

Well, the explanation is not long. You shall have it in his own words.—It would be desirable (he says) to revive—

" that good exercise which was practised in the Church for some years and afterwards put down (by order indeed from the Church, in respect of some abuses thereof inconvenient for those times, and yet against the advice and opinion of one of the greatest and gravest prelates of this land) "—

This was Archbishop Grindel, whose expostulations about it to Queen Elizabeth you may see in Fuller's " Church History.

—" and was commonly called prophesying; which was this,—that the ministers within a precinct did meet upon a week-day in some principal town, where there was some ancient grave minister that was president, and an auditory admitted of gentlemen or other persons of leisure; then every minister successively, beginning with the youngest, did handle one and the same piece of Scripture, spending severally some quarter of an hour or better, and in the whole some two hours; and so the exercise being begun and concluded with prayer, and the president giving a text for the next meeting, the assembly was dissolved. And this was, as I take it, a fortnight's exercise; which was in mine opinion the best way to frame and train up preachers to handle the word of God as it ought to be handled that hath been practised. For we see orators have their declamations, lawyers have their moots, logicians their sophisms, and every practice of science hath an erudition and initiation before men come to the life; only preaching, which is the worthiest, and wherein it is most danger to do amiss, wanteth an introduction and is ventured and rushed upon at the first. But unto this exercise of prophecy I would wish these two additions: the one, that after this exercise, which is in some sort public, there were immediately a private meeting of the same ministers, where they might brotherly admonish the one the other, and especially the elder sort the younger, of anything that had passed in the conference in matter or manner unsound or uncomely; and, in a word, might mutually use such advice, instruction, comfort, or encouragement, as occasion might minister (for public reprehension were to be debarred). The other addition that I mean is, that the same exercises were used in the Universities for

young divines before they presumed to preach, as well as in
the country for ministers. For they have in some colleges an
exercise called a Common-place, which can in no degree be
so profitable, being but the speech of one man at one time."

There you have Bacon's proposition for educating
preachers in their business. What do you say to it? Might
the Church, think you, still profit by the hint?

A.

That is a question not easily answered on the sudden.
If you look to the progress of opinion, you would say No;
for opinion seems to run the other way. Lawyers have
given up their moots; orators their declamations; logicians
and their sophisms are alike obsolete; only the names and
forms remain (or did remain in my time) at the Universities;
empty ceremonial observances which do not even affect to
be of any use. And yet, on the other hand, if you look to
the fruits, you would hardly say that the change in this
respect has worked well. Nay, it would seem too that the
want is practically felt by those who wish to learn, though
not recognized by those who have to teach: witness in all
places of education the springing up of debating-societies,
which are nothing but schools for practice, only without the
schoolmaster. .

But we shall never get this review despatched if we stop
to reform the Church by the way. I see what you mean.
And I grant that the object Bacon had in view was great,
and the occasion pressing; for preaching was not so harmless a thing then as it is now, and the times had not so much
leisure to wait upon the leisure of the Bishops.—Well, and
how did he propose to exclude incompetent preachers?

B.

That was simple enough; only by taking better care to
ascertain the competency of those that were admitted;—
making ordination a more careful and solemn matter:—that
is, by taking order (it is best to use his own words) for—

"a more exact probation and examination of ministers;
namely, that the Bishops do not ordain alone, but by advice;

and then that ancient holy order of the Church might be re-vived, by which the Bishop did ordain ministers but at four set times of the year, which were called *Quatuor Tempora*, which are now called *Ember weeks*; it being thought fit to accompany so high an action with general fasting and prayer and sermons, and all holy exercises; and the names likewise of those that were to be ordained were published some days before their ordination, to the end exceptions might be taken if just cause were."

A suggestion to this effect also, or something like it, was contained in the Petition of 1584.

A.

That of the *Quatuor Tempora* was of course meant for times when fasting had still some meaning in it.

B.

Yes; translate it into the language and spirit of our own, and it will be—I do not very well know what—but whatever outward observances are best fitted to impress upon the occasion a character of gravity, solemnity, and sanctity.

A.

The Bishops might give four dinners.

B.

Hush! The business we are talking of was high earnest in its own day.

It appears also that besides the parishes which were served by preachers not properly qualified, there were many that had not the benefit of any preacher at all. For remedy of this evil, he would have had an end put to non-residence, and some arrangement made (until the number of preachers could be sufficiently increased) either for such a permutation of benefices as might enable each preacher to attend more than one parish, or for the appointment of some preachers " with a more general charge to supply and serve by turn parishes unfurnished."

Then, in addition to these deficiencies, there were some particular abuses (as especially that of excommunication) which brought the Church into disrepute; and some stumbling-blocks to nice consciences that were needlessly insisted on; as especially the cap and surplice, which being objected to by the dissentient party as superstitious, the Church must needs enforce by articles of subscription!—grave matters both in the year 1603, however worn out of date now; the one fallen from a living judgment to a dead letter; the other from a point of conscience to a point of foppery, which the authorities of the Church cannot do better than leave to find its own way to the limbo of vanity; but questions then of most serious import, pregnant with all distraction, commotion, and civil war.

A.

The difficulty there, I suppose, was not in devising the remedy, but in persuading the authorities to apply it. There could be no difficulty in putting a stop to the abuse of excommunication, or in ceasing to. quarrel with ministers otherwise pious and competent on account of the cap and surplice.

B.

Just so. Excommunication, as the greatest of earthly judgments, he would have had strictly confined to the greatest causes, and would have had proceed under the gravest forms; some ordinary process being allowed to the Ecclesiastical Courts for dealing with offences of lesser degree. And as for the cap and surplice, he would have had them treated as matters indifferent, which had nothing to do with the unity of the Church, but only with uniformity; therefore as questions of policy, not of religion. He would have had them tolerated, not by connivance, but authority; and the subscription reserved for its proper office, which was to "bind in the unity of the Faith," not to enforce points of outward government.

His remarks upon the Ritual, which was the fourth point,

are scarcely worth dwelling upon. Our modern Prayer-book might almost have sat for his sketch of the Liturgy as it should be. And the parts which he points out as objectionable have either been altered or become so familiar that the objection is obsolete. At the time they were all points (no doubt) which nice consciences or superstitious apprehensions started at; as in fact they would do at this day if they were new questions; and his policy was to remove all things to which that objection applied, so long as they were in themselves indifferent. Some good people, for instance, were scandalized at the word *priest ;*—then why not use *minister,* at which no one was scandalized? Others objected to the form of general absolution ; why retain it,—being, as it was, "both unnecessary and improper "?

A.

Does he say, or can you tell me, how that form of general absolution ever came there ? I have always wondered what was the use of it,—especially as forbidden to be read by anybody but a priest. For I could never make out that it was anything more than the assertion of a fact, which would be just as much a fact if announced by the deacon as by the priest, or by the clerk as by the deacon. It is right, no doubt, on account of its solemnity, that it should be read by the highest functionary present; just as the blessing is ; but when no priest is there, why the deacon should not be allowed to read it, I never could understand.

B.

Bacon's opinion is, that it was "allowed at the first *in a kind of spiritual discretion ;* because the Church thought the people could not be suddenly weaned from the conceit of *assoiling,* to which they had been so long accustomed."

A.

A real rag then of the scarlet woman? What a noise there would be about it if it were a new thing now !

B.

Yes; but pray do not wake it, being so happily asleep as it is!

Well then—the practice of the Church in those days seems to have caused some misgivings as to the meaning and purpose of the Confirmation Service; as if it were meant for a *Confirmation* of the previous *Baptism ;*—an idea shocking to the Puritans, and indeed not intentionally countenanced by the Bishops. Upon this point he suggests that there was no difference, but only a misunderstanding; the accidental alterations of time and circumstance having made it seem like a "subsequent to Baptism," when it was in fact only "an inducement to the Communion;" and the misunderstanding seems to have been set right at the time.

A.

Was he right in that? I think our modern authorities, —Palmer in his *Origines Liturgicæ*, Bingham in his *Christian Antiquities*, and Jeremy Taylor in his *Worthy Communicant,*—are all against him.

B.

I cannot pretend to decide that question myself. But I doubt whether there be any of our modern authorities that know more of the matter than Bacon did. I fancy the Hampton Court people were all with him.

A real abuse (which also appears to have been set right) was the practice of private baptism by women and lay persons. And he makes two criticisms upon the Marriage Service,—of little importance in themselves, but worth mentioning, as illustrative, the one of his own taste, the other of the progress of the age in refinement and conventional delicacy. If the question were a modern one, I think we should all agree with him on both; viz. first, that the putting on of the ring is "a ceremony *not grave ;* specially to be made (as the words make it) an essential part of the action ; "—and secondly, that "some of the other words are noted in common speech to be not so decent and fit."

These however (as I said) are matters of small interest for us now. If they were new they would raise great disputes ; but they are above two hundred years old, we are all used to them, and they do very well. No judicious man would care to disturb them. What I wish you to remark and bear in mind is, the general purpose and principal features of this paper ; as showing the spirit in which Bacon worked on all occasions when he went out of his way to take a part. My own impression is that it was not only well meant, but well aimed ;·and that if his advice had been followed, the succeeding centuries would have had quite a different history. For as in differences between neighbours, the question whether two families shall be friends or enemies for years to come, depends upon the temper of the first answer; so in the larger theatres of the world, the entertainment of the first motion for reform decides whether there shall be peace or war half a century after.

A.

And what did your friend the King say to these suggestions ?

B.

Judging from Fuller's account of the Hampton Court conference, I think he was disposed to adopt some of the smaller ones ; but being still, as it were, in the honeymoon of his new reign, and overflowing with kindness towards episcopacy, he allowed himself to be easily overruled by the Bishops, and upon the whole, one may say that they were thrown away. This was indeed James's own special province, and he managed it after his own fashion, which as in most other things was rather well-meant than effectual. The Bishops had their way in the end, and the agitations went on. It was not however till after James's death that the Church began to go with full career in the opposite direction ; and you know what was the end of that. In the

mean time the credit which Bacon retained with the Church
reform party in the House of Commons may be taken as a
strong argument in favour of the policy which he recommended. In the conference which was held between the
two Houses in 1606 concerning ecclesiastical grievances,
the setting forth of the first head, which related to the
silenced ministers, was intrusted to him; so also was the
report;—and these were parts far too important to be assigned to any one who was supposed to be lukewarm in the
cause. Nor do I find that he ever declined from his
original opinion; to the justice of which, indeed, the events
which followed must have been daily bearing witness.—But
that was after. At present I want to keep within the first
year or two of James's reign, while most of these questions
of state were in a manner new.

A.

You mean when they were reopened upon a clear stage.

B.

Yes; while they were *res integra*, as they say.
Well. The opportunity of applying effectual remedies
to this, the main seat of the disorder under which the State
laboured, was, as I say, lost. That Hampton Court conference—(an ill-advised measure, which I will answer for it
Bacon never advised or hoped any good from),—was rather
calculated to drive the disease inwards. There was no hope
for the present of a cure; and it was all the more necessary
to keep the patient free from other complaints and from
accidents of weather. If the divisions of the Church were
not to be healed, divisions in State might yet be avoided.
The King and the Puritan clergy had parted with mutual
dissatisfaction. But the King and Parliament might still
meet on good terms and proceed harmoniously. Not without wary steering, though; for there were some dangerous
rocks in the way. Parliament met on the 19th of March,
1603-4; and in the very first week behold breakers ahead!
The election of Sir Francis Goodwin for Buckinghamshire

(which finds a conspicuous place in all histories as an important landmark in the constitution) threw the Commons at once in collision with the Court of Chancery, the House of Lords, and the King himself. And the management of the matter is well worth considering,—as an example from which the Commons might have learned how to carry all their other points of constitutional privilege at once most rapidly, most effectually, and with least disturbance.

A.

I hope you are going to explain particulars, for I remember no more of the matter than that it ended in a recognition of the right of the House to judge of returns to its own writs.

B.

All the particulars which are necessary to make what I am going to say intelligible, are easily told :—

In the Proclamation for calling the new Parliament, a clause had been inserted forbidding the election of outlaws. Sir Francis Goodwin, who had been outlawed, was elected for Buckinghamshire ; but the return being refused by the Clerk of the Crown on the strength of that clause, a new writ was issued from the Chancery, and Sir John Fortescue, a privy councillor, was elected instead. This was before Parliament met. Immediately upon its meeting the case was brought before the House of Commons ; upon a full consideration of the question, it was resolved that Sir Francis had been duly elected ; the Clerk of the Crown was ordered to file the first return ; and Sir Francis took the oaths and his seat. In the debate which ended in this resolution Bacon took a prominent part, but no record remains of what he said ; nor do we know even which side he took, only that we may infer from the subsequent proceedings that he was not dissentient. This was on Friday, March 23rd ; and thus far they were at issue only with the Court of Chancery, upon the question of jurisdiction,—to which of them it belonged to judge of the validity of the return.

But on the following Tuesday the Lords desired a conference upon the subject. This the Commons declined; as conceiving that it did not stand with the honour or order of the House to give account of any of their proceedings. So now they were at issue with the Lords. But this was not the worst; for the same day came another message, signifying that the King, having been made acquainted with the matter, and finding himself touched in honour, desired that there might be a conference on it between the two Houses. So now they were fairly in collision with all three; the Chancery whose judgment they had reversed, the Lords with whom they had refused to confer, and the King who had taken part with the Lords. Upon this, they moved for access to the King himself, which was granted the next morning; when the Speaker, attended by a select committee, explained to him their whole proceeding and the grounds of it; heard his answer to the several points (for new as the question was to him he argued it himself, and argued it they say with great ability), and received his charge; which was that they should first resolve among themselves, then confer with the Judges, and report to the Council.

And now came the real difficulty. For they were now engaged in a direct dispute with the King himself, not merely upon the question of conferring with the Lords, but upon the entire constitutional question and each several point of it. And now what shall they do?

A.

I suppose there is no doubt that the King was in the wrong?

B.

There is no doubt now; because the doubt which then was—(a considerable one, seeing that all the Judges were on the King's side; and as we all assume that whenever he differed from them there was nothing to be said for him, we ought to suppose that there was something to be said for him when he agreed with them)—that doubt, I say, was then set at rest. But this is not the difficulty which I mean. I know very well that to modern patriotism the difficulty seems small enough; the Commons had only to insist, the King and the Judges had only to give way. But in the year 1604 this was an arrangement not so easily effected. All things are done in England by precedent, and there was no precedent exactly in point. When Queen Elizabeth got into a contest with the Commons which seemed likely to prove a tough one, her way was to give them a rough reprimand and send them about their business,—taking good care however that by the time they met again the cause of contention should have disappeared. In that way the Commons had carried many points against the Crown; but none, I think,—unless in times of disorder and danger—by persisting in a course of flat opposition. Here Prerogative and Privilege (which had not yet settled which was master by a stand-up fight) found themselves suddenly face to face in a narrow passage. Either one must stand aside to let the other pass, or each must be content with half the causeway. Upon one point the Commons seem to have been at once and unanimously resolved,—to stand fast by the principle that they were judges of their own returns, sole and unaccountable. No one talked of a compromise on that point. But upon the question how they should proceed in asserting it, opinions were much divided. And here it was that Bacon became, as I take it, an important actor in the matter. His advice was,—so far as it can be gathered from the notes of his speech that remain in the Journals,—not to enter into a contest with the King upon the particular case; but to turn the dispute upon the general principle and improve the occasion so as to get that ascertained and settled for the future. The King had desired that they would argue the question before the Judges;—consent to do so; and in the mean time " consider and resolve of the material questions which will fall out in the debate of it."

This advice was not exactly followed by the House; was indeed in one very material point overruled; for they resolved *not* to confer with the Judges, but to address themselves directly to the King;—a resolution by no means judicious, if we may judge by the event; since they were forced before a week was over to abandon it. With this exception however they acted firmly and wisely. A committee was appointed to consider the King's objections and to frame an answer in writing. On the 3rd of April the answer (in the drawing up of which Bacon—as I suspect from its correspondence with what remains of his speech—had a principal hand) was reported, and a select committee was appointed to take it up to the Lords ;—Bacon being spokesman, with a commission to read it to them, and desire their co-operation for the King's satisfaction ; but not to amplify, explain, or debate any question that might arise upon the perusal. So the answer (which was in the form of a petition to the King) was read, and there the matter ended for that day.

The next day the inconvenience of thus proceeding without previous conference with the Judges was made manifest. The King sent for the Speaker, told him that he had received the petition, that he had heard his Judges and Counsel in the matter, that he was now distracted in judgment, and that for his further satisfaction he " commanded as an absolute King " that they would appoint a select committee to confer with the Judges in presence of the Council ;—the Council being present not as umpires to determine, but as witnesses to report.

Here was a new dilemma. For the question of conferring with the Judges had been twice raised in the House and absolutely resolved in the negative. Out of this there was no way but back again. And the same member who had before been most vehement not only against conference, but apparently against compromise of any kind, was now foremost to retreat. " The Prince's command," said Yelverton— (for it was he, not Bacon, that broke silence)—" is like a thunderbolt. His command upon our allegiance is like the roaring of a lion. We must obey ; the only question is how." Another suggested that the King should be petitioned to be himself present at the conference, to hear, judge, and moderate the cause in person. And a select committee was thereupon appointed to confer with the Judges in presence of the King and Council, with commission to fortify and explain their written answers, but *not* to enter into any new argument.

This was too delicate a matter to be entrusted to any hand but the best they had, and Bacon was accordingly selected to conduct the conference. He spoke for the Commons; the King presiding and speaking for himself. The notes which remain of what passed are so few and disconnected, that one can hardly gather from them what form the discussion took; much less the particular arguments urged on either side. Nor is this of much consequence, except that one would be curious to know how Bacon contrived to steer clear of a disputation; which seemed almost inevitable, and could hardly have had a peaceable termination. If in order to avoid it, he was compelled a little to exceed his commission by entertaining the question of a compromise,—which there is some reason to suspect,—it was a wise liberty, and the Commons were not disposed to quarrel with him on that account; for upon hearing his report of what had passed, they agreed to a proposal, (in which Sir Francis Goodwin expressly acquiesced, and which it was understood would satisfy the King,) that *both* returns should be set aside and a new writ issued.

A.

Then in fact the Commons gave way?

B.

Upon the particular case both Commons and King gave way; that is, each was content with half the way, and so the quarrel ended. But upon the *principle* the Commons stood out, and carried their point: their right to judge of such returns was never afterwards questioned. And thus by that small immaterial concession,—(the proposal of which by Bacon, had it been resisted by the Commons and led to a dissolution or to an endless quarrel, would no doubt have been branded by our popular historians and biographers, as base, servile, and unconstitutional,)—they did in fact obtain quietly, orderly, effectually, and at once, the recognition for ever of a most important constitutional privilege. By giving way to the King for the moment they had their own way ever after.

I know that all this is a tiresome recapitulation of bygone matters which no longer concern us. I know that the House of Commons does not want to be told how to make good its privileges against Queen Victoria. But though the question does not concern us directly, it concerns us indirectly through those with whom we are concerned. This question of privilege was not bygone when Bacon had to deal with it, but new-come; with an army of similar questions in its rear not yet come; and if you want to understand his life, you must endeavour to see it as it seemed to him. I said the management of it was worth considering, because it is in fact the best example I have met with of his method of effecting what I called the harmonious adjustment of the relation between the Crown and the Commons; of the rival pretensions of Prerogative and Privilege; which was the perpetually recurring problem of his times. The best example, I say, out of very many of the kind. And why the best? Because in this instance his advice was allowed, though not exactly (which would have made it better still), yet substantially and ultimately, to prevail. As it was, that first refusal to confer with the Judges (which was *against* his advice) had nearly shipwrecked all. And had the high privilege party been a little stronger, or had the management of the matter been entrusted to a man who had less courage with his discretion, less discretion with his courage, or less address with both, it could hardly have escaped miscarriage in one or other of the houses,—either in the conference itself or in the debate upon the report of the conference. The difference was now happily accommodated; and I do believe that if the Commons had only been wise enough to act always in the same spirit, there was scarcely one of the differences that arose between them and the King which might not have been accommodated as satisfactorily,

—the King yielding to them upon the point of substance, they to him upon the point of credit and honour. Ecclesiastical grievances, impositions, monopolies, everything, might have been adjusted almost as they would, if they could only have been content to let him feel that in so adjusting them he was *using* his prerogative and not abandoning it. So, at least, I am persuaded that Bacon thought; and the result in the present case must have encouraged him to believe not only that it could be done, but that if he could keep his credit with both parties, he was the man who could do it. Now I say that this was an object of such paramount and pressing importance, that a man who foresaw the opposite issues to which the diverging paths (between which they had now or never to choose) must conduct the nation, and who at the same time felt that he could himself do something to keep them in the path which led to liberty through order and peace—such a man, I say, must have been wanting in public spirit and masculine virtue, if either out of preference for a quiet life, or intolerance of human folly, or a fastidious self-respect, he could be content to stand aloof and see them take the wrong turn. I do not quarrel with Socrates or Plato, because I do not know what opportunities they had ; but commend me to Pericles and Demosthenes. The complexion that bears wind and weather is the complexion for a man, be he citizen or be he subject.

A.

You said that this was one example out of many.

B.

I might almost have said that it was a sample of all. But there was no " Hansard " in those days ; and the records of the proceedings in Parliament are so scanty and imperfect that I cannot reduce them into a narrative without making larger guesses than I should like to be responsible for. To recount all the cases however in which there is good evidence that Bacon's services were found available during this session for keeping those uneasy neighbours, Privilege and Prerogative, from coming into rough collision, would hold me till to-morrow. If you will look through the Commons' Journals you will find that, notwithstanding his daily occupation in the great business of the Union, as soon as any other business becomes critical or difficult the management of it generally falls upon him.

A.

Was there not—yes, I am sure I remember something about another question of Privilege, which gave a great deal of trouble about that time.

B.

The case of Sir Thomas Shirley.—Yes, a very important privilege (I am not so sure that it was a very desirable one) was made good in that case too after much difficulty. But the case was not so critical. For the quarrel was not with the King, the Lords, or the Courts, but only with the Warden of the Fleet; and though it seemed more likely to lead at the time to open violence, the consequences would not have been so dangerous. However as Bacon took, at one stage of it, an unusually prominent part (for he was allowed to speak three times on the same question), we may as well tell the story.

On the day of the King's solemn entry into London, Sir Thomas Shirley, attending by command and being a member of parliament, was arrested at the suit of a goldsmith named Sympson, and sent to the Fleet. This Sympson is an old acquaintance,—" a man much noted for stoutness and extremities upon his purse,"—the same who five or six years before arrested Bacon when he was (like Falstaff) "upon hasty employment in the Queen's affairs." Indeed it seems that this man had a pleasure in arresting his debtors, not so much when he could most easily catch them, as when the arrest would be most inconvenient to them and the disgrace most public. On that occasion, though he might have arrested Bacon any day in London, he chose to do it when he was engaged in the investigation of a newly-detected conspiracy to poison the Queen, and was returning from the Tower. And on this occasion he had certainly obtained his writ of execution against Sir Thomas Shirley six weeks before; and it was supposed (how truly I do not know) that the serving of it had been forborne until this solemn day by special understanding between him and the sergeant. At any rate we must suppose that there was something unusual in the proceeding, because both Sympson and the sergeant were committed to prison for it by the Lord Chancellor. However the dispute did not turn upon that point. Sir Thomas was a member, and the detention of a member from the House was a breach of privilege. For this, as a contempt, they forthwith committed Sympson and the sergeant to the Tower, and ordered a warrant to be issued for producing the body of Sir Thomas. But before they proceeded further, (because they would not have the privilege abused for the avoidance of just debts,) a bill was brought in for securing to Sympson his interest in the debt and saving the Warden of the Fleet harmless. Bacon was indeed of opinion that Sympson's interest in the debt would be good as the law stood; but other eminent lawyers were of another opinion, and the point appearing to be doubtful, they resolved to settle it by passing a special act for the purpose. This bill was passed through both Houses; and they were on the point of moving the King to promise his assent to it, when it was suggested that such a proceeding would be " some impeachment to the privilege of the House." And sure enough it would. By going so far out of their way to ensure the Warden, before they demanded the release of their member, they would seem to admit by implication that they could not legally demand him without such assurance. The caution was approved, and a writ of *habeas corpus* was awarded for the bringing of Sir Thomas's body into the House the next day. But the Warden refused to give him up until the act for his security should have actually received the royal assent. Upon this they committed him to the Tower, and again sent the Sergeant-at-arms for Sir Thomas's body. But the Warden's wife, who had all the keys, would do nothing without her husband's authority; and the Sergeant, though armed with *habeas corpus* and mace, could make no impression upon her. Meantime the King had intimated his intention to assent to the bill, and next day the Sergeant was sent again, armed as before, and (privately informing her of the King's promise) again demanded Sir Thomas; but she would act on no authority but her husband's. He took her by the arm, but she screamed. To go further was beyond his commission, and so all three—Sergeant, *habeas corpus*, and mace—came back empty as before. Upon this, the Warden himself was brought to the bar; was formally acquainted with the King's promise; was reasoned with; being found inexorable, was ordered into closer confinement in a dungeon significantly called "Little Ease;" * and when this produced no effect, some members were sent to see whether the order had been really complied with. They found (it seems) that he had not been made uneasy enough; and upon their report to that effect a most distracted debate followed. One would have the Lieutenant of the Tower fined 1000*l.* for not executing the order. Another would have the Warden himself fined 100*l.* a day until he relented. A third was for an act of parliament disabling him from all offices, &c. A fourth would have the Lessee of the Fleet sent for, and get at their member that way. A fifth proposed that six members of the House should go with the Sergeant and deliver Sir Thomas by force. A sixth would have the House rise and strike work until they had power to execute their privileges. And so the House seemed to be at a nonplus,—every man giving an opinion, and no two opinions alike. All this time I do not find that Bacon had taken any part whatever in the matter since he gave his opinion upon the legal point, as before mentioned;—I do not know why, for he was on the Committee of Privileges to which it

* "A fourth kind of torture was a cell called '*Little Ease.*' It was of so small dimensions and so constructed that the prisoner could neither stand, walk, sit, nor lie in it at full length. He was compelled to draw himself up in a squatting posture, and so remain during several days."—*Lingard*, vol. viii. p. 522.

had from the first been referred; perhaps his hands were too full of other business; perhaps he abstained from delicacy, as being liable to a suspicion of personal bias on account of his own former complaint against Sympson in a case so nearly resembling the present;—which is more likely; but, for whatever reason, it is certain that (with the above-mentioned exception) his name does not appear as connected with it till now. Now however the case was growing critical, and he not only spoke, but spoke, as I have said, three times. His advice was—not to send any of their members to assist the Sergeant in delivering Sir Thomas by force,— for being judges they could not be ministers,—but to petition the King to appoint some persons for that purpose. And the debate ended in a resolution that the Sergeant should be sent again with a new writ, that the Warden should be carried to the door of the Fleet, that the writ should there be delivered to him with commandment from the House to obey it; the Vice-Chamberlain being at the same time privately instructed to go to the King and humbly desire that he would be pleased (as from himself) to command the Warden upon his allegiance to set Sir Thomas free. This measure at last succeeded; they got their member, and established their privilege; and the Warden and other prisoners were in due time, after making due submission, released; our friend Sympson having to pay all the costs.

A.

But I hope they passed the Act all the same, to secure Sympson his debt and to save the Warden harmless.

B.

O yes, they never had any scruple on that point. It was only for the sake of making good the point of privilege that they proceeded without it. With that however Bacon had nothing to do. It was not till the Commons seemed to be in imminent danger of getting into a scrape, in attempting to vindicate their right which was clearly constitutional by

means which were clearly not constitutional, that he inter-
fered in the business at all. In this case, as in the other, I
believe the privilege was never afterwards called in question.

A.

Then the House seems to have done tolerably well for
itself this session. But how for the country? I do not
hear of any great matters accomplished in the way of reform.

B.

No; but some very great matters weighed anchor, and
by skilful piloting passed in safety through some hidden
shoals and rocks. The tender question of grievances, especially in matter of wardships, purveyors, trade, and ecclesiastical discipline, was opened, and so opened as to be
graciously entertained; and though it is true that they were
dropped and that nothing was effectually done in them, yet
at the end of the session they were by no means where they
were at the beginning. Both parties had had an opportunity of surveying their ground, and each understood
better how the other was to be dealt with. A good entrance
is half-way through, and this no doubt they felt. Accordingly the first movements in this delicate matter (which was
opened in the first week of the session) appear to have been
entrusted to the hands of Bacon; for I find that the first
proceedings of their own committee were reported by him
to the House; so was the first conference on the subject
with the Lords; and the first petition to the King (which
related to the grievance of purveyors was presented by him
with an introductory speech,—a true report of which fortunately remains to show how he discharged services of this
kind. The several heads of grievance were afterwards proceeded with separately and committed to several hands.
And they seem to have been proceeding prosperously
enough, at least not to have met with any decided obstruction, until other accidents intervened which wore out the
time and patience requisite for carrying them through, and
they were by general consent postponed to another session.

A.

What kind of accidents?

B.

Many kinds. One obstruction after another in the settlement of the Union;—a complaint against a yeoman of the
guard for refusing the Commons admittance to hear the
King's speech at the opening of Parliament, which was only
satisfied by his speaking it over again for the special benefit
of the Lower House;—the dispute about the Goodwin case;
—the troubles and delays about the Shirley case; the pressing of Church matters, which the King had settled to his
own satisfaction at the Hampton Court conference just
before, and which brought the Commons into direct disagreement with the Bishops;—some disappointment in the
troublesome matter of supplies;—all these had gradually
worn out the scanty measure of patience with which nature
had armed James, and provoked him to make a speech
of remonstrance, which hurt the feelings of his faithful
Commons and provoked them in their turn to draw up an
address of " satisfaction," as they called it—which (being in
fact a strong and decided justification of their conduct
point by point) must have acted, had it been presented, like
the stroking of a sore. Meanwhile matters were made worse
by the appearance of a pamphlet in which they were severely
taxed for meddling with causes they had no business with;
and which, turning out to be the production of a bishop,
brought them into collision with the House of Lords. Then
the Lords themselves got into a dispute with them upon
some point in a money-bill. And the year was already
drawing towards the end of June, so that it was no fit time
for pressing the subject of grievances; and if they could
contrive to part friends, it was as much as could be hoped.

A.

And had Bacon to accommodate all these differences as
well as the others?

B.

In almost all of them his name becomes conspicuous in the Journals as they become critical and require delicate handling. The first two or three communications with the Lords about the Bishop's pamphlet were managed by Sir Henry Hobart; but the last conference, in which the Bishop received his censure and made his submission and the quarrel was effectually made up, was managed by Bacon. In the conference which ended in the adjustment of the difference about the money-bill, it was Bacon who was chief actor and relator. And with regard to the "Address of Satisfaction" to the King,—though it may be true as Hume asserts (apparently upon a misunderstanding of the title as given in Petyt, where he found it) that he had a principal hand in drawing it up, yet it is distinctly stated in the Journals that he spoke *against* the presenting of it.

And so on the 7th of July the King and his first parliament parted on reasonably good terms,—each knowing more of the other than they had done, though both had still a good deal to learn. The country gentlemen went to their counties, the King to hunt, and Bacon to his study, to take a survey and a measure of all the questions which would fall under the consideration of the Union Commissioners, who were to meet in October;—a business which must have found him plenty of work for the rest of that year. This commission was referred to by Bacon long after in his Essays as a "grave and orderly assembly," in which "matters were propounded one day and not spoken upon till the next;" and in an introductory paragraph which he had prepared at the time to open the Commissioners' report with, he represented it as so blest with the spirit of unity, that "though there was never in any consultation greater plainness and liberty of speech, argument and debate, replying, contradicting, recalling anything spoken where cause was, expounding any matter ambiguous or mistaken, and all other points of free and friendly interlocution and conference, without cavillations, advantages, or overtakings,"—yet there did not happen from their meeting to their breaking up either any altercation in their debates or any variety in their resolutions, but " the whole passed with a unanimity and uniformity of consent." This, in a case where thirty Englishmen and thirty Scotchmen were met to make a bargain, was a good deal to say ; and though it seems to have been premature, since one of the Commissioners refused at the last moment to sign the report, and the proposed introduction was therefore withdrawn, I have no doubt that it represents fairly the general character of the consultations. They concluded their work on the 4th of December; from which time till the 5th of November following Bacon had nothing that I know of (except the business of his profession) to prevent him from pushing on the " Advancement of Learning," of which he had not yet finished more than the first book, and which I suppose him to be all this time extremely anxious to bring out as soon as possible, while the King's heart was still beating under the impulse and agitation of his new fortune, his imagination awake, his habits unfixed, his direction not yet taken ; well knowing that if the royal fancy should once set in towards other objects, he would not easily find leisure for a work so great and so new as it was the object of the " Advancement " to put him upon.

A.

Suppose then we leave him to his studies for to-night ; for it grows late, and we cannot leave him better employed.

EVENING THE EIGHTH.

A.

We left Bacon busy with the second book of the "Advancement of Learning;" hurrying it forward, you say, in the hope of awakening the King's interest in the argument, and preoccupying his mind with an ambition to become the great Instaurator of Philosophy.

B.

Yes. I can hardly doubt that he had some such dream in his head when he resolved to press it forward so fast as to have it out by the end of the year. He had published no part of it before ; and though his interest and industry about it never cooled or slept, he published no more of it for sixteen years after: so that his general plan must have been to allow it the full period of gestation. But on this occasion he was certainly in a hurry. There is a kind of disproportion in the parts of the work itself which indicates a somewhat premature birth. The first book, if you observe it,—which he himself "accounted but as a page to the latter," and which in reference to the main and permanent object is of least importance,—is nevertheless very full and elaborate ; while the second is in many parts professedly unfinished. And accordingly we find that when he afterwards corrected and enlarged it into the " De Augmentis," —(which is the completest in itself of all his philosophical works), he added nothing to the first book, but rather curtailed it; whereas he expanded the second into eight, making it more than twice as long as it was. And even then it did not exactly fit into the place reserved for it; but in offering it for the first part of the "Instauratio," he was obliged to guard it with a kind of apology. All this indicates not only some haste in the first instance, but also some departure, with an eye (we may suppose) to some immediate and temporary object, from the prefigured course. And this would be well enough accounted for on my supposition. When he began the "Advancement," he was thinking, as we have seen, to "meddle as little as he could with the King's causes," and to "put his ambition wholly upon his pen." He commenced therefore according to the measure of the subject which he had taken in his mind; and his immediate aim being to awaken the King's interest in it, he dwelt the more copiously upon the dignity and merit of the undertaking,—which is the theme of the first book. But before he could advance further he found himself involved in more business than ever; and foresaw, no doubt, that from that time forth his intervals of leisure were not likely to come often or last long. Such an interval, however, did occur in the vacation of 1605, and it is then that I suppose him to have resolved to make the most of it by getting done what he could in so limited a time.

A.

He was not long (I take it) in finding that the King was not likely to be of much use to him.

B.

Probably not. The King does not seem to have had any better ideas on that subject than the rest of the world. I do not know that he ever took any serious interest in natural philosophy; and his brains were busy with a hundred other things. However that could not be helped. The chance was worth trying at any rate; for much would have been gained by a hit, not much lost by a miss.

But all this is only a speculation of my own, upon which

I do not care to insist. If you think it strained, you can leave it, and invent something of your own instead. This will at all events remain true, that we left Bacon busy with the "Advancement" in the beginning of 1605; and that (except for his letter to the Lord Chancellor recommending the appointment of some fit person to write a History of England,—which is indeed only a leaf taken out of the "Advancement" for immediate use,) we hear no more of him till the end of that year, when we find him sending copies of the book to his friends. And now we must leave it to make what impression it may upon the King's fancy, and follow Bacon into less congenial occupations.

A.

If it did not make a good impression, it was not for want of unction. Dedications, you will say, are privileged; or you must admit that he stretched a point there.

B.

I should rather say that dedications are *compliments*. They are meant to please, and they are restrained from censure. Therefore they are, in their nature and of necessity, partial; they present the good, and not the bad. But I do not myself allow that their privilege extends further. I do not allow that a man ought, even in a dedication, to say that he thinks what he does not think; but what he thinks *well* he may speak out; what he thinks *ill* he may keep to himself. Is there any harm in that? Is it not the very thing which, under the name of *good manners*, is universally practised throughout civilized society? When you meet with a man who tells everybody all that he dislikes in them as well as all that he likes, what do you call him, as soon as his back is turned?

A.

A bear. But you do not mean to say that Bacon really thought all the good he said of the King in that dedication?

B.

Why not ?   What did he say that was not true ?

A.

It was not true that James was a wise man.

B.

Many men have had a great reputation for wisdom and much less to show for it. But Bacon did not say that he was a wise man. He said that he was a man of very large capacity, very faithful memory, very swift apprehension, very penetrating judgment, and great powers of elocution. Was he not ?

A.

Oh, but he says far more than that. He says he was the wisest man that ever was in Christendom.

B.

I beg your pardon. The *most learned* man. Nay, not even the most learned man ; only the most learned "of kings or temporal monarchs."

A.

And the greatest divine.

B.

Yes, among kings. Can you name any king that excelled him in learning, human or divine? But don't you see that a man might possess all these gifts, natural and acquired, and yet be very far from a *wise* king, in the sense in which you use the word when you deny that James was wise ? Many of our wisest and most learned men at this day would attribute every one of these qualities to Coleridge ; De Quincey calls him the largest and most spacious intellect since Aristotle ; and yet Coleridge would have made a very indifferent king.

Besides, when you speak of James's character, you are

thinking of the history of his whole reign. Remember that
when Bacon wrote that dedication, James had not been
three years on the throne. His defects had not had time to
show themselves. Set aside all that happened after the
year 1605, and then tell me what are the mental and moral
qualities in him of which you have any evidence—even the
questionable evidence of libellers and satirists. You have
evidence that he was a great scholar, a man of deep and
various reading, of ready wit, of remarkably quick apprehension ; a very good writer and speaker ; with views decidedly
large and liberal, a strong sense of justice, a great desire to
please everybody, and a heart as transparent as if it had
been the crystal which he said he wished it was. Add, by
way of drawback, certain high notions of the royal prerogative, an irritable temper, and a good deal of that self-import-
ance which a man cannot easily be without who was never
less than a king ; and I really believe you have all of his
character that, if Guy Fawkes had blown him up, would have
come down to us. Why then should I plead the privilege
of dedications ? You cannot doubt that James was a very
fit person to dedicate such a work to, even if you do not believe (as I do) that it was actually composed then and in that
shape because he *was* so fit. And you surely would not have
had Bacon take that occasion to tell him in the face of the
world that his tongue was too large for his mouth, that he
shuffled in his walk, or that he was too fond of talking.
And as for those graver defects which prevented him from
taking rank with the truly great governors, I do not see how
Bacon could have told him of them if he would. They had
not been publicly displayed, and there is no reason to suppose that either Bacon or any one else as yet suspected
them ; moreover, if you will consult what records remain of
the opinion of the people of that time,—(I do not mean what
people said to him in dedications or of him in public, but
what they said of him privately in their communications
with one another,)—you will find that Bacon ascribes no
more merits to him than were generally believed to be
his due.

A.

I will do that some other time. I did not mean to charge the flattery upon Bacon as any fault. I suppose there is flattery wherever there are what we call manners ; and I do not know why it is worse to flatter a king than a neighbour ; except that in one case you are supposed to do it for reward, and in the other from humanity.

B.

Whereas you do it in both cases alike, because it is agreeable to be agreeable.

A.

Well, now for the less congenial occupations. One of these, I suppose, was the prosecution of Guy Fawkes.

B.

I do not know. Bacon had to attend the indictments in January, (though he did not take any part in the proceedings,) and he was most likely employed in the previous examinations, which are stated to have occupied the Government for six months. But I have not yet ascertained any of the particulars. In a letter to his friend Tobie Mathew who was then abroad, he encloses a "Relation" "which carries (he says) the truth of that which is public." This may very likely have been an account of the discovery of the plot ; but as I have not met with any traces of it or any other allusions to it, I can say no more. Only if you happen to take up Mr. Jardine's history of the plot, and find there something more about "garbling" and about Bacon's method in drawing up narratives of state matters for public satisfaction, remember our last interview with him and be easy. There was a " Discourse of the manner of the Discovery of the Powder Treason," published by authority at the time, for the very desirable object of satisfying the curiosity and quieting the alarm of the public during the interval (necessarily a long one) between the apprehension of the traitors and their trial. This discourse was currently ascribed to the King himself; and Mr. Jardine has two ideas of his own about it:—first, that it is a false narrative, and secondly, that it was probably drawn up by Bacon. Now that it was a correct narrative any one may satisfy himself by comparing it with Mr. Jardine's own statement, from which it does not appear that it contains any one material inaccuracy. And that it was not written by Bacon, any one familiar with Bacon's style may satisfy himself by reading the first three pages. It may very likely have been founded upon some narrative of his. But the *dressing* is evidently the King's own workmanship; and it was afterwards published as his in an authorized edition of his works. Into which works, by the way, if you would take the trouble to look for an hour or two, I think you would find reason to modify your contempt for King James and his reputed wisdom. If you could put into the heads of those who laugh at him a little of his wit, they would not laugh quite so loud.

A.

My dear fellow, you really must not ask me to begin the study of King James's learned garrulities. I once tried one of his speeches.

B.

Very well; then I shall only ask you not to assume that he was a fool until you have succeeded in reading one through. You know Hume thought his speech on the Union very nearly as good as Bacon's.

A.

Be it so then. The terms I admit are fair, we will make peace upon them. What next?

B.

Next comes James's second parliament, or rather the second session of his first parliament.—Yet stay. Since I have avowed an opinion which most people will think ab-

surd, namely that Bacon was ill-fitted to work his fortunes
up through a Court, I may as well tell you first that in
the autumn of this year another opportunity had occurred
for advancing him to the Solicitorship (the second, remember,
since James's accession), and no advantage had been
taken of it. In August, 1605, Sir Edmund Anderson, Chief
Justice of the Common Pleas, died. This was a convenient
opportunity for advancing Sir Edward Coke to that office,
and so making room for Bacon either as Attorney, if Dodderidge
were not advanced, or as Solicitor if he were. Why
this was not done I do not know; but Coke remained where
he was, and on the 26th of August, Sir Francis Gawdy became
Chief Justice. Moreover, since Bacon has the popular
reputation of a mere sycophant and mendicant in his pursuit
of place, I may add that I find no traces of any application
whatever in his own behalf, either on this occasion or the
last. The only allusion I find to this second disappointment
(if disappointment it was) is in the letter to Tobie Mathew
which I quoted just now, and it is in these words;—" The
death of the late great judge concerned not me, because the
other was not removed." You may remember also that, on
a previous occasion in Queen Elizabeth's time, when both
Essex and Egerton wanted to have him made Master of the
Rolls, he declined to make any application for himself. All
which you may reconcile as you best can with the character
of an unblushing beggar for promotion. My own belief is
that his experience in 1593, 4, and 5, had sickened him of
the character of a suitor; and it is a fact that these new repeated
experiences of the consequence of *not* canvassing, and
of the fallacy of the ground on which, at James's accession,
he had augured better for his own fortunes,—namely that
" the canvassing world was gone and the deserving world
was come,"—these experiences, I say, (and this was not the
last of them,) never tempted him to resume that character;
further than by an occasional letter to his cousin the Earl of
Salisbury, to his old and constant friend the Lord Chancellor,
and latterly to the King himself; in remembrance of
his services and of such assurances as they had themselves

of their own accord held out to him. For what Lord Campbell says about the "deep resentment" which he expressed
on being passed over, though it is stated as a fact, is a mere
invention; a touch of what Lord Campbell felt to be nature,
introduced to give what he considered life to his narrative.
A few months after, there seems to have been a general expectation that room would be made for advancing Coke to
the Chief-Justiceship, by making Gawdy a Baron. And it
may have been on this occasion that Bacon reminded Salisbury that "in case Mr. Solicitor rose, he should be glad at
last to be Solicitor," but that he should make no further
suit. No change however was made till June, when Gawdy
died; and then Coke did succeed him. Still no preferment
for Bacon. Another new man, Sergeant Hobart, came in
above him as Attorney; and though the King had promised
that he should not be forgotten, and an arrangement was
soon after suggested by the Lord Chancellor to make room
for him in the Solicitorship by promoting Dodderidge to the
rank of King's sergeant, yet he was allowed to remain as he
was, with nothing but his fee of £40 and his pension of £60
for a full twelvemonth after.—You see therefore that rapid
as his rising sounds when the several steps are huddled together in a flowing sentence, he had in fact much more
reason to complain of James than ever he had of Elizabeth,
for "refusing him the professional advancement to which he
had a just claim;" much more reason to suspect some unfriendly influence in high quarters, and to think himself
(all circumstances considered) a much-neglected man. All
which things I should hardly have thought it worth while to
mention, but that they are at once so unlike the man as he
is commonly painted and so characteristic of the man as he
really was: nor do I mention them now to claim for him
any merit of magnanimity in holding on his course of duty
all the same, but merely to discharge him from the popular
imputation of being, in his civil and personal character, a
mere follower of his own fortunes. You may possibly be
able to reconcile the facts with that imputation, but I cannot guess how. Was it that he did not understand the arts

of rising? or was it that he was too scrupulous to use them? or was it that advancement was not his principal object? or what was it?

A.

How do you know that he did not write other canvassing letters, or make personal canvasses, which you are not aware of?

B.

Nay, if you appeal to unknown possibilities of that kind, how do you know that anybody is not a villain? It is the business of those who make the charge to produce the evidence. I have much reason to think that I know all the evidence to that effect which is known. And I only wish you could tell me of any place where such letters or such records are likely to be found. I am confident that they will accord with my view of his character, and not with the popular one.

A.

Well, I certainly cannot help you to any myself. And I must confess that after reading the chapter in the " Advancement " on the art of raising a man's own fortunes, it is hard to think that he did not understand the theory; and after seeing how well he kept his standing in the favour of so many opposing parties, it is as hard to think that he wanted address to practise it. It does seem to follow therefore either that he was unwilling to use the necessary means, or that he had other ends in view. However, I do not feel bound to decide the question at present. Therefore move on. You have a good deal to explain yet.

B.

By all means. Only remember that he is now in his forty-sixth year, and still bears a good character.

I am not aware that any charge has been brought against him for anything that he did during the parliament which met on the 21st of January, 1605-6, unless I must except his

marrying the alderman's daughter, an act which has not
escaped injurious remarks. Indeed I do not find that anything occurred in it to try him. It was upon the whole a
loyal parliament. The Gunpowder Plot had effectually
awakened the sympathy of the Commons. The bill of At-
tainders passed with general consent. The Union was in
abeyance. Grievances were handled tenderly, and supplies
were voted liberally. Bacon's services were used in the
same way as before; and when the parliament was prorogued
on the 26th of May, he seems to have stood as well as ever
in the favour both of the Commons and the King.

Of his employment during the following vacation I
cannot give any particular account. The wedding tour was
not, I believe, at that time an English institution. If it was,
it had to wait on this occasion for the prorogation; for the
wedding itself had taken place on the 10th of May, in the
thick of the Parliamentary business, and at a rather critical
time, when it was to be contrived that an answer should be
obtained to the petition of grievances before the Subsidy
Bill was finally passed. The duties of the honeymoon may
have employed part of the vacation, and if you will look
through the "Opuscula" and the "Impetus Philosophici"
(most of which were probably written between 1606 and
1612), you will find enough in them to account for the rest.
The "Cogitata et Visa" we know was in circulation among
his friends before the end of 1607. As for his marriage, and
for any criticisms which the charity of modern biographers
and reviewers may have made upon his choice of a wife and
his motives in choosing her, you are to understand that all
we know of the matter is this:—that in his forty-sixth year
he married a handsome young woman with a good fortune,*
whose father was an alderman, and her mother (I believe) a
shrew; that he lived with her for twenty years without any
disagreement or scandal that we know of; that a few months
before his death (when reputation, fortune, health,—every-

---

* It appears from a manuscript preserved in Tenison's Library, that he
had about £220 a year with her, and was to have about £140 a year more
upon her mother's death.

thing in short but his heart, his hope, his genius, and a few faithful friends, had forsaken him) he made or desired to make for her out of the wreck of his fortunes a special and honourable provision ; but afterwards " for just and great causes," the nature of which he does not specify, retracted it and " left her to her right only ; " and that she not long after his death married her gentleman-usher, (who, scandal says, was no better for the bargain,) lived for twenty-four years longer, and was buried at Eyworth in Bedfordshire on the 29th of June, 1650. If any one chooses upon these grounds to assume that his marriage was a mercenary and disgraceful act, I cannot help it. I can throw no further light either upon his motives in choosing her, or upon the occasion of his displeasure. I know well enough what to think of the judgment and moral taste of those who undertake upon these data to condemn him ; but to determine the merits of a domestic disagreement two hundred years old, of which I know no particulars whatever, is beyond me.

A.

I shall not press that point.

B.

Well then.—On the 10th of November, 1606, parliament met again, and continued with one or two short intermissions till July. It was a very busy session, though it produced very little. The main and almost the only subject which occupied it was the Union ; and the object of the Government was to carry a measure, or rather a series of measures, founded upon the report of the commissioners. That report (or instrument, as it was called) had been completed, as you may remember, in December 1604 ; and had it been adopted and acted upon, would have laid a broad foundation for a solid and permanent Union between England and Scotland. It would have provided, first, for the abolition of all traces of hostility between the two countries ; secondly, for the introduction of such a consent between their several laws as would have prevented the course of justice from being broken in its passage from one to the other ; thirdly, for complete freedom of internal trade; fourthly, in matters of foreign commerce, for an equal participation by both in all advantages enjoyed by either; fifthly, for a free admission of the *post nati* (that is, of all Scottish subjects born since the King's accession) to all rights and privileges of English subjects without reserve; sixthly, for an admission of the *ante nati* (that is, of all Scottish subjects born before the King's accession) to the like privileges; excepting only offices of the Crown, of judicature, or of parliament. In short, (leaving their several laws and forms of constitution for the present unaltered,) it would have abolished at once and for ever all traces of hostility, all marks of separation and distinction, and whatever else either impeded intercourse or rendered it unequal. And no doubt if such a foundation had been timely laid, all the rest would have followed in due season.

In practically carrying out these objects, there were of course many just doubts and substantial difficulties to be encountered. But the worst difficulty of all was an inward jealousy which got into the heads of the popular party in the House of Commons, lest the Scotch should have the best of the bargain; which jealousy, working in the brains of lawyers, begot such a brood of objections and obstructions, that they could not agree upon so much as a general measure for naturalizing even the *post nati*. This was the subject of that Conference between the Lords and Commons, in the reporting of which (on the 2nd and 3rd of March, 1606-7) Bacon's health, as I told you, broke down; after which for about a month I do not find his name mentioned in the Journals. The business fell into other hands, and dragged on with little progress, until (just before the Easter recess) some one either out of unwise zeal, or (as the King seems to have thought) out of mischief, endeavoured to put it in a new track, by substituting for the easy and simple measure of a general naturalization, a project at once premature and hopeless for a perfect Union. Upon the first suggestion of this, Bacon again took part in the debate; and in that "speech on the motion for Union of Laws" of which he has himself preserved a report, endeavoured to guide the question off that shoal. His endeavour, however, was not successful. The project for a perfect Union was revived after the recess; and after wasting much time and breath, was at length by common consent abandoned. The measure for general naturalization sank with it; and an act for the abolition of hostile laws—that is, of the laws which had been expressly made for a state of hostility between the two nations—was all that could be saved from the wreck. And so ended the labour of those eight months.

A.

Bacon being still unpreferred?

B.

No. He was made Solicitor-General at last, just before the parliament was prorogued; being half-way through his forty-seventh year.

A.

Had he to pay anything for it?

B.

No; he never in all his life, so far as I can discover, either paid or offered to pay anything for any office. Indeed I do not think that he was ever even suspected of either buying promotion for himself or selling it to others. And this is a fact which ought not to be forgotten; for this buying of offices, judicial offices too, became afterwards—whether it was at this time or not I do not know—but it became afterwards very common, and indeed, in my judgment, the greatest of all the abuses of the times.

And now we come to another interval of comparative leisure for him. For parliament did not meet again for some two years and a half; and though his place and his profession must have consumed much of his time, he does not seem to have occupied himself otherwise in public affairs. Salisbury had the management of everything; and though he treated Bacon (for anything that appears) in a frank and

friendly manner, he was evidently unwilling to use him out
of the circle of his office. Which is à strange thing. For
Salisbury had no easy sailing of it. He could not have
doubted Bacon's ability to help; he would certainly have
found him willing to lend both his best advice and his best
industry; he could hardly have feared to be overshadowed
by him, for Bacon had never shown any disposition to thrust
people out of their places, or to use their help in order to
step over their heads. He may indeed have feared that he
would draw men's eyes away from himself, and for that
reason may have wished to keep him in a subordinate
position; for that " he loved to have the eyes of all Israel a
little too much on himself" was Bacon's own censure of
him, and no doubt a just one. And yet I am myself inclined
to ascribe it rather to a consciousness in Salisbury of certain
radical and fundamental differences between them, both as to
ends and methods of proceeding. That Bacon did deeply
disapprove of Salisbury's whole course of policy during the
last two or three years of his life, we know; and, whether he
expressed it or not at the time, Salisbury no doubt felt that
it must be so. Indeed there is a remarkable passage in one
of Bacon's letters to him, written several years before, from
which we may infer not only that he had long observed
certain cardinal defects in his statesmanship, but also that
he had not been used to make any secret of his observation.
You remember that paper of advice about Irish affairs in the
beginning of 1602, of which I gave you an account at our
last sitting. You remember that he recommended the
subject to him as one by which he might do great good and
gain great honour. But I think I did not mention the
particular points in which he conceived that Salisbury might
raise his reputation as a statesman by it. The expressions
are worth quoting, for they contain by implication the best
judgment upon his character as a minister which I have met
with :—

" If you enter into the matter (says Bacon) according to the
vivacity of your own spirit . . . you shall make the Queen's
felicity complete, which now as it is is incomparable;—and for

yourself you shall show yourself as good a *patriot* as you are thought a *politic;* and make the world perceive that you have not less *generous ends,* than *dexterous delivery of yourself* towards your ends ; and that you have as well *true arts and grounds of government,* as the facility and felicity of *practice and negotiation ;* and that you are as well seen in *the periods and tides of estates,* as in *your own circle and way."*

The criticism, you see, is civilly conveyed, but it clearly implies an opinion that Salisbury wanted both sounder principles of government and worthier ends. Being addressed to Salisbury himself (then only Sir Robert Cecil) at a time when there was no other man in power or in prospect of power with whom he had any interest, it cannot have been meant for detraction. And being accompanied with the best possible piece of advice, it may be fairly taken for what it professes to be,—the friendly suggestion of a kinsman, meant to do good, and therefore the plainer spoken ;—another example of that "natural freedom and plainness" which Essex had remarked as characteristic of the man. Now Salisbury (if I conceive his character truly, for it is not very easy to make out) was very likely to receive such a criticism without any show of offence, but was not at all likely to forget it, or to admit such a critic into his counsels and confidence. Indeed if one may trust the censures which men of all kinds are said to have passed upon him after his death, when they were not afraid to speak out, there is too much reason to think that his ways were not such as he would have liked to expose to an eye like Bacon's. " Certain it is," says Mr. Chamberlain, (a very impartial, well-informed, and clear-judging observer,—writing to a private friend about two months after his death,) " that they who may best maintain it have not forborne to say that he juggled with Religion, with the King, Queen, their children,—with nobility, parliament, friends, foes, and generally with all." And even if we reject these imputations as vague and un-authentic, there were certain main points of his later policy which Bacon so strongly disapproved that the two men could never have worked harmoniously together. At any rate the fact is undeniable that Salisbury did choose for his instruments men of a very different stamp. A large collection of his papers during the reign of James is preserved in the State Paper office, including several letters addressed to him by Bacon. But these are all about matters falling directly within the duty of Solicitor-General,—such as draughts of proclamations, bills in parliament, reports on patents to be drawn or on petitions, &c. There are no traces either there or elsewhere of any employment of him by Salisbury in business of a higher nature; no confidential consultations; no memorials or advices on business of state, such as he abounded with after Salisbury's death. The other letters which we have belonging to the first two or three years of his Solicitorship (and they are not many) relate almost all to the progress of the Instauratio. We have also various essays and fragments printed under the head of Opuscula. Of these,—(though neither the date nor the order in which they were composed can be fixed I fear in many cases with exactness)—yet enough may be ascertained as to the time when some of them were written, to show not only that he was busily employed upon them at this period, but also that the figure, purpose, and idea of the total work were already shaped out in his mind; and that his chief anxiety was to bring it before the world in such a manner as to secure for it a favourable audience. To us who are used to regard Bacon as the acknowledged leader of a philosophical revolution,—a kind of dictator for whose words the world was waiting,—it is curious to observe in how different a position he seemed to himself to stand; what inattention, incredulity, and opposition he anticipated; what pains he took to obtain access to men's ears and understandings; with what obsequious attentions * and courtly arts he studied to propitiate the learned public, and to avoid rough collision with the prejudices of the times,—

"Yea curb and woo for leave to do them good;"

---

* *Atque, quod in intellectualibus fere res nova est, morem gerimus, et tam nostras cogitationes quam aliorum simul bujulamus. Omne enim idolum vanum arte, atque obsequio, ac debito accessu subvertitur, etc.*

by how many handles he seems to have tried in turn to take up his subject; into how many different shapes he had cast the substance of that portion of the argument which he lived to complete, before he finally fixed upon that in which we have it; what broad and deep foundations he had laid for those portions which he did not live to complete, and what a world of labour and time he must have sunk in them.

A.

Yes, I dare say. But before you go on I wish you would satisfy me on one point, upon which I have hitherto sought satisfaction in vain. What after all was it that Bacon did for philosophy? In what did the wonder and in what did the benefit consist? I know that people have all agreed to call him the Father of the Inductive Philosophy; and I know that the sciences made a great start about his time, and have in some departments made great progress since. But I could never yet hear what one thing he discovered that would not have been discovered just as soon without his help. It is admitted that he was not fortunate in any of his attempts to apply his principles to practice. It is admitted that no actual scientific discovery of importance was made by him. Well, he might be the father of discovery for all that. But among all the important scientific discoveries which have been made by others since his time, is there any one that can be traced to his teaching? traced to any principles of scientific investigation originally laid down by him, and by no other man before him or contemporary with him? I know very well that he did lay down a great many just principles;—principles which must have been acted upon by every man that ever pursued the study of Nature with success. But what of that? It does not follow that we *owe* these principles to him. For I have no doubt that I myself,—I who cannot tell how we know that the earth goes round, or why an apple falls, or why the antipodes do not fall,—I have no doubt (I say) that if I sat down to devise a course of investigation for the determination of these questions, I should discover a great many just

principles which Herschel and Faraday must hereafter act
upon, as they have done heretofore. Nay, if I should
succeed in setting them forth more exactly, concisely, im-
pressively, and memorably, than any one has yet done, they
might soon come to be called *my* principles. But if that
were all, I should have done little or nothing for the
advancement of science. I should only have been finding
for some of its processes a better name. I want to know
whether Bacon did anything more than this; and if so,
what? In what did the principles laid down by him
essentially differ from those on which (while he was thus
labouring to expound them) Galileo was already acting?
From all that I can hear, it seems evident that the Inductive Philosophy received its great impulse, not from
the great prophet of new principles, but from the great
discoverers of new facts; not from Bacon, but from Galileo
and Kepler. And I suppose that, even with regard to those
very principles, if you wanted illustrations of what is
commonly called the Baconian method, you would find
some of the very best among the works of Gilbert and
Galileo. What was it then that Bacon did which entitles
him to be called the Regenerator of Philosophy? or what
was it that he dreamt he was doing which made him think
the work so entirely his own, so immeasurably important,
and likely to be received with such incredulity by at least
one generation of mankind?

B.

A pertinent question; for there is no doubt that he was
under that impression. "*Cum argumentum hujusmodi præ
manibus habeam* (says he) *quod tractandi imperitiâ perdere et
veluti exponere* NEFAS *sit*,"—He was persuaded that the
argument he had in charge was of such value, that to risk
the loss of it by unskilful handling would be not only a
pity but an impiety. You wish to know, and the wish is
reasonable, what it was. For answer, I would refer you to
the philosophers; only I cannot say that their answers are
satisfactory to myself. The old answer was that Bacon was

the first to break down the dominion of Aristotle. This is now, I think, generally given up. His opposition to Aristotle was indeed conceived in early youth, and (though he was not the first to give utterance to it) I dare say it was not the less his own, and, in the proper sense of the word, original. But the real overthrower of Aristotle was the great stir throughout the intellectual world which followed the Reformation and the revival of learning. It is certain that his authority had been openly defied some years before the publication of Bacon's principal writings; and it could not in the nature of things have survived much longer. Sir John Herschel, however, while he freely admits that the Aristotelian philosophy had been effectually overturned without Bacon's aid, still maintains Bacon's title to be looked upon in all future ages as the great Reformer of Philosophy; not indeed that he *introduced* inductive reasoning, as a new and untried process; but on account of his "keen perception and his broad and spirit-stirring, almost enthusiastic, announcement of its paramount importance, as the alpha and omega of science, as the grand and only chain for linking together of physical truths, and the eventual key to every discovery and every application."

A.

That is all very fine; but it seems to me rather to account for his having the title than to justify his claim to it;—rather to explain how he comes by his reputation than to prove that he deserves it. Try the question upon a modern case. We are now standing upon the threshold of a new æra in the science of History. It is easy to see that the universal study of History must be begun afresh upon a new method. Tales, traditions, and all that has hitherto been accounted most authentic in our knowledge of past times, must be set aside as doubtful; and the whole story must be spelt out anew from charters, names, inscriptions, monuments, and such like contemporary records. Now an eloquent man might easily make a broad and spirit-stirring announcement of the paramount importance of this process, as the only key by which the past can be laid open to us as it really was,—the grand and only chain for linking historical truths and so forth. But would he thereby entitle himself to be called the great reformer of History ? Surely not. Such a man might perhaps get the credit, but it is Niebuhr that has done the thing : for Niebuhr was the first both to see the truth and to set the example.

B.

So, I confess, it seems to me. And if I thought that Bacon had aimed at no more than that, I should not think that his time had been altogether well employed, or that his sense of the importance of his own mission to mankind was altogether justified. For surely a single great discovery made by means of the inductive process would have done more to persuade mankind of the paramount importance of it, than the most eloquent and philosophical exposition. Therefore in forsaking his experiments about gravitation, light, heat, &c., in order to set forth his classification of the " Prerogatives of Instances," and to lay down general principles of philosophy, he would have been leaving the effectual promotion of his work to secure the exaltation of his name, than .which nothing could be more opposite both to his principles and his practice. If his ambition had been only to have his picture stand as the frontispiece of the new philosophy, he could not have done better indeed than come forward as the most eloquent expounder of its principles. But if he wanted (as undoubtedly he did above all other things) to set it to work and bring it into fashion, his business was to produce the most striking illustration of its powers,—the most striking· practical proof of what it could do.

Therefore if I thought, as Herschel seems to think, that there was no essential or considerable difference between the doctrines which Bacon preached and those which Galileo practised ;—that Galileo was as the Niebuhr of the new philosophy (according to your own illustration), and Bacon only as your supposed eloquent man;—I should agree with you that Bacon's right to be called the Reformer of Philosophy is not made out. But when I come to look at Bacon's own exposition of his views and compare them with the latest and most approved account I have met with of Galileo's works, I cannot but think that the difference between what Galileo was doing and what Bacon wanted to be done is not only essential but immense.

A.

Nay, if the difference be immense, how comes it to be overlooked? It is from no want of the wish to claim for Bacon all the credit he deserves in that line.

B.

No. Rather perhaps from the wish to claim too much. We are so anxious to give him his due that we must needs ascribe to him all that has been done since his time; from which it seems to follow that we are practising his precepts, and that the Baconian philosophy has in fact been flourishing among us for the last 200 years. You believe this, don't you?

A.

People tell me so; and I suppose the only doubt is whether it be exclusively and originally his;—there is no doubt, I fancy, that it *is* his.

B.

Certainly that appears to be the general opinion; and it may seem an audacious thing in me to say that it is a mistake. But I cannot help it. It is true that a new philosophy is flourishing among us which was born about Bacon's time; and Bacon's name (as the brightest which presided at the time of its birth) has been inscribed upon it.

> " . . . . Hesperus, that led
> The starry host, rode brightest—"

not that Hesperus did actually *lead* the other stars; he and they were moving under a common force, and they would have moved just as fast if he had been away; but because he shone brightest, he *looked* as if he led them. But if I am to trust Herschel, I must think that it is the *Galilean* philosophy that has been flourishing all these years; and if I may trust my own eyes and power of construing Latin, I must think that the *Baconian* philosophy has yet to come.

If Bacon were to reappear among us at the next meeting of the Great British Association,—or say rather if he had appeared there two or three years ago (for there seems to be something great and new going on now), I think he would have shaken his head. I think he would have said, " Here has been a great deal of very good diligence used by several persons; but it has not been used upon a well-laid plan. These solar systems, and steam-engines, and Daguerreotypes, and electric telegraphs, are so many more pledges of what might be expected from an instauration of philosophy such as I recommended more than 200 years ago; why have you not tried that?—You have been acting all the time like a king who should attempt to conquer a country by encouraging private adventurers to make incursions each on his own account, without any system of combined movements to subdue and take possession. I see that wherever you have the proper materials and plenty of them your work is excellent; so was Gilbert's in my time; so was Galileo's; nay even Kepler—(though his method was as unskilful as that of the boy who in doing a long-division sum would first guess at the quotient and then multiply it into the divisor to see whether it were true; and if it came out wrong, would make another guess and multiply again; and so on till he guessed right at last;)—because he had a copious collection of materials ready to his hand, and enormous perseverance however perversely applied, and a religious veracity,—did at last hit upon one of the greatest discoveries ever made by one man. But what could Kepler have done without Tycho Brahe's tables of observation? And what might Galileo not have done if he had had a large enough collection of facts? This therefore it is that disappoints me. I do not see any sufficient collection made of materials,—

that is, of facts in nature—or any effectual plan on foot
for making one. You are scarcely better off in that respect
than I was; you have each to gather the materials upon
which you are to work. You cannot build houses, or weave
shirts, or learn languages so. If the builder had to make
his own bricks, the weaver to grow his own flax, the student
of a dead language to make his own concordance, where
would be your houses, your shirts, or your scholars? And
by the same rule if the interpreter of Nature is to forage for
his facts, what progress can you expect in the art of interpretation? Your scholar has his dictionary provided to his
hand; but your natural philosopher has still to make his
dictionary for himself.

"And I wonder the more at this, because this is the very
thing of all others which I myself pointed out as absolutely
necessary to be supplied,—as the thing which was to be set
about in the first place,—the thing *without* which no great
things could possibly be done in philosophy. And since
you have done me the honour to think so very highly of the
value of my precepts, I am a little surprised that you have
not thought it worth while in so very essential a point to
follow them. And to say the truth, I could wish for my
own reputation (if that were of any consequence) that you
had either honoured me a little more in that way, or not
honoured me quite so much in other ways. You call me
the Father of your Philosophy, meaning it for the greatest
compliment you can pay. I thank you for the compliment,
but I must decline the implied responsibility. I assure you
this is none of mine.—May I ask whether any attempt has
been made to collect that "*Historiam naturalem et experimentalem quæ sit in ordine ad condendam philosophiam,*" concerning which I did certainly give some very particular
directions;—which I placed as conspicuously as I could in
the very front and entrance of my design;—of which I said
that all the genius and meditation and argumentation in
the world could not do instead of it, no not if all men's
wits could meet in one man's head; therefore that this
we must have, or else the business must be for ever given

up? *—If this has been fairly tried and found impracticable or ineffectual, blot me out of your books as a dreamer that thought he had found out a great thing but it turned out nothing. If not, I still think it would be worth your while to try it."

A.

I partly comprehend your meaning! but I should prefer it in a less dramatic form. You think that the difference between what Galileo did and what Bacon wanted to be done, lay in this—that Bacon's plan presupposed a history (or dictionary as you call it) of Universal Nature, as a store-house of facts to work upon; whereas Galileo was content to work upon such facts and observations as he collected for himself. But surely this is only a difference in degree. Both used the facts in the same way, only Bacon wanted a larger collection of them.

B.

Say rather, Bacon wanted a collection large *enough* to give him the command of all the avenues to the secrets of Nature. You might as well say that there is only a difference of degree between the method of the man who runs his simple head against a fortress and the man who raises a force strong enough to storm it,—because each uses the force he has in the same way, only one wants more of it than the other:—or between stopping *all* the leaks in a vessel and stopping as many as you conveniently can. The truth is, that though the difference between *a few* and *a few more* is only a difference of degree, the difference between *enough* and *not enough* is a difference in kind. According to Galileo's method, the work at best could be done but partially. According to Bacon's (so at least he believed) it would be done effectually and altogether.

I will put you a case by way of illustration. Two men

---

* *Neque huic labori et inquisitioni et mundanæ perambulationi, ulla ingenii aut meditationis aut argumentationis substitutio aut compensatio sufficere potest, non si omnia omnium ingenia coierint. Itaque aut hoc prorsus habendum aut negotium in perpetuum deserendum.*

(call them James and John) find a manuscript in a character unknown to either of them. James, being skilled in languages and expert in making out riddles, observes some characters similar to those of one of the languages which he understands; immediately sets himself to guess what they are; and succeeds in puzzling out here a name, and there a date, with plausibility. Each succeeding guess, if it be right, makes the next the easier; and there is no knowing precisely how much may be made out in this manner, or with what degree of certainty. The process is inductive, and the results, so far as they go, are discoveries. John seeing him thus employed comes up and says, "This is all very ingenious and clever, and far more than I could do by the same process. But you are not going the right way to work. You will never be able to decipher the manuscript in this way. I will tell you what we must do. Here (you see) are certain forms of character which continually recur. Here is one that comes more than once in every line; here another that comes once in every two or three lines; a third that comes only twice or thrice in a page; and so on. Let us have a list made of these several forms, with an index showing where and how often they occur. In the mean time I will undertake, upon a consideration of the general laws of language, to tell you, by the comparative frequency of their recurrence, what parts of speech most of these are. So we shall know which of them are articles, which conjunctions, which relatives, which auxiliaries, and so on. Setting these apart, we shall be better able to deal with the nouns and verbs; and then by comparing the passages in which each occurs, we shall be able, with the help of your language-learning, to make out the meaning first of one, then of another. As each is determined, the rest will be easier to determine; and by degrees we shall come to know them all. It is a slow process compared with yours, and will take time and labour and many hands. But when it is done we shall be able to read the whole book."

Here I think you have a picture in little of the difference between Bacon's project for the advancement of philosophy

and that which was carried into effect (certainly with remarkable success) by the new school of inductive science
which flourished in his time. If we want to pursue the
parallel further, we have only to suppose that John, after
completing in a masterly manner a great portion of his
work on the universal laws of language; after giving particular directions for the collection, arrangement, and classification of the index; and even doing several pages of it
himself by way of example; is called away, and obliged to
leave the completion of the work to his successors; and
that his successors (wanting diligence to finish, patience to
wait, or ability to execute,) immediately fall back to the
former method;—in which they make such progress and
take such pride, that they never think of following out
John's plan, but leave it exactly where he left it. And here
I think you have a true picture of the state in which the
matter now rests.

A.

I see. The manuscript is the volume of Nature. The
learned linguist and expert maker-out of puzzles is Galileo
or one of his school. The work on the laws of language
is the Novum Organum. The index is the Natural and
Experimental History *quæ sit in ordine ad condendam
Philosophiam.* The making-out of the words one by one is
the Interpretation of Nature—

B.

And the ultimate reading of the whole book is the
" *Historia Illuminata sive Veritas Rerum ;* " the " *Philosophia
Secunda ;* " the sixth and last part of the " Instauration ; "
the consummation which Bacon knew that he was not to
be permitted himself to see, but trusted that (if men were
true to themselves) the Fortune of the Human Race would
one day achieve.

A.

And you think that they have not been true to themselves ?

B.

Why what have they done with this work since he left
it ? There it lies to speak for itself, sticking in the middle
of the Novum Organum. No attempt has been made, that
I can hear of, to carry it out further. People seem hardly
to know that it is not complete. John Mill observes that
Bacon's method of inductive logic is defective ; but does
not advert to the fact that of *ten* separate processes which
it was designed to include, the first only has been explained.
The other nine he had in his head, but did not live to set
down more of them than the names. And the particular
example which he has left of an inductive inquiry does not
profess to be carried beyond the first stage of generalization,
—the *vindemiatio prima,* as he calls it.

A.

It may be so ; but *why* have they not attempted to carry
his process out further ? Is it not because they have found
that they can get on faster with their old tools ?

B.

Because they *think* they can get on faster; you cannot
say they have *found* it until they have tried.

A.

Have they not tried Bacon's way partially, and found it
not so handy ? Has not Sir John Herschel, for instance,
tried the use of his famous classification of Instances, and
pronounced it " more apparent than real " ? And is it not a
fact that no single discovery of importance has been actually
made by proceeding according to the method recommended
by Bacon ? I am sure I have heard as much, reported upon
the authority of a very eminent modern writer upon these
subjects.

B.

So have I. And I can well believe that the use of
Bacon's " Prerogatives of Instances," *in the way they have*

been used, is not much ; and for the reason given by Herschel, viz. because the same judgment which enables you to
assign the Instance to its proper *class,* enables you, without
that assignation, to recognize its proper value. Therefore
so long as the task of gathering his Instances as they grow
wild in the woods is left to the Interpreter of Nature himself, there is little use in a formal classification ; he knows
exactly what he wants ; what is not to his purpose he need
not trouble himself with ; what is to his purpose he can
apply to that purpose at once. And each several man of
genius will no doubt acquire a knack of his own by which
he will arrive at his results faster than by any formal
method. But suppose the Interpreter wants to use the help
of other people, to whom he cannot impart his own genius
or his peculiar gift of knowing at first sight what is to the
purpose and what is not. He wants them to assist him in
gathering materials. How shall he direct them in their
task so that their labours may be available for himself?
I take it, he must distribute the work among several, and
make it pass through several processes. One man may be
used to make a rough and general collection,—what we call
an *omnium gatherum.* Another must be employed to reduce the confused mass into some order fit for reference.
A third to clear it of superfluities and rubbish. A fourth
must be taught to classify and arrange what remains. And
here I cannot but think that Bacon's arrangement of Instances according to what he calls their Prerogatives, or
some better arrangement of the same kind which experience
ought to suggest, would be found to be of great value ;
especially when it is proposed to make through all the
regions of Nature separate collections of this kind such as
may combine into one general collection. For though it
be true that as long as each man works only for himself, he
may trust to the *usus uni rei deditus* for finding out the
method of proceeding which best suits the trick of his own
mind,—and each will probably pursue a different method,—
yet when many men's labours are to be gathered into one
table, any collector of statistics will tell you that they must

all work according to a common pattern. And in the subject we are speaking of, which is coextensive with the mind of man on one side and with the nature of things on the other, that will undoubtedly be the best pattern which is framed upon the justest theory of the human understanding;—for which distinction Bacon's would seem to be no unlikely candidate.

However, I am here again getting out of my province. It may be that Bacon's project was visionary; or it may be that it is only *thought* visionary, because since his death no heart has been created large enough to believe it practicable. The philosophers must settle that among themselves. But be the cause what it will, it is clear to me on the one hand that the thing has not been seriously attempted; and on the other, that Bacon was fully satisfied that nothing of worth could be hoped for without it; therefore that we have no right to impute to him either the credit of all that has been done by the new philosophy, or the discredit of all that has been left undone.

A.

Certainly not; if you are right as to the fact. But I still think there must be some mistake. How is it possible that among so many distinguished men who have studied Bacon's philosophy with so much reverence, such a large feature can have been overlooked?

B.

I cannot pretend to explain that. But an appeal to one's own eyes is always lawful. Here is one passage which is enough by itself to settle the question. If you are not satisfied with it, I can quote half-a-dozen more to the same effect: "*Illud interim quod sæpe diximus etiam hoc loco præcipue repetendum est——*"

A.

Translate; if you would have me follow.

B.

" I must repeat here again what I have so often said ;—that though all the wits of all the ages should meet in one,—though the whole human race should make Philosophy their sole business ;—though the whole earth were nothing but colleges and academies and schools of learned men ;—yet without such a natural and experimental history as I am going to describe, no progress worthy of the human race in Philosophy and the Sciences could possibly be made : whereas if such a history were once provided and well-ordered, with the addition of such auxiliary and light-giving experiments as the course of Interpretation would itself suggest, the investigation of Nature and of all sciences would be the work only of a few years. Either this must be done, therefore, or the business must be abandoned. For in this way, and in this way only, can the foundation be laid of a true and active Philosophy."

A.

Where does he say that ?

B.

In the Preface to what he calls the *" Parasceue ad Historiam naturalem et experimentalem,"* which is in fact nothing more than a description of the sort of history which he wanted,—such a history as a true Philosophy might be built upon,—with directions to be observed in collecting it. He published it (somewhat out of its proper place) in the same volume with the Novum Organum, in order that, if possible, men might be set about the work at once ; of such primary importance did he hold it to be. If you distrust my translation, take it in his own English. In presenting the Novum Organum to the King, after explaining the nature and objects of the work and his reason for publishing it in an imperfect shape, he adds, "There is another reason for my so doing ; which is to try whether I can get help in one intended part of this work, namely the compiling of a natural and experimental history, *which must be the main foundation of a true and active philosophy."* And again

about a week after, in reply to the King's gracious acknowledgment of the book,—" This comfortable beginning
makes me hope further that your Majesty will be aiding to
me in setting men on work for the collecting of a natural
and experimental history, which is *basis totius negotii*." And
this was no after-thought, but an essential feature of his
design as he had conceived it at least sixteen years before.
There is extant a description of this proposed history, which
appears to have been written as early as 1604; and though
the only copy that I know of is in an imperfect and muti-
lated manuscript, enough remains to show that in all its
material features it agreed exactly with the description set
forth in the *Parasceue*.

Now you know I am not going to discuss the merit of his
plan. It may (as I said) have been all a delusion. But
grant it a delusion,—still it was a delusion under which he
was actually labouring. If every man of science that ever
lived had considered it and pronounced it puerile and ridiculous, still their unanimous verdict could not, in the face
of his own repeated and earnest declarations, persuade me
that it was not an essential part of Bacon's scheme; that it
was not (in his perfect and rooted judgment) the one key
to the cipher in which the fortunes of the human race are
locked up,—the one thing *with* which all might be done;
without which nothing. And this is all that is necessary for
our present business. For we are not discussing his philosophical capacity, but his personal character and purposes as
illustrated by the tenour of his life.

Going back therefore to where we left him, you will be
pleased to remember that when the prorogation of parliament in July, 1607, and the indisposition of Salisbury to
use his abilities in matters above his office, left him with
another interval before him of comparative leisure, he was
brimful of this great idea, and really believed that in the
argument of which he found himself by some odd accident
the solitary and single-handed champion, were contained
the hopes of the human race for the recovery of their lost
dominion over nature and the final conquest of all the

necessities and miseries of mortality. And if you will like-wise remember that it was not as a man might entertain such a speculation in these faded times when astonishment itself has become an every-day matter of idle curiosity,—that it was no curious speculation but a real and moving hope, such as the promise of that great intellectual spring-time, when the volume of Nature was opened (one may say) for the first time and the world was waiting in expectation of the issue, might well awaken in the soberest mind,—if you will remember this, you may partly conceive how solemn a thing such an idea was, falling into such a mind.

To this argument, accordingly, all the leisure which his professional and official duties allowed him, appears at this time to have been devoted. At least among his unprofes-sional works that have come down to us, I think there are only two (not bearing directly upon it) which seem to have been composed at this period.

A.

· Which are they?

B.

The paper on the Plantation in Ireland, and the Latin memorial of the Felicities of Queen Elizabeth.

A.

I thought the paper on Ireland had been earlier.

B.

The title does indeed state that it was presented to the King in 1606. That however (in the shape in which we have it) it cannot have been ; for it alludes to the death of Chief Justice Popham, which did not happen till June 1607. The date (for the original manuscript had none) has been added, I think indeed by Bacon himself, but probably several years afterwards, when it was easy to make a mis-take of a year or two. And that there was some doubt about the exact time is clear, for 1605 had been written first. But the true date may be determined with tolerable precision to be the 1st January, 1607–8.* And the paper was written (I suppose) in reference to certain measures taken by the Government upon the flight of Tyrone from Ireland, which took place in the preceding autumn. In a letter to Sir John Davies of the 23rd October 1607, Bacon says in allusion to that event,—" I see manifestly the beginning of better or worse. But methinketh it is first a tender of the better, and worse followeth but upon refusal or default." And the time being critical, the object of the paper (which was presented to the King for a new year's gift) was to guide the project right while the stage was yet clear. The scheme of colonization, in furtherance of which it was drawn up, was the most successful measure, I believe, in the whole course of the policy of England towards Ireland ; and the principles laid down in it must (making allowance for altered circumstances) be still our guides if we hope to do any good in that region.

The memorial of the Felicities of Queen Elizabeth was written in 1608 ; partly to discharge his debt of reverence to the memory of his old mistress, partly as an important contribution to the history of the times, which no one else was so well qualified to supply. It is short, and touches only some principal points ; yet it ought in my opinion not only to find a place in every history of that reign, but to be laid as a foundation for the study of it, being the deliberate testimony of the man who of all others best understood the times he was writing of, given at a period when there was no inducement whatever to flatter them. The importance which he himself attached to it may be inferred from the fact that in one of his wills he specially directed that it should be published. And undoubtedly the report of such a man concerning the affairs of the days in which he lived,

---

* Mr. Gardiner (*History of England*, i. 554) dates it a year later, 1608–9. Rightly. Allusion is made in the paper to the project as " digested already *for the County of Tyrone.*" Now on the 12th of December 1608 a scheme for the settlement of the County of Tyrone was submitted to the Government by the Commissioners, and on the 9th of January 1608–9 for the other five counties. So New Year's Day 1608–9 would suit.

ought to be received by the historian as the weightiest
evidence that can be had. For there you have the two
great requisites in their greatest perfection,—the eye that
can see what is material, and the pen that can set it down
correctly.

The rest of his leisure seems to have been devoted entirely to his great work (for the " Wisdom of the Ancients,"
if not strictly a part of it, is made up of its surplus materials)
—until at the next meeting of parliament Salisbury's unhappy device of the " Great Contract " set the King and the
Commons together by the ears, and put the relation between
them so completely out of tune, that how to set that right
became the great problem of state in which all others
merged, and for the solution of which every man who had
any interest in the State must have felt bound to contribute
his best endeavours.

A.

Then this is too large a chapter to enter upon to-night.
But are you aware of the rock you are running on ? You
are trying to make out for Bacon so magnificent a mission
in the philosophical department,—magnificent according to
his own idea and belief,—that it must be a strong case which
will justify him in turning aside to pursue objects incompatible with the effectual prosecution of it.

B.

I am quite aware of that. And as it happens, I do really
think he would not have turned aside for a light one. But
you speak as if I were bound to prove that he never made a
mistake. Did I ever undertake to do that? Surely not.
The best man that ever lived, if he had to make the journey
over again, would in many places take a different road. I
am quite content that, if you see occasion, you should regret
the course he took as a misfortune, or even censure it as an
error. We know that he *regretted* it himself. That he *re-
pented* it (which is so commonly assumed) is not so clear.
But what if he did? Human life must always be in some

measure a game of chance. The wisest choice will often turn out the unluckiest; and however we may *wish*, after the event is known, that we had made some other, still if it was the wisest it was the right choice to make, let it turn out as unluckily as it will. Whether Bacon's choice on this occasion was the wisest or not, I am not prepared to say. But I do say—and I expect you to agree with me—that the occasion was one in which a man who had the public good at heart might easily doubt which choice to make. I am in a hurry to keep an important appointment; but if I meet by the way with a man who has fallen among thieves, I must stop to bind up his wounds, even though by the breach of the appointment some better man loses more than the wounded man gains by my surgery. And if I should say afterwards (as I very likely may) that I am sorry I did not keep the appointment, I hope no one will understand me as deliberately wishing that I had left the man to bleed to death. Bacon was in a hurry to finish the "Instauratio Magna." But he fell in by the way with a great accident which called for present help. A breach was opened between the King and the Commons, which was destined to grow every year wider and wider, till it led to a civil war, which issued in the violent subversion, first of the old government, then of the new, to make way for a third worse than either. It is surely possible to conceive that to one who foresaw in the distance some such possible issue, the first opening of that breach may have seemed like an accident which called all hands to the rescue.

But we will talk further of that when we come to it. In the mean time it is well that you should know what about this time was Bacon's own idea of his vocation in the world. I have given you my notion of the principles upon which he was acting and the ends at which he was aiming, as I have been able to collect them from the traces which remain of his actual course. I will now give you his own as he had himself recorded it, somewhere about this time. I say *had* recorded, because the record is contained in an old paper which he had laid by long before he gave his great work to the world; and which no doubt represents his feelings at the time when it was written. The exact date I cannot tell. It was found among his papers, and was published many years after his death with no explanation beyond the title. It bears evidence however in itself that it was written about the middle of his life, before he had attained any success in his civil career, and probably at the time when he meant his great work to be comprised in three books, under the title of *Temporis Partus Masculus, sive de Interpretatione Naturæ.* It is headed " *De Interpretatione Naturæ Proœmium,*" and if he had completed the work in that form and at that time, would I suppose have stood as the introduction. I translate freely, as far as the expression is concerned; but only that I may give the true meaning and effect the more exactly.

De Interpretatione Naturæ,
Proœmium.

" Conceiving that I was born to be of use to mankind, and that the care of the Common Weal is a kind of common property, which like the air and the water belongs to every-body, I set myself to consider in what way mankind might be most effectually served, and what I was myself best fitted by nature to do.

" And upon the first point I concluded that of all the benefits that can be conferred upon the human race, the greatest is the discovery of new arts, endowments, and com-modities for the benefit of man's life. For I saw that among the rude people in the primitive times, the authors of rude inventions and discoveries were consecrated and numbered among the gods. And it was plain that the good effects wrought by founders of cities, law-givers, fathers of the people, extirpers of tyrants, and heroes of that class, extend but over narrow spaces and last but for short times; whereas the work of the Inventor, though a thing of less pomp and show, is felt everywhere and lasts for ever. But above all, if—instead of striking out some particular invention, how-ever useful—a man could kindle a light in Nature herself,— a light that should in its very rising touch and illuminate all the border-regions that confine upon the circle of our present knowledge ; and so spreading further and further should presently disclose and bring into sight all that is most hidden and secret in the world ;—that man (I thought) would be the benefactor indeed of the human race, the propagator of man's empire over the universe, the champion of liberty, the conqueror and rooter out of necessities.

" Then, turning to myself, I found that I was fitted for nothing so well as for the study of Truth ; as having a mind nimble and versatile enough to catch the resemblances of things (which is the greatest point), and at the same time steady enough to fix and distinguish their subtler differences ; as being gifted by nature with desire to seek, patience to doubt, fondness to meditate, slowness to assert, readiness to think again, carefulness to dispose and set in order ; and as being a man that neither affects the new, nor admires the old, and hates every kind of imposture. So that I thought my nature had a kind of familiarity and relationship with Truth.

" And yet because my birth and education had seasoned me in business of State ; and because opinions (so young as I was) would sometimes stagger me ; and because I thought that a man's own country has some special claims upon him more than the rest of the world ; and because I hoped that if I rose to any place of honour in the State I should have a larger command of ability and industry to help me in my work ;—for these reasons I both applied myself to acquire the arts of civil life, and commended my services, so far as in modesty and honesty I might, to the favour of my powerful friends. In which also I had another motive ;— for I felt that those things I have spoken of (be they great or small) reach no further than the condition and culture of this mortal life ; and I was not without hope (the condition of Religion being at that time not very prosperous) that if I came to hold office in the State, I might get something done too for the good of men's souls.

" When I found however that my zeal was mistaken for ambition; and that my life had already reached the turning-point; and when my breaking health reminded me how ill I could afford to be so slow; and when I reflected moreover that in leaving undone the good which I could do by myself alone, and applying myself to that which could not be done without the consent and help of others, I was by no means discharging the duty which lay upon me,—I put all those thoughts aside, and (in pursuance of my old determination) betook myself wholly to this work. Nor am I discouraged from it, because I see signs in the times of the decline and overthrow of that knowledge and erudition which is now in use. For though I do not apprehend any more barbarian incursions (unless possibly the Spanish empire should first recover strength to crush other nations by arms, and then sink under its own weight), yet the civil wars which may be expected, I think, (judging from certain fashions that have come in of late,) to spread over many countries,—together with the malignity of sects, and those compendious artifices and devices that have crept into the place of solid erudition, —seem to portend for literature and the sciences a tempest no less fatal; and one against which the Printing-office will be no effectual security. And no doubt but that fair-weather learning which is nursed by leisure and blossoms under reward and praise, which cannot stand out against the violence of opinion, and is liable to be abused by artifices and quackery, will sink under such impediments as these. Far otherwise is it with that Knowledge whose dignity is maintained by works of utility and power.—For the wrongs therefore which the times may threaten, I am not afraid of them; and for the wrongs which men may offer, I am not concerned. For if any one charge me with seeking to be wise overmuch, I answer simply that modesty and civil respect are for civil matters; in contemplations nothing is to be respected but Truth. If any one call on me for *works*, and that presently, I tell him frankly, without any varnish at all, that for me,—a man not old, of weak health, my hands full of civil business, entering without guide or light upon an argument of all others the most obscure,—I hold it enough to have constructed the machine, though I may not succeed in setting

it to work.   Nay I will admit further that it would be
an error in me to make the attempt ; for that the Interpretation of Nature, rightly conducted, ought, in the first steps
of the ascent, until a certain stage of Generals be reached, to
be kept clear of all application to works.   And this has been
in fact the error of all those who have heretofore ventured
themselves at all upon the waves of experience, that, being
either too weak of purpose or too eager for display, they
have all at the outset sought prematurely for works, as
proofs and pledges of their progress, and upon that rock
have been wrecked and cast away.—If again any one ask
me, not indeed for actual works, yet for definite promises
and forecasts of the works that are to be, I would have him
know that the knowledge which we now possess will not
teach a man even what to *wish*.—Lastly (though this be a
matter of less moment)—if any of our politicians, that use
to value everything according to persons or precedents,
must needs interpose his judgment in a thing of this nature,
—I would but remind him how (according to the old fable)
the lame man that kept the course beat the swift man who
left it ; and that there is no thought to be taken about precedents, for the thing is without precedent.

" Now for my plan of publication, it is this. Those
parts of the work which have it for their object to find out
and bring into correspondence such minds as are prepared
and disposed for the argument, and to purge the floors of
men's understandings,—I wish to be published to the world
and circulate from mouth to mouth ; the rest I would have
passed from hand to hand with selection and judgment.
Not but that I know it is an old trick of impostors to keep a
few of their follies back from the public which are indeed no
better than those which they put forward ; but in this case
it is no imposture at all, but a sound foresight, which tells
me that the formula itself of Interpretation, and the discoveries made by the same, will thrive better if committed
to the charge of some fit and selected minds, and kept
private.

" However, the risk is none of mine. In so far as the

issue depends upon others, it is indifferent to me,   I am not
hunting for fame; I have no ambition (heresiarch-wise) to
found a sect; and to look for any private gain from such an
undertaking as this, would be as ridiculous as base. Enough
for me the consciousness of well-deserving, and those real
and effectual results with which Fortune itself cannot interfere."

A.

What a magnificent overture !   Why did he suppress it,
I wonder?

B.

You know the case had changed before he published the
" Novum Organum." He had re-engaged himself in politics,
—was no longer wholly betaken to this work. But indeed
he rather altered than suppressed it. The substance of the
more material part of it is to be found in the first book of
the " Novum Organum." It is distributed through several
different aphorisms, and brought out more fully and perfectly. But I think it is all there, except the autobiogra-
phical part, and the prophecy of civil wars ; both of which
are interesting, though I dare say he was quite right to
leave them out. The latter seems decisively to disprove
the assertion, commonly (though I think negligently) made,
that he had no foresight of the danger with which the
Government was threatened from the progress of popular
opinion. And the former is, I believe, the only piece of
autobiography in which he ever indulged. In the preface
to the " Novum Organum " he leaves it with a simple " *De
nobis ipsis silemus.*"

A.

Which I like still better.

B.

Yes, the silence is great; but we should not have known
how great, without knowing as we do from this, how much
lay beneath it,—what it was that he did not think it necessary to say.

A.

The interval of repose, then, carries him to the end of his forty-ninth year.   I shall be curious to hear what it was that brought him back into the turmoil.   The reviewer gives us no light upon the subject.

B.

No.   He must wait a little longer till we come up with him.

EVENING THE NINTH.

B.

I undertook to explain the nature of the emergency which interrupted Bacon in the prosecution of his great work, and called him back to the service of the State. And if you will be content with a general explanation, I do not know that I need be long about it. But if you look for details and authorities—

A.

O never mind the details. Make me understand generally what was the matter. I can ask for particulars afterwards if I like.

B.

The matter was the disease for which Falstaff could find no remedy,—the consumption of the purse; an awkward disease in itself for a King, and one which was fast breeding others of a more dangerous character. King James, to say the worst of him, could not easily deny himself any pleasure; and unfortunately one of his chief pleasures was to give to those whom he liked whatever they wished to have; in consequence of which he soon had much less than nothing left of his own. He had reigned with this infirmity for six years, when his Lord Treasurer, the old Earl of Dorset, died; leaving the Exchequer in a miserable condition. The ordinary expenditure exceeded the ordinary income

by 81,000*l.* a-year; besides which there was a debt of
1,300,000*l.*; and this at a time when the regular revenue
of the Crown was expected to meet all its ordinary occasions
without any assistance from parliament.

Salisbury was made Lord Treasurer, and lost no time in
setting his brains to deal with the difficulty; and if diligence,
subtlety, activity, and finesse, had been enough for the task,
perhaps there was no man more likely to succeed. But he
had here a new case to deal with, and the event showed that
he did not thoroughly understand it. It may be doubted
indeed whether, when he began, he understood it at all.
For though he succeeded in reducing the debt by 900,000*l.*
and in considerably increasing the ordinary revenue, yet the
amendment was but partial, and it was effected chiefly by
measures which stood directly in the way of the only remedy
that could be really effectual and satisfactory. He had
not been long in office, however, before he did understand
thus much, that that remedy must come from parliament;
and that, since the precedents of parliament showed no
instance of a supply at all adequate to the emergency, some
new occasion must be created that should lie out of the
region of precedents. Nay, he probably saw likewise that
it would be necessary to place the Crown and the Commons
permanently in a new relation to each other, so far as
revenue was concerned. Such a necessity was certainly
coming on fast. As the wealth and population of the
kingdom grew, the expenses of Government could not but
increase; yet the Crown revenues were not increasing in
anything like that proportion; and in the mean time the
value of the old parliamentary contribution,—the "one
subsidy and two fifteens,"—was rapidly diminishing. The
subsidy was indeed at this time less by at least a third than
it had been in the beginning of Queen Elizabeth's reign.

A.

How do you mean?

B.

I mean that three subsidies in James's time did not
bring as many pounds into the Exchequer as two did fifty

years before. I cannot tell you why; but so it was. And therefore it may well be doubted whether the Government, even with the strictest economy in the husbandry as well as in the distribution of its means, could have gone on much longer upon the old system. But however that may be, there could be no doubt that the immediate necessity with which Salisbury had to deal, made some extraordinary course absolutely indispensable; and the very ticklish terms upon which Prerogative and Privilege then stood made the choice of that course extremely difficult and hazardous.

A.

I can easily believe that:—an admission of the *truth* being, I suppose, hardly practicable.

B.

An exposure of the truth *naked* being at least very undesirable. Where it is the fashion to wear clothes, you know, Innocence herself must go drest, or she will be mistaken for something quite different. But in this case the danger was not so much in letting the truth be known (if it had been possible to know it fully), as in letting the questions be agitated through which it was to be approached. The boundary-line between the power of the Crown and the power of the Commons had not yet been laid down.

A.

Was not yet correctly understood, you mean.

B.

No; that is just what I do *not* mean. I mean what I say,—that it had not yet been laid down. I mean that there *was* no boundary-line. And it is important to keep this distinction in mind; because modern writers are too apt to talk as if the principles of the constitution had always been there and always been the same; only had not always been properly understood;—as if this thing might be spoken of as in itself constitutional, and that thing as in itself unconstitutional, without reference to the time of which you speak. Whereas in fact not merely the knowledge of the constitution but the constitution itself was *growing;* growing, and changing as it grew; nor is there any period of its growth in which a different combination of accidents might not have made it grow in a different way. Is it constitutional, for instance, that Privy-Councillors should sit and vote in the House of Commons?

A.

Yes; beyond all question.

B.

Beyond all question *now,* I grant. The accidents have so settled it. But in the year 1614 that very point was so far from being beyond question, that it was actually under discussion and within an inch of being settled the other way. That the Attorney-General should sit and vote in the Commons was actually decided to be *unconstitutional.* Of course I do not mean that decisions of such questions are merely capricious. They are meant to be decided according to reason. But reasons turn chiefly upon precedents; and precedents are for the most part determined by accident.

This, however, is all a digression; and for our present purpose it is not necessary that we should agree on the point. It will at any rate be admitted that many constitutional questions were as yet undetermined. Now in the case before us, the question which remained to be determined was this—how far, according to the laws and usages of the land, was the King dependent upon the House of Commons for means to carry on the Government? That he could not carry it on comfortably or prosperously without their help, was plain enough: but could he carry it on at all? Now tell me: Do you think it was desirable, as things then stood, to push such a question, or allow it to be pushed, to a definite issue? And before you answer, remember what practical inferences must have been immediately drawn from it, and what momentous consequences were involved in them,—especially if the answer were " No."

A.

If the King could not carry on the Government constitutionally without assistance from the House of Commons, it followed (you would say) that the Commons had constitutionally a *veto*, such as it has now, upon all the proceedings of the Government?

B.

Precisely. Do this, or we stop the supplies.

A.

It would have been a revolution, no doubt; and a revolution (I do think) far too great to come safely upon the nation, if it came suddenly. Even coming as it did after the civil war,—(for the civil war itself may be considered, I suppose, rather as the answer to the question than as a consequence involved in the answer)—great preparations were found necessary for the entertainment of it.

B.

Yes. The art of packing and corrupting the House of Commons, which had been scarcely thought of in James's time, and was then reckoned unconstitutional, had to be studied and brought into fashion. And if it had been studied less diligently or practised with less success, we hardly know now whether the State could have borne without some great disorder the full recognition of the dependence of the Crown upon the Commons. And in prospect, it must of course have looked more alarming than we can guess from our retrospect.

A.

Well: the problem then was, to induce the Commons to supply the King's necessities without tempting them to inquire too curiously into the extremity of his case, or to ask what would happen to him or to them if they left .him unsupplied. Yes. I see the difficulty of it. It was such a case as two wise men acting solely for themselves and upon their own judgment might have found hard to adjust, and for two such parties as a legitimate King and a popular House of Commons to settle it between them, must have been a very formidable enterprise. And yet I think great use might have been made of the occasion by a man of real ability.

B.

Ay; if a man could have been found who had sense and courage enough to understand the whole case and all its possible issues; who had public spirit enough to sympathize with both parties and desire their common good; who had enough of the confidence of both to be listened to on either side with respect and without suspicion; who had address enough to keep them both from treading too near the dangerous places;—such a man might have turned the difficulty to an excellent account, and have brought out of it a result greatly to the advantage of all. He might have rendered a service to his country as nearly immortal as anything in this world can be. But unfortunately Salisbury was not such a man. That he did not fully understand the case is unquestionable; for he had it in his own hands and it signally failed. And one would almost think (as I said just now) that when he first took it up he did not understand it at all. At least if he had been deliberately looking out for an obstacle to throw in the way, I hardly know what he could have found more effectual than his first measure.

A.

What might that be?   .

B.

I dare say you know that the question of *Impositions* had already been agitated in the House of Commons: the question (I mean) whether the King had a right by his prerogative to impose duties without the sanction of parliament upon goods exported and imported. It was true that a case which turned upon that question had been recently argued in the Court of Exchequer, and the Judges had decided that the King *had* such a right. But it was also true that in the last parliament that very decision had been complained of and controverted; and it was quite plain that it had by no means set the question at rest. It was just one of those stretches of prerogative of which the Commons were most jealous; perhaps with most reason. Yet the very first thing Salisbury did, after he was made Lord Treasurer, was to stretch this very power further than it had ever been stretched before;— to lay on at one clap, by the sole virtue of this disputed right, duties to the amount of 60,000*l.* a year. Whether it was done in inconsiderate haste, as the readiest shift to make the ordinary receipts equal to the ordinary expenditure and stop the accumulation of debt; or whether he had some further reach in it,—as thinking perhaps to enhance the value of a prerogative which he meant to sell, or by increasing the burden to make the Commons more eager to bargain for the removal of it,—I cannot say. But so it was. And a very mischievous measure it proved.

A.

I dare say it was only to enhance the value of his own services in the King's eyes, and so establish himself in his new seat.

B.

Well, that may be. It is the simplest explanation, and very likely the true one. And now you mention it, I remember something which rather confirms it. There is a curious paper in the British Museum drawn up by Sir Julius Cæsar, who was then Chancellor of the Exchequer. It contains a journal record of Salisbury's services during the first two months of his Treasurership; and seems to have been drawn up (in perfect good faith, I do not doubt) for the express purpose of magnifying to the King the merits of his new Lord Treasurer. The particular business of the Impositions is thus recorded:—

"On Saturday the 11th of June, the Lord Treasurer, attended by the Chancellor and the Barons of the Exchequer, went to the Custom House, and there in the assembly of the chief merchants of England, assembled from all the principal parts of the land, did make an excellent speech to prove that Impositions might lawfully be imposed by sovereign kings and princes on all merchandises issuing out or coming into their ports;—that no King, living or dead, doth or ever did deserve better for the continuance of that privilege than our sovereign King James, who in his excellent virtues, natural, moral, and political, surmounteth all other kings living or dead;—that his present necessities occasioned for the use of the public, especially for Ireland, contrary to his own will and the admirable sweetness of his own natural inclination, have occasioned him to use this lawful and just means of profit;—which speech he had no sooner knit up with a particular repetition of Impositions now seeming burdensome and ordered by his Majesty for the ease of his subjects to be lightened, and likewise most things of necessary important use to the poor to be excepted from any imposition, than every man, after some little contradiction, assented to this general imposition now established;—which will prove the most gainful to the King of any one day's work done by any one Lord Treasurer since the time of King Edward III."

The whole journal of Salisbury's services during these two months is summed up in these words:—

"He hath moreover, to the King's great honour, lessened the Impositions upon the commodities of currants, sugars, and tobacco; and hath, to the King's great profit and the benefit of his posterity, increased his revenue by new Impositions general upon other merchandises to the value of 60,000*l.* a year; and likewise hath raised a like benefit of 10,000*l.* a year increase upon ale-houses licensed.

"So that, besides his other continual employments both in this high place and other his important and great places, he hath in the space of two months and twenty days directed and signed 2884 letters, and gotten to the King in money 37,455*l.* and in yearly revenues 71,100*l.*; which I dare confidently affirm was never done by any Lord Treasurer of England in two years. God's name be glorified for it, and honoured be our gracious

Sovereign, who made the choice of so diligent and gracious a servant: and recommended be that servant who hath the conscience to discharge his duty to so gracious a Sovereign, whose long experienced judgment can rightly deem of men's deserts, and wisely distinguish between truth and falsehood."

So the good Sir Julius; Salisbury himself (we may suppose) not being unwilling that all this fuss should be made about him. His uppermost object, I dare say, was to make the King feel that he could not spare so diligent and so profitable a servant. It was his best defence against the rising influence of Carr, and the machinations of his Court enemies. But we are wandering again.

All this was done. But all this was not nearly enough. The Crown still laboured under a debt of 400,000*l.* and a large annual deficiency. The next step therefore was to think of some benefit to the people, in return for which (being conditionally offered) the Commons might be induced to vote a supply adequate to the wants of the Government. And certainly the scheme which Salisbury devised with this view was a large and imposing, and (had it been wisely digested and prudently carried) might have proved a very happy one. The revenue of the Crown was in those days drawn from many sources besides its patrimonial property; chiefly from certain tenures and privileges,—such as Wardships, Knights'-service, Purveyance, and others,—the particular nature of which I cannot undertake to explain :— remnants of the feudal system, which the times were fast outgrowing ;—privileges which had come to be burdensome to the people in a degree much greater, I fancy, than they were valuable to the crown; and what was worse, (the system and occasions out of which they originally grew being forgotten,) had come to be looked upon and felt as grievances. Yet that these rights did belong to the Crown and formed a regular and legitimate source of revenue was not disputed. Here therefore were all the essential elements of a just and advantageous arrangement for both parties. A fixed revenue of equal amount derived from taxation would have been better for the King. And even a considerably larger revenue so supplied would have been much better for the people. There remained only the old difficulty, incident to all the bargains that are made under the sun,— the difficulty of inducing the contracting parties to deal frankly and openly, with just and reasonable desires on both sides ; instead of higgling and trying above all things to overreach one another, or (which is almost as bad) taking care above all things not to be overreached. It must be admitted, however, that this difficulty was in the particular case unusually great. The Commons,—jealous, ambitious, conscious of their advantage, many, and full of lawyers ;— the King, irritable, impatient, loose-tongued, conscious of his disadvantage and struggling to face it out, his heart full of anxiety about his estate, his mouth full of prerogative and divine right ;—how were two such parties to come to an understanding on such a subject ? Everything would of course depend upon the discreet opening and conducting of it by those ministers who stood between the two and had influence with both. And here again it must be admitted that Salisbury, with all his experience, dexterity, and practised diplomatism, made great mistakes ; so great as to give some colour to the suspicion that he had some other end in view, and did not sincerely wish the negotiation to succeed according to the professed design. Such was certainly Bacon's impression ; though I cannot find that he had any definite conjecture as to what the real end was.

A.

Stop ; you are going a little too fast for me. What kind of mistakes did he make ?

B.

I will tell you as well as I can. But our accounts of the progress of the business and the causes which broke it off are so imperfect that much must be left to conjecture ; and I must confess that the best conjectures which I have myself been able to make leave much unexplained and unaccounted for. But there are two principal features in his

management of the negotiation concerning which there is no
doubt; and I think we may safely (especially after the
event) pronounce them great mistakes.

In the first place, whatever might be the causes in which
the proposition originated, the proposed arrangement both
professed to be and was for the good of the State. It was to
establish the necessary powers and revenues of the Crown
upon a foundation less inconvenient and obnoxious to the
people. Now in such a case what would you have set forth
as the ostensible motives and inducements to the measure ?

A.

The benefits which it promised, of course.

B.

Exactly so. The necessities and embarrassments of the
Crown should have been kept out of sight; and the substantial benefits of the measure, as a thing good for the commonwealth, should have been boldly relied upon as the only and
sufficient recommendation of it. But what did Salisbury
do ? He began by a public and official proclamation of the
King's pecuniary distress, the amount of his debts, the insufficiency of his ordinary income to meet his ordinary expenditure, and his utter inability to extricate himself from
his embarrassments without a very liberal supply from the
benevolence of the people. As if a man, going to borrow
money of a Jew, were to begin (by way of inducing him to a
reasonable bargain) with saying, " Here is a schedule of my
debts; my creditors are impatient and unrelenting ; therefore you see I am entirely at your mercy." Surely this was
to tell the Commons in so many words that they had the
King at a disadvantage and might make what terms they
pleased. For *they* need be in no hurry. *They* were in no
extremity. On the contrary, they were flourishing in a
wealthy peace. The burdens they suffered could hardly be
called oppressions. The cry of grievances was not the cry
which is sometimes wrung from a people by burdens increased till they become intolerable ; rather that of a people

whose burdens are just heavy enough to irritate, but not heavy enough to oppress. And of these they were in fact rapidly relieving themselves, and rapidly winning the game. It was the exultation of success, not the agony of despair, that made James's parliaments difficult to manage. They kicked because they had waxed fat.

Well, the foundation being thus ill-laid, and the distresses of the Crown being officially proclaimed and thrown into the House of Commons to be examined and discussed,—then came the second great mistake. By way of remedy the Commons were invited to provide for the King both a present supply sufficient to relieve him from his present necessities (for which 600,000*l.* was asked), and a permanent income for the future, sufficient for the annual expenditure of government (which was laid at 200,000*l.* a year); and by way of retribution for this provision, it was intimated that the King was ready to hear and redress all their grievances.

A.

Including Wardships, Purveyance, &c., I suppose?

B.

Why yes, I suppose the design was to include them. It could hardly have been hoped that the arrangement would proceed otherwise. But they were as yet kept in the background. The redress of *grievances* was held out in the beginning as a sufficient retribution. The sacrifice by the Crown of a portion of its legitimate revenue was not spoken of; and when it came to be proposed afterwards was treated as a matter for a separate bargain, worth another 100,000*l.* a year. However, though Salisbury would not show his whole budget at first, I cannot doubt that he was from the first prepared to fall back upon these as the bargain proceeded, and meant them in fact to form the substantial part of the retribution.

A.

Of course he would not throw away his whole "bag of equivalents" until he had felt his footing. But where was his mistake? I thought you admitted just now that such a change would be good for both parties.

B.

No doubt, it was better that the King should receive his 50,000*l.* a year (or whatever the sum might be) from a well-ordered tax or duty than from the Court of Wards; I do not find fault with that. But do you think the Commons were so dull as not to see, that if they both paid off the King's debts and assigned him a permanent income large enough to enable him to carry on the government without an occasional subsidy from them, the tables would be turned and they would be thenceforward at *his* mercy? Give him money enough, and what need would he have to call any more parliaments? or what should hinder him from calling them only to do his work, and dissolving them the moment they began to do any work for themselves?

A.

Yes, I see. It must indeed have been a large concession that would have made it their interest to give up that hold upon him.

B.

Would any conceivable concession have been large enough? Would it not have been fatal to the popular element in the constitution? Even the best-devised laws for securing the liberties of the people could not have been trusted when that check was taken away. Take away the fear of parliaments, and the lawyers would have made the laws mean just what they liked.

"Certainly," said Bacon, writing to the King two or three years after, "when I heard the overtures last parliament carried in such a strange figure and idea, as if your Majesty should no more (for matter of profit) have needed your subjects' help; nor your subjects in that kind should no more have needed your graces and benignity; methought, besides the difficulty (in next degree to an impossibility) it was *animalis sapientia*, and almost contrary to the very frame of a monarchy and those original obligations which it is God's will should intercede between King and people."

It is very doubtful to me whether any true friend to the entire constitution could have wished for the consummation of such an arrangement. It was very certain that the Commons (being, as a body, true friends only to their own half of the constitution) would be stimulated by such a proposal to rake up every possible grievance that might be thrown as an additional weight into their own scale, and to stir every disputed question which, being decided in their favour, would disparage the value of the concessions which the King was prepared to make. And what could a negotiation so commenced be expected to lead to but turbulent and irritating litigation while it lasted, and in the end to a fruitless breaking-off with mutual dissatisfaction?

With regard to the details of the actual proceeding we have a good deal of scattered information, partly in the fragmentary notes preserved in the Commons' Journals (too fragmentary to be understood), partly in general reports of the progress of the session sent from one friend to another and preserved in collections of contemporary correspondence; but hardly sufficient to ground a faithful narrative upon. Enough remains however to prove beyond doubt that the proceeding was full of offence and irritation, and that the end was utter failure, which left the relation between King and Commons in a worse condition than ever, and all chance of a satisfactory adjustment thenceforward greatly diminished.

The first thing was a general raking-up of grievances; a thing which of itself could hardly end pleasantly : for they were sure to light upon some which could not be redressed, and these would but smart the more for being probed. But it was impossible for them to get through the list of grievances without falling upon the question of Impositions. Salisbury's much-vaunted day's work made this inevitable. The valuation of the concessions offered by the King could not proceed a step until it was determined whether so important and indefinite a power as that of setting duties upon imports and exports at his own will, were his to concede or not. The very entrance upon the question, as might have been expected, bred trouble. Angry speeches passed between the Upper and Lower House. The King with characteristic precipitation forbade the Commons to discuss his right, and, upon their remonstrance, with characteristic facility withdrew his objection—but not till thoughts had been suggested and words spoken which were like sparks in the neighbourhood of gunpowder. The discussion ended, as might also have been anticipated, in a vote that the King had *no* such right; and though they abstained from a formal resolution to that effect, which would have been a direct censure upon the judgment in the Court of Exchequer, they yet took care to introduce it in the petition of grievances in such a manner as distinctly to imply a denial of the King's right; whence it followed that his consent to pass an act depriving him of this power for the future, (and to this he did afterwards consent,) which would have been received as a great boon had it come before that discussion, now went for nothing. Then came searching inquiries into all the other points of prerogative and the proper value of them; and then all the higgling incident to a bargain in which neither party knew how much the other was prepared to give. And in this also it must be added as another proof of Salisbury's mismanagement, that the huckster-spirit was more glaringly displayed on his side than on the other.

Nevertheless the time was certainly favourable. There appears to have been an eager desire to conclude an arrangement upon the proposed basis, and great hope that it would be effected. Intelligent men who were by no means blind to the difficulties of the case did certainly expect that it would end at last in some great beneficial arrangement for the commonwealth: and at one time it seemed upon the very point of adjustment: for by the latter end of July the Commons had formally agreed to assure to the Crown, in consideration of certain specified concessions, an annual revenue of 200,000*l.*; while the King, on his side, had intimated his willingness to make the concessions and accept the money. In short, they had agreed on the substance of the bargain; and it only remained to give and take effectual securities on either side for the due performance. In this no doubt there were many difficulties still to be encountered. But this preliminary agreement (to which the Commons had been brought at last and reluctantly by a sudden intimation that if they did not agree at once the negotiation would be broken off altogether) was thought a good enough resting-place for the time: whereupon they were prorogued for three months, with an understanding that at their next meeting they should take up the business where it had been left off.

A.

A fixed revenue of 200,000*l.* a year, assured to the Crown for ever, and not requiring any renewed sanction from parliament, I suppose. But stay—that was only for the *support.* What became of the proposal for a present *supply?*

B.

True: for which Salisbury had asked 600,000*l.* Why, for the present, little or nothing. They had voted one subsidy and one fifteenth; the smallest contribution ever voted, I believe;—not above a fifth part of the demand. However that was of no great consequence, considering the time. It would have been hardly reasonable to expect a full contribution until the rest of the bargain was concluded. To vote *that* would have been to give up their present advantage. Many accidents might · frustrate the bargain yet; and after all—(though but a few days before the close of the session they seemed "like to part on the lovingest terms that ever any subjects of England did rise from parliament ")—their final leave-taking was not auspicious. The greater part of the petition of grievances had hitherto remained unanswered. The answer was reserved until the day of prorogation, and when it came was very far from satisfactory. So they were sent into the country to meditate for three months upon what they had done and what they were to do, in no very good humour.

A.

And how did it all end ?

B.

Ask me *in what* it ended, and I can tell you easily enough :—in nothing at all, but mutual disappointment and vexation. *How* it ended, is a question which (strange to say) nobody can answer. Most of our historians impute the change to the House of Commons. When they met again (it is said) they were out of love with the project ; and instead of setting themselves to conclude the arrangement which they had agreed upon, took to the exhibition of fresh grievances or the ripping up of old grievances anew. And certain it is that within a month of their meeting they were in full cry upon that scent, and in very bad humour. That they were in that disposition when they met I should think probable, not so much from any evidence that I can find of the fact, as from the nature of the case. Three months spent in talking over their bargain with their constituents or with one another would naturally tend to diminish their satisfaction with it. All opinions would concur in exaggerating the sacrifice they had agreed to make, and in undervaluing the retributions for which they had stipulated. I should have been contented therefore with this explanation of the commencement of the breach, if it were not for some expressions dropped by Bacon, (and in letters to the King, to whom he would not offer an *unlikely* story,) which would seem to ascribe the breaking-off of the contract to Salisbury himself. In a letter written not long after Salisbury's death, —the object of which was to persuade the King to call a parliament, and to show that the failure of the last need not cause him to despair of good from another,—he concludes his examination of the grounds upon which he builds better hopes for the future with these remarkable words :—" Lastly, I cannot excuse him that is gone of an artificial animating of the *negative;* which infusion or influence now ceasing, I have better hope : "—clearly charging Salisbury with having secretly encouraged the opposition. And again in another letter written with the same object a few years later, (when after a second trial of a parliament and a second failure, he yet wanted to encourage the King to try once more,) I find the following passage in allusion to Salisbury's Great Contract. He is endeavouring to account for the "dryness" (as he calls it) of the last two parliaments, and to show that it arose from accidents and mismanagement, not from the natural disposition and constitution of the Lower House. Former parliaments, he shows, had been liberal :—

"But in the succeeding parliament *in septimo*, when that the Lord Treasurer that last was, had out of his own vast and glorious ways to poor and petty ends, set a-foot the Great Contract, like the Tower of Babylon, building an imagination as if the King should never after need his people more, nor the people the King; but that the land should be no more like the land of promise watered with the dew of heaven, which sometimes was drawn from the earth and sometimes fell back upon the earth again ; but like the land of Egypt watered by certain streams and cuts of his own devising ;—and afterwards, either out of variety, or having met with somewhat that he looked not for, or otherwise having made use of the opinion, *in the end undid the baby that he had made*,—then grew the change," and so on.

Now is it not clear from this that Bacon thought the breaking-off of the Contract was Salisbury's own doing ?

A.

It would seem so. But what could have been Salisbury's motive ? It is surely a most unaccountable proceeding.

B.

A man so much given to finesse as Salisbury may have served, or hoped to serve, some end by it which we cannot guess at now. In endeavouring to account for his mismanagement of this business, I have several times stopped to consider whether he was not trying to lead the Commons into a trap ; hoping to draw from them in the first glow of their expectations a large present supply; and meaning when that was secured to take some occasion for breaking off the contract. When he found that they were too wary for him, he may have thought it his policy to bring about a breach and yet not to appear himself as the author of it, and for that purpose may have thrown secret obstructions in the way. However it is hardly fair to fix so grave an imputation upon him without some corroborative evidence; and I have not met with any, unless the general charge of having "juggled" with parliament, with the King, and with everybody, (which we know from Mr. Chamberlain was so freely urged against him immediately after his death,) may be considered as a corroboration. Only I think Bacon would hardly have expressed such an opinion to the King, who must have known whether there was any truth in it, unless he had believed it to be true. And I do not know who was so little likely to be deceived in such a matter.

A.

To a person who did *not* know whether there was any truth in it, you think he might possibly have expressed such an opinion whether he believed it or not?

B.

Excuse me. *I* do not think so; but you do. Because of the hardness of your heart, I am obliged to make this concession. If I were to assume that Bacon never said a thing which he did not believe to be true, you would charge me with begging the question. When we have followed him to the end of his career, I may perhaps ask you *what* thing he ever said that he did not believe; for it is a thing I have yet to learn; but so long as his character is the subject of controversy, we must not treat his veracity as above suspicion.

A.

Then it seems you have no decisive judgment to pronounce upon Salisbury's motives in this great matter.

B.

None that I am perfectly satisfied with. And indeed why should we trouble ourselves to clear them up? Our business is not with the motives or management, but only with the issue; and about that there is no doubt. Whatever or whoever may have been to blame for the miscarriage of the negotiation, there is no doubt that it was a disastrous business;—a disaster hardly to be retrieved; for success was never more important and failure was never more complete. Of the terms upon which, after all this talk and expectation, the King and his people parted, here is a lively and authentic picture. On the 25th of November 1610, about six weeks after the last meeting of the parliament, Sir Thomas Lake wrote to Salisbury from the Court at Royston:—

"That the King hath received by Sir Roger Aston a copy of the order set down against the next meeting of the House; which his Majesty doth collect into three points. 1st. To give reasons why they should yield to no supply. 2nd. To examine the answers to the grievances, and wherein they were not satisfactory. And 3rdly, to consider what further immunities and easements are to be demanded for the people. His Majesty doth also perceive, both by my Lord of Montgomery and by Sir Roger Aston, that you would wish his Majesty and your Lordships might have a meeting to consult of his affairs in parliament.

"To both these his Majesty willeth this to be written:—

"That he maketh no doubt that the cause of your late advice to adjourn the House was for that you foresaw that they would do worse on Saturday than they had done on Friday; and how you are now assured that when they meet again on Thursday they will not be in the same mood, his Majesty would be glad to know. For he assureth himself that if your Lordships thought the House would follow the same humour, you would not advise their meeting. His Highness wisheth your Lordship to call to mind that he hath now had patience with this assembly these seven years, and from them received more disgraces, censures, and ignominies, than ever prince did endure. He followed your Lordships' advices in having patience, hoping for better issue. He cannot have asinine patience; he is not made of that metal that is ever to be held in suspense and to receive nothing but stripes; neither doth he conceive that your Lordships are so insensible of these indignities, as that you can advise any longer endurance. For his part, he is resolved, though now at their next meeting they would give him supply, were it never so large, and sauce it with such taunts and disgraces as have been uttered of him and of those that appertain to him (which by consequence redound to himself), nay though it were another kingdom, he will not accept it.

" Therefore, touching the other point of his meeting with your Lordships, either by his coming nearer to you or by any of your coming to him, his Highness thus answereth. That no man should be more willing to take pains than he, when there is hope of good to come by it. But as things now stand in appearance, for him to put either himself or you to the labour of an unpleasant journey without likelihood of comfort; but on the contrary when you meet together to find the pains of your bodies aggravated with vexation of spirit, or to part irresolute as at the last conference you did,—his Majesty doth not see to what end such a meeting should be. But for aught he seeth in his own understanding, he taketh no other subject of consultation to be left, than how the parliament may end quietly, and he and his subjects part with fairest shows; which he conceiveth must begin with some new adjournment until Candlemas term or the end thereof in respect of the nearness of Christmas. And in the mean time your Lordships and he may advise both how to dissolve it in the best fashion, and fall to consultation about his affairs.

* * * * * * *

" Another subject of this despatch is to let your Lordships know that his Highness findeth the speeches uttered (whereof your Lordships sent him a breviate, sent in a letter to me) were so scandalous, reproachful, and intolerable, as his Highness doth require your Lordships every one for his part to gather particular notes and information of the words used and of the authors who spake them ; for that his Highness doth conceive that some of them reach very near to the point of treason ; or are at least so scandalous (as his Majesty is informed) that he thinketh he shall have just ground to call the speakers to account for them."

One of these speakers was Wentworth, son of Peter Wentworth who used to trouble Elizabeth in the same way ; and it occurred to James that he might take a leaf out of Elizabeth's book. For I find him about a week after sending to the Council to know what evidence she had when she punished " this Wentworth's father,"—and adding, with better logic than policy, that " seeing the Lower House were so quick and eager in producing every day new liberties and privileges for themselves, he saw no reason but he ought to be as careful to keep the forms and customs which his progenitors had used in matters falling between the Lower House and them." Fortunately he seems to have been content with his logical advantage ; for he was easily persuaded to desist from the prosecution.

In such fashion, then, and in such temper on both sides, did the King and his parliament part. So ended Salisbury's project for reconciling their interests and removing all causes of collision for ever. Instead of 600,000*l.* gift, by which he had hoped to put the King at ease for the present, he had got only about 120,000*l.* Instead of a permanent independent yearly support of 200,000*l.* he had got nothing. But that was not the worst, nor nearly the worst. Had that been all, it would have been a simple failure, leaving things only as bad as they were before. But it did in fact leave the discontents of the Commons aggravated and exasperated by discussion and disappointment, and the King's finances worse embarrassed than ever ; because the notoriety of his necessities and the utter failure of this great effort to relieve them, from which so much had been expected, left him not only without money, but without credit. So that the terms on which they parted, though displeasing alike to both, were infinitely to the disadvantage of the King. The Commons had lost nothing ; nothing at least that touched their particular pockets or feelings (for of the general evils of a distracted government they came in of course for their share). In spite of their unredressed grievances, they could make money, build houses, feed themselves, clothe themselves, marry and give in marriage, as merrily as ever. But the King could not borrow 100,000*l.* of the aldermen, to pay his most pressing debts.

A.

Poor old King! It was a hard case, I admit, for a divine-right monarch to digest. But I dare say it was his own fault.

B.

In part perhaps it was. A man whose tongue lay so very near his heart as James's did, can hardly be supposed to have managed such a case with perfect judgment. But the question for us is not who was to blame for the disaster, but in what condition that disaster did actually leave the kingdom. Was it not a case of real national embarrassment? a case to justify anxiety and alarm? a case which, as I said, called all hands to the rescue? And if there was a man standing by who had watched the progress, who understood the causes, foresaw the dangers, and *thought* he knew the most likely remedies of that disease, is it necessary to suppose that in offering his services for that end he was only moved by vulgar ambition, and was basely misemploying his talents and his time?

A.

Why do you ask me that? I beg you will not confound me with those people to whom the more vulgar motive seems always the more probable. There are such people, I know —people who have so little experience in themselves of unselfish motives that they hardly believe in the existence of them, or at any rate think no explanation of an action so incredible as that it sprung from the predominance of an unselfish desire. Tell lawyer Scout that perhaps parson Adams is thinking of his duty and not of his fee,—he will receive the suggestion with a smile of superior incredulity; and there are doubtless more eminent members of the same honourable profession who have a good deal of lawyer Scout in them. But you cannot have less respect for them than I have. And therefore let us leave them to their own natural enjoyments. And tell me what had Bacon (for of course he is the man you are hinting at) been doing all this time? What part had he taken in these negotiations while they were going on?

B.

The same part, so far as his path can be traced, in which he has always appeared hitherto;—the part of a mediator and composer of the waters. But the notes which survive of the proceedings are so scanty, and it is so difficult to know what was merely formal and what was important, that the most careful conclusions one can draw from them must after all rest upon a very doubtful foundation. With the original suggestion and proposition of the measure, I cannot find that he had anything whatever to do. But after the opening of the negotiation (which was taken up at first with great good will, and the preliminaries conducted on the part of the Commons with much moderation and good temper), his name appears in all the principal proceedings. In the nice point of obtaining the King's leave to treat of a composition for Wardships and Tenures (the first in which there was any danger of a split), the management of the proposition appears to have been entirely left to him, and to have been perfectly successful. His manner of doing that we know, for we have a report of his speech preserved by himself. Again, in preparing the schedule of grievances (also a very tender point) he seems to have taken a prominent part, and with the full confidence and approbation of the House, until they fell foul of that dangerous question of Impositions. Of the jar which that produced, the fragments of the debates bear distinct evidence. And as Bacon differed from the majority of the Commons on the point of law, it must have been impossible for him to take a leading part with them where that question was involved. And accordingly he appears after this chiefly as a dissuader of rash counsels; interfering on one occasion to moderate the language of an answer to a message from the Lords; on another to dissuade them from making a needless difficulty about receiving messages from the King or Council through their Speaker; on a third, to deprecate a proposition for flatly refusing all supply until they should first hear the King's answer to all their grievances;—in all which attempts he seems to have been successful. Whether he took any part in their petition to the King for liberty to discuss his right to impose duties without consent of parliament,—or, as it may rather be called, their remonstrance against being forbidden to discuss it,—I cannot discover; but after leave was obtained, he spoke in defence of the King's right. After the grievances were collected, he was one of a sub-committee appointed to sort them and prepare some inducement or preamble to the petition. And when the petition was ready, he was selected "as their mouth and messenger" to present it to the King.

A.

Was that after the debate on the right of imposing, or before?

B.

A few days after.

A.

Then the part he took in favour of moderation and in defence of the King's prerogative did not lose him the confidence of the House of Commons?

B.

Clearly not.

A.

Then why should it lose him mine? But how did he steer through the next session; which from your account must have been a trying one?

B.

Of that we know nothing whatever. The Journals of that session are lost; and though there is a tolerably full account of it in one of the Cotton MSS., it is confined to the things done and the questions resolved; it gives no particulars of the debates and mentions no names.* As for Bacon, his name is not mentioned anywhere in the accounts of this session that I know of, except once in a private letter. And that tells us nothing except that he was one of some ten or twelve leading members of the Lower House whom the King sent for one day, in a very irregular manner, to expostulate with them about their proceedings. It was just after the Contract had—upon their refusal (as it would seem) to vote any further supply,—been broken off, and when they came, James bluntly asked them whether they believed that he was in want or not; to which question, says the narrator, "when Sir Francis Bacon had begun to answer in a more extravagant style than his Majesty did delight to hear, he picked out Sir Henry Neville, and commanded him to answer according to his conscience," &c. This is all we hear concerning Bacon during this last session; and it would not have been worth mentioning, were it not that the modern meaning of the word "extravagant" might lead a modern reader into a mistake. "Extravagant" meant nothing more than *indirect.* It was obviously undesirable, as things then stood, that such a question should be directly answered; and Bacon would no doubt have contrived to throw some veil over the nakedness of it, if he had been allowed to go on.

A.

Yes; I see no harm in that. But now for the drift of all this. You think, I suppose, that if Bacon had been Lord Treasurer the business would have been better managed?

---

* This was written before Mr. Gardiner's discovery of the notes of the debates in that session; which show, I think, clearly that the final breach was the choice and act of the Government, though they leave us still in doubt as to the motives. For a full account of the whole negotiation, written with the help of those notes, see "Letters and Life of Bacon," vol. iv. ch. 5 and 6. The account written here, when I had only the printed journals for my authority, is not (I think) substantially inaccurate, though very imperfect.

B.

I have little doubt of that. At any rate he *thought* he could have done better, and would certainly have done differently. What mistakes he might have made in other ways, or what difficulties he might have found in the King's humours, it is of course impossible to say. But in general you will find that the measures and methods of proceeding which turned out unfortunate were not those which he advised. This, however, is not the point I was driving at. I have no reason to suppose that he had anything to do with the measures we have been speaking of either as persuader or dissuader. No opportunity had been given him for interfering either way. Nor had he been induced to change his course in consequence of them. The meeting of parliament called him away from his studies ; the dissolution sent him back to them. The change which I undertook to account for did not take place till after Salisbury's death, about a year and a half later.

A.

But, stay ; how did the Government get on in the meantime ?

B.

Very badly. The emptiness of the Exchequer, the shifts and perplexities of the Lord Treasurer, became the common talk of the town. Ambassadors were told that they must wait for their salaries. Pensioners were forced to turn duns. The Paul's-walkers entertained themselves with wondering how Salisbury would scrape together money enough to provide the usual Christmas festivities.

A.

And what did Salisbury himself propose to do next ?

B.

Salisbury appears to have been nearly at the end of his devices ; or, if he had any left, they do not seem to have

succeeded any better. For at his death the ordinary annual
expenditure exceeded the ordinary annual revenue by
160,000*l.*; and the debt had increased from 400,000*l.* to
500,000*l.*

A.

And during that period (a year and a half I think you
said) Bacon had nothing to do with business of state?

B.

Nothing beyond what fell to him as Solicitor-General.
Indeed while Salisbury lived he had no opening. Not but
that he would have gladly lent his services; indeed, he made
offer of them; but Salisbury for some reason or other
neglected to use them. So that he was still spending his
leisure in carrying forward the "Instauratio," in writing
more essays, and in collecting and correcting his miscellaneous papers and speeches and law arguments.

A.

Did he not try to make up to Sir Robert Carr?

B.

If he did, all traces of the application are strangely
obliterated. But indeed, while Salisbury lived and continued at the head of affairs, it was not much that he could
have done. The only chance of retrieving the King's affairs
was by such a change of policy as could hardly have been
accomplished without a change of persons. It was necessary
that the King should appear in an entirely different character to his subjects, and that his subjects should feel
that the new character was his own, and that the one in
which he had last appeared was not his own. The death
of Salisbury happened opportunely and was the critical
moment. If James could but have been persuaded, and
been able, to seize that moment for an entire change in his
own ways,—if he could from that moment have laid his
former character aside and shown himself a new man,—he
might, I think, have succeeded. It would have been

thought that his true nature had been obscured till then by his minister, and appeared now in its natural lustre. Nor is it impossible that a *successful* experiment of that kind might really and permanently have changed him. For certainly he would have felt more comfortable and more at home as a man of the people than as a high-monarchy man. A different creed would have agreed better with his real feelings; for all his anti-popular opinions seem to have been doctrine, and doctrine only; while his untaught sympathies and natural impulses were always with the people and human nature. You have seen a man whom accident has made a dignitary, when nature meant him for a good fellow?

A.

Yes, and generally found him trying to supply his want of natural dignity by superfluous starch; and losing all the love due to his good nature without procuring any of the respect due to his office.

B.

Well, that was just James's case. And I cannot help thinking that if he had once tried the experiment of wearing his prerogative a little more carelessly, he would have found it so much more comfortable and becoming, that he would have continued the fashion.

But if this was to be done, it must be done suddenly. *Opportuni magnis conatibus transitus rerum.* It is in times of change that new impressions may be wrought in so as to last; let them once settle, and the new will never incorporate with the old.

Now therefore was the time. And now once more was Bacon tempted to step out of his course. Hitherto the very few, and (as I must still maintain) the very modest, applications which he had made to the King in his own behalf, had been merely for ordinary advancement in the regular course of his profession. But upon Salisbury's death, it could not but occur to him, as it must surely occur to everybody who now looks carefully into the state of those times, that the

King might have much more important use of him as a Councillor of State than merely as a State lawyer. He was a modest man, it is true ; but in times of emergency modest men become sensible of their worth ; and it is not to be supposed that Francis Bacon, armed as he was with all the outward as well as all the inward accomplishments of a statesman, could have looked on for above thirty years (he was now fifty-two) at the doings of other men, and have seen so many mistakes made and paid for, without feeling that he could do better. For my own part, I believe that at this crisis James had one thing to do,—and that was to make Bacon his prime minister and do whatever he advised. Bacon should have been to him what Burleigh was to Queen Elizabeth ; and then the whole subsequent history of England would have been quite different.—How say you ? Shall we conclude that in such circumstances he was to blame for wishing that the King would try him ?

A.

Certainly not for wishing.

B.

For asking, then ?

A.

That depends upon the manner of the asking. The motive, I agree, we have no right to call in question. And to tell you a secret—(let no man hear us)—indifference to *power* is not in my opinion a virtue, or a sign of virtue, in a man. Not to care about *glory* is a greatness ; but not to wish for *power*, or to shrink from using all honourable means to attain it, is an argument, I fear, either of selfishness or of pusillanimity or of conscious incapacity.

B.

Well, then, for the *manner* of the asking. Be so good as to read these two letters. The first was written within a week after Salisbury's death. The second has no date ; but evidently refers to the same occasion, and was probably written about the same time. I want you to read them all through ; both because I would have you judge for yourself, and not depend upon my report, which may be suspected of partiality; and because it is the fashion to refer to such letters as these, without quoting them,—or at most quoting a few isolated expressions,—in evidence of what Coleridge (who should have known better, only that I dare say he knew nothing about it) calls the "courtly—alas the servile, prostitute, and mendicant ambition" of Bacon's later life.

A.

Is this it? Vol. vi. p. 52. "To the King, immediately after the Lord Treasurer's death ; 31st of May, 1612." Does this come out of Bacon's own collection ?

B.

Out of the collection of drafts and copies which he kept for himself. Not out of that which he made to be preserved.

A.

" It may please your excellent Majesty,—
" I cannot but endeavour to merit, considering your preventing graces; which is the occasion of these few lines.
" Your Majesty hath lost a great subject and a great servant. But if I should praise him in propriety, I should say that he was a fit man to keep things from growing worse, but no very fit man to reduce things to be much better. For he loved to have the eyes of all Israel a little too much upon himself, and to have all business still under the hammer and like clay in the hands of the potter, to mould it as he thought good; so that he was more *in operatione* than *in opere*. And though he had fine passages of action, yet the real conclusions came slowly on. So that although your Majesty hath grave councillors and worthy persons left, yet you do as it were turn a leaf, wherein if your Majesty shall give a frame and constitution to matters before you place the persons, in my simple judgment it were not amiss. But the greater matter and most instant for the present is the consideration of a parliament, for two effects ; the one for the supply of your estate; the other for the better knitting of the hearts of your subjects unto your Majesty, according to your

infinite merit; for both which, parliaments have been and are the ancient and honourable remedy.

" Now because I take myself to have a little skill in that region, as one that ever affected that your Majesty might in all your causes not only prevail, but prevail with satisfaction of the inner man ; and though no man can say but I was a perfect and peremptory royalist, yet every man makes me believe that I was never one hour out of credit with the Lower House; my desire is to know whether your Majesty will give me leave to meditate and propound to you some preparative remembrances touching the future parliament.

" Your Majesty may truly perceive that, though I cannot challenge to myself either invention, or judgment, or elocution, or method, or any of those powers, yet my offering is care and observance : and as my good old mistress was wont to call me her watch-candle, because it pleased her to say I did continually burn (and yet she suffered me to waste almost to nothing), so I must much more owe the like duty to your Majesty by whom my fortunes have been settled and raised. And so craving pardon, I rest

" Your Majesty's most humble servant devoto,

"F. B."

Well, I must say this fits very well into your account of the matter. And I see nothing that can be found fault with. The disclaimer of pretensions is rather large ; but that is only manners : a kind of polite way of putting them forward, and I think not altogether insincere. Such disclaimers are often suggested by a genuine emotion, even when they cannot be sanctioned by the deliberate judgment. And no one can deny that the object of the letter is constitutional. But there is no application for place or power here. He merely asks leave to offer some advice.

B.

No. But now read the next.—" To the King," p. 54.

A.

" It may please your excellent Majesty,—

" My principal end being to do your Majesty's service, I crave leave to make at this time to your Majesty this most humble oblation of myself. I may truly say with the Psalm, *Multum incola fuit anima mea;* for my life hath been conversant in things wherein I take little pleasure. Your Majesty may have heard somewhat that my father was an honest man, and somewhat you may have seen of myself, though not to make any true judgment by, because hitherto I have had only *potestatem verborum;* nor that neither. I was three of my young years bred with an ambassador in France ; and since, I have been an old truant in the school-house of your Council-chamber, though on the second form ; yet longer than any that now sitteth hath been on the head form. If your Majesty find any aptness in me, or if you find any scarcity in others, whereby you may think it fit for your service to remove me to business of state,—although I have a fair way before me for profit (and by your Majesty's grace and favour for honour of advancement), and that in a course less exposed to the blasts of fortune,—yet now that he is gone *quo vivente virtutibus certissimum exitium,* I will be ready as a chessman to be wherever your Majesty's royal hand shall set me. Your Majesty will bear me witness that I have not suddenly opened myself thus far : I have looked on upon others ; I see the exceptions ; I see the distractions ; and I fear Tacitus will be a prophet, *magis alii homines quam alii mores.* I know mine own heart ; and I know not whether God that hath touched my heart with the affection may not touch your royal heart to discern it. Howsoever I shall at least go on honestly in mine ordinary course and supply the rest in prayers for you, remaining," &c.

B.

This is from the rough draft in his own handwriting.

And now I have said nearly all I have to say in answer to your questions at our last sitting. You now know what the case was which drew him aside from the prosecution of his great work, and made him desire once more to "meddle in the King's causes." I undertook to convince you, not that the course he took was the wisest he could have chosen, but that the occasion was one in which a man who had the public good at heart might easily doubt which course to choose. Are you convinced?

A.

I suppose I am. At least I do not see clearly why not.—
But before I go, tell me what was the result of this step of
his. Did the King make any use of him after all ?

B.

A good deal of use; but (unluckily, as I think, for the
King himself) not the right use. He gave him employment
and audience, but not authority. Perhaps indeed he could
not have given him that without using a sterner resolution
than he had ever shown himself master of,—without becoming in fact a different man ; an experiment which it was
late to try.

However we had better leave this for another time. The
occasion opened new opportunities, and may therefore open
a new chapter. You are content for the present to admit
that in re-engaging himself in business of state, Bacon may
have been actuated by other motives than vulgar and venal
ambition ?

A.

I am content.

B.

He is now fifty-two years old. Has he done anything as
yet inconsistent with the character of an honest man and a
good patriot ?

A.

Not that I know of. But I am taking his case entirely
upon your showing.

B.

True; but that is only because his accusers are silent.
In all the points upon which Macaulay founds anything
like a definite charge, you have had the benefit of his own
statement. The previous charges you admitted were not
made good; during the last ten years no charge is made.
Still therefore I claim for Bacon the benefit of general good

character; and if I find him hereafter doing anything which may be traced with as much plausibility to a good motive as to a bad one, I may still, if I like, suppose him to have been actuated by the good motive.

A.

Certainly, until it appears that good motives were less familiar to him.

B.

Which has not appeared yet.

A.

Not upon your showing. And certainly I have nothing to show against you.

B.

Then you admit that, so far as we have gone, any one who had rather believe that Bacon was an honest man than a rascal, may, without violence to his own instincts or to historical probability, indulge his inclination?

A.

Yes.

B.

Then suppose we stop here for the present. For to those who would as soon believe him a rascal as an honest man, I have nothing to say. I know there are such men; plenty of them. There is not a more universal attribute of low minds than a disposition to be pleased when anything occurs to damage the character of an eminently great or good man. A discovery that Wilberforce had been seen drunk, or the Duke of Wellington running away, would at this moment be received with delight by thousands. But as these are persons whom I do not wish to be on the same side with, I shall take no pains to convert them. If all men who would be glad to think that Bacon was in the main a virtuous man can be brought to think so, I shall be quite contented;— provided always that they are brought to think to by fair means and upon just grounds. For I am far from wishing either to believe myself, or to persuade any one else to believe, that he was what he was not; or to pay idolatrous honour to intellectual power, by representing it as incompatible with moral weaknesses or depravities with which it is not incompatible. I should no more think of pleading the intellectual gifts for which Bacon has credit with all men, as an argument that he had no faults, than of urging the beauty of Cleopatra as a presumption that she was chaste. We know very well that the highest intellectual powers, as well as the most perfect corporal beauty, are often joined with moral deformity. And though we may wish it were not so, yet as long as it is so, no true man can wish to *think* that it is not. But there is a certain form of beauty in the human countenance which I do believe to be incompatible with deformity of mind; and where there is an apparent exception, I shall always be glad to see it removed. In like manner there are certain forms and manifestations of intellectual greatness which I believe to be unattainable without moral goodness; and where a case is quoted in which the greatness seems to be there and the goodness seems not to be there, I cannot but wish to find that there is some mistake. And this I think we ought all to feel in the case of Bacon.

A.

No doubt the moral character of the man will more or less modify and guide the working of his intellectual faculty. Therefore whatever reveals to us the one, must reveal something of the other, if we can read the signs rightly. But I doubt whether the distinction is of much practical use; for those who cannot see any traces of goodness in a man's way of living will hardly recognize them in his way of thinking; and such men will deny that Bacon's intellect has that character which you ascribe to it. However I think you will find most people prone enough to think men good whom they feel to be great. The fault lies generally on that side. It is only the disbelievers in goodness and greatness who rejoice when the characters of good and great men are damaged. They are impatient of men's *reputation* for virtues; not of the virtues themselves; for in them they do not believe.—At any rate I can answer for myself in the case of Bacon. I would certainly much rather believe him an honest man than a rascal.

EVENING THE TENTH.

A.

Now I suppose we may go on with Macaulay again.

B.

I forget where we left him. Read the last sentence over again.

A.

"Unhappily he was at that very time employed in perverting those laws to the vilest purposes of tyranny. When Oliver St. John was brought before the Star Chamber for maintaining that the King had no right to levy benevolences——"

B.

Oh no! we are not ready for that yet. I cannot consent to skip the addle parliament. It was a very important feature in James's reign; a great fact; and has a great deal to do with Bacon.

A.

The addle parliament!

B.

Yes. The parliament which met in the beginning of April 1614, and was abruptly dissolved in June without passing a single act. It makes but a slight figure in our histories; I suppose on that account. But though it did nothing, it signified very much, as all great failures do.

That failure, with all the circumstances of it, must have entered as a most material element into all James's subsequent calculations; and must by no means be forgotten by us if we would pretend to understand and judge his subsequent conduct.—But we had better take up the subject where we left off.

A.

That was with the death of Salisbury.

B.

Yes. The King had "as it were turned a leaf." He had to choose a new prime minister, which in this case was almost as much as forming a new administration. Whom had he to choose from? He had in his council the Lord Chancellor; a man bred under Elizabeth, but now nearly worn out, chiefly occupied with the business of his court, and never much of a politician. He had the Earl of Northampton; a man in high repute for learning and talent, especially as a writer (being indeed a great artist with his pen according to the fashionable taste of the day); but unpopular from a suspected leaning to Popery; and not a man of any real judgment or ability (so far as I can make him out), nor patriotic in his ends, nor scrupulous in his methods of pursuing them. He had Robert Carr, now Lord Rochester; an inexperienced and uninstructed youth, given to pleasure, greedy of gain, intoxicated by his sudden elevation, disliked by the people because he was a Scotchman and getting all good things, and having an interest in the King's affections which gave him an influence over his counsels greater probably than the King was aware of. The rest were either instruments, or cyphers, or quiet people who minded only their own business, and did not affect to interfere with the management of the state. By far the best head in James's council was his own. And a very sufficient head it would have been if it had been steadily applied to its work. If it had been enough to have sound *opinions* as to the best method of proceeding in each conjuncture, he would have made (as I believe) a very politic King. But he was far too easy a master both to himself and to those about him. He was for ever excusing himself from following his own judgment,—from doing what he would have advised any one else to do in the same situation,—when it was opposed by his favourites or disagreeable to himself; and on that account, in such times as he had fallen upon,—with a debt of 500,000*l.*, an annual deficiency of 160,000*l.*, and a House of Commons newly awakened to a sense as well of his necessities as of their own powers, and determined to make the most of their advantage,—he was no fit man to be his own prime minister.

A.

And Bacon?

B.

Bacon was still only Solicitor-General. It is true that he became now a more important person, because the King encouraged him to offer advice on the greater matters of State, listened freely to him, and was I think generally disposed to act upon his suggestions. I say *disposed* to act; for between the disposition to do a thing and the doing of it, there was unfortunately in James's case a great gap. And Bacon was not in a position to do more than give the suggestion; he was not near enough to watch and guide the working of it in the King's mind, or to control the execution. Now no man can fairly be held answerable for the fruit even of his own counsels, unless he have opportunity both to answer objections and object to alterations, and also to criticise final determinations; a privilege which Bacon certainly had not now, and can hardly be said to have had afterwards when he was at his highest; for the final determinations were always taken by James himself: often when he was far away from his council; not unfrequently without inviting any second communication or leaving room for any remonstrance. It must often therefore have been in the power of a subtle or a favourite courtier to defeat the policy of the council; and Bacon, you are to remember, was of the council; not of the court.

A.

When he was Lord Chancellor he must have had liberty of access as often as he wished.

B.

Why, yes. I suppose the King was always ready to receive a communication from him, and generally to see him if he desired it. But the King spent very little of his time in London; much of it a good way off. And at any rate Bacon was not living in the Court; he could not be near the King at his meals and recreations; and those are the seasons when the influence of a courtier can be most effectually used.——

But where was I?—Oh, as to the influence of the courtiers,—I met the other day with a little thing which rather confirms what I just said, and seems to show that the inconvenience of this Court influence had already been perceived and felt. In the autumn of 1612, not long after Salisbury's death, Bacon published an enlarged edition of his essays. Of these essays there is a fair transcript in the hand of one of his secretaries (evidently made before they were published) which contains a sentence that you will not find in the printed copy. It is in the Essay on Counsel, where, after speaking of the true use of counsel to Kings, he notices the inconveniences which have been found in it. " For which inconveniences (he adds) the doctrine of Italy and the practice of France in some kings' times have introduced cabinet councils,—a remedy worse than the disease." There the printed copy stops. But the MS. goes on—(be interested, for not a soul knows this besides ourselves)—the MS., I say, goes on thus:—" which hath turned Metis the wife into Metis the mistress; that is, councils of state to which princes are married, to councils of gracious persons, recommended chiefly by flattery or affection."—It is easy to guess why he struck that sentence out.

A.

He was thinking of Rochester, I suppose?

B.

No doubt: the application would have been too obvious and personal.

A.

It should be put in again now; for it explains the meaning of that sentence, which I never understood before; the cabinet council being in our days precisely such a council of estate as he did *not* mean.

B.

Precisely that kind of council from which, by the word "cabinet," he meant to distinguish it. Yes, I think it should be reinstated; within brackets.—But whither are we wandering? We left James labouring under his debt and deficiency; with a very difficult and delicate task before him, and a very indifferent body of confidential advisers to help him in the execution of it. We left Bacon putting himself a little more forward than belonged strictly to his place, for the purpose of recommending the King to lose no time in calling another parliament, and offering all the help which he could render. Unfortunately, upon this vital question of calling a parliament there were divisions in the council. The Earl of Northampton, who from his age, his rank, his reputation, his abilities, and especially from his influence with Rochester (an influence natural enough in itself and greatly increased by Rochester's interest in his niece,—for that unhappy business was already on foot), was now become one of the most powerful men in the kingdom, is known to have been strongly against it. Rochester himself cannot be supposed to have had many ideas of his own on so difficult a subject. The King had ideas enough, and probably very good ones. But with a council so constituted he had very imperfect opportunities of knowing the truth, and with so fresh a recollection of recent disappointments and disgusts, would naturally incline to the opinion of those who promised to set his affairs straight without risking an appeal to that troublesome assembly. In such circumstances, one cannot wonder that he resolved not to try a parliament, or at least put off the resolution to try one, till all other methods of rectifying his estate should be put in force. It happened that his case could ill bear any such delay. Delay itself was bad, and perhaps the manner in which the interval was employed made it still worse. But kings and councillors have often made mistakes for which there was less excuse.

Well: so it was to be. The consideration of a parliament was suspended for the present; and the council were set hard at work to find all possible means of abating the expenditure and improving the revenue. Upon this they were assiduously employed for the first year; Northampton taking the lead in council, and Bacon being among the most active of the sub-commissioners appointed to assist. We need not trouble ourselves with the details; but the sum total of their year's work (as I find by a memorandum of Sir Julius Cæsar's, dated 18th March 1612–13) was an increase of the ordinary revenue by abatements and improvements amounting in all to 35,776*l.*, and a collection (from the coming in of debts, from fines, forfeitures, the sale of land and of baronetcies, and other extraordinary items) of 309,681*l.*

A.

And that to supply an annual deficiency of 160,000*l.* (I think you said) ;—upon what total of revenue ?

B.

Under 450,000*l.*; which was the total, according to Hume, in 1617.

A.

To supply an annual deficiency then equal to more than a third of the total revenue, and to pay off a debt of 500,000*l.*—No prospect of a cure, then ; only a mitigation of the painful symptoms.

B.

And no very considerable mitigation. The leak let in
about four quarts while the pump threw out one. One good
effect however this report must have had. It must have
made it clear that, at whatever risk, a parliament must be
tried ; for though it might still be deprecated by some of
the councillors and courtiers whose fortunes fared no worse
but perhaps better for the distresses of the State, and who
thought that the vessel would float long enough for them,
yet the manifest hopelessness of remedy from any other
quarter must have carried the question against them; and
accordingly it was determined some time in the course of
this year—(the precise date of the final resolution I have not
been able to ascertain, but it was as late as July)—that a
parliament should be summoned with as little delay as
possible. The result of this step was indeed (as the council
had reported to the King the year before) " very uncertain ; "
probably more uncertain now than it was then. Never was
there a measure of State which required more boldness and
yet more delicacy in the handling ; and perhaps never a
council of State less favourably constituted for handling it
well ; for it was as easy to go wrong through too great an
anxiety to further it as through too much obstinacy in
opposing it : too much faith and too little might be equally
fatal. On one side there was Northampton, who had so little
hope from a parliament, that he seems to have been not only
against its being tried, but desirous that it should miscarry.
On the other side were a party of parliament men, who out
of confidence in their own experience and influence with the
Lower House were rash enough to undertake the management of it, and to engage that if the King would follow their
advice, his business should be carried to his satisfaction.
At the head of these was Sir Henry Neville, an able and
public-spirited man, with large and just views as to the state
of the times, with sympathies well balanced between the
people and the Crown,—earnest for the redress of grievances,
yet hoping to be made Secretary of State,—and possessing,

it would seem, much influence over Rochester, which was the best opening for influence over the King. Several memorials and advices of his are extant, which refer to this period; and it cannot be doubted, I think, that his *ends* were wise and patriotic. But the case was new and difficult, and the event proved that he did not thoroughly understand his ground. He knew the harbour which was to be steered for, and in which it would be good for all parties, and satisfactory to all parties, to arrive; but he had not thoroughly fathomed the depths and shallows of popular judgment in such an assembly as the Lower House had now become. The sands at the bottom were rapidly and secretly shifting, and the currents at the top were shifting with them. It was not either ancient experience or recent experience that could tell a man where the safe course now lay; but only the combination of experiences both old and new with that prophetic sagacity which is derived from a profound insight into the nature of man, and is reserved for original genius of the highest order. It was no great blame therefore to him and his associates if they ran the vessel aground; nor any great blame to James that he took them for his pilots. But I think he had the choice of a better.

That Bacon, had he been prime minister, could have carried the business through successfully, it is of course impossible to say. But I have evidence to prove that, though aiming at the very same ends (for I do not know that he would have objected to any one of the measures which Sir Henry Neville proposed to carry), he would have proceeded in a different manner; and that too from an apprehension of danger in the very quarter where the event proved that it really lay. We have seen how strongly he disapproved of the contract-policy which was pursued with the last parliament, and how strongly he advised that no time should be lost in calling another. And you would like to know what course he would have had the King take with it in order to recover the ground which he had lost?

A.

I should like very much indeed to know that. It ought to be worth all the speculations of all the historians put together. If we had a Bacon among us now to write the history of those times, it would supersede all others; and yet he could not know nearly so much about them as the real Bacon did then. But it must be what he really did advise; not what you suppose he would.

B.

Surely. Though for want of evidence I am sometimes obliged to guess at his views, I hope I always report them as guesses. I report nothing as his but what I have historical evidence for. In the present case you shall have his own words, which may still be seen under his own hand.

Here is a letter addressed to the King, at what exact date I do not know; but sometime between September 1612 and December 1613; most likely in the spring or summer of 1613. But for our present purpose it is not material to fix the exact date; it is enough to know that it was written while the question of calling a parliament was still under consideration. You may as well read it through, for it has never been printed.

A.

How comes that? Has it been inaccessible till lately?

B.

Not at all. The original is among the Cotton manu-scripts in the British Museum; and there is a copy in the Lansdowne collection; both of which are entered in the general index under Bacon's name.

A.

" It may please your excellent Majesty,
" Before your Majesty resolve with your Council concerning a parliament, mine incessant care and infinite desire that your Majesty's affairs may go well hath made me in the case of Elihu,

who though he was the inferior amongst Job's counsellors, yet saith of himself that he was like a vessel of new wine, that could not but burst forth in uttering his opinion.

"And this which I shall write I humbly pray your Majesty may be to yourself in private. Not that I shall ever say that in your Majesty's ear which I will be either ashamed or afraid to speak openly; but because perhaps it might be said to me after the manner of the censure of Themistocles, 'Sir, your words require a city;' so to me: 'You forerun: your words require a greater place.' Yet because the opportunity of your Majesty's most urgent occasion flieth away, I take myself sufficiently warranted by the place I hold, joined with your Majesty's particular trust and favour, to write these lines to your Majesty in private."

B.

You see therefore that this letter has a peculiar value, as containing Bacon's own private and original opinion. What a man writes or speaks concerning matters in which a resolution has been already taken by others or in concert with them, does not necessarily indicate his own personal opinion. He may be only making the best of a course which has been chosen against his judgment and advice. But where a man goes out of his way to offer his opinion in private upon matters which are still under consultation, and that too with a view to influence the decision, there we may be sure we have his own genuine views. There is nothing to restrain him from recommending exactly what he thinks best.

A.

Very true. And I see also how unjust it is to hold Bacon responsible for the measures of the Government, when he could not so much as offer an opinion about them without an apology and a request that it should not be divulged. The "place he held" was still Solicitor-General, was it not?

B.

I think so. He became Attorney-General in October; and I should guess that this was written earlier; but I cannot be sure. You observe also how strongly he is im-

pressed with the *critical* character of the time; the urgency
of the occasion, and the opportunity flying away. One
might indeed, without this evidence, have given him credit
for that motive. You see, however, that it is no comment
of mine, but a fact.

A.

Certainly. Well, let us see what his views are.

"The matter of parliament is a great problem of estate, and
deserveth apprehensions and doubts. But yet I pray your
Majesty remember that saying, *Qui timide rogat docet negare.*
For I am still of that opinion (which I touched in general in
my former letter to your Majesty), that above all things your
Majesty should not descend below yourself; and that those
tragical arguments and (as the schoolmen call them) ultimities
of persuasions which were used last parliament should for ever
be abolished; and that your Majesty should proceed with your
parliament in a more familiar, but yet a more princely
manner."

B.

Mark that paragraph well, for it is the groundwork of
the whole advice. The "former letter" I suppose to be one
dated 18th September, 1612, in which Bacon urges the
King not to let "these cogitations of want any ways trouble
or vex his mind," nor be tempted, "in respect of the hasty
freeing of his estate, to any means or degree of means which
carrieth not a symmetry with his majesty and greatness;"
and goes on to pass a severe censure upon that ostentatious
display of his necessities and those shifts to relieve them, of
which Salisbury was the author. At all hazards and in
spite of all inconveniences to preserve before the world the
face of confidence and majesty was Bacon's constant advice,
both now and afterwards when it was much more difficult to
do. The tone of his counsel reminds one of that inspiring
speech of Faulconbridge to King John—

"But wherefore do you droop? why look you sad?
Let not the world see fear and sad mistrust
Govern the motion of a kingly eye.
Be great in act as you have been in thought.

> . . . . . . So shall inferior eyes,
> That borrow their behaviours from the great,
> Grow great by your example," &c., &c.

The worst of it was that James had now not only to preserve this appearance, but to recover it. And how was that to be done ?

A.

Let us see.

" All therefore which I shall say shall be reduced to two heads.

> " First, that the good or evil effect likely to ensue of a parliament resteth much upon the course which your Majesty shall be pleased to hold with your parliament; and that a parliament simply in itself is not to be doubted.

> " Secondly, what is the course which I would advise were held as safest from inconvenience and most effectual and likely to prevail.

" In both which parts your Majesty will give me leave to write not curiously, but briefly; for I desire that what I write in this argument may be *nihil minus quam verba.*

" For the first my reasons are :—

1. I do not find since the last parliament any new action of estate amongst your Majesty's proceedings that has been harsh or distasteful : and therefore seeing the old grievances (having been long broached) cannot but wax dead and flat, and that there has been no new matter either to rub up and revive the old or to give other cause of discontentment, I think the case much amended to your Majesty's advantage. It is true there have been Privy Seals, but it is as true they were never so gently either rated or pressed. And besides, Privy Seals be ever thought rather an attractive than a repercussive to subsidies."

B.

I do not know exactly how the law stood with regard to Privy Seals, or what was the limit of the King's power to borrow money in that way. But a privy seal was in fact an order served upon an individual to advance a specified sum of money to the King upon condition of repayment within a specified time, which order he, was bound either by law or custom to obey. I suppose it was a relic of the ancient arbitrary authority of the Crown, not yet formally taken away. The issue of Privy Seals was an indication that the exchequer wanted replenishing; and it was thought better to replenish it by subsidies,—that is, by a common tax which fell equally upon all,—than to force the Crown to use those arbitrary powers which it still retained and the burden of which fell chiefly upon the rich; the rich having the power of taxation in their hands, and being very willing to relieve *themselves* at the expense of the people, however chary they might be of relieving the King.

A.

" 2. The justice upon my Lord Sanquir hath done your Majesty a great deal of right; showing that your Majesty is fixed in that resolution,

Tros Tyriusque mihi nullo discrimine agetur,

which certainly hath rectified the spleen-side, howsoever it be with the liver."

B.

Lord Sanquir was a Scotch nobleman, whose eye had been put out by a fencer five years before. In revenge (which he had cherished all that time) he procured a man to murder him. Great pains were immediately taken to apprehend him and procure evidence. Upon his trial he confessed his guilt, and was hanged. The hanging of a Scotchman, and a Scotch nobleman,—especially as his demeanour at his trial moved general pity,—was an instance of impartiality for which the English public would hardly have given James credit,—so jealous as they were of his over-partiality to his countrymen.—Well?

A.

"3. Let it not offend your Majesty if I say the Earls of Salisbury and Dunbar have taken a great deal of envy from you and carried it into the other world, and left unto your Majesty a just diversion of many discontents.

" 4. That opposition which was the last parliament to your

Majesty's business, as much as was not *ex puris naturalibus* but
out of party, I conceive to be now much weaker than it was,
and that party almost dissolved. Yelverton is won; Sandes is
fallen off; Crew and Hyde stand to be serjeants; Brocke is
dead; Nevell hath his hopes; Barkley I think will be respective;
Martin hath money in his purse; Dudley Digges and Holys are
yours. Besides, they cannot but find more and more the vanity
of that popular course; specially your Majesty having carried
yourself with that princely temper towards them, as not to
persecute or disgrace them, nor yet to use or advance them.

"5. It was no marvel the last parliament, men being possessed with a bargain, if it bred in them an indisposition to
give; both because the breaking left a kind of discontent, and
besides Bargain and Gift are *antitheta*, as the Apostle speaketh
of Grace and Works; and howsoever they distinguished Supply
and Support in words, yet they commixed in men's hearts, and
the entertaining of the thoughts of the one did cross and was a
disturbance and impediment to the other.

"6. Lastly, I cannot excuse him that is gone of an artificial
animating of the Negative; which infusion or influence now
ceasing I have better hope."

B.

Mark again the last paragraph but one, as containing
another essential feature of Bacon's policy. It was not
merely the loss of majesty in his people's eyes (which could
not but follow when he began to dispute about bargains
with them) that was to be deprecated. If it had been the
readiest way to disembarrass the exchequer, the disembar-
rassment would indeed have been ill purchased at that price.
But it was not the way. On the contrary, by setting them
on to make specific bargains, you put them further off from
making those contributions which were really wanted. To
conclude such a bargain as would have made the Crown and
the people independent of each other for the future, was a
thing not to be wished even if it had been practicable. And
by once teaching them to look for a *quid pro quo* in that
matter; by teaching them to expect in return for each vote
of supply some particular boon from the Crown of cor-
responding value; you led them away from the considera-

tion of their true function, which was to furnish the government with the means of governing well; so to maintain the
Crown that the Crown might be able to maintain the people.
For certainly the duties which the King owed to his subjects
were not of a nature to be appraised and reduced to a value
in money. What they were worth was not what they might
be sold for, but what it might cost to get them done. Therefore however it might be desirable to bestow largely upon
the people particular boons of pecuniary or other relief, the
better to quicken their affection and strengthen their confidence, yet to offer these by way of equivalents for subsidies was utterly wrong, and tended to defeat its own purpose. When Queen Elizabeth consented to revoke a long
list of monopoly licenses, did she ask for another subsidy in
consideration of the value given away? No; she let them
drop from her hand like a thing taken up by mistake which
did not belong to her. And when the Commons insisted
upon coming to thank her, did she tell them how grateful
they ought to be, and how large a supply they ought to
vote? No; she told them it was herself that should have
thanked *them* for having informed her of the error. Their
subsidies she valued as the measure of their affection and as
the means of better discharging the duties she owed them :
for she desired to reign no longer than she might reign with
their loves,—to live no longer than she might see their
prosperity.

"And as I am that person " (she went on) " that still yet
under God hath delivered you, so I trust by the almighty power
of God that I shall still be his instrument to preserve you from
envy, peril, dishonour, shame, tyranny, and oppression,—partly
by means of your intended helps, which we take very acceptably
because it manifesteth the largeness of your love and loyalties
unto your Sovereign. Of myself I must say this; I was never
any greedy, scraping grasper, nor a strait fast-holding Prince,
nor yet a waster. My heart was never set on worldly goods, but
only for my subjects' good. What you do bestow on me I will
not hoard it up, but receive it to bestow on you again. Yea,
mine own properties I count yours, to be expended for your
good. Therefore render unto them from me, I beseech you, Mr.

Speaker, such thanks as you imagine my heart yieldeth but my tongue cannot express."

That was no doubt the style in which Bacon would have had it done, if James had been equal to the part.

But I wanted you to remark that passage in the letter, the rather because this point was not attended to ; and the not attending to it was a chief cause of the miscarriage of the business.

A.

Well; so much for the grounds upon which he hopes for better success with a new parliament; or rather does not despair of good from it. Now we come to his second division.

"For the course I wish to be held, I most humbly beseech your Majesty to pardon the liberty and simplicity which I shall use. I shall distribute that which I am to say into four propositions. The first is—

"1. That your Majesty do for this parliament put off the person of a merchant or contractor, and rest upon the person of a King. Certainly when I heard the overtures last parliament carried in such a strange figure and idea as if your Majesty should no more (for matter of profit) have needed your subjects' help; nor your subjects in that kind should no more have needed your graces and benignity,—methought, besides the difficulty (in next degree to an impossibility), it was *animalis sapientia*, and almost contrary to the very frame of a monarchy, and those original obligations which it is God's will should intercede between King and subjects."

—Surely I have seen that before. I thought you said none of this was in print.

B.

I quoted it at our last meeting. But never mind; it will bear a second reading.

A.

Yes; it seems to come out of the depths.

"Besides as things now stand, your Majesty hath received infinite prejudice by the consequence of the new Instructions for the Court of Wards. For now it is almost made public that the profits of the Wards being husbanded to the best advantage (which is utterly untrue) yet amounteth to a small matter; and so the substance of your bargain extremely disvalued."

B.

The Wardships, you remember, formed a principal item in the Great Contract. The improvement in consequence of the new Instructions appears to have been very considerable compared with the total revenue from that source; but the total was not much. For, if I may trust a schedule entitled "improvements," in Sir Julius Cæsar's handwriting, the actual increase in the revenue from Wardships in the year after Salisbury's death was 20,000*l*. But in the general tables of receipts for the two or three years following, the total annual revenue from them is set down as only 25,000*l*. Now Salisbury, in 1610, had asked 100,000*l*. of annual support for giving them up.

A.

"2. My second proposition is that your Majesty make this parliament but as a *coup d'essay*, and accordingly that your Majesty proportion your demands and expectation. For as things were managed last parliament, we are in that case, *optima disciplina mala dediscere*. Until your Majesty have tuned your instrument you will have no harmony. I, for my part, think it a thing inestimable for your Majesty's safety and service, that you once part with your parliament with love and reverence. The proportions I will not now descend into; but if the payments may be quickened, there is much gotten."

B.

There, again, is a principal point which was not provided for. If the King would recover his proper position and dignity in the eyes of his people, it was necessary to avoid not only the appearance of solicitude while the business was going on, but of disappointment in case it went ill. We agreed, I think, the other night, that too sudden a discovery of the growing dependence of the Crown upon the Commons would have been dangerous to the State. The tendency in that direction was indeed inevitable. It is probably no exaggeration to say that the Crown was already dependent upon the Commons ; that is, they had it in their power to withhold from the King the means of carrying on the government, and thereby to bring him to their own terms ; not indeed absolutely or at once ; but if they chose to persevere in refusing supplies until the conditions they demanded were complied with, to those conditions he must have come at last. But though this was the fact, it was a fact not yet declared ; and most desirable it was that for the present it should be disguised from popular observation. It was fit therefore that the King should act as if that assistance were not necessary to him which the Commons might constitutionally refuse. He must in fact be prepared to do without it, and let it be seen that he was so prepared. Bacon saw that to produce this impression was now the King's first object; a *sine quâ non;* that if he succeeded in that it would be enough, though he succeeded in nothing else ; and therefore that his true policy was to carry matters so that the hope of contribution might not seem to be a principal motive for calling the parliament, nor any disappointment in that respect a motive for proroguing it ; but to treat it as a thing comparatively immaterial, which was not essential to his purposes and did not affect his proceedings. How he proposed to effect this you will see presently. But what I want you to remark here is the importance which he attaches to the *parting* between the King and his parliament. That the King should "once part with his parliament with love and reverence" he holds a thing of "inestimable importance to his safety and service;" and therefore urges him so to proportion his expectations as at all events not to be put out by failure ;—a piece of advice which whether the King approved or not I do not know ; but certainly he did not succeed in acting upon it.

A.

I hope you are sure all this time that the King's cause was a good one ; or else—

B.

I think the King's cause, so far as Bacon tried to further it, was good. I think it was good that the framework of the constitution should be kept up, and repairs and reforms introduced gradually from within,—*by* authority, not *against* it. What might have been done by a king of ideal wisdom and magnanimity, I do not undertake to say. Such a king might possibly have found means to lay his power quietly down, to make over his revenue to the disposal of parliament, and resign his own functions in trust to a body of constitutional advisers holding their office during the pleasure of the House of Commons. The experiment would have been hazardous, and I doubt whether history has an instance that can be pronounced successful of sovereign power voluntarily abdicated before its time. To the largest experiment of that kind that I know of in modern times,—certainly the most praised,—we owe the constitution of the United States of America as it now is; but I do not think the issue can be pleaded in favour of it. And is it not true that the greatest reforming governors have all taken a different course ?—But whatever an ideal king might have done, it is clear enough that no such thing could have been got out of King James. And whether Bacon was right or wrong, there can be no doubt that his heart's wish was (and he thought it the wish of a true patriot) that the King should *not* give away his power from himself, but keep it and use it for the good of his people. If he is to be censured on this point, he must be censured for thinking so, not for acting as if he thought so.

A.

I think indeed he was much given to standing upon the old ways.

B.

Yes, till he could see which way to go. But no man knew better that he must go on.—But have we not stood long enough ourselves ? Suppose you go on.

A.

" And if it bo said that his Majesty's occasions will not endure these proceedings *gradatim;* yes, surely.   Nay I am of opinion that what is done for his Majesty's good as well by the improvement of his own as by the aid of his people, it must be done *per gradus* and not *per saltum;* for it is the soaking rain and not the tempest that relieveth the ground.

" 3. My third proposition is that this parliament may be a little reduced to the more ancient form (for I account it but a form) which was to voice the parliament to be for some other business of estate and not merely for money; but that to come in upon the bye, whatsoever the truth be.   And let it not be said that this is but dancing in a net, considering the King's wants have been made so notorious; for I mean it not in point of dissimulation but in point of majesty and honour; that the people may have somewhat else to talk of and not wholly of the King's estate; and that parliament-men may not be wholly possessed with those thoughts; and that if the king should have occasion to break up his parliament suddenly, there may be some more civil colour to do it.   What shall be the cause of estate given forth *ad populum;* whether the opening or increase of trade (wherein I meet with the objection of Impositions, but yet I conceive it may be to accommodate), or whether the plantation of Ireland, or the reducement and recompiling of laws,— throwing in some bye-matters (as Sutton's estate, or the like)— it may be left for further consideration.   But I am settled in this, that somewhat be published besides the money matter; and that in this form there is much advantage."

—What will the moral historian say to all this ?

B.

The moral historian may possibly be shocked ; but if he gets through the next week without doing something quite as shocking himself, I will undertake to say that he has but little to do in the world, and that none of the practical interests of society will fare the worse for losing him.   Some of these expedients may possibly not exactly square with his maxims.   But for my own part I think the cause of morality is ill served by the laying down of moral maxims which no man of sense or virtue can seriously resolve to act upon.

Many things must be kept secret in all civilized societies; and without some degree of dissimulation (which if you anatomise you will always find to include some falsehood) no secret can be kept. On the other hand, I do not think the cause of morality well served by attempting to define in words the exact boundaries between the lawful and the unlawful. Human language is not subtle enough or flexible enough to do it. The human heart duly exercised and awakened by a sense of responsibility, and bent earnestly on good ends, is the only judge. Ask any member of any government, I might say any father of any family, whether some of the best actions of his life,—actions in which he was least influenced by any selfish motive, in which he sees least to repent, of which he can least truly say that he would do otherwise if they were to do again,—ask him whether they did not involve some dissimulation; the keeping up of some false appearance for the sake of disguising the truth. But do not ask him to dissect them and call all the parts by their right names. Let that be dissembled too. As for the little points of dissimulation which Bacon here sanctions and recommends,—I do not ask you to remember the difference of the times in which he lived. Take our own times as they are. Can any man, who thinks what he says and says what he thinks, maintain that at this day a prime minister ought to enter upon his office with a resolution to lay bare to public view all the secret motives and purposes of the government;—to give nothing forth *ad populum* beyond or beside his real intentions?

A.

I am afraid he would not be prime minister long.—However I grant that in the case before us the insincerity is of a very mitigated kind; and may perhaps be called reserve rather than dissimulation; and under that name I will let it pass. It is in truth rather the profession than the thing, that even the moral historian would start at. But here is more of it.

" Lastly, as I wish all princely and kind courses held with

his Majesty's parliament, so nevertheless it is good to take away as much as is possible all occasions to make subjects proud, or to think your Majesty's wants are remediless except by parliament. And therefore I could wish it were given out that there are means found in his Majesty's estate to help himself (which I partly think is true), but that, because it is not the work of a day, his Majesty must be beholding to his subjects; but as to facilitate and speed the recovery of himself rather than of an absolute necessity."

B.

Observe that he wishes " it were given out ; " he does not wish the King himself to go and proclaim it.

A.

Yes.

" Also that there be no brigues or canvasses, whereof I hear too much ; for certainly howsoever men may seek to value their services in that kind, it will but increase animosities and oppositions ; and besides will make whatever shall be done to be in evil conceit with your people in general afterwards."

B.

Once more take notice of that. That is another most important point in which Bacon's advice was not attended to. There was a great deal of canvassing, and (what made it worse) with no great success. On the 3rd of March, 1613–14, Mr. Chamberlain writes to Sir Dudley Carleton :— " Here is much justling for places in parliament, and letters fly from great personages extraordinarily ; wherein methinks they do the King no great service, seeing the world is apt to censure it as a kind of packing." And in his next letter (a fortnight after) he tells him that " letters and countenance were not found so powerful as was imagined even in the meaner boroughs." What the consequences were in the parliament itself we shall see presently.

A.

Here is but one sentence more :—

" Thus have I set down to your Majesty my simple opinion,

wherein I make myself believe that I see a fair way through the present business, and a *dimidium totius* to the main. But I submit all to your Majesty's high wisdom, most humbly desiring pardon, and praying the Highest to direct you for the best.

" Your Majesty's most humble servant,

"FR. BACON."

B.

Well, here you have, as I conceive, a piece of genuine Baconian advice; from which you may safely draw inferences as to the policy he would have pursued had he been in a place of authority. There is another paper of his in the same place, entitled " Incidents of a Parliament ; " consisting of questions for consideration—what course may be taken to accomplish this and avoid that; but as the questions are only proposed and not answered ; and as the letter you have just read seems to contain all the fruit which his meditations had then yielded; at least all the definite advice which he was then prepared to ground upon them ; they add little to our knowledge of what he would have had done. They show rather what difficulties lay in the way, than how he was prepared to meet them. But in the foregoing letter we have enough for our purpose. We see here at any rate the principal things which he thought should be *avoided :* as 1st, all appearance of *necessity,* as if the King were constrained to call a parliament by the pressure of his own wants, and not for the general good of the kingdom. 2ndly, all appearance of *diffidence,* as if he had any doubt of their good-will to supply him with all that was needful for his affairs ; or of *dependence,* as if he relied upon their help and could not do without it. 3rdly, all appearance of *solicitude,* as if money were the great matter, and if that failed all failed. 4thly, all appearance of *bargaining ;* weighing gift against gift, value to be bestowed in concessions against value to be received in subsidies. 5thly, all *canvassing to form a party in the House ;* everything (to take the words of the paper of " Incidents ") " which might have the show, or the scandal,

or the nature, of the packing or briguing of a parliament."
6thly, all risk of an unkind or undignified parting. And
7thly (which I may add on the authority of the same paper,
though it is only hinted at in the letter by the way), all
secret interference by great persons with the proceedings of
the House. The words are, "What course may be taken
to let men perceive that a guard and eye is had by his
Majesty that there be no infusions, as were last parliament, from great persons; but that all proceedings be
truly free."

A.

And what said the King to all this advice?

B.

What he said I do not know. All I know is that he did
not act upon it. Sir Henry Neville and his party, whose
purposes (to do them justice) appear to have been truly
patriotic, and whose policy was at least very plausible, and
being much less bold than Bacon's probably seemed much
safer, succeeded in carrying the matter their own way.
These were the celebrated "Undertakers." They were em-
phatically the King's party; and undertook, if he would
make such concessions as they recommended, that his business should pass to his satisfaction. And here by the way
we have a proof (if it were needed) of the decision and
confidence of Bacon's foresight in this matter. For such
being their professed object and their service being accepted,
an ordinary man in his place (or indeed he himself had he
been the sort of man he is taken for) would naturally have
joined them. Yet he certainly did not. I have another
letter here, written not long before the parliament met,
which proves I think decisively that he disapproved of their
policy and expected no good from it. It would seem that
the King had been consulting him upon the subject; and
the tenour of his advice may be gathered from this letter,
evidently written by way of reminder.

"I most humbly pray your Majesty," he says, "to receive

into your royal remembrance that one point whereof you spake
unto me; which was this,—To put this case to those gentlemen
who profess to do you service in parliament and desire (as
they say) but to have some matter whereupon to work :—' If
your Majesty be resolved not to buy or sell this parliament, but
to perform the part of a king and not of a merchant or contractor,—what they can devise or propound for the satisfaction
of your people?'

" Of this three uses may be made.

" First, if they fall upon an answer as to say that the parliament is now so in taste with matters of substance and profit,
as it is vain to think to draw them on but by some offer of that
nature; then for my part I shall little esteem their service, if
they confess themselves to be but brokers for bargains.

" Secondly, if they do devise and propound anything that is
fit,—then that it be followed and pursued, because they are
likest to be in love with their own child and to nourish it.

" Thirdly, if they show good will to devise some such thing,
but that their invention proveth barren in that their propositions be not such but that better may be found; then that they
may be holpen by some better proposition from your Majesty
whereupon to work.

" This, because time runneth, I beseech your Majesty may
be put to them by some such mean as your Majesty is pleased
to use, as soon as may be."

A.

Where does this come from ?

B.

From the same volume as the last : one of the Cotton
collection. It is the original, all fairly written in his own
hand.

A.

Well I admit this as conclusive evidence that he is not
answerable for the errors of the Undertakers, whatever they
may have been. And what was the issue of it all ?

B.

For a full answer to that question we must plunge again
into the Journals of the Commons and the volumes of con-

temporary correspondence; and it will make too long a story for to-night. But if you will be content with Bacon's own report of the matter, I can give you that in a moderate compass. And it is as well perhaps that while his views beforehand of what ought to be done and what ought not to be done, and of what was to be hoped and feared, are still fresh in your memory, you should hear also his own account of what *was* done and what was the consequence of it. It is contained in a paper which has never been noticed (so far as I know), but which may be seen in the Inner Temple Library. It is addressed to the King; relates to matters concerning which the King must have been perfectly well-informed; and was written not more than a year and a half after they took place. It can hardly be supposed therefore to contain any intentional misrepresentation; and if it does contain a true representation of things as they appeared to Bacon, it has a historical value infinitely above that of any other account which can be had of that period.

The object of the paper, I should tell you, is to persuade the King not to be discouraged by the ill-success of this parliament from calling another; to show what were the true causes of the failure, and by what precautions a similar result may be guarded against another time. The only part which concerns us at present is that which explains the causes of the failure.

After speaking in the same spirit as before, but more explicitly and earnestly, of the ill-success of the Great Contract in the parliament of 1610, in damping " the generous disposition of free giving unto the King, and the politic arguments of persuading it upon reason of state," he proceeds—

" Then in the last assembly of parliament after four years' intermission, when the realm had paused from subsidies a good while, and when it had been time to forget these byways and to have reduced things to ancient course, the rather for that the leader of those ways was gone to another world,—then did certain gentlemen (whom I love and prize in particular, but nevertheless I will never spare in this)—being but merely empirics

of parliament, and those whose wisdoms reached but to that
they had observed last, not well seen in the rules of estate and
the pulses of people's hearts, and out of zeal perhaps to do
well overvaluing their strength,—revive again those former
errors of merchandising, and add a far greater error of new.

" For first, it being given out and professed that the end and
cause of calling a parliament was to pay the King's debts and
supply his wants— "

The very thing, you remember, which Bacon had especially dissuaded.

—" which of itself did great hurt by putting upon the King
the person of a mendicant, and was contrary to the honourable form of all former parliaments (wherein were the cause
of want never so manifest it was never acknowledged by the
State, but fell in upon the bye), they straightways fell into
the old track of gathering together certain heads of donatives
and graces, whereby they thought fit to invite the parliament to an ample gift; which being propounded, I cannot
forget that his Majesty seemed to be in heart and in his own
opinion against it; wherein he showed his great wisdom and
foresight; and nevertheless being persuaded unto it, he did
likewise as much as the wit of man could devise help it, in
carrying it in the best form by disclaiming all merchandising and making it but a mutuality and interchange of
love; the parliament having in contemplation the case of the
King, and the King having in contemplation the case of the
people, and not as in contract, either party looking to his own
advantage— "

This by the way (if the accounts we have of the King's
speech do it justice) is a version of his words much improved by the reporter. It was the colour which Bacon
himself put upon them in the House of Commons, and
coming from him as a member of the House, the effect is
very good. In the King's mouth it did not tell quite so
well; and I am ready to admit that Bacon stretched a point
in saying that the King took the most effectual course
" which the wit of man could devise " to remove the imputation of bargaining, by the manner in which he disclaimed
it. If he had made the King's speech for him, I think his

own wit would have devised some better turn. It is true the King was trying to act upon Bacon's advice, but he showed a singular want of tact in the attempt. Bacon had advised him to "put off the person of a merchant and contractor and rest upon the person of a king;" the King, with a simplicity which makes one love him, went and assured the House of Commons that he had done so, and that his offered graces were to be taken as springing from love, and not as if he meant to trade with them like a merchant. Never was such an instance of a man turning his wit the seamy side without. It was as if King John, when Faulconbridge implored him not to betray his fears before his people, had gone to his army and begged them not to suppose he was afraid. Therefore I cannot but think that Bacon did know of a man whose wit could have devised a better remedy for the error.

A.

He should have said "as much as *your Majesty's wit* could devise," then. But that would have been disrespectful. I shall not quarrel with him for that little piece of politeness.—Well?

B.

"—But yet it was not possible so to overcome or disguise the nature of things, but that it fell into the old way. For though it were not matter of mere contract as in the former parliament, yet it was a kind of valued gift, which made men take weights and measures into their hands, and those not the truest; so that in the end those graces came to be despised and to be termed *Veneficia* instead of *Beneficia*, and that cedars were cut down and shrubs given to browse upon, and such other unfit speeches: Which error was likewise accumulated with another circumstance which likewise did great hurt; in that they were all offered, and not first desired and sued for; contrary likewise to his Majesty's own opinion, who ever thought that offer would be vilified and that it is appetite that makes sweetness.

"But the second error (as I said) was the greater; which was that, through indiscretion, or vain-glory, or what it was, it was voiced abroad and carried as a thing notorious,—insomuch as people (who are evermore godfathers to such things) gave it

the name of *Undertaking* or *Undertakers*,—that certain persons
had undertaken to value themselves with the King by the service of preparing and inducing a parliament to pay his debts
and supply his wants—"

You remember how he had warned the King that
brigues and canvasses would only increase animosities and
opposition.

" —which did stir up a kind of indignation even in those that
were very well and honestly affected, that a house of parliament should become the shadows and followers of a few, and
that thereby they should at once lose money, liberty, and thanks.
But then this was taken hold of also and exasperated by all
such as under this fair pretext were glad and took boldness to
cover and convey their own secret averseness towards the King's
business and other their private drifts.

" Upon this grew also divers branches of inconvenience; as
first that there was great suing, standing, and striving about
elections and places; which joined with this general noise of
undertaking and likewise with the opposition thereunto made
by others, made the wisest and ablest persons of the kingdom
not willing to be of the House; as loth to offer themselves to
opposition and fearing lest it might be a turbulent and factious
parliament, and therefore choosing rather to sit quiet at home.
And these are the persons in whose hands the King's business
ever prospereth best, as being most interested in the State and
most respective in their opposing.

" Upon the same ground it came to pass that three parts of
the House were such as had never been of any former parliament, and many of them young men and not of any great estate
or quality; and they are wonderfully mistaken in their principle who think that such men will give most because they have
least: for such are ever more forward to oppose upon bravery,
than the gentlemen of the country or wealthy merchants are
upon dryness. And besides, that greenness of the House leeseth
the modesty and gravity by which great matters have passage
and turneth it into a kind of sport or exercise; which also is
a thing most pernicious (if it be truly looked into) unto the
liberty of a parliament; for howsoever they may ruffle once or
twice, yet if they leese their gravity and dignity they will
grow in contempt both towards the King and towards the
people abroad.

" Another inconvenience was by the said occasion that those gentlemen and their friends and associates (who to do them right were of the best voices of the House and the best able to persuade if they stood clear and unprejudged) were by this means turned unprofitable and of no credit in the House; so that every one of them could have done more in the parliament before than all together could do this parliament.

" There was also another shrewd dependence of this last inconvenience; which was that the same persons, finding that they had lost the House, were forced to regain reputation and to ingratiate themselves (as they term it) with the House by being forward and running violent courses in causes of popularity, as in the matter of Impositions and other pretended grievances, wherein the King's power or profit were interested : and so upon the matter but to beg credit one day to spend it another; wherein they found themselves only able to row with the stream, but had no arms or power to row against it. But in the meantime this bred a spirit of boldness and immoderate liberty to oppose in the King's causes; and the King himself was fain to pass over divers things which it had been fit to stop at the beginning, upon expectation that the end would make amends for all.

" Another inconvenience which followed was the manifest distraction which reigned in the House between the Undertakers and the Anti-undertakers ; which made the House more troubled with their appeals the one against the other than with anything else ; and made them also look rather upon the persons one of another how they were sided, than regard the matter they spake; crossing the matter for the person's sake ; which did cut off all means of persuasion and consent.

" But that which was of all others most pernicious, this distraction had entered into the King's house and council and amongst his great men; insomuch as my Lord Privy Seal "—

That was the Earl of Northampton.

" —who had discounselled the parliament and hated the persons almost of the Undertakers,—what for the glory of his opinion and what for the blasting of their services,—declared himself in that manner as he set up a kind of flag unto all those that opposed the Undertakers and would frustrate the success of the parliament.

" Lastly, contrary to all custom of parliament. and to the stirring of infinite animosity and distaste, the King's business was urged to be put to a point at the very first : and this was done that the weakness of the Undertakers, whose strength was more in noise than in strength,* might not be perceived before the King's turn was served; which point of time being unpleasing to every man and therefore soon overruled, made the House to find their strength ; which stumbling at the threshold was never after recovered.

" This then being a true description of the last parliament, I see no reason why it should cast a fear for the holding of another, no more than the opening of a body dead of a disease ought to fear a man in health ; but it may warn him somewhat to observe in the regiment of his health.

" Of this that hath been said there is a double use; the one for the removing of too much apprehension or discouragement concerning the calling of a parliament; the other because the notation of those errors carrieth in itself by rule of contrary a kind of direction or platform what course is now to be held. For I do not think there can be a more true or compendious advice how to carry things concerning a future parliament than this—to do just contrary to that was last done."

He then proceeds to give his " affirmative counsel " for the future parliament; which is exactly in the same spirit with the advice that he had previously given for the last, which we have just seen; only more large and elaborate and earnest, and entering further into detail. I have something to say about that too when its turn comes; but for the present we may as well stop here. The next thing will be to inquire from independent authorities what part he actually took in this "addle parliament," and how far it was consistent with his principles and views expressed both before and after, as they are expounded in the letters we have read to-night. Our information on that point is in truth very imperfect ; but it is better to bring forward all we have, that we may see how the footmarks lie, and that we may leave as few blank leaves as possible for the moral historian or the popular biographer to fill up from his own fancy.

A.

How far have we advanced now ?

* So in MS.

B.

In point of *time*, not far to-night: for Bacon is only about a year and a half older than he was when we began ; being just turned fifty-three. But in our knowledge of him and of his life, as it seemed to lie before him looking forward into the uncertain future, we have made, I conceive, a considerable step.

We have seen how clearly he perceived that the times were out of joint, and how strong an opinion he had as to the proper method of proceeding to reduce the dislocation, and the fatal consequence of delay in adopting it. The result of each succeeding attempt to set it right by a different treatment only proved more and more that he was correct. His influence with the King, though far from paramount, was nevertheless increasing. The events of this year cannot but have tended to improve it still further. The policy of the King, with all its errors, was surely not so hopelessly depraved that an honest man was bound to forsake his cause : and it has not yet appeared that in any single instance Bacon attempted to gain influence with him by encouraging him in his errors : on the contrary it is clear almost to demonstration that he used his influence so far as it would go to correct or modify them, or to ward off the consequences. His patriotism, it is true, was not like that of the extreme popular party of his day, which seems to be regarded by the liberal writers of our own as the only possible form of patriotism. It did not consist in an endeavour to defeat the King and strip him of his prerogatives. Does it follow that it was false or insincere ? Does it follow even that it was mistaken ? Surely no thinking man can say so. —What was the end which Bacon most desired to bring about ? A reconciliation between the King and the Commons :—not that the Commons should prevail against the King : but that the King and Commons should prevail together against dangers and disorders within and without, and proceed harmoniously in the great operations of good government. His end therefore you must allow was good. Then as to the means. *How* did he propose to effect this reconciliation? for there were many ways in which it might have been attempted. By helping the King to prevail *against* the Commons? No: but by showing him how to prevail *with* them; by guiding him into such a course of policy as should command their confidence and consent. So far you must allow his means to be good also. Once more then, as to the means of the means. How did he propose to command that confidence and consent? By intriguing, and forming parties, and overbearing their deliberations, and silencing dissentients? for those are the unpatriotic arts. The very contrary. One of the principal points which he insisted on as essential was this—that there should be no interference either with the elections in the country or with the proceedings in the House, but that " all proceedings should be truly free." Or if it be too much to say that he was against *all* interference with elections,—for it is true that he would have had measures taken if possible to bring in fit men and keep out unfit,—yet he expressly stipulated that those measures should be such as to satisfy two conditions:—first, they were to be " *bonis artibus*, without labouring or packing; " secondly, they were to have for their end the procuring of a really good House.

A.

Ay; but what was his notion of a really good House? Your constitutional critic will say that he meant a House with a majority on the King's side.

B.

I expected that ; but the constitutional critic will be mistaken. Bacon no doubt expected, as one of the *incidents* of a good House, that it would have a majority on the King's side; just as a man who believes that his cause is just believes that a good judge will decide it in his favour. But ask him what he means by a good judge,—he will say, a man of learning, integrity, judgment, and impartiality. Suppose in like manner we ask Bacon what he means by " a really good House of Commons." Here is his answer :—

" I wish by all means that the House may be compounded not of young men, but of the greatest gentlemen of quality of their country; and ancient parliament men; and the principal and gravest lawyers, sergeants, and readers; and the chiefest merchants ; and likewise travellers and statesmen ; and in a word, that it be a sufficient House worthy to consult with in the great causes of the Commonwealth."

Have you any objection to that ?

A.

No; the cause that prospers in such a House should be a good one. Certainly if it asks no more favour than a fair hearing in a House so composed, it must at least think itself a good one.

B.

Then you admit that the *end* which Bacon wished to bring about was good ; and that the means by which he proposed to bring it about, and the means of obtaining those means, were fair and constitutional ?

A.

It should seem so.

B.

Then you have no objection to make to the manner in which, and the purposes for which, he used what influence he had with the King ?

A.

None at present.

B.

If then you find him endeavouring to maintain and improve that influence, will it shock or surprise you ? Shall you be at a loss for his motive ? Or will you be content to suppose that his wish to improve his influence with the King may have arisen naturally out of a natural wish to serve his country ?—I do not ask whether that was his *only* motive. Sugar tasted sweet to him as to other men. But suppose he did feel such a wish,—that he had some care for the prosperity of King and kingdom,—was not that motive sufficient ?

A.

I confess I think it was.

B.

And do you not think we may go a step further yet? You admit that, upon that motive alone, he might naturally endeavour to advance in the King's favour. Could he, think you,—supposing that motive strong,—have *not* endeavoured to do so? Such being the state of things, such his views, such his position,—if you should find him *not* endeavouring to improve his influence with the King, should you not infer that his wish to serve his country was *not* strong?

A.

Stay, stay. That is too much at once. I must first know how he used his influence afterwards, when he had succeeded in improving it. If not in a patriotic spirit—

B.

Excuse me. That does not affect the present question. When we come to that, you shall judge it freely. What I ask you now you can answer now. I ask you whether a man in Bacon's position, fully persuaded that if he had but more influence with the King he could be of material service in extricating the country from a dangerous embarrassment, and yet wilfully neglecting to improve that influence,— whether such a man could be supposed to care much whether the country were extricated or not. Translate the case into our own times. A man thinks he knows how Ireland may be saved. He thinks too that he might himself be a material instrument for doing it if he were to put himself forward. He does *not* put himself forward. What may I infer?

A.

That he cares more for his own quiet than for the salvation of Ireland, I suppose.

B.

Of course. Well then if Bacon had not put himself forward?

A.

Yes, but you *assume* that he thought that by putting himself forward he could extricate the country?

B.

Assume! You cannot expect a demonstration of the secret thoughts of a man who has been dead ·two hundred years. Yet you can hardly call it an assumption either. You must at least admit that if he did not think so, he acted most unaccountably; and that if he did think so, he must have acted just as he did.

A.

Certainly I must admit that he had no motive for giving the advice he did, except a conviction that it was sound. For he seems to have been in a very small minority.

B.

A minority of one, so far as I can discover.

A.

Well then I admit that whatever other motives he may have had, that motive was sufficient of itself. Having such a motive, he is not only excused for wishing to keep and improve his influence with the King (not that I have ever said he needed any excuse), but he could not well have done otherwise. I hope that will content you.

B.

Perfectly.

END OF VOLUME I.

PRINTED BY WILLIAM CLOWES AND SONS, LIMITED, LONDON AND BECCLES.

www.ingramcontent.com/pod-product-compliance
Lightning Source LLC
Chambersburg PA
CBHW021339110726
47900CB00005B/1530